D0248382

KRISTINA OHLSSON

THE
FLOOD

Translated by Marlaine Delargy

**SIMON &
SCHUSTER**

London · New York · Sydney · Toronto · New Delhi

A CBS COMPANY

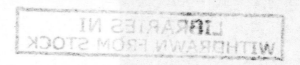

First published in Sweden by Piratförlaget under the title *Syndafloder,* 2017

First published in Great Britain by Simon & Schuster UK Ltd, 2019
A CBS COMPANY

1 3 5 7 9 10 8 6 4 2

Simon & Schuster UK Ltd
1st Floor
222 Gray's Inn Road
London WC1X 8HB

Simon & Schuster Australia, Sydney
Simon & Schuster India, New Delhi

www.simonandschuster.co.uk
www.simonandschuster.com.au
www.simonandschuster.co.in

A CIP catalogue record for this book
is available from the British Library

Paperback ISBN: 978-1-4711-6993-9
eBook ISBN: 978-1-4711-6995-3
Audio ISBN: 978-1-4711-8559-5

Typeset in the UK by M Rules
Printed and bound by CPI Group (UK) Ltd, Croydon, CR0 4YY

THE
FLOOD

To Annika, one of the very best

THREE LOST MEN
APRIL 2016

The First Man:

THE WILL

All these decisions. During the last months of his life, this was what he would think about the most. All the questions that needed an answer, all the answers that were in fact decisions. How he wanted to live, how he wanted to die. And which secrets he wanted to share, how many he would take with him to the grave.

He was in no doubt: she deserved to know. However, he was less certain whether she really needed to know while he was still alive what he'd hidden for all those years. He thought their relationship would be better off if he continued to keep quiet. The time was so short, and he still had so much to do. To use a clichéd expression: it was time to atone for the sins of the past.

So one rainy morning in April he sat down at his desk and wrote the most important letter of his entire life. Every word had to be chosen with extreme care, every sentence polished to perfection. When he had finished he read through it over and over again. Eventually he was satisfied. Or rather resigned. This was the best he could do, and he would never know how she reacted when she found out what he'd done. Exhausted, he got to his feet. He needed lunch, a rest, a walk. He needed to get away, but suddenly he was overwhelmed with fear and anxiety.

He sat down.

Again, he thought. *I have to read the letter again.*

And so he did.

My darling,

Some months have now passed since we were given the worst possible news. When you read this, I will be gone. The day of my death has been decided, and we both know exactly when it will be. It is incomprehensible – impossible to grasp – that I am sitting here writing, yet I am aware that my time is measured out. It always has been, to be fair, even if we human beings often choose to believe that death will come to others and not to us, as if there is a third option somewhere between eternal life and eternal rest. As if we can come and go as we wish through the portal that separates the living from the dead. Trust me, that option does not exist.

Perhaps I don't deserve any better than this. Perhaps the fact that I will be snatched away sooner than either of us would have wished is actually a kind of justice. That's why I'm writing this letter, because I am so afraid that I deserve the death that awaits me.

I did something very stupid a number of years ago. Do you remember just after our daughter was born, when I was still recovering from the car accident? Of course you do, it was a terrible time. No doubt you also remember the tablets I was taking, how we both laughed and said they

*were strong enough to knock out a horse. God knows I
needed them to function in my everyday life, to regain my
strength and to cope with my body. But you were right –
neither my brain nor my eyes were clear until the pain
went away and I managed to free myself from the grip of
the morphine.*

*I was careless just once. Once. But that was enough to
ruin another person's life. It was a Tuesday. This is what
happened. I got in the car and drove to Uppsala to meet
my boss in connection with a dinner that was to be held
later that evening. In spite of the fact that I was signed
off work due to my injuries, in spite of the fact that I had
mobility problems. And in spite of the fact that my senses
were befuddled because of the medication. I have never
forgiven myself for driving. I should have taken the train.
But I didn't.*

And I ran into someone.

*Yes, you read those words correctly. It's appalling, and
impossible to undo. The sound when she hit the bonnet,
when her head thudded against the windscreen. And
then the utterly bizarre sight of her lying lifeless on the
road behind the car. Less than three seconds had passed.
I remember staring into the rear-view mirror, I couldn't
understand how she'd ended up there.*

However, I understood everything else with great clarity.

*Either I stopped and took responsibility for what I'd
done, in which case my life would be over. I might even
lose you and our child. Or I drove on and pretended
nothing had happened. I looked around; there wasn't a
soul in sight. No witnesses, just silence. So I chose the
latter option. I left her there on the road. I thought that*

the decision would have to be made only once, and there could be no remorse. I don't really recall what thoughts were going through my head as the car began to move – probably not too many. But the guilt and the shame were embedded in my very bone marrow, and since then there hasn't been a single day when I haven't struggled with the memory of what I did. The story was in the papers, of course, and I secretly read about the woman I'd hit. She actually survived, much to my surprise. I say survived, but everything she had once been was gone. That's what we do, unfortunately – we keep people alive at any price.

By this point I'm sure you are deeply shocked, castigating me for my cowardice, wondering what the hell I was thinking. I was thinking about myself – that's the short answer. And you and our daughter, and later our son. And that's the way it stayed until a few months ago, and the day when everything changed. When everything came crashing down and I learned something about my own death that I could never have suspected. That's when I decided I had to take responsibility for that terrible mistake. To atone for my crime.

So that's what I've done. I've tried to compensate my victim, as far as possible at least. I'm afraid that in doing so I have inevitably left a trail. That's why I'm writing this letter, because I think there's a risk the police will start digging into the accident I caused, and might well track me down. Track me down and discover that I am dead, and of course that's not how you should find out what I did. You need to hear it from me.

I ran into a young woman and left her lying on the road without attempting to help her. Others have done similar things, behaved atrociously and evaded all responsibility, but I don't want you to remember me that way. That's why I want to tell you that I'm different from those people. I am actually trying to take responsibility, in spite of all the years that have passed. As an author once said: I am putting everything right.

I'm afraid I can't do any more.

I love you more than anything.

The Second Man:

THE HOUSE

Just as the man who knew when he was going to die was signing his written confession, another man was contemplating a house that was more like a secret. The air was cold and raw, irritating his windpipe when he inhaled. The April weather was changeable. This was going to be good. Very good. The house had been built by hands so discreet that hardly anyone knew it existed. Hardly anyone. That was enough for the man, who turned to the woman standing beside him.

'Could I take a look indoors?' he said.

'Of course.'

The man glanced around. The garden was pretty large, and beyond it lay a small field, then nothing but forest as far as the eye could see.

Perfect.

The woman unlocked the front door and held it open for him.

'The construction was completed just under five years ago. There was nothing illegal about the project, but we were very careful to keep it quiet as far as we could. The house isn't linked to the municipal water supply or the sewage system. We dug a well, and we have a septic tank that we empty ourselves. We also have our own electricity supply thanks to a diesel generator.'

'I understand,' the man said, even though he really didn't.

To think that such a place could exist. It was astonishing. It also made him feel more than a little naïve. Was this how it felt when time slipped away? Or was it simply that this house was a consequence of a society that was growing colder and colder? He knew who the property developers behind the project were, knew their history.

As he stepped inside he felt at the front door. It was thicker than a normal door, seemed to weigh a ton.

The woman seemed pleased.

'Both the windows and doors are designed to withstand gunfire,' she explained. 'The glass was ordered especially from a supplier in Germany and is strong enough to take dozens of blows with a hammer or something similar without breaking.'

'Sounds like the windows in the Oval Office,' the man said.

His companion laughed.

'We actually had the White House in mind when we designed this bunker. I think we did pretty well.'

The man raised an eyebrow.

'Bunker?'

'We don't want anyone to forget that it's no ordinary house.'

Stunned into silence, he walked from room to room. His pulse rate increased; never in his wildest dreams had he imagined there could be such a simple solution to his problem. The house was perfect, absolutely perfect.

'How long can I rent it for?' He couldn't do anything about the hoarseness in his voice.

'It's available for at least six months. Do you think that'll be enough?'

All of a sudden he wasn't sure.

'I don't know. The thing is, I don't need it until later in the spring. When my daughter returns from overseas.'

The woman placed a hand on his shoulder.

'I heard what happened to you. Dreadful.'

The sun was shining in through one of the windows, and it was clear that the light was affected by the thickness of the glass.

'It certainly was,' agreed the man who was going to rent the house. 'But much worse for my daughter and her family than for me. It would be fantastic if they could find sanctuary at long last. I mean, they can't hide overseas forever.'

The woman straightened her shoulders.

'I can guarantee they'll be safe here. No one will be able to find them. So unless their situation changes before they come home . . .'

'It won't.'

'. . . then they're welcome here.'

The man allowed himself a smile.

'Excellent,' he said. 'Excellent.'

The Third Man:

THE EMPTINESS

And then there was the third man. The man who felt no need to confess his sins, or to find a place of sanctuary for someone close to him. The man who had lost so much that he was no longer himself.

He was sitting in his office staring silently at the wall. He didn't react when his boss walked past his door and came to a sudden halt.

'I didn't realise you were here,' his boss said. 'I thought you were off duty.'

It was obvious from the tone of his voice that he didn't like what he was saying. And 'off duty' wasn't the right phrase under the circumstances.

'I had a few things to sort out.'

His boss lingered.

'I can see you're not feeling too good,' he said. His voice was soft; he really wanted to help.

'I'm fine, I just don't want to be at home all the time.'

His boss cleared his throat.

'You need a break – this isn't working.'

'I'm sorry?'

His boss looked troubled. More than troubled.

'I can't have you flying off the handle at everybody over every little thing,' he insisted quietly. 'Your attitude, your lack of balance – it can't go on. That's why we suggest you take some sick leave.'

Silence.

So the words had finally been said. The words he'd been waiting to hear for so long. He wasn't welcome, they didn't want him around.

'Fuck off,' he said. 'I don't want to go on fucking sick leave.'

His boss took a step backwards, but only one.

'I want you out of here today,' he said. 'I've already given you more chances than you deserve.' He walked away, still somehow hesitant.

The man behind the desk knew he would be left in peace now. No fucker dared approach a man in the throes of grief, especially if that man had also been insulted. None of his friends or colleagues would come near him, because they didn't know what to say. Not that he blamed them; he himself found it hard to put into words what he was going through right now. It must be impossible for someone else.

The hours passed much too slowly. He stayed where he was, staring at the wall. That was what he looked like when he was thinking. His boss had said he wanted him out today, but he hadn't given him a time. An idea was slowly taking shape, and he felt the need to develop it in peace and quiet. He had messed up plenty of things, but he had to get this right. Not only for his own sake, but for the sake of many others. All those who were unable to gain redress themselves, all those who had been abandoned.

Time had become something he had both too much and too little of. On this particular day it was too much. But at last evening came, and he had to go home. Home to what was called life, home to emptiness, desolation.

I can never make everything right again, he thought. *But I can make it better.*

He got to his feet and walked out of his office.

INTERVIEW WITH ALEX RECHT
06-09-2016

Present: Interrogators one and two (I1 and I2),
Detective Chief Inspector Alex Recht (Recht)

I1:   Thank you for making time to see us
        today. I believe you're going to the
        funeral tomorrow?

Recht: That's correct.

I2:   Must be difficult.

Recht: To be honest it's unbearable.

I2:   Do you miss her?
        (silence)

I1:   We know that you and Fredrika ... If you
        don't feel able to talk about her at the
        moment, we'll try to work around it. We
        realise you're under pressure, but we do
        have to conduct this interview. A colleague
        has been accused of committing a criminal
        offence, and we need to speak to someone
        who was involved from the start.

Recht: In that case you need to speak to someone
        else. Because I wasn't involved from the
        start. None of us were.

I2:   What do you mean?

Recht: I mean we were blind to what this whole story was about. I mean things would have been easier if we'd understood some of the basics - like how many victims we would be faced with, for example, and in what order those individuals were killed.

(silence)

I1: Okay, let's make that our starting point. Who was the first victim?

(silence)

Recht: A man who was like the rest of us.

I2: Sorry?

Recht: I said a man who was like the rest of us. A man who was nothing more than a human being.

SATURDAY

It was in the middle of the summer that would be the longest of all that the first grisly murder was committed. It began on a Saturday, a day that could have passed like any other but was destined to be one that radically changed the lives of a number of people. Henry Lindgren was one of those people, but he didn't know that.

It was 8.45 in the evening when Henry left his apartment to go and buy a newspaper, one of those with plenty of crosswords in it. There was nothing worth watching on TV, and he always slept well if he completed a crossword before switching off his bedside light. If he'd known what that brief excursion would cost him, he would have stayed home.

It was raining and a little chilly, so Henry put on the autumn jacket he'd been wearing for almost a year thanks to a mild winter, a cold spring and a cool early summer. He also picked up his umbrella. He was heading for the newsagent's on the corner, and wouldn't have to go far in the bad weather. Which was just as well – the wind tore at his umbrella as soon as he stepped outside, and his trouser legs were soon soaked through. A bell tinkled as he pushed open the door of the shop.

'What a summer,' said Amir, the owner.

'Could be worse,' Henry replied. He liked the fact that

the summer brought both sun and rain. He paid for his paper and left.

The shadow came from nowhere. Not particularly large or tall, but very clearly in his way. Henry stopped and tried to make out who was blocking the path.

'I need help with my dog,' the man said.

Henry looked around. There was no sign of any dog.

'Oh?'

The man took a step closer.

'My dog,' he repeated. 'It's not well. Can you help me carry it up the escalator?'

That should probably have rung a warning bell in Henry's brain, but it didn't. He assumed the man was on drugs and was hallucinating about both the dog and the escalator.

'I'm sorry, but I don't think there's anything I can do,' he said, trying to get past.

He hurried back to his apartment block and keyed in the four-digit code. He shook his umbrella and closed it. Too late he discovered that the man had followed him into the building. The outside door clicked shut behind both of them.

Damn. This wasn't good, but Henry Lindgren kept his composure. It was important not to panic, he'd read that so many times. Never panic when faced with an unpredictable individual.

He didn't dare wait for the lift, but took the stairs instead. He lived on the top floor, and his knees were already protesting by the time he reached the second storey. The man seemed to have stayed put; Henry couldn't hear any footsteps behind him. By the third flight of stairs he was breathing heavily; he was running out of steam, finding it hard to focus. He concentrated on keeping going, making sure he wasn't being followed. Unfortunately he failed to notice that the lift was on its way up.

Henry was on the point of bursting into tears by the time he reached his own front door. He fumbled for his key and inserted it in the lock just as the lift came to a halt. Then everything happened so fast that an elderly person like Henry could be forgiven for not reacting in time. It was as if the man flew into his apartment. He slammed the door and locked it. Henry stood there in the hallway clutching his dripping umbrella.

Then the man uttered the words that changed – and possibly explained – everything.

'Forget the dog. I want you to keep an eye on my daughter. The thing is, I made a terrible mistake. I left her on the train, she was asleep when I got off. I was only gone for a couple of minutes, but that was enough. Now I'm standing on the platform and she's all alone on the train. Can you keep an eye on her?'

Henry slowly shook his head as his field of vision shrank. He was paralysed and struck dumb with shock. He couldn't say a single word. He just wanted to know why this man had turned up to remind Henry of the biggest mistake of his life.

Can you keep an eye on her?

I thought I could. I really thought I could.

'What do you want?' he whispered, his voice hoarse with tension. Henry was afraid.

Terrified.

The man didn't reply. Instead he struck Henry across the throat with such force that everything went black and his legs gave way. Lying on the floor, incapable of speaking or even swallowing his own saliva, Henry was only vaguely aware of what was happening. Unstructured thoughts filled his mind, too many to grasp. They turned into a warm flow of energy surging through his body as he felt the man grab the hair at the back of his neck and push his head forward. A few thoughts flashed with sudden clarity, broke through. Strangely enough, he didn't think 'Why me?' His killer had already answered that question, for which Henry was grateful. What he didn't understand, however, was the man's need to mete out punishment. Not a day went by without Henry cursing what he had done and the consequences of his action.

Henry Lindgren was nothing more than a human being. And that obviously wasn't enough.

The fire in the tiled stove was burning much too fiercely. Malin was well aware of it, but didn't do anything about it. Not at first. She had become both numbed and over-sensitive, as if her nerves were on the surface of her skin while at the same time her capacity for dealing with a crisis had virtually disappeared. Panic destroyed the body in so many different ways. The brain was worst affected, the ability to think. And it just went on and on, Malin had realised. The panic never ended, it had become part of her everyday life.

She sat there in front of the heat and watched as the flames found their way out of the stove, yellow-red monsters briefly licking the white tiles before withdrawing equally quickly. Only when she heard her son's voice behind her did she react.

'Mummy – that's dangerous!'

Malin hurried over and closed the doors of the stove. The fire would soon be suffocated. Just like everything else.

The boy wrapped his arms around her legs.

'I'm boooored, Mummy!'

She moved across the room, dragging him behind her. He was too old to carry on like this, but it was a game he'd loved when he was little. Clinging to her legs as she walked.

'Have you asked Hedvig what she's up to? She might want to do something that's fun.'

She had no idea what time it was; maybe the children ought to go to bed soon. But all that kind of thing – like bedtime routines – had become so difficult to maintain. Rules they had stuck to for years had disappeared, been forgotten. Or rather cast aside. So many things from their old life had no relevance in this new one.

Not when they were permanently terrified.

Her son let go and slumped down on the floor.

'Hedvig doesn't want to play,' he informed her. 'She wants to read.'

Please don't let the books run out. Malin didn't know what her daughter would do if that happened; reading was the only thing keeping Hedvig sane. Without them she would become like her mother. A wreck.

'I was thinking of doing some baking,' she said to her son. 'Would you like to help me?'

She didn't actually want his help, she just wanted to be alone for an hour, quarter of an hour, five minutes, one minute. But it never happened. One of the children was always there, around her, on top of her. All day every day.

The boy's face lit up.

'Cinnamon buns!' he said.

'Not today, Max. Today we're going to make teacakes.'

When had they last made cinnamon buns? Last week? Or was it the week before? She didn't know, but thought it was when the food was delivered. The days blended into one, it was no longer possible to distinguish between weekdays and the weekend. She had tried at the beginning, but now it was harder. The children's father refused to help. He almost looked as if he was wondering what the hell she was doing, why she was bothering. She had explained, over and over

again, and each time she had seen him being driven further
and further away from her and the children.

Routine.

Wasn't that what they needed most of all?

Routine.

*The very cornerstone of crisis management in a situation
like this.*

Why was that so fucking difficult to understand?

They went into the kitchen. Malin took yeast, milk and
butter out of the fridge while her son fumbled with the
bag of flour.

'Be careful – it's full,' Malin said.

'I know!'

Malin melted the butter, added the milk, warmed it gently.
Max crumbled the yeast into the bowl.

'Can I pour?'

Malin nodded and the boy allowed the milk to trickle over
the yeast as Malin whisked. The yeast dissolved, turning the
mixture beige.

'And a pinch of salt,' she said.

Max ran to fetch the salt cellar. Malin glanced out of
the window. It was raining, so heavily that it looked almost
misty. She could still see that the trees were green, the black-
currant bushes flourishing. The lawn was overgrown, the
fence leaning drunkenly. Sorrow overwhelmed her, made her
inhale sharply. She let out a sob as she exhaled.

'What's wrong, Mummy?'

The child's pale face was tense and anxious. Sometimes
Malin wondered how much he understood, how much he
was suffering.

'Nothing. I'm just a bit tired.'

Max followed her gaze and saw what she saw: the garden, the field. The fruit trees and the stillness. The desolation. And, in the distance, the forest that made them invisible.

'I want to go outside,' he whispered.

'I know, sweetheart. So do I.'

MONDAY

The ground around Malcolm Benke's impressive house had been softened by all the rain. The grass was flattened by the feet moving back and forth across the garden. Curious onlookers had already gathered by the fence, leaning over to see if they could work out why the police were so interested in the place.

'Has something happened? Is he dead?' asked a teenager with a skateboard under one arm.

Detective Inspector Torbjörn Ross contemplated him in silence, wondering what to say. He hadn't seen a skateboard for years – were they still a thing?

'Make sure they stay behind the fence,' he said to a colleague, gesturing towards the uninvited observers.

He trudged back to the house. The last few years had taken their toll on Torbjörn Ross; he'd even considered leaving the job. However, that would please far too many of his colleagues, those who couldn't wait to get rid of him, who regarded him as unreliable. Ross shook his head. There were always people who confused a normal sense of orderliness and perseverance with mental illness.

'Torbjörn!'

The voice reached him on the threshold of Benke's home. He didn't need to turn around to see who it was. Margareta Berlin.

'What are you doing here?' she snapped.

'I could ask you the same question,' he said.

Berlin sighed.

'This is Alex Recht's case.'

'I'm not sure that explains why you're here,' Ross countered calmly.

'I like to get out into the field.'

It was Ross's turn to sigh. Why did Berlin have to be the kind of boss who wanted to show the foot soldiers that she was one of the gang, that she didn't mind getting her hands dirty? Determined to ingratiate herself. Ross preferred a genuine approach, which he had learned to suss out.

'I thought Recht's team had been disbanded,' he said. 'Surely there's no room for special units in our new organisation?'

The last three words were dripping with contempt. Our new organisation. Everyone hated it. The biggest ever restructuring of the Swedish police service. Executed so badly, built on shifting sands. At least according to Ross.

'Alex's team has proved to be a successful concept over a long period,' said Berlin, who had obviously decided she wanted to call him Alex rather than Recht. 'So it stays.'

Ross shook his head. He didn't have much time for Recht's so-called successful concept. For example, Recht had led the investigation into the murder of a young girl who was found dead after having been missing for several years. He would never have solved the case without Ross. If there was anyone who deserved to move up through the organisation it was Ross. Not Recht.

'Seriously,' Berlin said, taking him by the arm. 'Go back to HQ. I have no idea how this situation arose, but of course I'm sorry you've come out here for nothing.'

He looked her straight in the eye; it was hard to suppress a smile when he realised she was afraid of him. If he refused to leave, she wouldn't have a clue what to do.

He fixed his gaze on a point somewhere behind her as he considered his next move. She had no idea why he'd turned up in Nacka. She had no idea about a lot of things. Long may it continue.

'Torbjörn?'

'I'm going.'

The relief on her face was unmistakable. She didn't understand that he was punishing her by cooperating. He and he alone knew the truth about the crime Recht would be investigating. Well, it served them all right. This time they would have to manage without his support. At least until they had the sense to ask his advice.

Torbjörn Ross went back to the car. He'd used his own Saab rather than wasting time picking up a car from HQ. He glanced over at his boss as he turned the key in the ignition.

Black clouds were gathering above Margareta Berlin.

If he'd been a less experienced driver he would probably have come off the road when he encountered the Saab. The brown car came hurtling along like a cannonball, way above the speed limit. And much too close to the white line in the middle. When DCI Alex Recht and the Saab met on a bend, Alex was a hair's breadth away from swerving and ending up in the ditch.

'Fucking idiot,' he muttered.

He didn't have enough time to go after the speeding driver; Berlin had sounded stressed when she called him.

'I want you and Fredrika to take this,' she said, before adding: 'Right now, Alex.'

Of course. He wasn't the kind of person to say no – not out of loyalty to his boss, but to the job. He would make that very clear to Margareta Berlin. She was capable of a meltdown on the scale of Chernobyl. A nasty piece of work. He had thought so ever since she went behind his back, questioned his competence after Lena's death. She had continued to overstep the mark in her role as head of Human Resources; many colleagues regarded her as a bull in a china shop, which was why it had come as a surprise when she not only applied for a senior operational post a year or so ago, but was actually appointed. Alex had expected her to stay put rather than progressing within the organisation.

Naïve, to say the least.

But all that had to be put aside when duty called. He arrived at the scene in Nacka less than an hour after Berlin's phone call. He noted the large house, the expensive cars on the drive, the attractive location by the sea. He pulled on protective clothing and went inside.

The deceased, Malcolm Benke, was sitting in a leather armchair staring blankly at a fire that had gone out long ago. He had been found that morning by the cleaner, who always came on a Monday. She had already been questioned, and Alex didn't think she would be of any great interest. The CSIs moved silently around him. The whole place was full of people, people Benke had never met and whose only purpose was to investigate his death.

Alex crouched down in front of the dead man and studied the bloodstains on his shirt. Malcolm Benke had been shot in the chest. The bullet had passed straight through his body and through the back of the chair before burying itself in the wall.

Who gets shot sitting in a favourite armchair in front of the fire? Alex wondered.

There were no obvious signs of a disturbance in the room, which could lead to the assumption that Benke and the killer had known each other. Or that Benke had been taken by surprise, hadn't even heard the perpetrator coming. It was this kind of tentative speculation you had to love if you were going to be a police officer. It was important not to jump to conclusions, and to avoid getting frustrated over all the things you didn't know.

'The bullet tore a substantial hole in his chest,' said Renata Rashid, the medical examiner, who was standing beside him. She gently moved Benke's shirt aside, exposing the wound.

Alex pulled a face.

'A horrible way to die,' he said.

Although that wasn't really what he meant. On the contrary – he had very few objections to the way in which Benke had died. A bullet in the back of the neck or the chest seemed like a dream in comparison with the way many others met their end. However, Alex did have a major problem with the location. He was always particularly angered when people were subjected to crimes in their own home, the one place on earth where they had the right to feel safe.

'As far as I can see there are no other obvious injuries,' Renata said. 'Although of course we won't know for certain until I've carried out the post-mortem.'

Alex looked closely at Benke's face. His expression was peaceful – or was it resigned? He'd seen faces frozen in horror at the moment of death. Not a pretty sight.

Benke was wearing a shirt, trousers, slippers. A jacket was draped over the back of the chair. According to records he was seventy-two years old and lived alone. He and his wife had divorced ten years earlier. They'd had two children, but only one was still alive. Their daughter had died six months before her parents split up, at the age of thirty. A quick internet search told Alex that Benke had been a successful property developer, involved in a number of notable projects in Stockholm.

A young colleague came to join him; much to Alex's embarrassment, he couldn't remember his name. He wasn't part of Alex's team, but had been deployed as an extra resource. He was bubbling with enthusiasm, the adrenaline coursing through his veins.

I was like you once upon a time. I used to think it was exciting when someone died.

'So what do you think?' said the young man.

'Nothing.'

'A disgruntled client who wanted to settle a score?'

Alex stared at him.

'Is that how you deal with builders you've engaged? By shooting them?'

The other man flushed.

'You have to think outside the box,' he mumbled before jerking his head in Benke's direction. 'Was he a poof?'

Alex was taken aback. A poof? Did he have the energy to point out that this was unacceptable language? To be the stickler who demanded political correctness? Who knew what the idiot would come out with next – maybe some racist term that would make Renata Rashid hit the roof. She was married to an Iranian, and knew exactly what it was like to be perceived as different. Alex suppressed a sigh. There were days when he seriously doubted whether talking could change the world, and this was probably one of those days, in spite of everything.

'What makes you think he was gay?' he asked, hoping his own choice of words and his tone would convey the right message.

'His hands.'

'His hands?'

'The rings. He's wearing a lot of jewellery for a straight guy – and isn't that a woman's ring?'

Alex frowned. He counted three rings: an ordinary signet

ring and a freemasons' ring, plus the one that his colleague thought was a woman's ring. It was on the little finger of Benke's left hand – gold, with what Alex assumed was a small diamond inset. Reluctantly he had to concede that it did indeed look as if it had been designed for a woman. Which didn't mean that a man couldn't feel good wearing it, of course.

But not this man, he thought grimly.

There was something archetypally masculine about Malcolm Benke and his home. Besides, the ring was too small, even for his little finger.

'Can we take a closer look?' Alex said to Renata.

She removed it from the finger, and Alex held it up, examining it by the light of the chandelier. The blasted latex gloves made his hands itch.

'There's an inscription.' His young colleague was so close he was almost on top of him.

ALWAYS AND FOREVER. BEATA AND RICHARD

'Beata,' Alex said.

'Wasn't that his daughter's name?'

'It was.'

He dropped the ring into an evidence bag and handed it to his colleague. If this was Malcolm Benke's daughter's wedding ring, then why was he wearing it on his little finger?

Hadn't this been the worst summer ever? Fredrika Bergman thought so. She had searched her memory for one that could be classified as worse, but without success. She could remember summers that had evoked anxiety – who couldn't? – but nothing like this.

I don't want to do this any more.

That phrase was acceptable only when uttered by a child, not an adult. Sometimes when Fredrika allowed her thoughts to roam free, usually at night when sleep refused to come, she would remember how easy everything had been when she was a child. No conviction had been stronger than the one that told her anything was possible.

How she missed that feeling, that illusion.

She was over forty now, and knew all too well that so many things we wish for will never happen. Never.

It had been Spencer's idea to take an early holiday. He had come up with the idea back in January, long before anyone even thought of booking their annual leave, long before life fell apart. He got his way in the end, and they went to Italy, rented a villa in Tuscany. They spent the last few days back in Stockholm, surrounded by concrete and steel. When it was time for Fredrika and Spencer to return to work, the children joined their maternal grandparents at their summer cottage. The fact that she was working and the children were getting a taste of the summer they deserved kept Fredrika on an even keel.

'Why do you have to work with things the way they are?' her mother had asked. 'Why can't you take some time off, be together?'

With things the way they are.

Was that an adequate description of a life from which virtually every scrap of joy had been removed?

'Spencer doesn't want to do that,' Fredrika replied.

She could have expressed herself more clearly. She could have said that Spencer *really* didn't want to spend all summer on holiday.

'Why the hell would we do that?' he said when she broached the subject. 'So that we have all the time in the world to sit here and stare each other to death? No chance.'

His anger made her laugh then cry, but not until she had left the apartment to go shopping on her own.

Alex Recht called when she was in the car on the way to a music session. The violin that she had once hoped to make her career had become more important than ever. Music was her breathing space, her refuge.

'Fredrika.'

'Hi, Fredrika, it's Alex. How quickly can you get to Nacka?'

Fredrika sighed.

'I can be there first thing tomorrow morning.'

'How about in half an hour?'

'Alex, it's my day off.'

Spencer hadn't completely won the battle over their summer plans. Fredrika had sneaked in odd free days in July, days when she didn't go to work, but made time for reflection, for playing the violin. And – like today – time for a meeting that couldn't be postponed.

'That might be the case,' Alex said. 'But tomorrow and for many days after that you'll be investigating a murder.'

Fredrika didn't respond.

'I need you,' her boss said.

And that was all it took to make her turn the car around and head for Nacka instead. She would still have time for her meeting; it wasn't for a few hours. And the violin could wait. Alex had called on behalf of the dead; that wasn't something she could ignore.

The place was unusual, almost like a modern haunted house. If it had been in a children's cartoon it would have been festooned with cobwebs, dust and dirt, and the odd broken window. In reality it was clean and tidy, but soulless. Fredrika got out of the car and walked towards the front door, which was wide open. A colleague supplied her with protective clothing before she was allowed inside. This was no longer a private residence, but a crime scene where every trace of the perpetrator must be secured, every trace of the police noted and eliminated.

Fredrika slipped on her shoe covers and thought how easy it was to switch into work mode. The transformation was blissful; all the bad thoughts were temporarily sent packing when she disappeared into her professional role.

She found Alex in the living room, the deceased seated in an armchair. There was a corner sofa facing a TV, but Malcolm Benke hadn't been watching television when he died. He had been gazing at the open fire – at least that was how it looked to Fredrika.

'Is he known to us?' she asked Alex, wondering if he had a criminal record. She took in his silver-grey hair, his pleasant face.

He seemed to want to whisper 'welcome'.

'No,' Alex said. 'Not as far as we can tell.'

That didn't necessarily mean a great deal, and they both knew it. Benke could have been involved in criminal activity without the police being aware of it; there were an alarming number of felons out there.

Fredrika glanced around. The decor exuded gravitas and a conscious attempt to appear stylish, giving the impression that everything was expensive and carefully chosen. It reminded her of an exclusive hotel. This wasn't a home in the real sense of the word; it was just a place where Benke spent more time than anywhere else.

'I'll take a look around,' she said. Alex didn't answer; he was talking to one of the CSIs.

Fredrika moved silently through the house. The kitchen was one of the nicest she'd seen. Top-quality French tiles and glossy cupboard doors in a subtle shade. Perfect for someone who enjoyed cooking. But was Benke the kind of man who wandered into the kitchen and threw together a boeuf bourguignon? It seemed unlikely.

There was a loaf and a bread knife on a board.

'Was he eating when he died?' Fredrika asked a CSI who was busy examining the rubbish bin under the sink.

'There's an empty plate on the table next to the armchair,' he said. 'We think he made a sandwich and ate it in front of the fire.'

Fredrika wondered what Benke would have chosen if he'd known it was to be his last meal. Probably not a sandwich.

She continued into the hallway, past what appeared to be a study. There wasn't a single sheet of paper on the desk. She felt the same as she had in the kitchen: did he ever work in there? She stepped inside, examined the well-organised bookshelves (so well-organised that it was hard to envisage anyone ever picking out a book). She went upstairs and found more rooms with clear functions; again, she couldn't imagine Benke using them himself. Two guest rooms and a TV room furnished with two Chesterfield sofas. She tried one and thought it would be impossible to find a comfortable position. Finally she reached a large bedroom that must be Benke's. The bed was made, a tie lying on top of the covers. Yesterday's paper was on the bedside table.

She opened the wardrobe and stared at the shirts, trousers and suits. She didn't know what she was looking for, what she thought she might find.

She went back downstairs. Alex was on the phone to his partner Diana.

'I'm not sure when I'll be home – I'll call you later. Love you.'

Love you.

Wasn't that too personal? Or had Fredrika become over-sensitive? She'd never been one for exposing her private life, or for involving herself in the affairs of others. However, she knew she'd been unusually quiet during the spring – even for her. She never asked Alex if everything was okay at home, mainly to avoid similar questions in return.

How are things with you and Spencer?

Pretty bad, actually.

Fredrika blinked and focused on the living room. There were several large paintings on the walls, acquired presumably because they were expensive and impressive rather than because Benke appreciated the artists. There were only three framed photographs, arranged on the mantelpiece. They were all of children, and Fredrika guessed they were taken during the 1980s. Once again, the balance seemed wrong; why so little of a personal nature in his own home?

'How many children did he have?' she asked Alex, who'd finished his call.

'Two.'

Fredrika noticed the drinks trolley over by the wall, close to Benke's armchair. She frowned. There was a Polaroid snap next to the fruit bowl. She studied it for a long time, wondering why it was there and who the subjects were. Three men were gazing into the camera, their expressions serious. One was Benke; she didn't recognise the other two. It was impossible to establish any kind of context; none of them were dressed up. Benke was wearing a pair of chinos and a blue shirt with the sleeves rolled up. Fredrika's heart skipped a beat. There was a fourth man who looked as if he would rather be anywhere else. He was partly turned away, half his face in shadow. And yet she was sure.

She recognised him.

She showed Alex the photo.

'Do you know who that is?' she said, pointing.

'No. I'm guessing it was taken quite a while ago – Benke's much younger.'

Fredrika turned the picture over and was disappointed to see no names, no date on the back. She replaced it on the trolley. The CSIs would take it back to HQ, make a copy.

'The brutality,' Alex said, interrupting her train of thought.

'Sorry?'

'There's something about this murder that feels brutal. I mean more brutal than usual.' He sounded almost embarrassed.

'Depends what you're comparing it with,' Fredrika said dryly.

'Of course. Obviously we've seen much worse, but this is . . . unusual. Check the entry wound. The killer didn't want to risk failure.'

Memories of investigations that had driven her to the brink of insanity floated to the surface.

Brutal, Alex had said. And he was right.

Maybe I've become inured to it all. I don't react the way he does.

She took another look at the Polaroid. It must mean something to Benke. Or to his murderer.

Fredrika wanted to know what that was, but most of all she wanted to know who the fourth man was, the one refusing to look into the camera.

Could he really be the only one who suspected that something was wrong? Noah Johansson found it difficult to believe that was the case. He didn't even need to check his diary; if someone asked he could immediately tell them how many weeks and days Dan had been gone. And Noah hadn't a clue how he was going to get him to come back.

It was a horrible realisation, particularly as Noah had begun to think that time was running out. If he didn't find Dan soon, it would be too late. This was a fresh thought, and unbearably painful. However hard he tried, time just kept on passing, and soon there wouldn't be any left. Noah felt as if he was going crazy. He was so alone. The police weren't interested, and his friends didn't understand why he was so upset. Anxiety could punch great big holes in friendships. Of everything that had happened over the past few weeks, that was what had shocked him the most.

Roine, his oldest friend and one of the few who was still around, had been honest with him over a drink only last week.

'I'm trying to understand,' he'd said. 'But ... the way you talk, it scares me. Why can't you come to terms with the fact that your brother's gone to Australia? Get over it. Be your old self again.'

Australia.

Fucking Australia.

Noah had had to make a decision. Either he let the harsh words go unchallenged, or he would lose Roine. He chose to keep his friend. He couldn't cope with being any more isolated than he already was; he couldn't bear to lose Roine too. But he hadn't heard from Roine since that evening . . .

At first Noah had thought everything was okay with Dan and his family. They'd been talking about moving to Australia for several years. They hadn't actually emigrated; it was more of a family adventure. They were planning to live abroad for one or two school terms. They had discussed Thailand (too much sun), then London (too expensive). Finally they had decided on Australia. After New Year the details had been firmed up. Both Dan and his wife had applied for and secured interesting jobs, after online interviews. The children's school applications had been submitted, and eventually everything was settled.

'We're leaving two weeks before the end of term,' Dan had said. 'I've got a couple of meetings I need to attend in late May, and there's no reason why we shouldn't all travel out together. That will give us a few weeks before work and school kick in.'

Noah freely admitted that he'd never been keen on the project. He thought it was a frivolous idea, and unfortunately he'd expressed his opinion more than once. The brothers had fallen out, and when Noah was offered the chance to attend an industry conference in Majorca in the week of Dan's departure, he decided to go. He extended his stay on either side of the conference, took an early holiday. When he came back everything seemed so empty. Dan was gone, his house deserted. There was an envelope in Noah's mailbox containing the key and a note from his brother:

Can you look after the house as we agreed? Thanks.

Noah had been furious. They hadn't agreed any such thing! Someone else could do that. Besides which, Noah already had a key. One week passed, then two. Noah heard nothing from Dan. The silence soon became distinctly uncomfortable. They couldn't go on like this. He picked up one of the keys and went over to the house. He wanted to see what needed doing before emailing Dan to ask how things were going.

That was where he first got the feeling something was wrong. The house didn't look the way he'd expected, given the fact that the owner was planning to be away for a year. There was laundry hanging up in the airing cupboard. Dirty dishes in the dishwasher. And then there were the wardrobes: they were crammed with clothes. Were Dan and his family intending to buy everything new in Australia? Surely not.

Noah emailed his brother from his phone while he was still in the house, but didn't receive a reply until two days later. The tone was brusque, the words few. Noah needed to stop looking for problems, stop nagging. They would organise their trip however the fuck they wanted. *However the fuck they wanted.* That was what did it for Noah. Dan had never, ever sworn at him. That word, together with the key in his mailbox, convinced Noah that something was wrong. Very wrong. So he called the police.

Unfortunately they didn't take him seriously either, not even when he burst into tears and told them about finding his brother's bike on the drive on the afternoon when he'd realised there was a problem. It looked like any old bike, but Dan had inherited it from their grandfather, and never left it unlocked. After a very brief investigation the police concluded that Noah was simply imagining things. They claimed to have been in touch with Dan, who had confirmed that he'd gone to Australia and everything was fine. That was the end of the matter, as far as they were concerned.

But Noah couldn't let it go.

He had contacted the Swedish embassy in Canberra. They'd promised to check whether Dan and his family had arrived in the country, but couldn't guarantee that they'd be able to help. Someone would call him within a few weeks; it was holiday time, and the embassy was understaffed. Noah had continued to search, his stress levels increasing by the day, but he'd got nowhere. The airlines all had a duty of confidentiality, and were unable to confirm that Dan had flown with them. Noah went back to the police, but they refused to help. Obtaining lists of airline passengers was a huge task, didn't Noah understand that? Without real evidence that something was wrong, they wouldn't lift a finger.

Noah swallowed hard. His next client was due, and Noah needed to be on top of his game. This man had very specific requirements. Noah had actually intended to postpone the meeting, but hadn't got around to it. Which had to be the very definition of having too much to do – not even having time to clear his diary.

The client arrived, the bell over the door jingled. Noah took a deep breath and went to greet him.

'Good afternoon,' he said, with the smile that many people believed was largely responsible for his success.

A pleasant smile, a warm smile, but above all a smile that couldn't be interpreted as anything other than sympathetic. Not by those who were grieving, nor by those who knew they would soon die – as was the case with the man who had just arrived.

'My wife has reconsidered since our last visit,' the man said. 'She'd prefer me to be buried in the white coffin. The black one is too posh for her.'

He laughed, his teeth dazzling white against his tanned skin. No one would ever guess that he was less than two months from his own death.

Noah made a note. 'She's not with you today?' What a stupid thing to say. Obviously she wasn't with him today.

But the man didn't seem bothered by the funeral director's brain-dead comment. On the contrary, he seemed happy to respond.

'She's working.'

Noah nodded. 'Just one small detail: you say you and your wife have decided that you'll be buried in the white coffin rather than the black one.'

'Yes?'

'So does that mean you've also changed your mind about cremation and would prefer to opt for interment?'

The man recoiled and inhaled so sharply that Noah became concerned.

'What the hell . . . ? No, absolutely not!'

Noah calmed him down.

'I thought that was the case, but I had to ask.'

The man pursed his lips.

'Do people still go for that? Being buried in the ground?'

'Yes indeed. Many hate the idea of being incinerated, if you'll forgive my choice of words.'

The man shook his head.

'So they'd rather be eaten by worms and stink to high heaven. That doesn't make sense!'

Noah thought so too, but it wasn't his place to share his own preferences with his clients.

'And are we sticking to the date as agreed?' he asked.

The man's eyes changed in a second, as if a lamp had been switched off. Any trace of liveliness disappeared, replaced by two deep pools filled with such sorrow that Noah had to stop himself from reaching across the table to squeeze his hand.

'Yes. The first of September is the end, and the service will be held the following week as arranged.'

Noah's throat went dry. Money could buy a lot of things, including peace of mind. Which was just as well. The man sitting opposite him would have the death he wanted. He would die with dignity. What could possibly be wrong with that?

It's important not to lose hope, Noah thought.

Dan had been gone for almost eight weeks. How much longer would Noah be able to cope with the anxiety that threatened to suffocate him? How much longer before he lost all hope of being able to save his brother?

There was no stamp or postmark on the letter; it had been left in her mailbox in the foyer by someone who had gone to the trouble of delivering it in person. In person but anonymously.

Lovisa Wahlberg frowned as she examined the white envelope. No addressee, no sender's name on the back.

Strange.

The ancient lift rattled and screeched as it made its way upwards. Lovisa could have taken the stairs – should have taken the stairs – but she didn't have the energy. She was worn out after running on the treadmill for over an hour. She just wanted to get home, pull off her sweaty clothes, have a shower.

And open the letter.

She'd hardly got through the door before she dropped her bag on the floor and ripped open the envelope. It was so light, so thin. For a second she thought it might be empty. Or maybe it was meant for someone else – whoever had brought the letter could have slipped it in the wrong mailbox. That kind of thing did happen.

That kind of thing did happen.

But not to her.

Because as soon as she looked into the envelope, all such

thoughts disappeared. *This was meant for her and no one else*. A newspaper cutting. An article written in Spanish, printed on yellowing paper. She carefully removed it. The envelope fell to the floor, remained lying on the doormat. She could hear someone walking up the stairs.

She panicked, petrified of whoever was out there. She locked the door, backed into the kitchen, away from the footsteps.

Her mobile. She must get out her mobile. It was in the side pocket of her sports bag. She dashed into the hallway, dug out the phone, stopped dead and listened hard. Not a sound.

Her heart was pounding like a jackhammer and her mouth had gone dry. She returned to the kitchen. She hadn't heard the main door open and close, so whoever was in the stairwell must still be there. Outside her apartment? On the floor below?

Her hands shook as she stared at the cutting. The picture told her everything. Everything. It contained terrible information, evoked an unbearable feeling of guilt. She didn't need the article itself.

She hadn't meant anyone any harm, hadn't realised that by saving herself she was sacrificing someone else. She hadn't had the opportunity to grasp the violent consequences of her decision. She had known that her strategy was selfish, but fatal? No, that had been beyond her comprehension.

I just wanted to get home.

Her entire body was shaking as she crept into the hallway once more. She had no idea how long she'd been standing in the kitchen. All she knew was that she was shivering in her sweaty clothes; she ought to go and have a shower. But not until she'd peeped through the spy hole, made sure there was no one out there waiting for her.

She leaned forward cautiously, wanting and not wanting to know. At first she couldn't see a thing. The light had gone out automatically, and no one had switched it back on. There was no natural daylight in the windowless stairwell, but gradually her eye grew accustomed to the darkness. And then she saw him. The shadow among the shadows. He was standing motionless outside the lift, staring straight at her door.

Straight at her.

Lovisa ran into the bathroom and locked the door. She sank down on the cold tiles, drew her knees up to her chest and wrapped her arms around her legs.

How could she have been so stupid?

How could she have believed it was all over?

She felt incredibly naïve.

And terrified beyond all reason.

They gathered in the Lions' Den just after four to review what they knew so far. Everything was the same, nothing was the same. Alex Recht's special-investigation team seemed to be the only one that had survived the restructuring. He was grateful, but the problems that the team had experienced from the beginning still remained. It was still difficult to bring in additional resources and support when necessary, and it was still difficult to explain exactly where the team fitted into the new organisation, although of course there was an official answer to that question. They were in Margareta Berlin's department within the Stockholm police, and were based in police HQ at Kungsholmen. Fortunately they were able to work with a wide range of other departments; Alex would have gone crazy if he'd been working directly under Berlin.

Although on this occasion she had delivered, to be fair. They had been given additional personnel to help with the investigation into Malcolm Benke's murder; in fact so many new colleagues had appeared that there weren't enough chairs in the conference room. Alex noticed that Fredrika Bergman already seemed to have forgotten that this was supposed to be her day off. He must remember to thank her. He was really bad at expressing his gratitude and appreciation, as Diana often pointed out.

'Okay,' he said, raising his voice to silence the room. 'Let's make a start.'

A new body, a new murder. It must never become routine, but on the other hand there was no point in pretending they hadn't learned from previous cases. Alex often wondered how death's gloomy presence affected someone like Fredrika. She'd never intended to work for the police; she'd dreamed of an entirely different career. He knew she'd been deeply affected by what had happened during that dreadful winter when two Jewish boys had been shot dead out on the island of Ekerö, but things had been pretty quiet since then, hadn't they? There had been no spectacular cases since the murders of the two children. As far as Alex was concerned, life on the domestic front had also been unusually calm and harmonious. He'd looked after his grandchildren, read books, gone fishing, met up with colleagues for a drink after work. He felt he'd achieved a good balance – until a few months ago, when Berlin became his boss.

Is this when it all changes? he thought. *Is this when the peace and harmony slip through my fingers?*

When he got back to HQ after the visit to Nacka, he felt inexplicably uneasy. The feeling was inexplicable not because of what he'd seen – good God, the day he reacted to the sight of a dead body he'd know it was time to retire – but rather because of what he *hadn't* seen.

He tried to shake off his unease by focusing on the meeting.
The ring.
If only it hadn't been for that damned ring.

'Malcolm Benke,' he began. 'Where are we with his private life? According to the records he lived alone, but that doesn't tell us much.'

The younger officer who'd been at the scene of the crime spoke up. By this time Alex had learned his name: Ivan. A strange name for such a young man.

'Benke had a seat on two boards and one major interest group,' Ivan said. 'I haven't got very far yet, but I did manage to make a couple of calls during the afternoon. Apparently it's well known in Benke's circles that he had a relationship with Gudrun Manner a few years ago, and has been single ever since they broke up.'

'Gudrun Manner the fashion designer?' Fredrika couldn't hide her surprise.

'That's right.'

'Wow.'

If it hadn't been for Diana, Alex wouldn't have had a clue who they were talking about, but as it was Manner needed no further introduction. She was in her early sixties and had a shop in Östermalm. She was famous for using only three colours: black, white and grey. Alex had discreetly tried to dissuade Diana from shopping there; just walking past the window made him feel miserable.

'Anything else?'

Only a few hours had passed since the discovery of Benke's body. The picture they had begun to build up was based mainly on official records; they still had a lot to do.

'No, but I'm looking at his social network,' Ivan replied. 'The technicians are working on his computer and mobile phone. I've barely scraped the surface, but so far there's no indication that Benke had been subjected to threats, or was involved in any kind of dispute that might have led to his death.'

'Good,' Alex said. 'Good.'

What was so good about the fact that they didn't have a single lead? He turned to Fredrika.

'How about his family?'

She didn't answer at first; she seemed to be lost in thought. It took a few seconds before she glanced up and realised she'd been spoken to.

You're not yourself, Alex thought. *And you haven't been for a long time.*

'Right, yes,' she said, gathering the papers in front of her. She pushed back a strand of hair that had escaped from the thick braid hanging down her back. The braid had become her signature; no one could imagine her without it. Alex remembered exactly what he'd thought the first time he met her: that she looked like the kind of person who'd read too many books and met too few real people. That she didn't belong in the police. They'd come a long way since then – she even had silver running through her hair now.

The thought made him smile, and Fredrika frowned.

'What . . . ?'

'Nothing. Nothing.'

I'm smiling because you have threads of silver in your hair, and I'm embarrassed because I'm thinking that it really suits you.

'Benke had two children,' Fredrika said. 'His son, Bernhard, has been living in Vienna for the last ten years. He moved there when his sister died and his parents divorced. Benke's ex-wife, Karin, still lives in Stockholm. They had a prenuptial agreement that spelled out any eventual settlement. Virtually all the money was Benke's, as was the house they lived in.'

'So she left the marriage with nothing?' said a colleague who'd remained silent until now.

'Yes, but you could hardly describe her as poor,' Fredrika went on. 'She had plenty of her own money.'

'Her own money or inherited money?' Alex wanted to know; he thought there was a clear difference between the two.

'Inherited, I'm guessing,' Fredrika said. 'I've checked her tax returns and there's nothing there to explain how she can afford a summer cottage in the archipelago and a large apartment in Östermalm.'

Alex leaned back. The ring on Malcolm Benke's little finger – it gave him no peace.

'Do we know the name of the daughter's husband? If she was married, of course.'

'Richard – just as it said inside the ring,' Fredrika replied. The room fell silent.

'Anyone else have the feeling that Benke didn't usually wear his daughter's wedding ring?'

Several people nodded.

'We need to speak to the ex-wife,' Fredrika said. 'About Benke, but also about their late daughter.'

Alex felt the weight of unpleasant memories. The hardest memories of all – those involving parents who had lost one or more of their children. It was something they all seemed to learn to live with, but could never really put behind them. Alex had felt as if something died inside him the day his wife Lena passed away from cancer. One minute she was there, then she was gone. He had said it was the worst thing that could happen, and he had meant it. He had honestly believed that he loved her more than their children – until the day his son became entangled in a plane hijacking that could have gone badly wrong.

I would never have recovered, he thought. *It would have been unbearable.*

He pulled himself together. 'What do we know about the daughter's death?'

'Not nearly enough. She'd been living in England with her husband for several years when she died,' Fredrika informed him.

Alex looked around the room.

'Anyone else have anything to contribute? CSI – where are we with the murder weapon?'

'All I can tell you is that it's notable by its absence,' a female technician said. 'Our initial assessment suggests that the bullet came from a Colt 45. We've checked all the doors and windows – no sign of forced entry. And as those of you who were at the crime scene could see, there was nothing to suggest that a struggle had taken place in the house.'

'So Benke knew his killer,' Fredrika said. 'Well enough to let him in, at least.'

'Either that or he was taken by surprise,' the technician countered. 'It wouldn't be impossible to pick the lock on the front door and sneak inside – if you knew what you were doing.'

'In other words, the perpetrator has found his way through locked doors before,' Alex said slowly.

'Exactly.'

'Do we even know if the door was locked?' Ivan wondered.

'The cleaner who found Benke said it was locked when she

arrived in the morning. It's a classic dead latch – you don't need a key to lock it.'

Alex reached for the computer.

'How far have we got with house-to-house enquiries?'

'Ongoing,' Ivan replied. 'Nothing to report as yet.'

So no witnesses either. Great.

Alex clicked on the notes he'd made when Renata Rashid called him just before the meeting.

'In Renata's opinion, Benke had been dead for between ten and twelve hours when he was found at nine o'clock in the morning, so we're looking at between nine and eleven the previous evening. However, that tells us nothing about when the perpetrator arrived, how long they were together before Benke died.'

He glanced up.

'The only thing we know for sure is that the cause of death was the wound caused by the shot to his chest. That's not enough. I want more information about his contacts; we need to exclude the possibility of a threat that he was aware of. And I want feedback when the house-to-house is done.'

The ring. That damned ring.

'We also need to speak to the ex-wife as soon as possible.'

He slammed the computer shut and turned to Fredrika.

'You and I will go over there right now. We'll all reconvene in the morning.'

Chairs scraped against the floor as everyone stood up and left the Lions' Den. Fredrika was in front of Alex, head down, lost in thought.

'Is everything okay?' he asked.

She gave him a smile so fleeting it was hardly there.

'Of course.'

He immediately regretted the question. She was lying, which made him uncomfortable. It wasn't just that there was a problem – she wasn't prepared to tell him what it was. He cleared his throat, tried to put into words what was bothering him on a professional level.

'I can't get my head around this case,' he said.

Fredrika reacted with confusion.

'Surely that's nothing unusual at such an early stage?'

Alex ran a hand through his hair.

'That's not what I meant. It's . . . there seems to be a kind of symbolism about this murder, and I find it disturbing.'

At that moment Torbjörn Ross walked past, a coffee cup in his hand, Wellington boots on his feet.

'How's it going?' he said.

'Fine,' Alex replied, hoping his colleague would keep walking.

Which he did. Ross disappeared into the kitchen.

Torbjörn Ross had once been his friend. These days he was someone Alex preferred to avoid. The passing years had made Ross difficult, and his judgement was poor. Alex was aware that they were in the same department, but so were plenty of others. Ross kept himself to himself; Alex had no idea what he got up to, and he didn't want to know.

Fredrika shook her head when he'd gone.

'The ring,' she said.

'Exactly. Benke looked so calm, sitting there in his armchair – a grotesque contrast to what had happened to him.'

Fredrika agreed. 'Grotesque is exactly the right word.'

But no more grotesque than two Jewish schoolboys shot in the back, Alex thought grimly, allowing his mind to take him back yet again to the nightmare in which he and

Fredrika had found themselves a few years ago. It had been a bitterly cold winter, and an ice-cold killer had wandered the streets of Stockholm, closely followed by the legend of the evil Paper Boy.

And then.

The thought came out of nowhere, threatened to floor him.

'The photograph,' he said. 'The photograph on the trolley.'

Fredrika immediately straightened up.

'What about it?'

'I know who the fourth man is, the one who refused to look into the camera.'

'I've been thinking about him all afternoon,' Fredrika said. 'Go on – who is he?'

We thought he was dead. That was what Alex wanted to say, but in the heat of the moment he couldn't remember the man's name. Instead he simply came out with the name of his wife.

'Eden,' he said.

E den Lundell, who had been the head of Säpo, the Swedish security service, and who had chosen to leave Sweden after one of her daughters had been murdered. Her husband's name was Mikael. As far as Fredrika knew, the family lived in Israel. She shuddered when she thought about Eden, about the investigation in which she had been involved. No case had had more layers, more low points than the one that began with the shooting of a teacher at the Solomon school and ended with Eden losing a child.

Had Eden also lost her mind? Fredrika wondered as she and Alex drove over to see Karin Benke. *I would have done.*

The thought of any contact with Eden and her family filled her with dread.

I have nothing to say to someone like her.

Instead she focused on Karin Benke. All roads leading away from the darkness were equally welcome. As a child Fredrika had loved to play with the doll's house her grandmother had given her. It had been like travelling to a different place, a place that belonged to someone else, yet she was allowed to visit whenever she liked. She had experienced the same feeling when she started working for the police and was let into other people's homes in different situations, either to carry out a search or to conduct an interview. And sometimes to deliver terrible news.

Malcolm Benke's ex-wife had already been informed of his death when they arrived at her apartment in Östermalm. Fredrika had tried many times to define the difference between an apartment and a flat; in this instance it was crystal clear, for once. The high ceilings, the space, the impressive and well-preserved original details from the last century; there was no doubt that this was an apartment.

Karin, on the other hand, was a very ordinary, down-to-earth person, open and straightforward, with an unmistakable air of integrity.

'Our condolences,' Alex said when she'd let them in.

'Thank you.'

She led the way into the kitchen, where they sat down at the table. Orchids in the window, no curtains, white-painted walls.

I could live here, Fredrika thought instinctively.

Alex began tentatively, allowing small talk to shift into a standard interview without Karin really noticing the change. He was good at this, Fredrika said to herself, just as he was at so many other things. She felt an embarrassing sense of relief; it was important that Alex held it together when she was falling apart.

She couldn't help a faint blush rising to her cheeks.

I have to tell him. I have to tell him what's on my mind. But not now. Another day.

'What can you tell us about your ex-husband's life?' Alex said. 'Were you close?'

'No.'

'But maybe you met up through your son?' Fredrika asked.

'No. We preferred not to have any contact whatsoever.'

'I understand.' Alex sounded surprisingly empathetic.

Fredrika moved on to Beata. 'I believe your daughter lived in London?'

Karin's face closed down, trying to conceal the way she felt.

'That's right.'

'How long was she there?'

'Many years. She was at university there for four years, then she got a job.'

'So altogether . . . ?' Alex prompted her.

'Twelve years.'

'What did she study?' Fredrika asked.

'Languages – Latin and English. She worked as a teacher at a grammar school in East London.'

'Her husband was British – was that why she stayed in the city?'

Things were getting more difficult now. Karin was a woman who gave the impression of being in control most of the time, but grief and horror are not so easily subjugated. Fredrika knew that, and so did Karin.

'I think so. On the other hand, there was no mention of her moving back to Sweden even before she met him. She loved London.'

'Was her husband also a teacher?'

'No, he was a stockbroker.'

It struck Fredrika that she didn't refer to him by name; Karin's son-in-law was 'he' and nothing else. She thought about the ring on Malcolm Benke's little finger. Forensics had already established that there were no prints on it – not Benke's or anyone else's.

'What was he like?' Fredrika pushed a little harder,

keeping her voice quiet. 'Your son-in-law Richard, what was he like?'

Karin looked as if she was about to get to her feet, but remained seated.

'He was horrible. Really horrible.'

She didn't say any more. Horrible. A word Fredrika's children liked to use, frequently and sometimes at full volume.

'You're HORRIBLE!' her son would roar when Fredrika refused to buy him sweets in the supermarket.

Alex also reacted to Karin's choice of word.

'Horrible in what way?' he said.

Karin's face changed again, but this time it wasn't sorrow they could see in her eyes. She was angry – furious, in fact. She took a deep breath; she seemed to have a problem forcing the air out of her lungs.

'Horrible,' she repeated. 'That's the best way of describing him. Everything Richard did was horrible, everything had an ulterior motive. We didn't realise to start with, and nor did Beata. He was totally dysfunctional. He changed jobs as often as the rest of us change our underwear. And then there were all his ridiculous so-called investments. Money disappeared at an alarming rate, first from their joint account and then from Beata's own account.'

'So he was manipulative,' Alex commented.

'Incredibly.'

Fredrika hesitated, wondering how to formulate the question that had to be asked.

'Was he violent towards her?'

Karin looked away, unable to meet their gaze.

'Yes.'

Alex and Fredrika exchanged a glance. Alex ran a hand over the surface of the table, the scars pale pink against skin that had been burned on the day he saved a little girl from searing flames.

'She died ten years ago,' he said. 'If it's not too painful, could you tell us what happened?'

Karin didn't speak for a moment, then she looked Alex straight in the eye and said: 'He murdered her.'

'Richard?'

'Yes.'

'So he's in jail?' Fredrika asked.

'No.'

'No?'

'There was no evidence, but we all knew what he'd done, and so did the police.'

'They didn't look for another perpetrator?'

'At first, maybe, before they realised what had gone on.'

Fredrika swallowed hard. Karin's story was hardly unique. If reasonable doubt exists, there can be no conviction. Many people got away with crimes because society was unable to find the necessary proof. Some regarded this as a weakness in the justice system, others as an indication that the democratic process was working.

'So how come he got away with it?' she wanted to know.

Karin shook her head. 'They couldn't even prove he was home on the night she died, and they never found the murder weapon.'

Alex cleared his throat. 'This might sound like a strange question, but we were wondering about Beata's wedding ring.'

'Her wedding ring?'

Alex nodded. 'What happened to it after she died?'

Karin's eyes filled with tears.

'I've no idea. We did receive a package from the police containing the jewellery she'd been wearing when she ... when she was found, but I don't remember what happened to it. I took a pair of gold earrings that Beata had inherited from my mother, but as for the rest ... I don't even recall whether or not we discussed it. I was in a kind of fog for a long time. Excuse my language, but I can't imagine anyone would want that fucking wedding ring.'

'You used the word "we",' Fredrika said. 'Who received the package?'

'Me, Malcolm and Beata's brother, Bernhard.'

'Not her husband?'

'Absolutely not. They'd already arrested him by then.'

'Could Malcolm or Bernhard have kept the ring?'

'I suppose so, but why are you asking about the ring? Why is it important now?'

'I'll happily explain further down the line,' Alex said, 'but right now we have more questions than answers.'

Karin seemed satisfied with that. Maybe she just wanted them to leave. It was impossible to tell whether she was mourning her ex-husband; they didn't know enough about their relationship. Fredrika decided to try to find out why Karin and Malcolm had split up.

She made an effort to sound as warm and pleasant as Alex always did.

'You and Malcolm divorced in the year Beata died,' she ventured.

Karin looked up. 'Yes.'

'Forgive the intrusion, but can I ask why?'

Karin got up and went over to the sink. She filled a

glass with water and drank it without asking if anyone else would like one.

'Because grief doesn't necessarily bring people together,' she said eventually. 'That's how it was for us, and I know it's the same for many others.'

The honesty in her voice was clear, but the fact that she was keeping something from them was equally clear.

What is it you don't want to tell us? Fredrika thought.

Alex took over. 'How were things before Beata's death? Did you and Malcolm agree about your son-in-law?'

'Definitely,' Karin said firmly. 'We both disliked him equally.'

There. Another statement that wasn't a lie, but didn't reveal the whole truth. Fredrika's frustration was growing by the minute.

'But?' she said.

'But what?'

'You were in agreement, but not about everything. Tell us how your views differed.'

Karin shook her head. 'We both felt exactly the same.'

Fredrika believed her – so what had been left unsaid?

Alex had draped his jacket over the back of the chair; he turned, reached into the inside pocket, and brought out a copy of the Polaroid they'd found on the drinks trolley in Malcolm Benke's living room. The one that showed Eden Lundell's husband, Mikael, among others.

'Who are these men?' Alex asked, handing Karin the photo. Her face relaxed; someone or something in the picture had cheered her up.

She pointed to the men on Benke's left. 'These two were Malcolm's childhood friends, Eskil and Sten. Eskil died a few

years ago, but Sten's still alive. He's a really good person –
Sten Aber.'

'And who's this?' Alex pointed to Mikael.

'I don't actually know. Talk to Sten – he'll be able to tell
you when the photo was taken.'

'You weren't there?'

'No – I don't remember ever having seen it before. It must
be pretty old though, mainly because Eskil's there.'

Alex didn't seem entirely happy with Karin's answer. It
was the same old story; they had to speak to a hundred people
to find out what they needed to know, a time-consuming task
that would try the patience of a saint. It was enough to make
a sane person start climbing the walls.

They thanked Karin for making the time to see them,
and got ready to leave. Fredrika made a careful note of Sten
Aber's contact details, then Karin asked to see the photo
again. Alex passed it over.

'The wallpaper,' she said. 'I should have noticed it
right away.'

Fredrika took a closer look. The snap had been taken
indoors, and behind the four men she could just make out
wallpaper with a colourful pattern.

Karin's face was ashen. 'That's Beata's apartment. She
redecorated just a few months before she died, and she sent
me some pictures. But . . .'

'But?' Alex prompted her.

'But I didn't see it for real until I visited the apartment
after her death.'

When they emerged onto the street a little while later, the air
was cool and the sky overcast.

'We need to speak to Sten Aber,' Fredrika said immediately.

'And I guess we also need to speak to Eden's husband,' Alex said grimly.

Fredrika shifted uncomfortably from foot to foot. She still couldn't face thinking about Eden.

The ring, however . . .

It altered the picture of the murder, made it clear that this was personal as far as the killer was concerned. It also suggested that Malcolm's death had something to do with the murder of his daughter.

But they still had no trace whatsoever of the perpetrator.

Holiday brain – wasn't that what people suffered from in July? Malin thought so. Holiday brain felt quite different; it was a slower version that mixed up days and times, but you could always make the excuse that you'd been off work for too long, setting all duties and obligations to one side. 'Oh, I didn't realise you were coming today – I thought it was tomorrow.'

She sorted the children's clothes into two piles. She had switched on the washing machine at some point over the weekend, she thought, but then she'd forgotten all about it until her daughter informed her that she couldn't find any clean knickers. Only then had Malin emptied the machine and dried the laundry.

The effect of a traumatised brain.

She took a deep breath.

What would she give to regain her everyday life and security?

Anything.

However, while she waited for life to get back to normal (if that day ever came), she had to focus on keeping her head above water.

Routine.

The word came back to her several times a day.

They needed routine.

She'd read it in countless articles and books about people who'd been deprived of their freedom for long periods: how they'd survived in captivity, where misery and impotence threatened to break them.

They created routines. Without them they'd have gone crazy.

Hedvig came into the bedroom.

'Want some help?'

Malin shook her head. 'I've finished.' She passed Hedvig her pile of clean clothes. A very small pile.

Hedvig swallowed. 'How long . . . ?'

Malin shrugged. 'I don't know, sweetheart.'

Hedvig left the room without another word, and Malin sank down on the edge of the bed. She hated her weakness, her inability to provide answers. Was this the last memory the children would have of her?

Was this where the whole family was going to die?

The article that had been left in her mailbox gave Lovisa Wahlberg no peace. She burst into tears several times during the day and evening. She'd called friends, talked and talked, but hadn't dared to put into words what she really wanted to say.

She was scared.

She didn't want to be alone.

And her boyfriend had other plans, so he wasn't available to keep her company.

The only people she hadn't called were her parents. They would have asked far too many questions, messed with her head even more.

'Tell me you're not having problems again!'

That was exactly what her mother would say.

Then she would sigh.

Sigh and groan and shake her head.

I'm such a disappointment.

Lovisa went and lay on the sofa, pretended to watch TV, but stayed there for only a few minutes. Resting, trying to switch off, just made her panic. Someone was after her, there was no doubt about it.

I ought to call the police.

She dismissed the idea immediately. They wouldn't listen

to her, not after what had happened, everything that had come out. The police knew she'd been lucky to get away with it. Things could – should – have ended very differently for Lovisa. The officer who'd interviewed her on her return to Sweden had made that very clear.

'Don't imagine we're not aware that you should have gone down too,' he'd said. 'I hope you're not under the illusion that we regard you as a victim in all this.'

Lovisa stared blankly at the newspaper article. No, she hadn't been a victim. Not last time.

But maybe this time . . .

She shuddered and went into the hallway yet again. Just like before, she held her breath as she peered through the spy hole.

No one there.

Only shadows.

No one there.

Only shadows.

So why was she so convinced that someone was following every move she made?

'The art trail in Österlen in August,' Diana Trolle said. 'What do you think?'

'I think it sounds just about as boring as counting grains of sand on the shore,' Alex Recht replied.

'Oh, Alex!' Diana couldn't help laughing.

'Seriously – how long have we been together now? You know I'm nowhere near as interested in art and ... culture as you.'

'But you like Österlen.'

'I like most places. You wander round the art trail and I'll find something else to do in the meantime – I'll go and lie on a nice beach and read my book.'

Diana smiled and went into the kitchen, leaving Alex in front of the TV. He'd just finished vacuuming the entire house, and now he wanted to watch a film or an interesting programme. Something entertaining. *I'll go and lie on a nice beach and read my book.* Had he really said that? He could understand why the comment had amused Diana; Alex rarely had time to read books, and as for lying on a beach ...

The new me, he thought. *Beach boy 2016.*

He could hear the clink of crockery and cutlery as Diana emptied the dishwasher. The sounds of everyday life. The best of the best. Alex couldn't understand people who constantly longed to escape from the power of habit, the pattern of routine. He loved the lack of change. He loved the fact that he had a life that felt whole.

Diana was without doubt the best thing that had happened to him since Lena's death. The realisation made him feel alive, made him love her. When Lena died he hadn't thought it would be possible to find his way back to becoming a functioning human being. He and Lena had been married for what seemed like an entire lifetime; neither of them had ever wanted anyone else. They had created a home together, two children, security and intimacy. Summarising their marriage in those few words made it sound pathetic, almost clichéd, but he had experienced a contentment that he found difficult to describe to his children. They had families of their own now, but it was as if they couldn't sit still in their nests. There were dancing lessons and cookery lessons and couple time and alone time. Just listening to them made Alex feel nervous. Tired.

The television had nothing suitable to offer. Alex sipped his coffee and wondered whether to call his daughter. He was much better these days at nurturing his relationship with the children, saw them more often.

His work mobile rang, making the decision for him. He had a bad feeling; it was nine o'clock. Had there been another death?

The last thought bothered him. *I have to stop expecting the worst.*

However, he couldn't shake off the nagging worry that had been there since he saw Malcolm Benke's body; the visit to Karin Benke hadn't exactly helped.

The ring, the ring, the ring.

If it wasn't for the ring, Alex thought things would have been different.

'Hi, it's Ivan,' a voice said when he answered.

Ivan? It took Alex a few seconds to place his younger colleague.

'Yes?'

'I just wanted to let you know that I spoke to the police in London about Beata Benke's death. One of the detectives who worked on the case is on a course in Stockholm right now; she's happy to meet us, talk us through the inquiry.'

'Great,' Alex said, then he fell silent. Was this a sidetrack worth pursuing, or not? He still hadn't got his thoughts in order after the conversation with Karin; he didn't really know what to think. They needed to speak to Sten Aber, the man in the photograph. And Mikael Lundell. And Malcolm Benke's son, who lived in Vienna. Did they really need to drag a British detective into the circus as well?

'It can't do any harm to pick up more information, can it?' Ivan said when the silence went on.

'Okay.'

Ivan exhaled audibly.

'Good – she's coming in tomorrow at four.'

'Okay,' Alex said again.

He spent the rest of the evening watching a useless crime thriller, unable to get Malcolm Benke's death out of his mind. Nor could he forget the change that he'd noticed in Fredrika. It had happened gradually during the late winter and spring. She had many excellent qualities, but she was still much too private, kept too many aspects of herself hidden from others. He could count on the fingers of one hand the few occasions when she'd dropped her guard and let him in.

The last time had been when they were out drinking wine. A lot of wine. A unique experience within their relationship; Alex had never seen Fredrika drunk before. It was the evening back in February when they'd found out that Margareta Berlin was to be their new boss.

'This is such fucking bad news I can't get my head around it,' Alex had said. 'Let's go out and drink Berlin into oblivion.'

And they had.

Several years too late, Alex thought now. *The two of us could have done with that evening when Fredrika was new to the job.*

What worried him most was her reaction to Berlin's appointment. At first she'd been just as angry and upset as Alex, but then – more or less straight away – it was as if all the frustration simply left her. As if she'd capitulated.

Surely she hadn't given up, for God's sake?

He could see that something was bothering her, making her unhappy.

His heart rate increased.

Just as long as he wasn't left alone in Berlin's empire. Then he would be lost.

Evening came, night came. Fredrika crawled into bed and reached for Spencer. He rolled over onto his back so that she could rest her head on his arm. Her hand found its way to his chest and stopped over his heart. The body's most amazing muscle.

She breathed deeply, in, out.

'Tough day?' Spencer said.

How was she supposed to answer that? She couldn't even remember a day that hadn't been tough, and it was nothing to do with her job. Life itself was hurting her, in a way that she couldn't fix. She didn't want to say it out loud, though. She was keeping quiet in too many places, both at home and at work. Spencer didn't need to wonder what was wrong; he knew. But Alex couldn't even begin to guess.

'It never ends,' she said in response to Spencer's question.

'What never ends?'

'The horrible stuff. It just keeps on happening.'

Spencer sighed. Was it her imagination, or had his body tensed?

'And this is news?'

Fredrika pressed her face against his skin; she loved every millimetre of this wonderful man.

'Do you think I'm naïve?'

He laughed. 'Not exactly. You're far too cynical to be naïve.'

She raised her head.

'Cynical?'

'Yes – that's not news either, is it?'

Only Spencer could make such a remark sound like a compliment. Fredrika remembered what he'd said when they moved in together.

'We mustn't have unrealistic expectations of life, Fredrika. We mustn't dream of a future that can't be ours.'

He had said it as a gentle reminder that he was twenty-five years older than her, that neither of them had any right or reason to expect their life together to last forever. He probably hadn't realised that his words would stick in her mind, that they would come back to her over and over again. The perfect future belonged to someone else. It could never be hers. To a certain extent she found comfort in accepting such a simple truth. Some people got everything, some got considerably less. Fredrika had dreamed of a career as a violinist, but her dreams had been shattered by an accident when she was a teenager. After that she had been lost, drifted from one course to another at university, embarked on a relationship with Spencer, who was her professor. She hadn't thought for a moment that he would become the father of her children, nor that she would one day enjoy working for the police.

Fredrika had found her way home.

Then it had all turned to dust.

'Spencer, we—'

He interrupted her immediately.

'Let's talk about something else. Tell me about work.'

'There are a lot of things we ought to discuss,' she whispered.

'Not tonight.'

'Okay.'

After a brief silence she asked: 'How did the meeting go this afternoon?'

'Fine.' She hadn't made it; she couldn't have left work without drawing attention to herself. Spencer had sworn it was all right, that he was happy to go alone. All the details had been dealt with at the previous meeting when she'd been there.

That's how we function, she thought. *We don't abandon each other.*

She closed her eyes. 'Did you mention the colour?'

She could hear Spencer's heart pounding, couldn't imagine a time when it would stop.

'I said we'd changed our minds,' he said quietly. 'So the coffin will be white.'

Present: Interrogators one and two (I1 and I2),
Detective Chief Inspector Alex Recht (Recht)

I1:   So Benke had been murdered, and it was your
job to investigate. Was Bergman in a fit
state to work?

Recht: Absolutely.

I2:   Really? Her husband was extremely ill. That
must have affected her.

Recht: You're right, but let me tell you this: if
she'd felt for one second that she wasn't
up to the job, she would have signed
herself off sick.
(silence)

I1:   What did you think about Benke's murder?

Recht: The ring on his little finger bothered
me. It was an indication that this murder
was different.

I2:   Different in what way?

Recht: It was too early to say. But then the first
letter arrived . . .

I1:   Yes?

Recht (quietly): We didn't realise.

I2: You didn't realise what?

(silence)

Recht: That things were going to get worse. So much worse.

TUESDAY

If one more person told Noah Johansson to stop worrying about his brother's move to Australia, he would go crazy. *Because I know him, and I know there's something weird about what's going on here. Something dangerous.*

Noah sat down at his desk. It was early in the morning, the best time of the day to call. There was only one person he could contact to talk about his brother, a man who seized every opportunity to humiliate him.

'Yes?' a voice said wearily on the other end of the line.

Noah's heart sank. It was always the same; he felt strong before he phoned, but as soon as he heard that response every ounce of strength drained away. If Detective Inspector Stig Mattsson bothered to answer at all. He was a waste of space who had been designated as Noah's contact officer. Several weeks went by before Noah realised what 'contact officer' meant: some poor sod who'd been told to deal with Noah's agitated calls. Definitely not an indication that the police were following up his report. As far as Noah could tell they didn't even think there was a case to look into; today was no different.

'You again,' Mattsson said. He sighed so loudly that Noah could have wept.

He couldn't keep up this facade of politeness. He was

beside himself with worry, and was hardly sleeping. If this went on he'd have to take some time off, let someone else run the business. That couldn't happen.

'It's about my brother.'

'Again.'

'Again. It's three weeks since I last spoke to you; have you made any progress?'

Another sigh. Noah might as well have put the phone down; he knew what was coming, knew exactly what Mattsson was going to say. They'd taken note of his concerns, there was no indication that a crime had been committed, there was nothing to investigate, could Noah please stop calling (for fuck's sake).

'We've been over this several times. As I've already told you, we've been in touch with your brother and he's confirmed that there's nothing wrong. He—'

'Have you spoken to him on the phone?' Noah interrupted. 'Or are you just referring to those emails you received?'

He'd asked the question a thousand times, and always got the same answer.

'Noah, you know I've spoken to him on the phone. Very briefly, admittedly, but that was because he was on his way to a business meeting. Otherwise we've been in contact via email.'

Those emails. Mattsson always came back with the same counter-argument: if the family had disappeared against their will, then who was sending all those messages? Noah thought someone else could easily have taken their phones and forced them to reveal their PIN codes, but the police dismissed his objections. That kind of thing might happen in the movies, but not in real life.

'Remind me – what business meeting?'

'I didn't ask, as you know perfectly well.'

Noah was on the verge of panic; he had to come up with something else, something new, something different, something that hadn't already been said and done. He had to make it clear that the police were failing to do their job. But everything had been said, all the questions had already been asked. They weren't interested, and if Noah made a real effort he could understand why, to a certain extent. On the surface the situation looked precisely as it should. He wasn't sure exactly who the police might have spoken to, but every one of his brother's friends or acquaintances would of course confirm that they'd heard Dan talking about the move to the other side of the world. Noah had called Dan's father-in-law to ask if he was worried, but no. Apparently the family were due to fly out on the Saturday, and he'd spoken to them on Thursday to wish them bon voyage. This didn't make Noah feel any better. If everything had been fine on Thursday, what had happened on Friday?

He had mentioned his concerns, but to no avail. Noah was aware that his sister-in-law and her family weren't close; they spoke only a few times a year, and whenever they got together at Christmas, for example, the results were disastrous.

'We don't really know one another,' his sister-in-law had said. 'And that's fine.'

However, this was nothing like Noah's relationship with his brother, and he had to make the police understand that. He knew better than anyone else when something wasn't right.

'I have to go,' Mattsson said. 'If there's nothing else . . .'

Noah took a chance.

'What time of day was it when my brother said he was going to a meeting?'

'Funnily enough, I do remember that. I was having lunch and I happened to belch down the phone. I'd had a kebab, the best in town. Do you know that place in the Söder district, on Hornsgatan? They deliver if you order the day before.'

But Noah wasn't listening. He was online, checking out the time in Australia.

'So you called him around lunchtime?' he said.

'I just told you. I don't have time to talk to you any more.'

That pierced Noah's heart like a barb. Mattsson didn't have *time* to talk to him. Other matters took priority over the search for Dan.

'So I'm guessing we're talking about twelve o'clock, something like that?'

'Maybe.'

'Which is ten o'clock at night in Sydney,' Noah informed Mattsson.

Silence, then: 'So?'

'You said my brother was on his way to a business meeting.' Noah could feel his pulse rate increasing; at last he'd found concrete evidence for what he'd been trying to put across for so long. 'Who goes to a business meeting at night?'

Silence.

'And maybe you ought to reconsider this whole "business meeting" scenario,' Noah went on. 'My brother is a psychologist. He never uses terms like that. Just as he never swears at me the way he did in that email.'

He could hear Mattsson speaking quietly to someone else. He held his breath; surely the police had to take him seriously now?

'Listen, Noah.' Mattsson's tone was gentler now. 'We have a counsellor here at the station who'd be happy to see you – if you think that would help?'

Noah ended the call, absolutely devastated. He wouldn't contact Stig Mattsson again. He had to get hold of someone else who could help him, someone who understood how unbelievable it was that an entire family had been missing for weeks, and that the police had refused to look for them. Someone who would listen.

He closed his eyes and rested his head on his hands. Maybe there was one more lifeline. *Maybe.* The only problem was that Noah was hampered by what he could and couldn't do as a funeral director. There were certain contacts that could be exploited, others that couldn't.

At that moment the bell tinkled; someone had come in. He took a few seconds to compose himself, then went into the reception area to see who it was. A young woman was standing just inside the door. Noah had never seen her before, and yet she said:

'Hi – I don't know if you remember me? Tina.'

She smiled, but strangely enough the smile just made her look sad.

Noah shook his head, searched through his chaotic memory. Tina. Tina? No, he didn't recognise the name.

'I'm sorry, I don't. How can I help?'

Tina suddenly seemed unsure of herself. 'Maybe I shouldn't have come here . . . I feel so stupid.'

Her uncertainty gave Noah confidence.

'There's no need to feel stupid,' he assured her. 'So where did we meet?'

She fiddled with her handbag. 'At your brother's.' She

started to cry, a pathetic, feeble little effort. And then she whispered the words Noah had been longing to hear for months.

'Am I the only one who's wondering? Is no one else concerned? I'm so worried that something's happened to Malin and Dan.'

The television was yelling and shrieking. The children were watching a film. Again. The same film. The first time they'd watched it Malin had decided to switch it off after only a few minutes; it was much too unpleasant. But now, just like so many other things, it no longer mattered.

She had often thought that they ought to pull themselves together, that nothing could be more dangerous than giving up, allowing it all to end in disaster. Her brain stopped, stuck fast on the word 'end'. Because who knew how this was meant to end? Not Malin or her family, and that was what filled her nights with the most violent nightmares. Malin had even started thinking about her father; she missed him.

So very, very hard to bear.

All the relationships they hadn't had the chance to conclude, to acknowledge.

Noah. Noah must be feeling terrible right now.

Everyone else thought they were in Australia, but Noah must have realised something was wrong. Dan had been smart to begin with, before he lost the battle with his demons. He had persuaded their kidnapper (how difficult was it to take that word seriously under normal circumstances?) to leave a key in Noah's mailbox, said that Noah would start asking questions otherwise. In fact the reverse was true. They'd planned to leave a key with their neighbour, not Noah – he already had one. As did Tina, Malin's best friend.

But she probably believes we're in Australia, living the dream.

The opportunities to do something clever had been limited since the drama began. Malin was still overwhelmed with despair as she recalled their first few weeks in this ... prison. They had tried to stay awake at night, tried to work out how they were going to escape from the house, reach the outside world. They had attempted to talk to the man who'd abducted them, they had shouted and wept, begged and pleaded. But nothing had worked. It was impossible to leave the house, and the man refused to grant them any kind of amnesty – a realisation that could paralyse the strongest warrior.

Dan was sitting at the kitchen table with a mug of warm milk. He was pale and hollow-eyed, more haggard than the rest of the family. It infuriated Malin. What gave him the right to feel so fucking sorry for himself?

'Does that taste nice?'

She tried to hide the venom in her tone.

'Yes. It's delicious.'

So far the summer hadn't been too hot, which Malin saw as a blessing. The heat would have made being in the house even more intolerable.

'Good. I'm very pleased. Because you took the last of the milk. And we don't know when we'll get any more.'

Dan looked up, almost dazed, as if his brain was incapable of processing what she'd said. That frightened her. She couldn't face being the only adult in the house whose sanity was intact.

'I thought there was another litre in the fridge.' His voice was hoarse; he had spoken so little lately.

Malin pursed her lips and shook her head. 'You were wrong.'

She yanked open the fridge door and checked the contents of the half-empty shelves. Eggs, two cartons of juice, butter, cheese . . .

We won't starve. Not yet.

The fear came in waves, threatened to drown her. Her eyes filled with tears, scalding like acid.

'Do we know when the next delivery is due?'

Dan's only response was a shrug. Malin made a mark on the bread board with the knife each morning; it was their only way of counting the days. They lived in a restricted world with no clocks or watches, but several knives. And items that had been put there to make the place feel homely. Potted plants, for example. On one occasion she had picked up the largest of them and hurled it at the living-room window with all her might. The pot was smashed to pieces, but the window was undamaged.

'Did you really think it would be that easy?'

She hadn't noticed her son standing behind her, so his question struck her like a bullet in her back.

Did you really think it would be that easy?

No, of course not. But we have to try, don't we?

And they had to keep on trying.

She closed the fridge door.

'We need to work out a plan. Try to get out of here.'

She didn't recognise her own voice.

'Again?' Dan said. 'Make yet another pointless attempt?'

Then he went and sat with the children in front of the television, leaving Malin alone in the kitchen with her fear.

Spencer Lagergren was going to die, and Fredrika Bergman was going to become a widow. She had considered embroidering the words on a piece of fabric and framing the damned thing, just to make them easier to take in. Because however many times she repeated them to herself, they just didn't stick. They didn't mean anything.

A widow? Me? That can't be right.

'Are you having fun, Saga?'

Fredrika didn't know what her daughter was laughing at, but it didn't matter. The sound of the child's joy was enough to make her feel secure. The children were happy.

'We're going SWIMMING today!' Saga shouted down the phone.

'Isn't it a bit too cold?' Fredrika asked.

'No,' Saga said firmly.

Fredrika was in her office; she'd just arrived at work. She and Alex were due to meet Malcolm Benke's friend Sten Aber in one of the interview rooms shortly.

'Can I speak to Grandma, please?'

Her mother came on the line. 'How are you, Fredrika?'

For God's sake, how many times could she ask the same question?

'Fine, thanks. I just wanted to check that the kids were okay.'

'Well, I suppose so,' her mother replied. 'I mean they're alive, they're healthy.' And then, a second later: 'Forgive me! I'm so sorry, I don't know what . . .'

Fredrika couldn't help smiling. A new skill she had not only acquired, but was rapidly developing to world-championship level: the art of contemplating the destruction of her life with a smile on her face.

'It's okay,' she whispered, her voice close to breaking.

She heard her mother move away from the children.

'They're asking about you and Spencer. I think they can tell something's wrong,' her mother said after a moment.

'Of course they can – they know Spencer's sick.'

'But not *how* sick. There's a time and place for everything, and yours is here and now. You have to tell them.'

There's a time and place for everything. How could such an inaccurate assertion have endured for so long? Because whichever way you looked at it, there was no right time or place for death. Not in Fredrika's life, especially when death had come after one of the people she loved most.

'We'll talk to them when they get home.'

Her mother let out a sob.

'I'm sorry. I'm not trying to interfere, I just want to help.'

'It'll be fine, Mum. It'll be fine.'

But when the call was over and loneliness overwhelmed her, Fredrika couldn't hold back the tears. She put her head down on the desk and let them come.

Nothing would ever be fine again.

'Have you got a cold?'

Alex sounded genuinely concerned when they met outside the room in which Sten Aber was waiting.

The question was a matter of politeness; Fredrika had glanced in the mirror and knew exactly what she looked like. Swollen eyelids, bloodshot eyes.

'Sorry I'm late. I had to sort something out. And no, I haven't got a cold. It's an allergy.'

Alex touched her arm. 'If I can help in any way . . .'

Fredrika bit her lip and shook her head.

Don't cry don't cry don't cry.

But one question echoed inside her head, the question she didn't dare ask.

How did you cope?

Alex had travelled this same road. Watched as the love of his life was consumed by a disease, saw her die. Disappear from their shared existence, never to return.

Spencer won't even call me. How can I bear not hearing his voice for the rest of my days?

'Another time,' she said. 'There will come a time when I need your help. But not today.'

She pushed open the door of the interview room.

'Fredrika Bergman,' she said, holding out her hand to greet Sten Aber. Alex did the same.

Fredrika sat down on the cold, hard chair. Alex tried to catch her eye, but she concentrated on her notes, then focused on Sten.

'Thank you for coming in at such short notice,' she began. The standard opening comment always amused her; as if he had any choice. Whatever you chose to call this encounter, it was an interrogation. Not that Sten was suspected of any crime, but because there was reason to believe that he could provide important information. If he hadn't turned up, he would have been brought in.

'This has been a real shock,' Sten said. 'I'll help in any way I can.'

He seemed genuinely distressed. His eyes were tired, and it was clear that the news about Malcolm Benke's death had hit him hard. Fredrika had closely monitored what had appeared in the press so that she would know what he might have been able to find out. As usual the journalists had behaved like predators in their hunt for information, but had secured relatively few details. The headlines screamed 'murder', and they knew that Benke had been shot, but that was more or less all. They hadn't printed Benke's name. Not yet. Which was a good thing.

'So how did you know Malcolm?' Alex asked.

'We were in the same class at school right from the start, and we've been friends ever since. We did our military service together, and even went to the same university.'

'Both of you are – or rather were – engineers?'

'That's right.'

Fredrika checked her notes.

'You also ran your own construction company, just like Malcolm. Were you competitors?'

Sten gave a little smile.

'It would be foolish to pretend otherwise,' he said. 'However, I can't remember a single occasion when our rivalry led to any kind of conflict. We had an enormous amount of respect for each other.'

The smile faded. Fredrika liked his voice, his attitude. He had presence and focus. There was a precision in the way he expressed himself; he didn't want to be misunderstood.

He misses his friend, she thought. *And he's not the one who shot him.*

Alex brought out the photograph they'd found on the trolley.

'When was this taken?'

Sten took out a pair of glasses from the breast pocket of his shirt and put them on. He looked closely at the picture, and his face changed. The sorrow was replaced by something else, something . . . more severe.

'I don't remember,' he said, putting down the snap.

Fredrika picked it up.

'We're not expecting you to give us an exact date,' she said. 'But surely you can give us a rough idea?'

Sten folded his arms. 'It might have been on a business trip, but I can't remember which one.'

'A business trip? Okay – which country are we talking about?' Alex said.

Fredrika's eyes were fixed on the wallpaper Karin had recognised from her daughter's home in London.

'Probably France,' Sten said. 'We often went over there. Paris.'

Fredrika leaned back; every scrap of sympathy she'd felt for the man was gone in a second. So he was playing games? He would have cause to regret that. She folded her arms, mirroring his posture.

'I'm sure you did. Go to Paris, I mean. It's a wonderful city. But this photograph wasn't taken there, as you well know.'

The ensuing silence became uncomfortable for all three of them.

Tell us what you know, Fredrika thought. *Because we don't have the patience to play the waiting game.*

'Have another look.' Alex took the photo from Fredrika and passed it across the table.

Fredrika was in no doubt: Sten Aber knew exactly where it had been taken, but for some reason he didn't want to explain the context.

She cleared her throat and said firmly:

'Okay, let's temporarily ignore the fact that you're pretending you don't remember. Tell us who the other people are.'

The acrimonious tone of her voice provoked a reaction from both Alex and Sten. A smile played around the corners of Alex's mouth for a second, while Sten looked furious.

'I'm not pretending. I don't remember.'

'Whatever. So who are the others?'

Sten glared at her.

'Well, that's obviously Malcolm,' he said, pointing. 'The guy next to him is Eskil, a mutual friend of ours who died a few years ago.'

He fell silent.

'And the fourth man?'

To Fredrika's surprise, Sten leaned back in his chair and spread his hands.

'That's where my memory fails me again. I don't recall who he is.'

Alex and Fredrika couldn't believe their ears. It took a few seconds for the significance of what Sten Aber had just said to sink in.

Fredrika shook her head.

'Enough. You claim you can't remember when or where this photograph was taken. You can't even name everyone in it. Your friend Malcolm lived in a great big house; there were only three photographs on display in the whole place. Three. And then we found this one, on the drinks trolley. At the moment we don't know what it was doing there, but the very fact that it was in Malcolm's living room tells us that it must have meant something to him. Or possibly his killer – he or she might have brought it along and left it there.'

She broke off. It wasn't like her to experience such a surge of adrenaline during an interview.

It's because life has changed beyond recognition. And I hate it.

Sten didn't speak. It wasn't a cheap silence; trying to appear unconcerned was obviously costing him a great deal. Fredrika wanted to beg and plead, shout and scream. *Help us to help you!* But if there was one thing she'd learned during her time with the police, it was that the help she and her colleagues were prepared to offer wasn't always sufficient. People got themselves into the most peculiar – and sometimes dangerous – situations. Under those circumstances they often weren't prepared to confide in the police, either because they thought involving the cops would just make things worse, or because they had something to hide. She didn't know whether either of these applied to Sten Aber, but it infuriated her that he was preventing them from moving forward with the investigation.

Faced with Sten's continuing silence, Alex too was unable to hide his frustration.

'Let me give you a clue. This wallpaper is in Beata Benke's hallway in her apartment in London. And the man you claim not to recognise is Mikael Lundell. He's a priest, and he spent a number of years with the Swedish church in London.'

Sten opened his mouth then closed it again.

'So we already know where the photograph was taken and who's in it,' Alex went on. 'But we'd like to find out why it was taken, and why it was so important to Malcolm.'

Sten sighed.

'We went on so many trips together, Malcolm and Eskil and I. It's very difficult for me to remember the kind of detail you're asking for.'

'How many times were you in Beata's apartment in London?' Fredrika asked.

Sten thought for a moment. 'Ten, maybe?'

'Maybe,' Alex said.

And with that the interview was over.

They went back to Alex's office.

'Stubborn fucker,' Fredrika said.

Alex raised his eyebrows.

'Have you started swearing, fru Bergman?'

'I've been swearing since I was three years old, herr Recht.'

Alex smiled.

'What now?' Fredrika wondered.

Alex immediately grew serious.

'Now we contact our friends in Israel.'

Wishful thinking was something that took up far too much of Mikael Lundell's time. Whenever he'd been told that something was impossible, he'd thought that his determination and obstinacy, along with prayers to the higher powers of whose existence he was absolutely convinced, would make all the difference. He had genuinely believed that this was how you achieved the improbable.

Like the idea that he and Eden would live together happily ever after.

'I don't understand how you can delude yourself like this,' his father had said after meeting Eden for the first time. 'How could a woman like her ever be your wife? How could she be anyone's wife? She's like a wild horse – impossible to restrain. If you try, you'll just make yourself look ridiculous.'

Mikael had hated that gross comparison with a horse. Who would want to restrain another person? Not Mikael, or anyone he respected. What made Eden so attractive was the wildness that his father saw as an obstacle to a successful relationship. With hindsight, however, he had to admit that his father had been partially right. It *had* been difficult to create a life with Eden, and it had cost Mikael more than he could ever have imagined.

A child.

Or two, depending on how you looked at it.

Dani was dead, Saba was still here. But neither of the girls had been Mikael's – at least in the biological sense. That was the biggest sacrifice he had been willing to make in order to hold on to his relationship with Eden – realising the truth, then silently accepting the idea of being a father to children Eden had conceived with someone else. She had asked him how he'd known. He'd told her that he'd seen it the second they were born, but the truth was that he'd suspected as soon as she told him she was pregnant. The dates didn't work. They'd been going through a bad patch just before she revealed that she was expecting; it was easy to think back to the times they'd had sex, and it just didn't fit with her due date.

Wishful thinking. Maybe that was what made the impossible possible. That and his love for Eden. Mikael couldn't explain it any other way; as far as he was concerned, he had been Dani and Saba's father. When Dani was murdered, he thought he was going to lose his mind.

Even then I never considered leaving her, he thought.

He knew that love could be a senseless, destructive force. Many people had been driven to the brink of insanity by what they called love. Perhaps it was Mikael's faith in God that had kept him alive in the darkness, together with the fact that Eden had fallen pregnant again. And this time Mikael knew that the child on the way was his.

He could hear Eden playing with their daughter in the living room.

'Look at these lovely colourful bricks!' she said.

She'd never behaved like that with Dani and Saba. Her

approach to parenting had been to have as little as possible to do with the children.

And I allowed it to happen.

Mikael liked an orderly life, but not to the point of fanaticism. He was a pragmatic individual. The events of the past few years had made him a little more spiky, he was aware of that. He had grown harder, while Eden had grown softer.

He listened to Eden and their youngest daughter for a while longer. This couldn't last forever, and that was probably a good thing. There would come a day when Eden would want to go back to work, when being with her family wasn't enough to fill her life. Mikael had asked himself what they would do then. Eden could hardly apply for jobs in Israel, which meant going back to Sweden. At the moment that didn't tempt her at all.

Mikael went and sat at the computer. He wanted to check if there was anything new on Malcolm Benke's death. Eden had insisted that they couldn't be sure it was him – the newspapers hadn't named the victim – but Mikael was in no doubt that Malcolm was dead. And Mikael was afraid he knew why.

Eden wasn't happy; she didn't like the fact that he knew things about Malcolm, that the outside world was encroaching on their safe bubble. However, Mikael couldn't help it if he'd once been drawn into Malcolm's life. Or rather his daughter's. It was an encounter he was unable to forget. Not that anyone had blamed him, regarded his input as a failure, but that didn't stop him from feeling that way. Things had taken a very unpleasant turn, and he had withdrawn before it was too late. Too late for him. That was what he'd told himself at the time: he had to protect his own interests. And the question that haunted him was whether this was what had cost Beata Benke her life in the end.

That wasn't the only reason, he thought. *My failure wasn't the only thing that led to her death. But I was a part of it.*

At that moment a phone rang. Eden's. Saba had changed the ringtone to one so shrill that you answered immediately just to make it stop.

'Eden,' he heard her say.

Then: 'Yes?'

Like a question.

She moved into the bedroom, closed the door behind her. Mikael got to his feet, didn't hesitate for a second. When he pushed open the bedroom door Eden gave a start.

'Okay, fine,' she said, and ended the call.

'Who was that?' Mikael was using what he had begun to call the New Voice. The one that was so harsh it immediately made Eden and the children look uneasy.

She was holding her mobile with both hands.

'Who was that?' he repeated.

'Alex Recht.'

Mikael let out a sigh of relief. Alex was a good person, not the kind to bother them with unnecessary problems.

'Does he want you to go back to work?'

Eden was surprised. 'No. No, he didn't say anything about that.' She laughed. 'Anyway, Alex was never my boss.'

'So what did he want?'

He felt foolish – why was he asking the question? Eden didn't have to report back on conversations with former colleagues, if Alex fell into that category.

'He wanted to speak to you,' Eden said.

Now it was Mikael's turn to be surprised.

'Okay . . .'

'I said you weren't home.'

'What the—?'

She interrupted him.

'It was about the murder of Malcolm Benke. You were right – he is dead. I asked Alex to call back later.'

The air conditioning hummed quietly, bringing a welcome coolness. Alex had gathered the team for a quick run-through before he and Fredrika met their colleague from London. He wasn't sure whether that conversation would be of any use at this stage, but it was worth a try. He glanced at his watch, the second hand racing along. Time was passing, and they were getting nowhere fast.

'I'm assuming we've had the list of calls from Benke's mobile by now,' he began. 'Who's looked at them?'

A female investigator sitting next to Fredrika raised her hand. At that moment Alex's phone rang. Diana. For the second time that day he rejected her call.

'As far as we can see, Benke had only one mobile, and the phone company has been very helpful,' the investigator said. 'He might have had other phones, of course, but in that case they were pay-as-you-go, which means we can't follow them up. Unless we find them.'

'Nothing turned up when the house was searched?' Fredrika asked.

'No, and we've also checked his cars and his summer cottage this morning.'

'Okay, so we work on the theory that this was Benke's only phone,' Alex said impatiently.

His colleague nodded. 'The strange thing is that there seems to have been very little traffic. People often make and receive dozens of calls a day, but in Benke's case we're looking at no more than a handful.'

Alex shrugged. Disregarding work calls, how much did he use his phone? He spoke to the kids maybe once a week, Diana rang him now and again, but only when he was at the station or out on a job. If he was a pensioner and at home all day, there would be very few calls. The thought made him go cold. As far as he was concerned, retiring was something in the distant future. So distant it didn't seem real, even though in fact it wasn't that many years away.

Fredrika interrupted his train of thought. 'Okay, so who's Benke been in touch with?'

'Mainly business acquaintances. He was an active member of his company's board, and he spoke to his son in Vienna. He also contacted Sten Aber occasionally.'

'Isn't that a bit odd?' Ivan said eagerly. As always he was keen to find some interesting diversion. 'I'd have expected him to talk to his best friend more often.'

Alex couldn't suppress a smile. He had two best friends, and they rarely spoke. The idea of chatting on the phone to maintain relationships made his flesh crawl.

'No,' he said. He could see that most of his colleagues agreed with him. 'It's not at all odd.'

'Who was the last person he spoke to?' Fredrika wanted to know.

The investigator consulted her notes. 'His son in Vienna – at eight o'clock on the evening Benke died.'

Alex's phone rang again. Diana. He felt a stab of

unease. Had something happened? He rejected the call and switched his phone to silent. He would ring her after the meeting.

'Sorry,' he said to the others.

'We need to interview the son,' Fredrika said. 'For several reasons.'

'Do we know where he is right now?' Alex asked.

'He's still in Vienna,' Ivan informed him. 'I talked to him earlier today – he contacted us. His mother told him what had happened, and he's flying to Stockholm tonight.'

'Good – we can question him tomorrow.' Fredrika made a note in her diary.

Under different circumstances her pallor would have worried Alex, but right now there wasn't time for concerns of that kind. For the same reason he had pushed aside the thought of her red-rimmed eyes when she turned up late for the interview with Sten Aber.

He straightened his back. The chairs were uncomfortable, and the air con now seemed to have achieved some sort of turbo-charged level and was dispensing ice-cold air.

'What else have we got? Anyone checked Benke's emails?'

They hadn't. The technicians had discovered two accounts, both password protected. Alex sighed. If people only knew how much time it took to gain permission to access their email, even when they'd been murdered.

'There might be a short cut,' Ivan said.

'Not one I want to hear about,' Alex said firmly, before adding: 'Although of course I'd be interested in anything you find out.'

Ivan's cheeks flushed and he looked down. At that moment Alex couldn't believe he'd ever been so young and unspoilt, the kind of person who took short cuts, who blushed, who wanted so much.

That's the problem, he thought. *I don't want anything any more. Because I've already done everything.*

Fredrika reported back on the conversation with Sten Aber.

'We found out far too little,' she concluded. Then she moved on to other sources, and for the first time Mikael Lundell's name was brought into the frame. This quickly aroused everyone's interest.

'Are we sure he's in Israel?' a colleague asked. 'He couldn't have been in Sweden at the time of the murder?'

The question made Alex unreasonably angry. Mikael Lundell was the last person he wanted to suspect. Thank God Fredrika stepped in before Alex could explode.

'I've already checked. He and his family have been living in Israel for several years, and Mikael hasn't visited Sweden in recent months.'

Her statement made Alex feel better; she was much better at being objective than he was. She had made it a priority to exclude Mikael as a suspect.

He swallowed. Of course they couldn't be absolutely certain. Just because Mikael hadn't been in Sweden, it didn't mean he couldn't be involved. He and Fredrika exchanged a glance of mutual understanding.

They both knew the hell that Eden and Mikael had gone through.

They both hoped with all their hearts that Mikael had nothing to do with the murder of Malcolm Benke.

But they had both seen him in the mysterious photograph taken in London. If Mikael chose to follow the same path as

Sten Aber, to keep quiet about a truth that must be revealed at all costs, then they had a problem. A problem that would cast a shadow so dark and vast that it would reach all the way to Israel. That was why they had called and found out when he was available.

They ended the meeting and left the Lions' Den, which now resembled a fridge.

'We need to get that fixed,' Alex said to Fredrika, gesturing towards the air conditioning. 'Otherwise some tosser will go to the union and demand a change of venue.'

Fredrika smiled, highlighting the network of fine lines around her eyes.

'It's true,' Alex went on. 'The union—'

His mobile vibrated in his inside pocket. *Diana*.

'Hi.'

'Alex, you have to come home.'

He stopped dead. Diana wasn't the kind of person to worry unnecessarily. On the contrary, her calmness was one of the qualities he valued most. Something had happened – her voice was tense and shrill. Out of the corner of his eye he saw Torbjörn Ross. Twice in two days, for fuck's sake. Was it Alex's imagination, or was Ross deliberately ensuring that they bumped into each other? It was a ridiculous idea, and yet . . .

He went back to the Lions' Den for some peace and quiet.

'What's going on?'

'You've had a letter,' Diana said.

'A letter?'

'I'm sorry, I shouldn't have read it, but I was in a hurry, I was opening the rest of the post and I accidentally—'

Alex interrupted her.

'It's fine, Diana. *Tell me about the letter.*'

She was breathing hard. 'I don't know . . . there was something about the way it looked, what I thought it was. And what it wasn't.'

Fredrika came in looking concerned.

'Diana, you're babbling. I'm sorry, but you are. Read me the letter, please.'

His firm tone made Diana pull herself together, and she read out the words on the piece of paper.

Alex listened, his mobile pressed to his ear. The colour drained from his face. When Diana had finished reading the few short lines, it was the last one that reverberated in his head.

And I am putting everything right.

Before Fredrika Bergman started working for the police, she'd had only the vaguest idea of what the work involved. Above all, she'd found it difficult to imagine the kind of things that might come her way. She remembered the box of hair, which had been sent by courier to a mother after her daughter had been abducted. For Fredrika, it had been a watershed moment. It was after that event that Alex had acquired the scars on his hands, and Fredrika had seen for the first time what certain people were capable of doing to their fellow human beings. It had made her doubt herself; maybe this job was meant for someone else? Slowly she had come to believe that not only was she capable of making a difference, but she could learn to find the work interesting. Two children and a temporary post with the justice department had made the decision easier. Fredrika knew where she belonged: in the police, together with Alex.

Together with Alex.

She was on shifting sands here, just as she was elsewhere in her life. Alex was bound to stop working soon. He had a maximum of five years left until retirement, however hard he tried to pretend that wasn't the case. Many officers of his age had already chosen to leave.

Five years, Fredrika thought. *Who will I be in five years?* The question burned a hole in her soul.

She didn't even know who she would be in the autumn, when Spencer was gone.

She gripped the pen in her hand. *The message that had been sent to Alex.* That was what she must focus on. Was there a link to the murder of Malcolm Benke, or was it referring to something else?

'Are you coming?' Alex suddenly appeared in the doorway of her office. 'The letter's here, in the Lions' Den.'

Everything was icy. The air conditioning was still playing up, and relations between those gathered in the room were frosty. Alex, Fredrika and Margareta Berlin bent over the unprepossessing sheet of paper that had been collected and driven to HQ in a patrol car, blue lights flashing. They read the short lines until they knew them by heart.

> *I am doing what you cannot do and have never*
> *been able to do.*
> *I am making a difference.*
> *And I am putting everything right.*

The message had been in an envelope with Alex's name on the front, and nothing else. No address, no stamp. The sender had personally placed it in Alex's mailbox, or used a messenger to do so.

'Have you received anything like this before?' Berlin asked.

'Oh yes. I get so many fucking letters like this that it's hard to keep track of them all.'

Berlin sighed. 'Enough, Alex.'

'Of course I haven't had anything else like this.'

Berlin pushed her glasses up into her hair.

Fredrika knew Alex hated that gesture, along with everything else about his boss. It was because she'd been head of HR, and was far too pedantic for his taste. Fredrika had to agree. The woman had no leadership qualities. The day they found out she was taking over, Alex and Fredrika had gone out and got drunk after work – the first time in ten years, as far as Fredrika was concerned. It had been much needed, and extremely liberating.

'Time to go home,' Alex had said when midnight had come and gone. 'And tomorrow we'll find that we've drunk Berlin into oblivion, just like we wanted.'

How wrong he'd been. Neither Berlin nor the bad dreams had gone away. The memory of how the night had ended still made her cry. She'd been so happy, so tipsy, so high on life. She had done her best not to wake the children when she got home, but had still managed to knock over Spencer's beloved umbrella stand, scratching the parquet. She had collapsed on the floor, trying in vain to stop giggling. And suddenly there he was beside her.

'Sorry,' she'd said, attempting to adopt a serious expression. 'I'll buy you a new umbrella.'

As if she thought she'd broken them all.

She hadn't been able to stop laughing, or to pick up the stand. And there in the hallway she had experienced her last moment of pure happiness.

'Fredrika, there's something we need to talk about.'

She remembered the words with absolute clarity. *Something we need to talk about*. The laughter disappeared and never came back. *Something we need to talk about*. They went and sat in the kitchen, then came the next sentence, which had branded itself on her long-term memory.

'I have a brain tumour, and it's inoperable.'

And then yet more searing, inescapable pain:

'This is not the death I want.'

She had begun to cry, and the man who had been her professor before becoming her husband stroked her hair and whispered:

'I'm sorry.'

Brain tumour. Inoperable.

Not the death I want.

Sorry.

That had been back in February. Fredrika didn't want to think about how the intervening months had affected her, eaten away at her. She had seen Alex watching her, concerned but too preoccupied by Margareta Berlin to reach out.

Thank God.

'Did you hear what I said, Fredrika?' There was no mistaking Berlin's irritation.

I wish we'd managed to drink her into oblivion, Alex.

'Yes.'

'So have you? Had any messages like this?'

'Don't you think I'd have reported it if I had?'

Alex grinned and Berlin inhaled sharply. 'I want to know if there's a connection to the ongoing investigation,' she snapped.

'So do we,' Fredrika said calmly. She glanced through the letter again. Those words – *I am putting everything right* – she recognised them. She'd seen them somewhere, read them.

But where?

Where had she been over the past few days?

'We need to send the CSIs back to Benke's house,' she said slowly, speaking and thinking at the same time.

'I think one or two of them might still be there,' Alex said. 'What do you want them to do?'

Fredrika hesitated, wondering how far she dared push something she wasn't sure about.

'I think I saw a similar message at the house.'

Alex frowned. 'What do you mean?'

She shook her head. 'I don't know, I just feel I've come across parts of the letter in a different context. And I think it was at Benke's house.'

Her brain was full of slush, refused to cooperate.

Where had she seen those words?

Berlin sniffed. 'I'm not buying this. We don't even know if the message has anything to do with the murder.'

But it might have, Fredrika thought.

'I want to go back there,' she said.

Alex looked from the letter to Fredrika.

'In that case I'll come with you.'

Berlin tapped her pen on the table.

'And what about your colleague from London? Who's standing waiting in reception? Are you taking her with you? Forget it.'

Neither Fredrika nor Alex replied. They left the Lions' Den in silence.

'You agree with her – you think I'm imagining things,' Fredrika said.

Alex shrugged. 'I don't know what I think.'

The letter and its brief message were unpleasant to say the least.

And I am putting everything right.

Everything?

Everything?

At first Vendela thought it must be her imagination. Then she thought it must be down to the ventilation system. The apartment block was old, and it was no secret that they'd had problems for some time. Vendela had contacted the housing committee more than once; poor ventilation could cause damp, or air that was too dry. And very unpleasant smells.

The stench was coming from the kitchen. There was often a greasy haze in Vendela's apartment when her neighbours down below were frying food, but this was something different.

'Try leaving the window open in the afternoons,' the chair of the committee had suggested when she called to complain.

A ridiculous idea – how was that going to improve the situation? However, in spite of her scepticism, Vendela gave it a go. She left the window open for several hours, and when she closed it the odour was just as bad as before.

She went downstairs and rang the bell of the apartment on the far left; the occupants were a very nice family with small children. They even invited her to dinner occasionally. Elvira looked stressed when she opened the door. She was holding the latest addition, a two-month-old baby who was screaming so loudly that Vendela was quite taken aback.

'I'm a bit busy at the moment,' Elvira said. 'Is it urgent, or can I pop up and see you when things have calmed down?'

She smiled, as she always did, but the smile didn't reach her eyes. Vendela wished she hadn't come.

'I was just wondering if you'd noticed a strange smell over the past few days,' she said.

Stupid question – the whole stairwell stank. Elvira shushed the baby.

'Yes – Paul thinks there might be a dead rat somewhere.'

The same thought had occurred to Vendela. After all, Stockholm was practically heaving with the creatures. They must get into buildings and die there all the time. She shuddered and drew her cardigan around her body. It always upset her when something in the block went wrong. As a self-employed person with a home office, she was dependent on things functioning properly. Otherwise she couldn't get on and started missing deadlines, which didn't impress those who supplied her with work.

'I'll take a walk around, see if I can suss out where it's coming from,' she said.

She decided to start in the basement, see if she could locate the source of the problem. If it was a dead rat it ought to be down there where the laundry room and storage facilities were, or maybe on the ground floor. It seemed unlikely that it would have got into one of the apartments.

However, the further down she went, the less noticeable the smell became. By the time she reached the laundry room, it had disappeared completely. She scratched her head. Weird. She quickly turned and headed back upstairs. The smell made its presence felt on the second floor. On the third floor, where Elvira lived, it was worse. When she got to her own floor, the smell had become a stench. Slightly out of breath, she continued up to the top floor. It was unbearable up there. Vendela moved from door to door, sniffing. She glanced up at the attic and decided to check it out. It was damp and rather too warm during the summer, but the smell had noticeably diminished. It was like a little world of its own; the unpleasantness hadn't managed to get as far as the attic.

'Weird,' she mumbled again, and went back down to the fifth floor. She rang one of the doorbells, but no one answered. She tried the other three; no luck.

She returned to her own apartment; she had an advertising campaign to finish off. She closed the door and went into the kitchen to make herself a cup of coffee. She stood beneath the air vent inhaling the disgusting smell.

Something's rotting, she thought.

Lovisa Wahlberg didn't have much to be proud of, and plenty of people had felt the need to tell her this over the years – mainly her parents. She hadn't achieved a fraction of what they had expected of her.

'You need to get yourself a decent apartment,' her mother had said on her last visit.

By which she meant 'an apartment of your own', not one that belonged to someone else. As if it was just a matter of making the decision. As if absolutely anyone could buy an apartment in Stockholm, or magic up a rental agreement rather than a sublet. Lovisa had stopped listening. She'd been living here for over a year now, and would be able to stay for four more years. The owners were in Dubai and loved the life out there. No doubt Lovisa would have loved it too.

She didn't look around when she left the cake shop in the Söder district where she worked. She went straight across the street to her bicycle. The fear was in her blood, there was no getting rid of it. It made her focused and distracted at the same time.

She was just about to unlock her bike when the shadow appeared in her peripheral vision. The shadow that meant her harm. If she hadn't received the letter the previous day, she wouldn't have reacted, but now everything happened very fast, in spite of the fact that she was very tired after lying awake for most of the night. She didn't even raise her head to confirm her suspicions, she simply trusted her instinct that danger was close by. The lock came off, releasing the bike. People were passing by on the pavement, all preoccupied with their own affairs.

I'll scream if he tries to hurt me.

She got on her bike, pedalled down onto the road. There was a bump from the parcel shelf as the wheels hit the tarmac. Then, and only then, did she turn her head. She had to see who the shadow was, but he'd backed away, was partly hidden behind a bus shelter. Her heart was pounding, the adrenaline surging through her body.

Who the hell was he?

She cycled down the street, not caring whether she took a right or a left at the traffic lights, she just had to get away. A red light forced her to stop.

'Hey!' someone shouted behind her.

Red, amber, it would be green in a second.

I don't care if I get run over, I'm just going to go for it.

As she got ready to push down, someone came up alongside her – not the shadow, but a shorter, skinnier guy. He smiled at her.

'Sorry, I didn't meant to scare you. I just wanted to tell you that you're in danger of losing the book on your parcel shelf.'

She looked over her shoulder in confusion. She didn't have a book on her . . . She blinked several times. *What the . . . ?*

Someone had attached a book to the shelf. A green book with no pictures on the cover. The traffic began to move. She reached for the book, glanced over at the bus shelter.

The shadow was gone.

And the book was one she'd never heard of.

She read the strange title, trying to process what was going on:

I Am Putting Everything Right

Those who are grieving must be left in peace. Noah Johansson's parents had made that very clear when they were training their son, preparing him to take over the business.

'There's no payback,' his mother used to say. 'We're here to serve, and we do that with generosity.'

She meant that if a painter and decorator came to see them because his wife had died, they didn't save his phone number in case they needed someone to do up the kitchen in twelve months' time. They would call a different painter. Noah had always stuck to this rule, but not any more. He was faced with an emergency, and his parents would have understood if they'd still been alive. This was about their son, after all.

If only they were still around. They too would have realised that something had happened to Dan. Neither Noah nor Dan had expected to lose their parents so early, before Noah or his brother had turned forty. They had died in a car crash on the island of Crete. The dividing line between life and death was so thin, so thin.

One of Noah's clients had been a police officer, a man in his fifties whose wife had died of cancer. Noah searched his database for the man's name. Alex – or Alexander – Recht. There he was. A quick internet search brought up references that were no more than a few months old; Alex Recht had spoken out on some union issue. Good, in that case Noah dared to hope he was still with the police.

However, he wasn't sure if he had the right contact details. He wasn't too bothered about the address, but he wanted to be certain that he could reach Alex Recht on this phone number. He was utterly sick of the way the police had handled, or rather failed to handle, the disappearance of Dan and his family. It was beyond belief that someone could be missing for almost two months without anyone taking action.

Noah punched Alex's number into his mobile. Tina's visit had changed everything. She was the one who'd given him the strength, even though she didn't know it. He was no longer alone; someone else could see there was something very wrong with this move to Australia.

'I can't get hold of them,' she'd said. 'They're not answering their phones, and I've had these weird emails asking me to stop bothering them.'

However, something else had given Tina cause for concern. Like Malin's father, she had spoken to Malin on the Thursday, two days before they were due to leave.

'I've got a million things to do,' Malin had told her. 'Can I call you tomorrow? I should have time in the afternoon.'

She hadn't called. And Tina, who didn't want to be a nuisance, thought it best not to ring Malin in case she was busy. Instead she'd sent a text wishing them the best trip ever. A text that didn't get a reply. She texted again a few days later asking for their address so that she could send them some Swedish treats the children particularly liked. No reply. They'd already found a house and were planning to move in before the school term began and they both started working full time, but hadn't got round to passing on the address to their nearest and dearest.

If only I'd been more interested, Noah thought. *If only I'd been more positive, shared their enthusiasm about the adventure.*

Tina hadn't stayed long, but they'd arranged to meet up again. Before then Noah would try to speak to Alex Recht, hoping to find a new point of access to the police.

The phone rang several times before anyone answered.

'Alex Recht – I can't talk right now, but if you give me your name and number I'll call you back.'

'Hello . . . My name is Noah Johansson and I'm a funeral director. I . . . Am I disturbing you?'

Alex was clearly surprised. When he spoke again, his voice had changed.

'I remember you,' he said slowly. 'Very well, in fact. My children and I thought you were fantastic. You really helped us.'

Noah blushed, mainly because he was embarrassed at how happy Alex's words made him; such accolades always meant too much. But also because he felt a little spark of hope, the hope that Alex would be the one who listened.

Alex was speaking quietly to another person. Noah pressed the phone to his ear, wishing he'd gone to the police station and tried to see Alex in person.

'Listen, Noah, things are a bit tricky at the moment – can I call you later or tomorrow?'

Noah thought about all the days that had passed since his brother disappeared, and now Alex wanted to waste even more time.

'No problem,' he said.

He tried not to let his disappointment come through, but of course it did.

'Has something happened?' Alex asked.

Noah hesitated. How could he explain that the situation had been critical for weeks?

'My brother's gone missing.'

'I'm sorry?'

'My brother Dan has gone missing. Together with his entire family. They're supposed to be in Australia, but that's not true.'

Even though he was telling the story exactly as it was, he suddenly felt doubtful. It seemed so improbable.

'That sounds terrible,' Alex said, but the warmth in his voice had gone. 'It would be better if you call the main switchboard number, tell them you want to report a missing person, then someone will look into—'

'No,' Noah interrupted him. 'No, they won't look into anything, that decision has already been made. That's why I called you.'

Once again he heard Alex talking to someone else.

'I'll get back to you later,' Alex said to Noah. 'Okay?'

'Okay.'

Noah put the phone down on his desk and sank back in his chair. Then he sat there and waited. And waited.

There was something about colleagues from overseas, there was no denying it. Above all it was the fact that Alex rarely came into contact with them. He reminded himself of this when he and Fredrika sat down in one of the smaller meeting rooms with the investigator from London. The room was furnished with sofas rather than a table and chairs. Alex had seen the disappointment in Ivan's eyes when he hadn't been asked to join them; after all, it was Ivan who'd tracked down Linda Sullivan and arranged for her to come in. However, that couldn't be helped; the demands of the case had to come first, even at the expense of hurt feelings. Right now he needed Ivan to focus on Malcolm Benke's social network and any possible threats against him.

Fredrika caught Alex's eye as they sat down.

'Everything okay?' she said quietly in Swedish.

He gave a brief nod. He was okay. Even though he'd just spoken to the man who'd arranged Lena's funeral, even though someone had left an anonymous letter in his mailbox at home. He was okay, but that didn't mean he wasn't brooding over both those things. His blood pressure was rising and his hands felt cold.

'Who called you?' Fredrika went on equally quietly,

smiling at their British colleague as if to apologise for speaking Swedish.

Linda smiled back politely.

'Later,' Alex said.

Or not at all, depending on what Noah Johansson wanted. The conversation had been bewildering in every way. Alex didn't have a bad word to say about the man, but that didn't explain why he'd called Alex, talking about a missing brother. The whole thing made Alex uneasy. Something was wrong, and he wasn't sure he ought to get dragged into whatever it might be.

He turned his attention to their guest. Linda Sullivan appeared to be a few years older than Fredrika. She wore ripped jeans, which Alex hated, and smelled of cigarette smoke.

'Thank you for making the time to come in,' he began.

'No problem – I was in town anyway.'

'You were involved in the inquiry into the murder of Beata Benke?' Fredrika said.

'That's right. It was a while ago, but I hope I'll be able to help.'

'I'm sure you will,' Alex said. 'The only information we have comes from Beata's mother. We were hoping you'd be able to supply us with a more detailed account, and confirm what we've already been told.'

Linda's version largely overlapped with what they'd been told by Karin Benke. The Metropolitan Police had questioned Beata's friends, colleagues and members of her family, and had built up a picture of her life. At first everything had seemed promising for Beata and the man who later became her husband. He was the best boyfriend ever. The change took place at some point during the first year of their marriage. According to her friends, Beata had started to behave differently, pushing away those who were close to her. She wasn't very successful; they thought too much of her to accept it.

'So one day she was confronted by a small group of her friends. They eventually managed to get the truth out of her: Richard was controlling every aspect of her life. He beat her and threatened her, and the situation was rapidly deteriorating. However, she felt trapped, unable to get away from him no matter how hard she tried. One of the friends contacted Beata's family, told them what was going on. You can imagine how they reacted.'

There.

The detail Alex had been waiting for without realising.

'Tell me,' he said. 'How did they react?'

Linda made a dramatic gesture, spreading her arms wide.

'They were distraught. Furious. Her parents were very well off, as you probably know. They came storming over to London, did everything they could to help their daughter. But you know how it is – some things just can't be fixed.'

Ain't that the truth, Alex thought. *So the question is – what do you do instead?*

He suddenly felt grateful that Ivan had set up this meeting.

'You said they did everything they could – what exactly does that mean?' Fredrika asked.

'They talked to Richard, tried to get him to let Beata go. But he had her in a grip of iron, which Karin and Malcolm found incredibly frustrating. The thing is, he could be so sweet, so loving. Beata forgave him over and over again, with the result that she became smaller and smaller in every sense of the word. It was so difficult for those around her; she would ask for help, then immediately withdraw when anyone attempted to get close.'

'Did her parents contact the police?'

'Yes. They asked for help and advice just a few months before she was murdered, but Beata refused to cooperate, insisted she didn't need any support. Out of pure fear, I should think. The police frightened her more than anything else. And then the call came in to say she'd been found dead at home, and it turned into a murder investigation.'

The way such situations often ended – no one needed to put it into words.

'Who found her?' Alex realised he had slid too far down and shuffled to adjust his position. The shiny sofa was unforgivably ugly; he wondered where the hell they'd found it. No doubt tight-fisted Margareta Berlin was somehow responsible . . .

'Her husband. He called the emergency services in total panic mode.'

Alex suppressed a sigh.

'What made it so difficult to convict him?'

'He had an alibi. We worked like dogs to crack it, but we got nowhere. We couldn't prove he'd been at home when Beata was thought to have died, and that was the crucial point. Plus the murder weapon was never found.'

'Did you follow up on any other suspects?' Fredrika asked.

'No. I don't mean we didn't bother – we were open to the possibility that it could be someone other than Richard. Aggravated burglary, for example, but when there isn't a single piece of evidence, you can't really go in that direction.'

Another detail that stuck in Alex's mind. Not a single

piece of evidence to suggest that Beata had been killed in connection with an aggravated burglary. *Not a single piece.*

'Can you elaborate on that?' Alex could hear the thickness in his voice; it always happened when he was tense. 'What do you mean when you say there was no evidence to link Beata's death to a burglary?'

'There was absolutely no indication of forced entry into the apartment,' Linda explained. 'Which could mean that she'd forgotten to lock the door, of course, but all of her friends insisted that the front door was always locked. That left two alternatives: either she let the murderer in, or the person in question had a key.'

'And you concluded that the second option was the most likely?' Fredrika said.

'Yes. Because of the way she died, it seemed that she'd been surprised by the perpetrator and hadn't heard him coming.'

Alex frowned. 'Because of the way she died?'

'She was shot at close range. The bullet hit her in the chest; she would have died instantly.'

Alex and Fredrika looked at each other, both equally surprised. Alex could feel the unease clawing at his body. Beata had been killed in exactly the same way as her father. With a bullet to the chest. This was what he'd known all along, deep down: the murder of Malcolm Benke was hiding a bigger story. Maybe even big enough to encompass the letter writer who had sent Alex a cryptic message.

I am doing what you cannot do.

Fredrika crossed her legs. 'Do you happen to know whether Beata was wearing her wedding ring when she was found?'

Linda slowly shook her head.

'I can't remember, to be honest – but I can certainly check.'

There was a brief silence. Alex thought they were unlikely to get any further, and might as well bring the meeting to a close. Then Fredrika spoke:

'Where exactly was she when she died?'

'In the living room. She was sitting in an armchair in front of the open fire.'

The working day was drawing to a close. Fredrika had to think back a long way to recall a time when she had felt so powerless. She couldn't have predicted the turn the investigation would take, how surprised she would be. Nor could she have expected Alex to receive an anonymous message at home. Her stomach contracted with fear. Everything was out of balance, both at work and at home.

And I thought I'd be able to fix this.

She shouldn't have gone along with Spencer's suggestion that they should carry on working as normal, rather than 'sitting staring at each other' all summer. What the hell had they been thinking? This was Spencer's last summer – of course they should be sitting staring at each other!

So I ought to go home. Right now. And stare at him until my eyes fall out.

She looked at a photograph of Malcolm Benke, dead in his armchair with a bullet through his chest. Was it a betrayal if she changed her mind? Was she betraying Malcolm by going home to wait for someone else's death rather than pursuing the truth about his? Hardly. Alex would be fine without her.

I'll discuss it with Spencer tonight. Then I'll tell Alex.

But first of all she must contact Mikael Lundell in Israel. Alex had asked her to do it; he was clearly disturbed by the phone call he'd taken just before the meeting with Linda Sullivan. Fredrika took several deep breaths before she was able to make herself pick up the phone and key in the number. She and Eden had neither seen each other nor spoken since those terrible events. There had been no reason to do so. She suddenly felt nervous. What was she going to say when either Eden or Mikael answered? Should she offer her condolences? They'd been grieving for almost four years now.

A click on the other end of the line.

'Eden Lundell.'

Fredrika couldn't get a single word out. Eden's voice brought back countless emotions. Eden, who had rushed up the stairs and into her apartment to find that both her children had been shot.

'Hello?'

Fredrika cleared her throat. 'Sorry, I am here – it's Fredrika Bergman. I don't know if you remember me?'

'Of course I do.'

Eden's voice was just the same as before, deep and hoarse.

'I'm calling on Alex's behalf. He . . . Something came up.'

Death. What else?

'Okay.'

'I'd like to speak to Mikael, if that's possible? Or shall I call back later?'

Eden's reply was brusque. 'We agreed on five o'clock Swedish time and it's five o'clock now, so I don't see a problem.'

Fredrika was so taken aback by Eden's attitude that she didn't say a word.

'Mikael will be here in a second.'

With that Eden was gone. No exchange of pleasantries, and Fredrika hadn't even attempted to ask how the family were getting on. It wasn't a lack of politeness, she realised; she wanted to spare Eden the pain of answering that question.

Even as a child Fredrika had understood that an astonishing number of couples consisted of two people who were nothing like each other. Opposites attract, as they say. In Eden and Mikael's case this was particularly striking.

After Eden's harshness came Mikael's gentleness.

Fredrika asked him how he knew Malcolm Benke. 'They called me one Sunday,' he explained. 'Sorry, not they – he. Malcolm rang me one Sunday, said that he and his family needed my help. His daughter had told him that she'd turned to me for support on several occasions.'

Mikael's accent was difficult to place, but it was obvious that he'd moved around a lot, spent time in different parts of Sweden and the rest of the world. Fredrika let out a long breath when he began to speak. He wasn't being in any way obstructive.

'And why did Beata need your support?'

'Because she had problems with her husband.'

Was he allowed to tell her this? The question came into Fredrika's mind out of nowhere. Mikael was a priest; wasn't he obliged to respect the seal of the confessional, so to speak? She decided to let him take the lead; if Mikael didn't object, she would carry on. Always better to apologise than ask for permission.

As if he'd read her mind, Mikael said:

'The police didn't contact me after Beata's death, and I didn't seek them out. I read about the case in the papers, of course, kept myself informed as best I could.'

He paused, as if he'd run out of words and was wondering how to continue.

'You regret that,' Fredrika said. 'Although I can't see you did anything wrong.'

She could hear Mikael breathing heavily. 'That's only because you don't know what I knew.'

It was Fredrika's turn to fall silent.

'As I said, Beata had told Malcolm that I'd supported her, so one day he contacted me. On a Sunday, just after the morning service. He asked to see me, and I invited him round that same afternoon. I . . .'

A child shouted in the background, and the conversation was interrupted as Mikael put down the phone and disappeared. He soon came back.

'Sorry about that – my youngest daughter wanted help with something.'

Tears sprang to Fredrika's eyes. 'Congratulations.'

'Sorry?'

Fredrika clarified: 'I didn't know you'd had another child.'

Mikael let out a brief laugh. 'It was a few years ago, but thank you.'

Fredrika smiled, then returned to the matter in hand. 'So you met Malcolm Benke.'

'Yes – and his son.'

'His son?'

'Bernhard – he was a year or so younger than Beata. A real hothead, if I can put it that way. He was obviously furious with his parents.'

'Why?'

'He accused both of them, but mainly his father, of doing far too little for Beata. He feared for his sister's life, and of course he was proved right in the end.'

'What on earth did he expect his parents to do?'

Mikael didn't answer straight away, and Fredrika could feel his uncertainty.

'I think he wanted them to do anything, literally anything, for her.'

'I understand,' Fredrika said quietly.

'Of course it's possible that I was mistaken, but I don't think so. Bernhard was seething over his parents' weakness.'

'So why didn't he do something?'

'Quite. Maybe he thought they had less to lose by crossing the line, so to speak, and engaging in criminal activities in order to get Beata out of there.'

'And all this was played out in front of you?'

'It was. When their discussion spilled over into a stand-up row, I realised why Malcolm had contacted me. He wanted me to mediate between him and his son, but it was incredibly difficult. I had very little advice to offer, but I did tell them not to do anything stupid that they might regret.'

Fredrika continued to make notes; the conversation with Bernhard Benke was going to have a very different focus now.

Were you planning to murder your brother-in-law, Bernhard?

And did you murder your father because he failed to save your sister?

'How did your meeting end?' she asked.

'They left without my having managed to broker any kind of peace between them,' Mikael replied, sounding downcast. 'I didn't hear from them again until Malcolm turned up with his friends.'

Fredrika stiffened. 'What friends?' She opened her folder and took out a copy of the photo they'd found in Malcolm's house. The one that had been taken in Beata's living room at a time no one was prepared to remember.

'Two childhood friends – Eskil and Sten.'

Bingo.

She allowed Mikael to continue.

'They arrived in London ready for a fight, intending to confront Beata's husband mob-handed and, as they put it, scare the shit out of him. They were also going to offer him a large sum of money to disappear from Beata's life. They wanted me there as a witness to prevent him from claiming they'd beaten him up or something.'

'The mention of scaring the shit out of him sounds as if they weren't afraid to cross a line,' Fredrika said. She stared at the photograph. Mikael was clearly uncomfortable, refusing to look at the camera.

'I thought back to my previous meeting with Malcolm,' he said. 'I was afraid Bernhard had been working on him, persuaded him to do something stupid. And his friends didn't fill me with confidence; they didn't seem stable, they were much too emotional.'

'So you went along to make sure the encounter didn't end in disaster?'

'That was the general idea, but it was all a lot less dramatic than I'd feared. Beata's husband broke down completely as the three of them yelled at him. Eventually everyone calmed down, and we managed to discuss things on a more constructive level. I don't think I saw anything that could be described as criminal behaviour.'

You don't think?

'No threats were issued?' Fredrika asked.

'Not as far as I can recall. Well, no direct threats. No death threats anyway.'

Fredrika didn't press him to be more precise.

'Were any pictures taken on that occasion?'

'Yes – I thought that was very strange. Malcolm asked Richard to photograph us before we left.'

Fredrika wondered if she'd misheard.

'He asked his son-in-law to take the picture?'

She'd assumed Beata had been behind the camera.

'That's right.'

'Beata wasn't home?'

'No – God, no.'

The priest was blaspheming, which pleased Fredrika no end.

'Sten Aber claimed that he didn't recognise the photo,' she said. 'He even pretended not to recognise you. Can you think of any reason why he would do that?'

It was a shot in the dark; Mikael Lundell wasn't responsible for Sten's silence.

'I can imagine that Sten would have been very stressed after the event,' Mikael said. 'He wasn't the most driven of the three men; he might even have got it into his head that he was somehow to blame for Beata's death.'

So Sten Aber had lied to protect himself.

Not unusual, but it didn't exactly make him a model citizen.

'So what was your assessment of the situation when you left? Did you think you'd managed to improve things for Beata?'

'I'm embarrassed to answer that question,' Mikael said, 'but yes, I thought everything would be fine. It wasn't, of course. As I found out almost straight away.'

Fredrika was still looking at the picture.

'When did this meeting take place?'

Mikael's voice suddenly sounded thin.

'Two days before she died.'

Alex Recht was sitting with the phone in his hand, hesitating. He ought to call Noah Johansson back; he was curious to find out what the funeral director wanted. But first he had to staunch the flow of memories. Didn't Johansson realise what he'd stirred up?

No ordeal had been worse than watching Lena die. Nothing had torn at his heart more, weighed him down more. To experience such a loss was to become privy to a secret no normal human being wanted to get anywhere near. He had been so angry back then; sometimes he was still so angry now.

'Why didn't anyone say anything?' he'd shouted during a phone call to his son one evening when things were at rock bottom. 'Why the fuck didn't anyone tell me?'

His voice had been thick with tears, his whole body full to bursting with fear.

'Tell you what, Dad? I don't understand.'

And Alex had whispered:

'Why didn't anyone tell me this could actually happen?'

Because that was how it felt, as if the truth had been kept from him. People could die long before they achieved the eighty years or so they'd been promised, and he was not exempt from the effects of this terrible tragedy. Dying before you got old was unnatural. That was the only conclusion he'd managed to reach – or at least the fact that it had happened to someone close to Alex was unnatural. Shit happened to other people – and as part of his job, never in his private life.

He didn't remember how his son had answered his desperate question – with some pathetic platitude, no doubt. Nobody had known what to say when Lena died. Even Margareta Berlin, head of Human Resources back then, had come out with some meaningless nonsense, then gone behind his back and asked Fredrika to keep an eye on him. Unforgivable.

There's something damaged about that woman, he thought. *And it can't be fixed.*

He pulled himself together and made the call.

'Noah Johansson.'

'Alex Recht. Sorry it's taken me so long to get back to you.'

It was gone six; the hours had just slipped by.

Noah sounded eager (much too eager) and relieved:

'No problem, it's fine, absolutely fine. The important thing is that you've called. I can't thank . . . I was so afraid that . . . I didn't even know if . . .'

The forced jollity and the series of unfinished sentences worried Alex. What did Noah want? He'd mentioned a missing brother.

He coughed; the air in HQ was so dry. 'You said you wanted my help; could you be a little more specific?' He hoped this would encourage Noah to get a grip.

Which it did.

'Of course, of course. I don't quite know where to start. It's been several months . . . As I said, my brother's disappeared.'

Alex shook his head slowly. 'I'm very sorry, but as I explained before, you need to report him missing so that someone with more time than me can take a closer look at the situation.'

Noah's protest was immediate.

'I've already done all that. I called the police as soon as I realised something was wrong.'

Then he told the story again, this time in considerably more detail.

'It was a few weeks after I got back from a trip abroad. My first for several years – it's difficult for me to take time off. Anyway, that's just background really. The fact that I'd been away for a while. I went over to my brother's house, and I knew straight away that something wasn't right. The place was kind of untidy – as if the family was at home. A bike lying on the drive, a window left ajar. You don't leave a house like that if you're going to be away for a year.'

Too many words, too much stress in his voice. Alex was in the middle of another case; he didn't have time to wonder what had become of Noah's brother. As if from a distance he heard Noah talking much too fast about the many failings of the police, and about one officer in particular who couldn't even work out what time it was in Sydney. He also mentioned hidden messages from his brother in the form of a house key and a swear word.

'You need to calm down,' Alex said eventually. 'You say your brother's missing, that the house was a mess. The family were planning an extended trip to Australia, but you don't think that's where they've gone. So were they leaving their house empty?'

Noah's voice almost broke.

'As I understood it, yes. They did consider renting it out but Malin, my sister-in-law, didn't like the idea.'

'So maybe they left it in a bit of a state to give the

impression that they wouldn't be gone for too long? To keep the burglars away?' Alex suggested.

'No. I see your point, but this is different.'

'And the police believe they left of their own free will?' Alex said quietly. It was very clear that he should never have made this call.

'Exactly, and they're wrong. Totally fucking wrong. Excuse my language, but I don't understand how the police can get away with this. The summer will soon be over, and it's clear to me that someone is guilty of gross negligence at the very least. What if Dan and his family are dead?'

Noah began to cry, and Alex wanted more than anything to put down the phone. And yet ... He remembered the funeral director as a composed and competent person. A man in control of himself and life. There was no doubt that something had changed since then – but what? And why was it Alex's job to look into whatever it might be?

It's not my job. It's not my job.

'The officers you've been dealing with must have explained why they think your brother has chosen to stay away,' he said in a kinder tone.

'They believe all that nonsense about Australia, because they've sent messages to Dan's email address and received replies saying everything's fine.'

'Sorry if I sound confused, but are you telling me the police have been in contact with your brother?' Alex said.

'No, that's my point! Dan didn't write those messages, someone else is using his email account. The fact that I even need to point out something so obvious is just crazy. I know my own brother. He's not in Australia. Or maybe he is, but there's still something very wrong about the whole situation.'

Alex scratched his head, trying to work out what Noah was telling him and what he wasn't telling him.

'If the problem is in Australia rather than in Sweden, then you ought to contact the police over there,' he said. 'But you need to be sure they are there and not somewhere else.'

Alex allowed his thoughts free rein for a moment. There was clearly a problem, but did that problem lie with Noah, or were his claims about the family's disappearance true? Alex didn't really know the man, didn't know anything about his physical or mental health. People imagined things, especially those who had too much time and too little going on in their lives. Noah was a single man in his forties who ran a funeral business. Alex was wary of reading too much into that, but he wondered what Noah's relationship with his brother was like. Was Dan the most important person in Noah's life? If so, it was hardly surprising that he would be upset by the family's decision to move to the other side of the world, and had come up with a different explanation for their disappearance from Stockholm.

Disappearance.

That word made everything so difficult. According to Noah, an entire family had been abducted and were being held captive. Unless of course they were dead. Did that kind of stuff really happen? It was a question that had become less and less relevant over the years as far as Alex was concerned. Everything happened, and rather too often. But an entire family?

'I'm not the only one who thinks it's weird,' Noah said. 'One of my sister-in-law's friends came to see me – she's really worried too. Her name is Tina, Tina Antonsson.'

Alex jotted down the name and thought it was probably

the least important note he'd ever made. He'd already come to a decision. When he had time – and not before – he would contact the officer Noah had been dealing with, find out what had been done and what he or she thought.

'Tell me this – off the top of your head, why would someone do this to your brother and his family? It sounds so deliberate, so strange. Abducting a whole family is an extremely risky undertaking. Why would someone go to such lengths to harm Dan?'

Noah's breathing was shallow.

'I don't know. I mean, I suppose the kidnapper might have been after my sister-in-law, but Dan's a psychologist. He's worked with criminals, and he's certainly failed more than once.'

'Failed?'

'I'm not sure how to put it – that's not my world at all. But he's worked with deeply depressed individuals, and some of them – maybe two or three – have taken their own lives.'

A bird crashed into Alex's window, making him jump.

Noah interpreted his silence as an invitation to keep talking.

'He has a duty of confidentiality, of course; he says very little about his work. He was very upset last autumn though – he actually received threats.'

It was like quietly starting up an engine then allowing it to idle. Alex shuffled uncomfortably, not wanting to acknowledge what he was feeling. A spark had been ignited within him; elements of Noah's account had captured his interest.

'What happened last autumn?'

'It was all over the papers. A man shot his family, then himself. He was Dan's patient. And Dan didn't manage to stop him.'

Malin was moving through the house like an apparition. She was looking for Dan, calling his name.

'Dan?'

She hated the way her voice seemed to echo, bouncing off the walls. There were curtains and rugs, but it didn't make any difference. The house was like a sink hole they couldn't possibly fill.

She remembered with horror what the children had asked in the beginning:

'How long, Mummy? How long do we have to stay here?'

She'd answered:

'I don't know, but Daddy and I want to get out too.'

They'd stopped asking when they were going home. It was as if they'd capitulated, or as if something inside them had broken. They'd stopped – and started – doing so many things. Her daughter had stopped crying and started remaining silent. Her son had stopped talking about his friends and started wetting the bed at night. At her lowest moments Malin thought the decline she was witnessing was irreversible. If the children came out of this house alive (something she doubted more and more with each passing day), they would do so as damaged individuals.

'Dan?'

She went upstairs, the carpet stifling any sound.

Dan was in the bathroom. He'd had a shower and was standing in front of the mirror combing his hair. He'd refused to cut it ever since they arrived, and by now he looked like a hippie. It had been this long once before, over twelve years ago, when their relationship was still pretty new. Dan had lost his job, and had declared that he wasn't going to get a haircut until he found a new post. It had taken a good six months, by which time both Dan and his hairstyle had changed beyond recognition.

Malin thought back to what she'd said when unemployment threatened to break him.

'You can't give up. Things don't happen by themselves.'

The fact that he'd become so weak so quickly had terrified her. Did she really love this man? Was he the kind of person she ought to invest in? Would he be able to shoulder responsibility for their relationship, their life together? Would he want to? Then came the day when his face lit up; he had an interview. The day Malin found out she was pregnant. She'd pushed aside all her doubts; she didn't have time to worry about their future, it would have to take care of itself. On the whole it had gone pretty well. Their careers had flourished, their life had been so perfect that she'd sometimes wondered how one family could be granted so much happiness.

With hindsight, she knew better. Life was like any bank. If you withdrew too much, one day you would discover that the account was empty.

'Why don't you answer when I call you?'

Dan blinked at his reflection.

'I didn't hear you.'

'Nonsense – of course you did.'

Malin wanted to cry, to sit down on the cold tiles and let the tears flow, but she couldn't do it. Her legs refused to bend and her eyes were dry.

Dan walked past her into their room. He dropped the towel on the bed and pulled on a pair of underpants. Malin had no idea when they'd last had sex. Or when she'd last reminded him not to drop his wet towel on the bed.

Things that had once been important no longer seemed to matter. She followed him and closed the bedroom door behind them.

'We need to talk,' she said.

He stiffened, then began to pick out the clothes he wanted to wear. Shirt and trousers. No socks. His feet were just as white as hers. They didn't look as if they belonged to a living person. That was why Malin always wore socks – so she didn't have to see what their stay in this house was costing them.

She searched for the right words. It didn't go too well.

'We . . . we have to start doing something.'

Dan stared at her.

'Like what?'

'Something. Anything.'

Malin spread her hands wide; to her relief her eyes were no longer dry.

'Darling, we're falling apart,' she whispered. 'Soon we won't exist any more.'

His face grew stern, then shut down.

'Isn't that the point?' he said.

She wanted to scream, more than anything, but it was impossible. The children would hear, they'd be scared. They already had so many questions she was unable to answer.

'Of course that's the point!' Her voice was so strained that it was as hoarse as his. 'But that doesn't mean it has to be that way! Don't you understand? We have to start resisting, we have to . . .'

'Resisting?'

He spoke the single word so quietly that her blood froze. 'Resisting, Malin? Who do you suggest we . . . resist?'

She shook her head. If only the tears would flow. If only everything that had become so hard and solid would grow warm and begin to thaw.

'Him. We tried once, but . . .'

Dan took a few rapid (much too rapid) steps in her direction. 'Leave it.'

Malin automatically backed away as he came towards her. Gone were the days when she used to run straight into his open arms. Why wasn't he prepared to talk about how they could get out of here?

Maybe because he knew deep down, just as she did, that it was pointless.

Because they knew their every move was being monitored.

Because they didn't know how quickly the man who had done this could get to the house, they didn't know how far away he was.

Because a failed escape attempt could mean their deaths.

'We can't go on like this,' she said. 'The children . . .'

'The children feel like shit,' Dan said.

There. At long last. A single tear ran down her cheek.

'Exactly!' she said. 'Exactly. The children feel like shit. We can't allow this to continue. We have a responsibility as parents. This nightmare isn't simply going to end; we have to realise that, we . . .'

Dan stepped back, silencing her with the movement.

'I've already realised that,' he said in a voice that was too calm. It was filled with resolve, and it made her suspicious. He was also smiling – a joyless smile.

'I've been thinking,' he went on. 'It might work after all.'

His words should have brought relief, but Malin's reaction was the opposite. She was stressed, terrified.

'Yes?' she said.

He nodded. 'Yes. Yes. Wait a few days and you'll see.'

He didn't say another word all evening. Malin's fear grew along with the silence. Her heart was pounding so hard it was painful.

Two things were perfectly clear following her conversation with Dan.

First of all, he'd lost his grip on reality.

And secondly Malin now believed he was a danger to both himself and his family.

The evening sun caressed the tarmac on which Fredrika Bergman was walking. She was heading home from work. Away from the equally unpleasant and incomprehensible letter that had been sent to Alex, away from an investigation she didn't understand. Everywhere she looked she saw people hurrying along in the fine weather, hurrying to enjoy themselves. She thought that was a good answer to the question 'What is typically Swedish?': living in cold and darkness for so much of the year that the odd summer's day evoked anxiety more than happiness.

What happens if I don't enjoy myself enough?

When will the next opportunity come along?

Spencer rang as she was crossing Torsgatan and passing Vasa Park. He wanted to meet at the outdoor cafe on Odenplan, make the most of the sunshine. Of course. He had more reason than anyone to seize the day.

So many things to fit in.

So many things he would never have the chance to experience again.

Fredrika's lungs burned as she inhaled.

'Wouldn't you prefer somewhere by the water?' she asked, trying to keep her voice steady. 'Odenplan isn't exactly charming.'

'By the water? What difference does that make? I'm happy with good food and decent wine.'

She let him decide. This was his last summer; she had to allow him to make his own choices.

She dashed away the tears from her cheeks. More tears. She couldn't think of another summer when she'd cried so much, or another autumn she'd dreaded as much as the one that lay just weeks away. In her darkest hours she saw everything slipping through her fingers, the children being placed in foster care when she died of a broken heart. It was as if she needed to reach rock bottom in order to find the strength to climb up again.

The children.

It was for their sake that she would continue to put one foot in front of the other. Anything else would be unthinkable, unforgivable.

'What's the worst thing?' her mother had asked. 'What's the worst thing about what you're going through?'

Fredrika hadn't hesitated for a second.

'The certainty,' she'd said.

She hated – *hated* – people who insisted it 'must be good to know for sure'. As if the doctors' diagnosis brought peace of mind, according to the totally meaningless principle that 'it's better to know than to worry'. Only the lucky individual who'd never seen their worst nightmare become a reality could possibly think that way.

I won't accept it, she thought. *I won't.*

'Don't cry, Fredrika,' Spencer said on the phone. His voice was gentle, his patience endless. Unlike hers. Quite the reverse.

That was where it ended, in fact, right then and there.

I
won't
accept
it.

She stopped dead and voiced her despair.

'How the fuck can it be like this?' she yelled so loudly that people passing by turned around. 'How can you leave me? I don't get it!'

She was sobbing now, sobbing for all the things that would never be, all the things they hadn't got around to doing, for the children who were so small, and for her own pitch-black future.

'Do you know how it feels?' she whispered. 'It feels as if I'm going to die along with you.'

She heard Spencer's breathing and felt incredibly guilty.

The kingdom of sorrow was too cramped. There wasn't room for both of them.

'See you soon,' Spencer said in a muffled voice, and ended the call.

Fredrika wept all the way to the cafe. When she arrived Spencer was sitting at one of the round tables. Thinner than before he fell ill, but only someone who'd known him for a long time would notice. From a distance he looked strong and healthy. He spotted Fredrika and raised a hand in greeting.

She waved back, then hurried over and kissed him on the lips. Spencer opened with his favourite question:

'Hard day?'

'Same as usual.'

The events of the day had already been filed away in her mind, leaving the boundless love for the man she'd adored for virtually all of her adult life. Their time together might be limited, but her love was not.

'I want us to reconsider,' she said. 'I want us to give up work, be together instead.'

Spencer shook his head.

'Grief would drive us both crazy. It's out of the question – I don't want you to remember my last few weeks in that way.'

'But if we're talking about *my* memories, then surely I have the right to choose?'

'Sorry, I didn't express myself very well. It's not just about your memories, it's also about how I'm going to cope with the realisation that every single thing I do this summer will be for the last time.'

He sighed.

Fredrika swallowed. 'There are other options,' she said quietly. 'You don't have to stick to the choice you made.'

Spencer flinched.

'Are you crazy? What are you saying? Do you expect me to wait for a slow death that will inevitably be a living hell? To experience how it feels to lose control over my bodily functions, one by one? Never, Fredrika. We've already discussed this.'

And of course they had. And of course she understood his thought process. His brain encompassed everything that made him the man he was, and letting his illness slowly obliterate him was out of the question.

'I ordered you a glass of red,' he said.

'Perfect.'

'It's a Burgundy – the one we had at the Erlandssons' a few weeks ago. Heavy and voluptuous – do you remember?'

'I do.'

He took her hand and kissed it.

'That's what makes it easier,' he said, leaning across the table. 'The fact that you remember.'

Fredrika started crying again. Spencer put both arms around her and drew her close. The person who was dying consoling the person who was fit and well. And all he could say was:

'Why does it have to end like this?'

The letter weighed exactly thirty-two grams. Almost nothing at all. And yet Alex suspected that it made a huge difference. He looked at the copy he'd brought home. The short lines, the assertion that something needed to be put right, and that Alex was incapable of doing what must be done.

Diana had been shaken when he got back. She realised the letter was important, and was afraid it might also be dangerous.

'If we're under threat then I need to know,' she'd said.

Alex had calmed her, assured her there was no threat, that he had no idea why the letter had arrived. She'd looked resigned when she went off to meet a friend a little while ago, almost as if she didn't believe him.

Now he was alone in the house, slumped in the chair behind his desk. He had called forensics, learned that there were no fingerprints on either the letter or the envelope. No trace of the sender. Hardly unexpected, but a disappointment nevertheless. A couple of colleagues had made discreet door-to-door inquiries in the neighbourhood; no one had seen the letter being delivered.

He wondered whether to call Fredrika. They hadn't finished discussing the letter; in fact they'd hardly started, because as usual Berlin had got in the way with her stupid questions, making a fuss and showing off, pretending to understand what was going on. As if there was anything to understand at such an early stage.

Alex reached for his phone, then hesitated. He had other things to think about, such as the conversation with Noah Johansson about his missing brother. Alex was very sceptical about the idea that an entire family could have been abducted from their home and were being held in an isolated location without arousing suspicions. It just didn't make sense, even after Noah had passed on the story of the client who'd killed his family and himself. According to Noah, he was more or less the only one who thought something was wrong – apart from a friend of his sister-in-law. As far as Alex was concerned, this was a clear sign that Noah had got the wrong end of the stick.

Anyway, if they have been abducted they're no longer alive.

It was a troubling thought, but surely it was the only answer. In which case, would they ever find the bodies of the missing family?

His phone rang and he picked it up, trying to ignore the soreness and stiffness in his fingers. His father had taught him everything he knew about rheumatism, which was a hell of a lot more than Alex wanted to know. Alex didn't have rheumatism. He'd made the decision, and that was the end of the matter.

He glanced at the display: *Peder Rydh.*

His first feeling was a surge of happiness. Peder was a colleague he'd worked with for a long time, someone he'd missed ever since the day Peder had been forced to leave the police. Which led him straight to the second feeling: anger. Because for all that time Alex had been fighting to bring him back. At first it had seemed impossible, then things began to look a little more positive. That was immediately after the fatal shootings in the Jewish community, the Solomon Community, where Peder had been working as head of security. Unfortunately Peder had changed his mind, decided he didn't want to return to the police. He was happy on the outside.

In which case he could damn well stay there.

'Alex Recht.'

He couldn't help liking Peder. He wanted to hear his voice, find out how things were going.

'Hi, Alex.'

'Hi.'

That treacherous smile that kind of sneaked out of its cage and plastered itself across his face when he spoke to Peder.

'Hi,' Peder said again. 'I just wanted to see how you were. It's been a while.'

A year, Alex worked out. They hadn't been in touch for a year, and it was Peder who'd called him on that occasion too. Anger gave way to a guilty conscience.

'How are things?' he asked.

Peder gave a brief answer; he didn't seem interested in discussing the details. He mentioned that his sons were growing up, that they needed less care than when they were tiny.

'You remember, don't you?' he said. 'When they were babies and everything was crap?'

Alex remembered only too well. He'd had to take Peder aside and explain how you behaved towards female colleagues, and how you most definitely did not behave. He'd been forced to send Peder on a course to learn about equality in the workplace. Alex didn't think it was something that could be learned in a lecture room, but that was beside the point. The order had come directly from the head of Human Resources, so . . .

He suddenly sat bolt upright.

'Did you hear what's happened? Berlin's been promoted. She's head of department.'

'Which department?'

'Mine, among others. The whole place is a shambles since the restructuring. Berlin's in charge of an empire the size of a continent.'

Peder laughed so hard he started coughing.

'Jesus Christ!'

'It's true. I was so pissed off I managed to persuade Fredrika to come out and get drunk with me.'

'You're kidding me!'

'Absolutely not. You should have seen her. Being drunk kind of suited her. Well, you know what I mean.'

Peder knew exactly what he meant.

They carried on talking; Peder had a new job.

'I was with the Solomon Community for a long time. My temporary post was extended, and I finished up staying for several years. It was good, but now I'm working for a private security firm that helps big companies with background checks on job applicants.'

'Like being a secret agent?' Alex said.

'Kind of,' Peder laughed. 'Although it's a lot more comfortable and very well paid.'

Alex laughed too. He could just imagine Peder digging up people's secrets. He was capable of both efficiency and discretion, although he could also be restless. Alex couldn't help wondering why he'd left the Solomon Community. He hadn't been there that long, despite his assertions.

'Did it get too monotonous?' he wondered.

Peder didn't answer for a moment.

'No, it was more ... I just needed to do something different. I wanted a change – it was time. Once I'd made the decision it all happened pretty quickly.'

It was time.

That was the way you thought when you were young. In Alex's case the phrase 'well, it's too late now' was more prevalent. Too late for a change of career, too late to make something else of his life. His gaze fell on a framed photograph on his desk, a picture of himself with the children. Diana wasn't there. Nor was Lena.

He picked it up, thought back to the conversation with Noah. Tried to imagine a scenario where he and the kids disappeared in a way that meant no one would miss him.

Impossible.

He hesitated, then made up his mind.

'Peder, can I run a story by you?'

'A story?'

'Yes, a story someone told me today. The problem is I don't know what to do with it.'

The words came pouring out, how desperate Noah had sounded.

'The trouble is I can't just dismiss him as an idiot. He's not making this up.'

'Do you want me to check him out?' Peder said dubiously.

'No, no, that's not why I brought it up. I want to know what you think, whether it's something I ought to pursue.'

'If your colleagues have already looked into it and decided there's nothing in it, then what can you achieve?'

Peder's words should have made Alex feel better, but they didn't.

'I'm not sure . . .' he said.

'About what?'

'Whether Noah might be right after all.'

He could hear Peder tapping on a keyboard.

'If I tell you something in confidence, it stays between us – okay?' he said.

'Absolutely,' Alex promised after a brief pause.

'Before I got this post I spent some time with a security firm targeting small businesses that needed help with alarm systems, that kind of thing.'

Alex sighed.

'You're telling me you've fitted in another job since you left Solomon?'

He knew he sounded like a nagging parent, but he couldn't help himself.

'Do you want to hear what I have to say or not?'

Peder's voice was louder now, slightly stressed.

Alex backtracked; he didn't want to risk Peder hanging up on him. At the same time, he didn't like what he was hearing. Peder was a sensitive soul, and he had gone through a great deal in the past. As long as life was running smoothly he was fine, but over the years he'd had something of a tendency to go off the rails – often deliberately.

'I do,' Alex said, even though he was uncomfortable at not knowing where the conversation was heading. 'Sorry, I shouldn't be telling you what to do – you're all grown up now. So . . . you worked for another security firm for a little while?'

'Yes, what's so strange about that? Sometimes things don't turn out the way you expect.'

Alex suppressed another sigh. That was precisely Peder's weakness. He always had an explanation, an excuse when something didn't go according to plan. And Peder's voice . . . It wasn't just defensive. If they hadn't known each other so well, Alex would have thought it sounded threatening.

But why?

Adopting a conciliatory tone, he said: 'Okay, tell me what you know.'

'Noah Johansson contacted us. It must have been early autumn, just after I started there. He was scared, thought someone was after him.'

'What?'

'Exactly. That's more or less what I said – "What?" I told him I could help him with an alarm system and so on, but that he had to contact the police if he was being followed or harassed. He wasn't prepared to do that, and I never did find out why. To be honest, I think he was making it up. He was kind of volatile, talked a load of crap.'

Volatile, talked a load of crap.

An assessment directly at odds with Alex's own.

Not that it was unwelcome. If Peder was right, it would undeniably explain a great deal. After all, Alex didn't have personal knowledge of Noah's character; he couldn't assess his reliability from the brief contact they'd had.

He glanced over at the window. If he wanted to he could go out and enjoy one of the season's few warm, sunny summer evenings. However, he lacked both desire and company, and preferred to remain indoors.

'You don't think whoever was threatening Noah could

be holding his brother hostage to get what they want?' he said.

'If that's the case I'm pretty sure he would have told you. Or kicked off big time when the police insisted there was nothing to investigate. But honestly, Alex – I think he was making it all up. He's a fantasist.'

Alex felt a sense of relief. Peder was probably right.

'Do you know anything about Noah's situation today?' he asked. 'In terms of security systems, I mean.'

Peder didn't say anything at first; when he did speak, he'd lowered his voice.

'No.'

Alex heard a key in the front door; Diana was home. Warmth and happiness filled his body, as if she'd been away for years rather than just a few hours.

'I have to go,' he said, getting to his feet. 'Anything else you think I ought to know?'

Again Peder hesitated. Out in the hallway Diana was taking off her shoes, putting something heavy on the floor – maybe a bag of books? They absolutely didn't need more books, although of course Diana wouldn't be pleased if he expressed that particular point of view. According to her, books were not about *need*. It was worse than that. They were a *prerequisite* for all rational life on earth.

Love means compromising, Alex thought. *Every single day.*

He registered Peder's silence on the other end of the line, and sat down again. To hell with Diana's books. Peder clearly had more to say.

'I drove past Noah's funeral business by pure chance the other day,' Peder said quietly. 'I don't know if . . . Shit, maybe

I shouldn't be telling you this. It's so easy to jump to conclusions. He might be a bit of a fantasist, but that doesn't mean he's always wrong or always exaggerates.'

Alex leaned forward, feeling the hard surface of the desk beneath his elbows.

'Tell me,' he said. 'Tell me what's bothering you.'

He was acutely aware of Peder's uncertainty, felt it grow and infect him. And with that uncertainty came a change of heart.

Don't tell me, because I don't want to hear what you have to say.

But it was too late.

'I saw a man slam the door behind him as he left. Then he turned and stormed back inside. There are huge windows, so you can see what's going on. I pulled up, and I saw the man go over to Noah and grab hold of his jacket.'

'Okay . . .'

Noah was a funeral director. Death aroused strong feelings; there was nothing new about that.

'He shoved Noah against the wall,' Peder went on, 'so hard that Noah banged his head. If the man hadn't left straight afterwards I would have called the police. I stayed put until I was sure Noah was all right, then I drove off.'

Alex wasn't particularly impressed; where was Peder going with this?

And then, with no warning, he said:

'Alex, it was Spencer.'

'What?'

'The man who was so upset was Spencer, Fredrika's husband.'

'Are you sure you can't stay tonight as well?'

Lovisa Wahlberg was sitting up in bed with a blanket around her shoulders as her boyfriend got dressed.

He shook his head.

'Best if I sleep at home – I've got to be up at five in the morning.'

Lovisa thought about the letter she'd received, the book someone had left on her bike. The shadow hiding behind the bus shelter.

'That doesn't matter,' she said cheerfully. 'I like getting up early.'

Her boyfriend grinned and pulled on his trousers.

'Liar!'

Lovisa drew the blanket more tightly around her shoulders.

I don't want to be alone.

Socks, sweater. 'I'll see you tomorrow evening, won't I?'

He sounded worried; he'd noticed how quiet she'd gone.

'Of course.'

She got out of bed and went to the door with him, kissed him when he'd put his shoes on.

'When will you be home from work?' he asked. 'I thought I'd come over about four.'

'I won't be back by then. Take the spare key and let yourself in.'

'Okay.' He slipped the key into his pocket, kissed her and left. Lovisa closed the door and locked it, then padded back to the bedroom. She grabbed her bag and took out the book.

I Am Putting Everything Right

She'd never heard of the author, or the book. There was no blurb on the back cover, no indication of what it was about. The pages were yellowing; apparently the book had been printed in the 1940s.

Lovisa shuddered; she didn't want it anywhere near her. She pushed it into her bag and sat down on the bed.

Then she heard a key in the lock. Overwhelmed with relief, she rushed into the hallway.

He's come back! He could tell that I didn't want him to go!

The relief disappeared.

The sound wasn't right.

It wasn't a key – someone was messing with the lock.

Lovisa looked around frantically, desperately searching for an escape route.

Where can I go?

The door flew open and the man she'd thought of as a shadow was standing there. With slow, deliberate movements – he knew perfectly well that Lovisa was trapped – he closed the door behind him.

All Lovisa could think about was the article that had been sent to her.

'Now,' he said. 'Now you and I are going to put everything right.'

Present: Interrogators one and two (I1 and I2),
Detective Chief Inspector Alex Recht (Recht)

I1: Did you tell Fredrika what you'd found out about Spencer?

Recht: No, it was too vague. I decided we could talk about it later, if there was a reason to do so.

I2: Okay, let's leave that for the moment. You continued with the investigation into the murder of Malcolm Benke. What happened?
(silence)

Recht: Far too much.

I1: Seriously . . .
(silence)

Recht: There were more deaths. And more letters.

I1: Did you have any suspects at this stage?

Recht: No.

I1: But it wasn't long before the situation changed, if I've understood correctly.

Recht: No investigation is entirely without speculation.

I2: Surely it wasn't hard to predict that there
would be more letters?
(silence)

Recht: As far as I was concerned, it was. And that
also applies to my colleagues.

WEDNESDAY

Grass tennis courts. What a ridiculous idea. That was what Gustav's father had said when he heard about his son's latest little earner. Cutting the grass on the new tennis courts out in Saltsjöbaden.

'Absolutely lunacy,' he'd said. 'We're getting like the British – so conservative that we'd rather allow tennis players to break their legs than provide them with a modern surface to play on.'

Gustav knew nothing about either tennis or British traditions (and neither did his father, to be honest), but he knew how to earn money. He'd been the same ever since he was twelve years old, never letting an opportunity pass him by. He looked after babies, dogs, cats, sold Christmas magazines, ran errands for old Agnes who lived across the street. Gustav loved earning money. The more he earned, the closer he got to his goal: to pass his motorcycle test when he was eighteen. His parents would never agree to finance such nonsense; they'd made that very clear the first time he'd mentioned it at the age of ten.

The ride-on mower was waiting for him in the garage. It started at the first attempt and moved smoothly out of its hiding place. It was a glorious summer day, and Gustav was very happy. Above all he was delighted that the weather was good enough for him to be able to cut the grass. He also had a new girlfriend, and plenty of work. Sven at the ICA supermarket a hundred metres from Gustav's home had offered him a few hours on the checkout, which Gustav had gratefully accepted. It was wonderful to be on holiday from school. It was wonderful that everything was going so well.

He drove onto the court. The grass wasn't like normal grass; it was much denser, and there were no weeds. It also had to be cut unbelievably short. Gustav did exactly as he'd been shown: straight lines, sharp turns. The sun was in his eyes half the time, and he wished he'd remembered to bring his sunglasses. He screwed up his eyes, tried to shade them with his hand, but that didn't go too well; he had to hold on to the wheel at the same time.

Maybe that was why he missed the pale lumps protruding from the grass. He drove straight over them, felt the mower jolt, but kept on going. Fuck – were there stones on the court? If so, it must be sabotage. He stopped and turned around. There were four patches of red behind him.

Gustav frowned. What the . . . ?

He switched off the mower and went over to take a closer look, which didn't help at all. The red stuff was sticky, grainy, smeared across the green surface, mixed with something else. Something beige and white.

Gustav froze.

Beige, white . . . and fleshy.

Ten centimetres from his foot lay a thumb.

'I think I've changed my mind,' Spencer said.

Fredrika was standing in the bathroom wishing he'd said something else. He'd changed his mind. Really?

She put down her mascara and went into the bedroom, where Spencer was sitting on the bed with his tie draped around his neck. She crouched down in front of him.

'Would you like me to help you?' she said.

Spencer didn't answer, and Fredrika gently began to knot his tie.

'I want the children to come home this weekend,' he said.

'Okay – I'll ring Mum and ask her and Dad to bring them back.'

'Or we could go and fetch them.'

'It's fine, Mum and Dad enjoy a trip to town. And it'll give them more time with the children.'

'They'll have plenty of time with their grandchildren when I'm gone,' Spencer said.

Before Fredrika could come up with a suitable response, her mobile rang. Spencer reached over and passed it to her.

She tightened the knot of his tie before she took the call. Spencer stood up and left the room.

'Fredrika, it's Alex. You have to come out to Saltsjöbaden.'

She straightened up, felt the room sway. Nothing to

worry about, according to the psychologist she'd spoken too. Dizziness was a symptom of all the stress she'd suffered over the past few months.

Alex's voice sounded high, strained.

'What's happened?'

'I don't want to tell you over the phone. Just get here – I'll text you the address.'

'What's happened?' Fredrika said again. 'You must be able to tell me something.' And then, before she could stop herself, she added: 'Who's dead?'

She could hear crackling on the other end of the line; Alex was in a windy spot.

'Lovisa Wahlberg.'

The name meant nothing to Fredrika, but she wondered how this was going to work. They were already investigating one murder; they couldn't possibly take on another. Unless there was a connection.

Her heart skipped a beat.

'I hope she didn't die sitting in front of an open fire,' she said quietly.

Alex's voice almost broke as he answered.

'I need you here. This whole thing is so sick I can't understand what the hell is going on.'

Alex was waiting when she drove into the car park. He was smoking. Fredrika couldn't believe her eyes. She closed the car door and went over to him.

'What are you doing?'

'I'm sinning. This is my first cigarette in thirty years.'

He tossed it aside and set off.

'Don't say "this is the worst thing we've ever seen", because we both know it can't be,' Fredrika said as she followed him.

Alex didn't speak. The sun was burning down. Today of all days.

'Who found her?'

'A young lad who was cutting the grass. Ivan can question him later – he's in hospital.'

'Injured?'

'Suffering from shock.'

Fredrika remembered how old she'd been when she saw a dead body for the first time: nine. Her uncle had died during a family dinner. She recalled the commotion, the chaos. So many adults losing control at the same time. That had frightened her far more than the death.

They reached the tennis court. Fredrika's gaze swept the empty seats, the court itself.

'Have they already taken her away?'

'Oh no. She's over there.'

There was a cordoned-off area in the middle of the open green space, but Fredrika still couldn't see any sign of a body.

'Come with me,' Alex went on. 'I told them to leave her until you got here.'

His breath smelled of cigarette smoke.

My first cigarette in thirty years.

Fredrika's unease grew with every step. What was so bad that Alex had felt the need to smoke for the first time in three decades?

'So what do you think?' he asked when they were a metre or so away from the dead woman.

Fredrika gasped, then found she couldn't exhale. She thought she was going to be sick, then she wanted to turn around and go straight back home. She crouched down, wordless and empty.

'Are you okay?'

'No,' she whispered.

Someone had buried Lovisa Wahlberg beneath the smooth surface of the tennis court, but left her hands and feet sticking up out of the ground. The sharp blades of the mower had inevitably done a certain amount of damage.

'Her face?' Fredrika asked. She didn't want to find out the answer by looking for herself.

'Was far enough down, so it's intact. We just opened up the area around her head and shoulders to get an idea of who she might be.'

Fredrika rubbed her hands over her knees. People's inventiveness never ceased to amaze her. However, it was hardly surprising. If man could travel to the moon, then obviously he could come up with a million different ways to murder and degrade his fellow human beings.

'How did she die?'

'We don't know yet,' said a voice behind Alex and Fredrika.

Renata Rashid, the medical examiner, was holding her mobile phone. Her voice was so hoarse that many people assumed she'd smoked like a chimney for most of her life, which was incorrect. Her vocal cords had been damaged by throat cancer over twenty years ago. Fredrika knew this only because Alex had told her; Renata herself gave away very little about her private life.

Like me, Fredrika thought. *Like me*.

'I'll have a better idea when I've taken a closer look at her. The way things are now, I can't make any kind of assessment.'

Alex nodded to show that he understood.

'I wanted Fredrika to see this before we moved her. She's all yours now.'

It was Renata's turn to nod.

'Do we have any idea how long she's been here?' Fredrika asked.

'She was probably buried during the night. The court was in use until around nine o'clock yesterday evening.'

Fredrika straightened up.

'I'd like to make a start,' Renata said.

Alex and Fredrika automatically stepped back. Nobody wanted to get in Renata's way.

Fredrika gazed down at the dead woman and her grave.

'Didn't the guy on the mower see what was sticking up?'

'Obviously not,' Alex replied.

'So what did the surface look like when you arrived?'

'It was pretty creepy, to be honest. Everything had been done with absolute precision. The grass was perfect; there was no sign of damage.'

'How on earth did he or she manage that?'

'It's something we need to look into,' Alex said. 'The grass court is fairly new, so maybe it's easy to take up the turf and replace it. Or just put it back.'

Fredrika knew absolutely nothing about grass or gardening. Spencer would have liked to move from their apartment to a house, but Fredrika had vetoed the idea with some force. He might as well have suggested relocating to Ulan Bator.

'Why were we meant to find her here?' she wondered. 'There's something ritualistic about the way she's arranged.'

Alex had to agree. Lovisa Wahlberg lay in the ground as if she'd been crucified, directly on the central line of the court. The net had been taken down because of the mowing, but if it was put back up it would run straight across her hips.

'Wasn't there some trouble about this court?' he said.

'I don't remember.'

'I'm sure there was,' Alex insisted.

Renata called them over. She and her assistant had just lifted Lovisa Wahlberg and turned her over. There was a large wound in the back of her head.

'This could be pretty straightforward,' Renata said.

'You think she was killed by a single blow?'

'Possibly.'

'Let's not waste time speculating,' Alex said firmly. 'Let me know when you're sure.'

He and Fredrika set off for the car park, but within seconds Renata called them back.

'You need to see this.'

She was holding up Lovisa's wrist, showing them the underside. The skin was dirty, but traces of a tattoo were clearly visible. Fredrika couldn't work out what it was: dots and lines, plus a few apparently unconnected letters and numbers. Renata gently brushed away the soil.

'So she had a tattoo,' Alex said.

Renata was clearly unimpressed by his reaction.

'Can't you see what it is?'

Fredrika took a closer look.

'If I saw this in a different context I'd think it was a chemical formula,' she said.

Renata sighed. 'It *is* a chemical formula.'

Fredrika and Alex exchanged a glance, both equally grateful that the other hadn't been smarter.

'Cocaine,' Renata clarified.

'Sorry?' Alex said. 'She has the formula for cocaine tattooed on her . . . ?'

'Exactly. And it looks as if it was done fairly recently. Then there's this. It was in the grave beneath her head.'

Renata held up a red-painted face mask.

Alex frowned, and inside Fredrika's head the possibility of associations with occult movements exploded. But most of all she was still thinking about the unanswered question: what was she doing here? What did this murder have to do with them?

We can't do everything.

'Why are we here, Alex?'

He didn't answer.

'Made in Haiti,' Renata announced after checking inside the mask.

Fredrika put on a plastic glove and held out her hand. Haiti. A place where myths about voodoo and zombies originated. *What the hell was going on here?*

She turned to Alex.

'Tell me. Why are we here?'

'Because of this,' Alex said. He passed her an evidence bag containing a sheet of paper.

On the paper were the words:

I'm doing it again. Putting everything right.

And looking back, this was how they would choose to recount the story of property developer Malcolm Benke's strange death and everything that followed in its wake.

It began with his daughter's wedding ring on his little finger.

That was followed by a victim who was buried in such a shallow grave that her fingers and toes were sticking out.

And even when our perpetrator was kind enough to send us letters, we didn't dare call him anything other than an ordinary, run-of-the-mill killer.

They went into one of the smaller meeting rooms and closed the door. The place stank of curry. Alex tried to open the window, but without success.

'Is the air con working?' Fredrika asked.

'I think that's why we're in here instead of the Lions' Den,' Alex said.

Needless to say it was Margareta Bloody Berlin who'd decreed that the Lions' Den couldn't be used as long as the room temperature remained so low. Alex couldn't see the problem. If it was too cold, people could put on a jumper. But if it was too warm – which he thought it was in the smaller room – it was hard to do anything about it, since most people didn't find collective nudity particularly appealing.

'Sit down,' Fredrika said, pulling out the chair beside her. 'We've got food and we've got time to talk, which isn't always the case.'

She winked, and for a moment she was her old self. The relief made Alex take a seat and help himself to the lunch she'd picked up from the Thai place across the street. Chicken curry and rice – the best!

'The mask,' Fredrika said.

'The cocaine,' Alex countered.

'Was Malcolm Benke using?' Fredrika wondered. 'Or dealing?'

'I realise you're trying to find a link between the two murders, but I'm afraid it's not going to be that easy.'

Fredrika put down her knife and fork.

'Alex, we're going to have a ridiculous amount to do.'

'I know. Berlin suggested letting someone else investigate Lovisa Wahlberg's murder. We can keep each other informed, then bring both inquiries together when we see where the points of contact are. I think that might work very well.'

Unless Berlin snatched the case off him before then. She'd gone crazy when she heard about the new message. It had been on the tennis-club noticeboard for all to see. This wasn't a major problem, because hardly anyone understood the cryptic note, but there was no doubt about who it was addressed to. The name 'Alex' was written at the top of the page, and everyone assumed it had to be Alex Recht.

'Can you handle this?' Berlin had said. 'Seriously – can you keep your balance in a case that for some inexplicable reason seems to be targeting you?'

And Alex had done what he always did: he'd lied. Said that

of course he could handle it perfectly well. *Perfectly well.* He'd been a police officer for most of his life, he knew how to keep a cool head.

The truth, of course, was that he didn't have a clue what he was capable of, for the simple reason that, like everyone else, he had no idea what lay behind the messages. Berlin had asked him to write down the names of everyone he'd met professionally or in his personal life who might possibly be responsible for them.

So far there wasn't a single name on the list.

I don't have that kind of enemy.

'Are they bothering you?' Fredrika asked. 'The messages, are they stressing you out?'

No one else could ask such a question and expect an honest answer.

'I'd be lying if I said I didn't care.'

He avoided looking at her, didn't want to prolong the discussion. She took the hint.

'We're meeting Bernhard Benke in two hours,' she said. 'Yesterday I was prepared to regard him as a suspect, but now I'm not so sure – not while there's no clear link between Wahlberg and Benke.'

'Same here.'

They had proof that Bernhard had been in Vienna when his father was murdered, but that didn't mean he wasn't involved. However, Alex didn't believe that was the case, not after they'd found Lovisa, debased and defiled. He couldn't stop thinking about how her body had been treated.

Where would someone get such an idea from?

They ate in silence. He still hadn't told Fredrika about his conversation with Noah Johansson, nor Peder's call. He felt bad going behind her back, but that wasn't really what he was doing. Not intentionally. It wasn't his fault that Peder had contacted him, said things he maybe shouldn't have said. Besides, Alex didn't know what to do with the information, if anything. What had Peder actually told him? Only that he'd seen Spencer in an agitated state with Noah. Not much to build on. Alex reminded himself to get in touch with whoever had dealt with Noah's original missing-persons report, but he knew he wasn't going to make it a priority. It wasn't important, it wasn't his responsibility.

Why did Peder have to mention Spencer?

What the hell was Spencer doing with a funeral director?

'The ring on Malcolm's finger,' Fredrika said. 'His daughter's wedding ring. I keep coming back to it. The question is, if it weren't for the ring, would we have started to look into Beata's murder?'

It was a good point. A mouthful of curry went down the wrong way and Alex started coughing. Fredrika thumped his back. The last time she'd done that was when they were out drinking, although then it had been more of a pat than a thump. She'd said she thought the world of him.

'No,' Alex said eventually. 'I think we'd have missed the link to her death.'

'When you say link, what do you mean?'

Alex looked up in surprise.

'I mean that father and daughter were murdered in the same way, of course, but probably not by the same perpetrator. Beata was killed by her ex, her father by someone else.'

'Exactly.'

'Exactly?'

Fredrika poked at her food.

'This is more than an investigation, Alex. This is a drama. We have a murderer who doesn't want to be misunderstood, but also doesn't want to be stopped. That's why the ring was on Malcolm's finger – so that we'd know where to look. If it hadn't been for the ring, we'd have spent a huge amount of time trying to find a client or business partner with whom Malcolm had had some kind of dispute. Or someone else who might have been angry enough to put a bullet in his chest.'

Her words found their mark, and the realisation they brought made Alex's heart sink.

A murderer who doesn't want to be misunderstood.

A murderer on a mission?

In which case how many more victims will there be?

He broke out in a cold sweat, then pulled himself together.

'I'm wondering why the first letter arrived when Malcolm Benke was already dead, and the investigation was already under way, rather than at the scene of the crime, like the second letter.'

Fredrika focused on her food, stabbing at the strips of chicken as if she was trying to kill the bird all over again.

'I said yesterday that we ought to go back to Benke's place. I'm still convinced that I've seen the phrase "putting everything right" somewhere else. Maybe that's why the letter was sent, because we'd missed a clue that was left in the house. And so the killer decided to be less subtle the next time, and pinned his message on the notice board.'

Alex's phone rang.

'Yes?' he snapped.

'Hello? Alex?'

It took a second for him to recognise Linda Sullivan's voice.

'Yes, hi,' he said in English.

'I just wanted to let you know that I've looked into what might have happened to Beata Benke's wedding ring,' she said, making no attempt to hide her excitement. Fredrika noticed the change in Alex's expression, and put down her fork.

'She wasn't wearing it when she died,' Linda went on. 'There was a clear mark on her finger where it had been – you know how the skin is paler if you always wear a ring. It didn't register with us at the time, nobody thought it was strange, but now you've told us it was on her father's little finger, it's interesting to speculate on where it's been for all these years. Who took it.'

'Absolutely,' Alex said. 'Absolutely.'

He'd known from the start that the ring was important, known that it told them something about the perpetrator.

'Just an idea – what's Beata's husband doing these days?'

'You think he could have murdered his father-in-law too?' Linda said dubiously.

'I don't think anything, I'd just like to rule him out.'

'I've no idea what he's doing, but I'll look into it and get back to you.'

They ended the call with a mutual promise to speak soon, and Alex recounted the conversation to Fredrika.

'I don't think Beata's husband is involved,' she said. 'Nor her brother – not after what we saw today.'

'I agree, but we need to turn over every stone, see what crawls out.'

See what crawls out. Something that might possibly explain why a murderer took the life of an elderly man and a young woman who didn't appear to know each other. And how a ring made its way from London to Stockholm.

'When do you want to go back to Benke's house?'

Fredrika pushed away her carton of curry. 'How about now?'

Alex wiped his mouth and put down his napkin.

'Give me ten minutes to sort something out,' he said.

Fredrika didn't ask any questions. Alex went to his office, sat down at the computer and quickly found Noah's original report. He narrowed his eyes as he searched the internal database for further information. A detective by the name of Stig Mattsson had logged several conversations with Noah. His notes were characterised by frustration and sheer condescension. His final verdict was that Noah must be both mentally ill and a fantasist. 'Refuses to see counsellor in spite of this' he'd written.

Alex sighed. He was beginning to understand why Noah didn't have a very high opinion of the police. He carried on searching and found a decision not to conduct a preliminary inquiry. The investigation indicated that there was no reason to suspect that a crime had been committed, therefore there was no point in proceeding.

So why am I sitting here thinking they got it wrong?

Because that was how Alex felt when he read his colleagues' conclusions. They had been satisfied by limited contact with Dan Johansson via email and phone, taken this as proof that he hadn't been abducted against his will.

Alex glanced at his watch; his ten minutes were almost up. He gave Stig Mattsson a quick ring.

'What the fuck – has he started hassling you now?' Mattsson said when Alex explained why he'd called.

'Not at all – I'm just wondering who else was involved, apart from you.'

After reading Mattsson's notes he was hoping to hear that other officers had taken part in the investigation leading to the decision not to take things any further.

'There were several of us, obviously,' Mattsson assured him. 'Plus I consulted an inspector from your department.'

'My department?'

'He spent some time with us towards the end of the year, but he's back at HQ now. He's very knowledgeable and experienced, which was why I turned to him. He was very clear about the fact that it wasn't worth proceeding.'

'And who was this?'

'Torbjörn Ross.'

Vendela was woken by the phone. A friend wanted to borrow a book, could she call round? Vendela stretched in bed, wishing she hadn't worked so late. And then there was that horrible stench, seeping through the building.

Rotting excrement. That's what it smelled like.

'I can bring pastries,' her friend suggested. 'From the cake shop just around the corner from you?'

Vendela loved morning coffee. And afternoon coffee. She just loved coffee, to be honest. But that smell ... it was messing with her head.

'You're welcome to come over, but I'd rather go out for coffee. You'll understand when you get here.'

Her friend arrived less than an hour later. Her expression was one of pure disgust when Vendela opened the door.

'Sorry,' she said. 'But what the hell is that smell?'

Vendela gave a loud, theatrical sigh, but at the same time her heart had begun to pound. Deep down a suspicion had begun to grow. She thought she'd experienced the same stench before, when her grandmother hadn't answered her phone for several days, and Vendela and her mother finally went over to her house and let themselves in.

Grandma?

Grandma's sleeping, sweetheart.

'I was hoping you'd help me find out,' Vendela said. She slid her feet into a pair of slippers and went out into the stairwell. 'I think it's coming from up there.'

She set off up the stairs, followed by her friend, who was far from happy.

'Jesus!' her friend exclaimed when they reached the fifth floor.

'It's somewhere around here, isn't it?'

'Definitely.'

Vendela did what she'd done before – she rang each doorbell. Most of the residents seemed to be out, but a young woman opened one of the doors. Vendela couldn't remember ever having seen her before, but didn't like to ask if she was new. She didn't want to give the impression that she was keeping tabs on her neighbours just because she worked from home.

'Sorry to bother you, but it's about the smell,' she began.

'Oh, I know! My partner and I searched the whole flat yesterday, but we couldn't find anything that might be causing it. I rang the housing committee, but apparently they can't help. They don't have keys to our apartments, and they're not allowed access. Which is perhaps a good thing.'

Vendela's friend was busy going from door to door, pausing outside each one. Four doors, four potential sources of the smell.

'In here,' she said firmly. 'It's coming from in here.'

'Are you sure?' Vendela asked.

'Absolutely.'

Vendela and the young woman looked at each other, then at the door.

The one with 'Henry Lindgren' on the nameplate.

Malin and the children were sitting at the kitchen table. Thanks to her obsession with establishing routines, she'd decided they would attend summer school. Dan had yet to appear. Malin knew he'd had a headache during the night and had slept badly. This was nothing unusual; he'd suffered from migraine attacks on a fairly regular basis ever since they first met. However, he'd never had to endure them without pain relief. She couldn't shake off the feeling of horror that spread through her body when she thought about what all this was doing to him. Maybe this isolation was taking more of a toll on Dan than on the children.

They had to make sure he didn't draw them into the trap along with him. If there was any possibility of escape.

We have nowhere to hide.

'I don't understand this.'

Her son threw his pen across the table and sulked, his head drooping over his maths book.

Malin took a deep breath. She mustn't lose her temper. Not before lunch, or it would be a really bad day.

'Let's go over it one more time,' she said. 'Watch how I do it.'

School in the middle of summer. Just to make the time pass.

The children hated not seeing their friends, having only each other, and Malin hated being their teacher. Yet still she was driven by the need to create structure in their everyday lives, to achieve a kind of balance of terror.

All three of them were equally miserable, particularly as the sun came out and the temperature inside the house began to rise.

Malin had tried countless times to work out what they were a part of. She thought about the phones they'd been forced to give up, the emails they'd been forced to write – a few short lines to friends and family who got in touch. They must all believe the move to Australia had taken place. More emails to cancel planned meetings in Australia. They'd been too afraid to protest, they'd simply done as they were told. Malin had realised that it didn't matter who contacted them; the man would always have something appropriate to say. He would send his own emails and text messages. How long would it take before someone other than Noah (*because surely he must know that something had happened?*) reacted and sounded the alarm. The family was supposed to be away for a year; very few of their friends had expressed a desire to come and visit.

A year.

They could be gone for a whole year before it became obvious they weren't in Australia.

We'll never survive, Malin thought. And then:

What's supposed to happen to us during that year?

It was terrifying to think that the man must have been monitoring them for quite some time before he struck. He'd known about their travel plans, known exactly when they were due to leave. Although that wasn't so strange; they'd posted on

Facebook, talked extensively about what they were going to do. The children had been very busy on social media. Anyone who wanted to find out exactly what the family were up to needed nothing more than a mobile phone or a computer.

What do we do if no one misses us?

Malin was so frightened she could have wept. The children's friends would notice that Hedvig and Max had dropped off the radar, but they wouldn't be able to trigger a major search. If only she'd been closer to her father! And if only there were more people who'd realise something was wrong. Thank God for Noah – but who would listen to him?

'Mum, when can we go home?'

Hedvig. For the second time in a very short period.

'I still don't know.'

She heard a bang from upstairs that made her jump. Dan. A part of her wanted to oversee every move he made, check what he was doing, because she was certain he'd disappeared into a darkness where she couldn't reach him. He'd said he'd had an idea; he thought he'd found a way of getting out of the house.

I don't want to know. I just want to live.

No one is going to find us. Her heart contracted with fear.

'I'll get us some fruit,' she said, getting up from her chair. Her legs felt wobbly as she went over to the worktop and started to peel an orange. They would have to share it; she didn't know when they'd be given more fruit.

We're going to die here. Maybe today, maybe tomorrow. And no one will know.

She opened a drawer, looking for a knife to cut up the orange. She stared down blankly. She had expected to see a carving knife and a bread knife. Both were missing.

She closed the drawer, opened another. Found a small knife and began to divide the orange.

'Has either of you borrowed a knife?' she said to the children, fighting to keep her voice steady.

They both shook their heads.

'It's all right if you have. I won't be cross.'

'We haven't touched your stupid knives!' Hedvig snapped.

'Okay,' Malin said quietly.

Suppressed tears made her throat constrict, her eyes sting. Dan must have taken them. Panic spread through her body like wildfire.

What was he going to do with the knives?

The wallpaper was peeling in several places and the paint was flaking off the skirting boards. This used to bother Noah, but he no longer even noticed. He was sitting at his desk staring at a blank computer screen. If anyone had asked him how long he'd been sitting there, he wouldn't have been able to answer. It was as if he'd fallen into a trance.

Noah was many things, but he wasn't stupid. He'd heard the dubious tone in Alex Recht's voice. Noah's story hadn't been enough; he was going to have to come up with another way of motivating Alex to take up the search for Dan and his family. And that was where he'd got stuck. Because what else was there to do?

Only one thing.

Send Dan another email.

So far Noah had been careful not to mention the police in his messages to his brother. He was convinced that someone else was running Dan's account, and guessed that that person didn't have Dan's best interests at heart, so he hadn't wanted to give away what he was up to. Hadn't wanted whoever had taken Dan to know that the search was under way. Which it wasn't, to be fair, because the police were doing nothing, but Noah preferred to keep that to himself as well.

Until now.

He'd written that he'd been forced to contact the police, report Dan missing, and that an investigation was ongoing. Noah hoped that this bombshell would bring the status quo to an end. Whoever was checking Dan's mail would surely react when he or she realised that the police were involved. Noah had given a lengthy description of all the measures that were being undertaken in order to clarify exactly where Dan and his family had gone. To be on the safe side he also mentioned the Swedish embassy in Canberra, in spite of the fact that he'd heard nothing from them.

So now both the police and our diplomats are searching for you and your family. Hang on in there – help is on the way!

Noah was very pleased with how he'd expressed himself, simply and clearly. He'd called Tina and read the message to her over the phone. She'd listened and given her approval. She was a gift from the gods, Tina. She made him feel strong, because she too was beside herself with worry, convinced that something terrible had happened. However, she still had moments of doubt.

'What if we've imagined the whole thing?' she'd said. 'What if they're not missing at all? There's a microscopic chance that that's the case, in which case Dan will be furious when he gets your email.'

Noah had thought the same.

'But that's not necessarily a bad thing,' he'd said. 'If they really are okay but just don't feel like getting in touch, then they have only themselves to blame. I just want to know they're all right.'

Noah was close to tears when he thought back to the conversation with Tina. There was no chance whatsoever that Dan was okay, that he and his family were having a great time. There was no chance whatsoever that his terse messages were an indication that he was pissed off with Noah because he hadn't supported their Australian adventure. Dan wasn't like that.

I just hope it's not too late.

That was the worry constantly eating away at Noah. So many weeks had passed; did that mean they'd run out of time? Because where could you hide an entire family for that long? And why would you hide them and keep them alive? Wasn't the only logical conclusion that they were dead?

Noah's heart raced, panic threatened to swallow him whole. He had to keep a cool head, keep the hope alive. The email must provoke some kind of reaction, a reaction that would prove once and for all that there was a problem – and give him something to show Alex.

Help is on the way, Noah thought. *Help is on the way.*

The air inside Malcolm Benke's house was heavy and hard to inhale, as if someone had mixed it with smoke. Just enough to make itself felt, not enough to be visible. Fredrika hesitated in the hallway. What had got into her? Coming back here to play Sherlock Holmes. Actually, it was worse than that – she wasn't playing, she was taking the whole thing very seriously.

Alex was right behind her.

'Go on in,' he said. 'Let's get this over and done with.'

His breath smelled of curry, and for a moment Fredrika imagined what it would be like to kiss him. Not that she wanted to – just because. She'd had the same thought when they went drinking after finding out that Berlin was going to be their new boss. She'd been far from sober on that occasion; she didn't have the same excuse now.

Surely bottomless grief doesn't make you horny?

She moved into the living room, where Benke had been found. The CSIs were long gone, leaving traces of their meticulous work. Bernhard would be the first of Benke's relatives to see what the house looked like.

If that were me, Fredrika thought, *if I lived in Vienna and came home to see my parental home like this, in a mess and with stuff all over the place ... And the armchair*

*in which my father was found shot dead. I don't think I
could cope.*

She was known for her attention to detail and her intuitive-
ness. Her gaze swept across the walls, floor and ceiling with
laser-like precision. There was no sign of the words she was
looking for. *Couldn't it be easy, just this once?* In an attempt
to make the situation less embarrassing, she started searching
with an almost ferocious energy. Under sofas, behind paintings, beneath rugs – places where she couldn't possibly have
seen the words she was certain she recognised, words that
linked the deaths of Malcolm Benke and Lovisa Wahlberg.

Alex joined her.

'Did you find anything in the hallway?' Fredrika asked.

'I don't know what I'm looking for.'

That makes two of us.

His tone was neither accusatory nor condescending. If he'd
thought the whole idea was ridiculous, he wouldn't have come
with her. He might even have dissuaded her from returning.

He went over to the window, pushed his hands into his
pockets and waited for Fredrika to finish. She knew he'd
noticed the change in her, that he could see something was
tearing her to pieces, but until it was all over, she didn't
think she could talk about what lay ahead. A journey to
Switzerland, an assisted suicide, a professor who had taken
control of his own death.

She took a quick walk around the rest of the house.

'Okay, I give in,' she said when she came back to the living
room. 'I must have got it wrong – there's nothing here.'

Alex shrugged. 'I wouldn't say you got it wrong –
you thought you remembered something, so we needed
to investigate.'

Fredrika gave him a grateful smile.

Then she spotted the book on the table next to the armchair. It was upside down, but the spine was facing her. She read the title silently to herself and felt the floor give beneath her feet.

'Look,' she said to Alex, pointing.

'What do you think I am, an eagle? It's at least fifteen years since I was able to read something that far away.'

As he came closer, Fredrika read the title aloud.

I Am Putting Everything Right

Margareta Berlin had two pieces of information for Alex when they got back to HQ. Firstly, a decision had been made as to who would lead the separate investigation into the murder of Lovisa Wahlberg: Detective Inspector Torbjörn Ross. Secondly, Detective Inspector Torbjörn Ross was looking for Alex and Fredrika.

That fucking leech.

Who crawled along the corridors 'bumping into' Alex, who had decided that the inquiry into Noah Johansson's missing brother wasn't worth pursuing.

Alex was so stunned he didn't know what to say. When Berlin had gone, he turned to Fredrika.

'Ross? What the fuck? Is she out of her mind?'

Berlin was back in a second.

'Is there a problem?' she snapped.

Alex laughed dryly. 'Are you joking?'

'I thought he'd been deemed unsuitable for this kind of task,' Fredrika said.

Berlin folded her arms over her bosom. This wasn't entirely successful; her arms were too short and her breasts were too big.

'Because?'

'Because he behaved inappropriately towards Thea Aldrin.'

Both Alex and Fredrika preferred to avoid mentioning Thea Aldrin's name. She was an elderly children's writer whose books had had terrible consequences for far too many people, including Peder Rydh. His brother had been murdered, and Peder had been so angry that he'd shot the perpetrator, putting an end to his career as a police officer.

Alex's thoughts returned to the ongoing investigation, to Malcolm Benke in his armchair and Lovisa Wahlberg in the ground. Some people were capable of extinguishing life, under certain circumstances.

Does that apply to me too? Am I capable of murder? I'd really like to think the answer's no.

'That was a long time ago,' Berlin replied. 'Plus he's expressed an interest in this particular case.'

'Has he indeed.'

'Yes, he has. For *very good* reasons. He has *good* knowledge of Lovisa Wahlberg's background.'

Fredrika sighed and sat down on the visitor's chair in Alex's office.

'That's *good* news,' she said. 'And what background is this?'

Berlin ignored the sarcasm.

'Lovisa was suspected of drug offences a number of years ago. Not here in Sweden, but in Haiti. I think that's what he said. The Swedish police were involved on the periphery, and Torbjörn was the main contact.'

Alex pricked up his ears, noticed that Fredrika did the same. The tattoo on Lovisa's wrist, the chemical formula that neither of them had recognised.

'Cocaine,' he said.

'Exactly. It was thought that she'd been a courier between Scandinavia, Central America and the West Indies. However, she was cleared and allowed to return home. Since then she's had nothing to do with the police.'

Malcolm Benke. Lovisa. What was the connection? Alex wondered.

'Did Lovisa know Benke's daughter?' Fredrika asked, obviously on the same track.

'You'll have to ask Torbjörn,' Berlin said, then she was gone again. By tacit agreement Alex and Fredrika hadn't said anything about the book they'd found in Benke's house. They couldn't cope with her guesses and speculation before they'd had time to process the discovery themselves.

This time they waited until they were sure she couldn't hear them.

'This is unbelievable,' Fredrika began. 'How the hell can she give this case to Ross?'

Alex could only agree. 'But we need to make sure we collaborate effectively with him, otherwise this will go badly wrong before we've even started.'

And the next thought: *I'm not inviting him to a single fucking meeting.*

'He's not our only problem,' Fredrika said. 'I dread to think what will happen when the media realise that Lovisa Wahlberg was probably killed by the same person who murdered Benke.'

Another cause for concern – useless journalists who never missed a chance to put the boot in when it came to any police inquiry. Berlin had brought out the heavy artillery to make sure no one heard about the messages Alex had received; if that information became public knowledge, it would make their work immeasurably more difficult. The question was how long they could keep it quiet.

'The book,' Alex said.

Fredrika took it out of her bag. They'd followed the rules (well, mostly) and touched it only when they were wearing gloves. It was now in a sealed evidence bag: a green book with no motif on the cover.

'I'll ask Spencer about the author,' she said. 'Morgan Sander – I've never heard of him.'

Nor had Alex. They'd entered the name into a search engine, but found nothing.

'We need to decide what to do with it,' Alex said.

'We give it to forensics right away, and we brief Berlin and the team tomorrow, when I've had a chance to check out the author.'

Alex thought that was a good plan. 'I don't like this. The title, the words *I Am Putting Everything Right*. I don't get it – exactly the same as the messages sent to me.'

Fredrika was pale. 'Me neither.'

Alex's mobile rang: Torbjörn Ross. He pulled a face.

'We'll meet up later,' he said to Ross. 'Fredrika and I are just about to conduct an interview.'

'If it's anything to do with Lovisa Wahlberg, I want to be there,' Ross insisted.

'It isn't. It's about Malcolm Benke.'

There was a brief silence, then Ross asked: 'Is it his son?'

'Yes.'

'I was so sure . . .' Ross murmured. A murmur that made Alex press the phone closer to his ear.

What were you so sure about?

'Sorry?'

'I was so sure it was the son, right from the start. But apparently not – he has no connection to Wahlberg.'

'That's our view too,' Alex said, bringing the call to an end.

'Okay, let's go and see Bernhard Benke,' Fredrika said.

They headed for the lifts, each absorbed in their own thoughts. Alex couldn't shake off a feeling of unease after speaking to Ross. He'd been so sure it was Bernhard who'd shot his father. *So sure. Right from the start.* How the fuck was that possible? And why did it sound like a suspicion Ross had formulated long before Alex and Fredrika reached the same conclusion?

It was after four o'clock by the time Vendela decided to start searching for Henry Lindgren. The housing committee had finally woken up to the fact that there was an issue, but they weren't much use. Two representatives turned up, rang Henry's doorbell and called his landline, but there was no response. They simply stood there and shrugged. One of them had seen Henry leaving the building with a suitcase a few days earlier, and assumed he'd gone away. Vendela didn't think so.

She was so cross; she was going to have to do this herself. She called her nephew, who was good at solving problems. He was also good at finding things out, unlike Vendela. She'd tried to track down the names of Henry Lindgren's relatives, but without success.

'What exactly do you want to know?' her nephew asked.

'If Henry has any children who might have an idea where he is.'

Her palms grew sweaty as she spoke, because the suspicion in her mind had become a virtual certainty.

What stinks like that?

Death.

Her nephew called back a few minutes later.

'No children, but there's an ex-wife. Easy – you could have found her yourself.'

'Obviously not,' Vendela said.

She scribbled down the number and her nephew wished her luck. She thanked him for his help, then called the ex-wife. *Please let her answer, please don't let this be another dead end.*

The signal rang out eight times, then a hoarse voice said: 'Vera Lindgren.'

Vendela cleared her throat, almost dropped the phone, then said: 'Oh, hi, hello, my name is Vendela Nilsson.'

Oh, hi, hello? What's wrong with me? Get a grip!

The woman waited patiently. Vendela sat down on the sofa, moved a magazine and brushed a petal off the cushion.

'This is really embarrassing, but I don't have anyone else to contact. It's about Henry, your . . . your ex-husband. We're neighbours. Well, kind of.'

'Has something happened?'

Her reaction was so quick, her voice was so full of concern that Vendela immediately felt a sense of relief. Vera wouldn't have sounded like that if she couldn't bear to hear Henry's name.

Vendela cleared her throat again, unsure of how to continue.

'No. Or rather . . . I don't know. We can't get hold of him. There's something to do with the apartment block we'd like to discuss with him.'

'We' sounded better than 'I'. Stronger, more convincing. She didn't want the ex-wife to think she was a busybody with no life or interests of her own.

'I understand. Have you tried his mobile?'

'Several times. A member of the committee said he thought he'd seen Henry leaving with a suitcase a few days ago. I wondered if you might know where he'd gone?'

'I think I would have done if he'd been planning a trip. We have a very good relationship, Henry and I. We meet up on a regular basis, maybe once a week. I saw him last Thursday, and he didn't say a word about going away.'

'I don't suppose you have a key to his apartment?'

'I do, but I wouldn't give it to a stranger. What do you want it for?'

Vendela raked her nails down her cheek. She couldn't put it off any longer.

'We think ... we think there might be a problem in Henry's apartment.'

'What kind of problem?'

Vendela took her time, searching for the right words.

'There's a terrible smell.'

She spoke very quietly, almost inaudibly, but Henry's ex-wife heard not only what she'd said, but what she'd left unsaid.

There's a terrible smell.

I'm afraid that Henry's dead.

'I'll be there as soon as I can.'

We're not going to get much from you. That was Alex's first thought as he shook Bernhard Benke's cool hand. Bernhard. What kind of a name was that? Had he come up with it himself when he moved to Vienna? And, more importantly: did he know Lovisa Wahlberg?

Fredrika also seemed underwhelmed by the grieving son. She'd almost burst out laughing when they first saw him. Her cheeks flushed red, and however hard she tried, anyone could see the laughter bubbling up inside her. Alex couldn't blame her. Bernhard looked as if he'd come straight from filming *The Sound of Music*. And he smelled of cinnamon. However, Alex was prepared to forgive him everything; he'd made Fredrika smile, albeit unintentionally, and that was something no one else had managed to do recently.

Alex began by offering condolences on the death of Bernhard's father in such dreadful circumstances. His sympathetic expression provided a sharp contrast to Fredrika's rather more cheerful approach.

'So you didn't arrive in Stockholm until yesterday?' Alex said.

'I couldn't leave Vienna any earlier. I have my own cheese shop in the city centre, with very few staff members.'

He had his own cheese shop. Of course he did. Alex could

see the corners of Fredrika's mouth twitching, and looked away. If she didn't get a grip she'd start him off.

'I love cheese,' Alex said with no idea why.

'Excuse me.' Fredrika leapt to her feet, almost knocking the chair over. 'I have to . . .' She shot out of the room.

Bernhard stared at the door. 'Isn't she feeling well?'

'She's fine, she just has to take care of something.'

The room they were in was a cube. The walls and ceiling flowed together in different shades of white, and Bernhard's green clothing – trousers and jacket – glowed against the pale background.

'How would you describe your relationship with your father?'

'Virtually non-existent.'

Alex glanced up. 'Could you expand on that?'

'I don't know what else there is to say. We spoke on the phone a few times a year. I didn't visit him on his birthday, nor did I open the presents or cards he sent when it was my birthday. We didn't celebrate Christmas together, and when I come to Sweden I only see my mother.'

Clear and simple.

'How long has the situation been this bad?'

'A long time.'

'Can you be more precise?'

'At least ten years.'

You're like all the rest, Alex thought. *Someone who chooses not to tell me everything.*

'At least ten years? So I assume things were better when you were growing up. Did you fall out as a result of a particular event?'

Bernhard coughed and reached for the glass of water on the table.

'I wouldn't call it an event. We had different opinions about something. Very different opinions.'

The door opened and Fredrika came back in. She nodded to Alex before sitting down. *I've pulled myself together.*

'About what?'

'My sister Beata had major problems in her marriage. Her husband was a pig, to put it bluntly. He never missed a chance to humiliate and belittle her. She took a lot of abuse in that relationship – in every sense of the word. My father and I didn't agree on how much the family could or should intervene.'

Alex lowered his gaze, fiddled with the pen he was holding. Fredrika took over.

'What did you think the family ought to do?'

'Me? I wanted us to do as much as possible. Whatever we could, because Beata didn't deserve to be treated like that. No one does. My father agreed, in principle, but he wasn't prepared to do his utmost, and I couldn't accept that. Not then, and certainly not . . . afterwards. When she was gone and it was too late.'

Alex put down his pen.

'What do you mean when you say your father wasn't prepared to do his utmost?'

Bernhard's face was cold and hard.

'That doesn't matter now.'

'It matters to us,' Fredrika said.

Bernhard shook his head. 'I have nothing more to add on that point. My father was pathetic, I wanted to take a tougher approach. That's all there was to it.'

'Why do you think your father felt that way?' Alex asked.

Bernhard spread his hands wide.

'I assume he was afraid. Too busy putting himself and his reputation first rather than his own child.'

Fredrika didn't feel the slightest desire to laugh now.

'It sounds to me as if you would have had no problem in breaking the law in order to help your sister. Am I right?'

Bernhard folded his hands and placed them on his lap.

'Of course not.'

What else could we expect? Alex thought.

In spite of his anger, Bernhard must understand the seriousness of the situation. He was smart enough not to admit in a police interview that he'd wanted to kill his brother-in-law. If that was the case.

Fredrika tried a softer approach.

'It doesn't really matter what was in your mind back then. As far as we know Richard is alive and well, and he's never made a complaint against you or Malcolm for threatening or violent behaviour. All we're interested in right now is the conflict between you and your father.'

And whether you killed him, Alex added silently.

To his great surprise, Bernhard said exactly the same thing.

'You forgot to ask the obvious question – you want to know whether I killed him, or had him killed. The answer is no, I didn't. The idea never even crossed my mind. He could rot all alone as far as I was concerned; that was a far better punishment than death.'

He seemed pleased. Pleased that his father had been alone, that his life had been empty.

Alex broke out into a cold sweat. All these splintered families, all these parents and children who couldn't stand one another. Fate could be more than cruel when she brought together people who were doomed to be a 'family'.

'Do you know what happened to your sister's wedding ring after her death?' Fredrika asked.

'No.'

'Did she usually wear it?'

'Yes – her husband went crazy if she didn't have it on.'

Fredrika and Alex exchanged glances.

'Do you recognise the name Lovisa Wahlberg?' Alex said.

'No.'

Alex opened his folder and showed Bernhard the photograph they'd found at Benke's house.

'Have you seen this before?'

Bernhard gave a snort of derision.

'Yes, but it was a long time ago.'

'So it belonged to your father? It wasn't given to him by someone else?'

'No, it was his.'

'Where did he keep it?'

'How should I know? When he showed it to me he took it out of the tin box on the drinks trolley.'

Alex had a vague memory of seeing a metal box on the trolley. So Malcolm had taken out the picture before he died – to look at it himself, or to show it to someone else? His killer?

'You don't seem to like what you see,' Fredrika said.

'No, I don't. My father's pathetic attempts to fix things, his ridiculous efforts to help Beata. Useless. Plus I think he did it with the aim of repairing his relationship with me, rather than to change Beata's situation.'

Alex put down the picture.

'Do you blame your father for your sister's death?'

'I believe he could have saved her,' Bernhard said, the

strain clearly audible in his voice. 'But the only person to blame for her death is her husband.'

He picked up the photograph and looked at it again, his cufflinks glinting in the bright overhead light.

'I don't understand why you've brought this up. My father's "I-did-the-best-I-could" picture. A sop to his own conscience, but no use at all to Beata. I asked him not to show it to my mother; it would only upset her.'

Alex didn't say anything; he now realised why the photo had been so important to Malcolm, and why Karin hadn't recognised it.

Fredrika shuffled on the uncomfortable chair.

'Was Beata also disappointed in your father?'

Bernhard looked up.

'No.'

'She thought you and the rest of the family were doing everything you could to help her?'

'Beata didn't believe she could be helped – that was the big difference.'

Then, before they could stop him, he tore the photograph in half.

'Are we done here?' he said.

How many times had she tried to talk to him now? Five? Ten? So many times that Max eventually began to cry. Malin gave up, and Dan slipped away, without having said one word about where the knives had gone.

It wasn't only the knives he was keeping quiet about. Dan had stopped talking. He would sit alone for long periods, staring out of the window.

'I want Daddy to be like he used to be,' Max said, crying into Malin's shoulder as she tried to comfort him.

Malin wondered what 'like he used to be' meant to Max. She had forgotten – or suppressed the memory of – how they had lived and behaved when they took freedom for granted, when their lives were the same as everyone else's.

We argued sometimes.

That was one reason why they'd started talking about Australia, considering the possibility of staying there for a year or so. They needed to change tack, to get away from their daily routines and create new ones. Well, they'd certainly had some help in that quarter. All the old routines were gone, and this was definitely a different tack.

How she missed the life they'd had!

Max felt stiff and tense in her arms.

'Is Daddy dangerous?' he whispered.

Malin didn't answer, she simply stroked his head.

'Is he, Mummy?'

Malin took a deep breath.

'I don't think Daddy's very well.'

She spoke quietly, so that only Max would hear.

'Can't we ask a doctor to come to the house?'

'Apparently not, sweetheart.'

She had to pull herself together, come up with a plan. But above all she had to find the knives. She couldn't work out where he'd put them. She'd searched and searched, with Hedvig's help. Dan had watched them, an amused expression on his face. The knives were gone. Nowhere to be found.

She carried Max into the living room and put him down on the sofa next to Hedvig. She had to go on searching, because this was ridiculous. Dan couldn't leave the house, so where the hell had he hidden the knives?

Hedvig made a move to get to her feet, but Malin stopped her.

'No, you stay here and keep Max company.'

Max curled up beside his sister and they both sat there, equally afraid.

Tears sprang to Malin's eyes and she turned away.

The knives.

She had to find the knives.

Many people thought of death as a state, as the polar opposite of everything they regarded as living. Noah didn't think that way. For him death was a function, a mechanism. Death was what made life finite, which was a very good thing. No sane person would want to live forever. The only problem was when death came calling too early, too early in relation to what people had come to expect, too early in relation to what they had managed to experience so far.

Noah had imagined that he, like his paternal grandfather, would one day be a very old man. Old but as bright as a button. There was nothing he could do about the physical ageing process, but it was definitely possible to control one's mental faculties, if one had the strength and determination.

Dan and his children were an important part of Noah's vision of the future. He had nothing against Malin, but he didn't miss her when she wasn't around. They hadn't really managed to form a relationship; they had settled for mutual respect. That was often enough; it wasn't necessary to love and be loved by everyone.

Time was hanging heavy on his hands. He hadn't had an answer to his email, and he hadn't heard anything from Alex Recht, which was bitterly disappointing.

What would become of Noah if Dan was dead?

It was such a painful thought that his eyes filled with tears. He couldn't bear it if Dan had been dead all these weeks, and Noah hadn't known. Anxiety drove him back to the computer to check his email yet again. No new messages. He checked his phone; nothing from Alex either.

I'm going crazy. I have to get out of here.

He had no appointments booked, and the chances of a new client simply turning up were very limited. He shut down the computer and slipped his phone into his pocket. His shirt was sticking to his back; stress made him sweat.

The bell pinged as the door opened then closed.

Noah hurried out of the office, keys in his hand. His brain was working overtime; whoever this was would just have to go away and come back later.

'Unfortunately we're closed,' he said. 'But if you'd like to make an appointment and—'

He broke off when he saw who it was. He opened his mouth and closed it. For a second he couldn't place the man, but then his mind cleared. His heart skipped a beat.

'Hi!' He hoped he didn't sound too cheerful, too relieved.

The man who had just walked in had once helped Dan a great deal. Was that why he'd come to see Noah? To help Dan again?

The man moved slowly towards Noah. He was wearing a leather jacket even though it was the middle of summer, and he kept one hand in his pocket.

If only Noah hadn't been so exhausted, if only he'd been able to rely on his normal ability to think clearly, then he might have perceived the danger before it was too late. But that wasn't the case.

'How can I help you?' he said. 'Is it about Dan?'

The man took his hand out of his pocket.

He was holding a revolver.

A revolver?

Noah blinked. He'd seen guns in films, but had never expected to be confronted with one in real life.

'What do you want?' he whispered.

The gun was shaking slightly in the man's hand, but his voice was steady.

'I want to put everything right,' he said. 'And you're going to help me. Do you understand? You're going to help me. By keeping your mouth shut.'

Then he forced Noah back into the office. Once again Noah thought that death was no more than a function designed to bring life to an end, and that he would be utterly devastated if his time was already up.

They met in the Lions' Den – partly because it was the closest available space, but mainly to annoy Margareta Berlin by ignoring the note she'd stuck on the door, stating that the room was not to be used as long as the air conditioning wasn't working properly. The first thing Fredrika did was to switch it off, and the temperature immediately began to rise. Outside the sun was pouring down, caressing Kronoberg, doing its best to beautify the irredeemably ugly police HQ. Lovely weather didn't necessarily make the world a lovely place. Fredrika had known that ever since she was a child.

Torbjörn Ross had insisted on calling them to a meeting. Fredrika was trying not to show how unpleasant she found the situation.

'I thought it would be a good idea to get together and compare notes,' Ross said. He was wearing Wellingtons as usual; no doubt he was going fishing after work. Or maybe he'd spent his lunch hour fishing. You never could tell with Ross.

'Most of the information is already on the computer,' Alex pointed out, sounding more dismissive than he'd intended. And it was typical of him to say that the material was 'on the computer'. Since Fredrika's arrival the IT system had steadily improved, but they were still lagging behind, and in fact very little was 'on the computer'.

'I prefer to meet face to face,' Ross said.

That was generally how the team operated, but on this particular day Fredrika would have liked to get home a little earlier than usual. Spencer had called and promised barbecued steak for dinner.

'You're not going to barbecue on the balcony, are you?' Fredrika had said, only too well aware of what the neighbours on the floor above would think.

'I'm going to barbecue wherever the hell I like,' Spencer had replied.

She wanted to laugh out loud at the memory, wanted to scream because there wasn't enough time to make lots more memories. Because there would be too little to tell the children one day.

Do you know how much your daddy loved barbecuing on the balcony?

'The mask that was buried with Lovisa Wahlberg,' Ross began. 'I showed her parents a picture of it. We'd originally intended to keep that detail to ourselves, but they recognised it right away. Apparently she brought it back from the West Indies.'

'When she was accused of being a drug courier?' Alex asked.

'Yes. She said her boyfriend had given it to her. He stayed behind, which was why she kept it.'

A boyfriend who gave his partner a carnival mask. Which she kept. After being dragged into a narcotics investigation.

What did I do when I was young? Fredrika thought. She knew the answer before a ghostly voice whispered in her ear:

You were never like others. You were with Spencer, no one else. And you studied way too much.

'Why did he stay in the West Indies?'

'He was convicted of drugs offences. He's rotting in jail – if he's still alive. Apparently there's been no contact between him and Lovisa for years. I'm not interested in him; the question is how Lovisa's murderer got hold of the mask. And why he killed her.'

'And how her death is linked to Malcolm Benke's,' Alex said.

'Which is the main reason why we're all sitting here,' Ross agreed. 'If I've understood Berlin correctly, you're working on the hypothesis that Benke was killed by someone who was close to his daughter?'

Alex pulled a face.

'It's too early to start formulating any hypotheses,' he said. 'But obviously he was executed in the same way as Beata, and he was wearing her wedding ring when he was found.'

'And you don't think that's enough for a hypothesis?' Ross sounded weary.

'No. Not when we also have Lovisa's murder to take into account.'

Fredrika tried to redirect the conversation.

'I believe Beata and Lovisa were the same age?'

'Beata was two years older than Lovisa,' Ross informed her.

'Did they ever attend the same school, belong to the same riding club, anything?' Alex wondered.

'Not as far as we've been able to establish. From a social point of view the girls were very similar – they both had wealthy parents – but geographically they didn't grow up anywhere near each other. Of course that doesn't necessarily mean they couldn't have met somewhere, but so far we haven't been able to find any connections. Lovisa's parents didn't recognise Beata's name.'

Fredrika consulted her notes. Notes that would never end up 'on the computer'. She shouldn't accuse the police admin system of being old-fashioned; she wasn't particularly modern herself.

'So Beata moved to London as soon as she left school, and stayed there until she died,' she said. 'While Lovisa went to the West Indies and got involved in drug dealing.'

She glanced up at Ross for confirmation.

'There wasn't enough evidence to secure a conviction, but I'd say she certainly wasn't innocent. I do know the whole experience scared her; she was terrified by the thought of ending up in jail, so she got out as soon as she could.'

'Do you know this for sure, or are you just guessing?' Alex asked.

'We kept an eye on her for several years after she came home. If she'd put a foot wrong, we'd have known about it. She wasn't the sharpest knife in the drawer, and she found it difficult to lie low. I can always tell, though I say it myself.'

Though I say it myself. *Jesus, what a boring, arrogant fucker.*

'We need to find the point where our investigations intersect,' Ross went on, clearly unwilling to engage in any further discussion of the life Lovisa had lived.

Fredrika thought about what Alex had told her when they were on their way to meet Bernhard Benke: that Ross had expressed an opinion on how Malcolm Benke had died, who had murdered him. An opinion that had no basis in evidence.

Is that something we ought to ask him about? she wondered.

At that moment they were interrupted by a discreet knock on the door, and an admin assistant came in.

'Sorry to disturb you, but I have a Linda Sullivan in London on the line, wanting to speak to either Alex or Fredrika.'

'I'll take it,' Fredrika said.

She left the meeting room, realised she'd let out a long breath when she was away from Ross. The sun had disappeared behind the clouds; with a bit of luck it would start raining before Spencer managed to light the barbecue.

She sat down at her desk.

'Fredrika Bergman.'

'Linda Sullivan. I have news about Beata Benke's husband.'

Fredrika held her breath.

'Go on.'

'He's dead.'

'Sorry?'

'He's dead. He died several weeks ago. He'd been living in Manchester for a few years, which I didn't know. I contacted colleagues up there and found out that he died in an aggravated burglary. It happened in the middle of the night – no witnesses.'

Fredrika's mouth went dry.

'What was stolen?'

'I thought you'd never ask.' There was a hint of excitement in Linda's voice. 'His girlfriend identified the body, and was able to tell the police what she thought was missing – a necklace and a wallet. Guess what the necklace was like?'

'I've no idea.'

'According to the girlfriend, who'd been with him for over a year, he always wore a fine gold chain with a gold ring on it.'

'A gold ring . . .'

'Exactly. A gold ring with a diamond set in it. Way too

small to fit on his fingers. He claimed it was his mother's, and that he'd kept it to remember her by. But I'm assuming that's not true.'

'Definitely not.'

When they ended the call, Fredrika hurried back to the meeting room, but there was no sign of Ross or Alex. Then she heard Alex's voice behind her.

'The meeting's over. Ross had a call too.'

'Anything important? Because I have very interesting news from London.'

However, Alex didn't appear to register what she'd said.

'I've just spoken to Renata Rashid,' he said. 'The tattoo on Lovisa Wahlberg's wrist – her parents practically screamed when they saw it. They insisted she would never have done something like that of her own free will.'

Fredrika remembered Renata saying it was fairly recent.

How recent?

'Renata now thinks it was done only hours before she died,' Alex said in answer to her unspoken question.

'By the killer.'

'Exactly. And do you know who else had that same tattoo? Lovisa's ex, the one who dragged her into all that business with the drugs. Her parents recognised it right away, and insisted their daughter would never have wanted it.'

'But she got it anyway,' Fredrika said slowly. 'Just as Malcolm Benke got his daughter's wedding ring.'

Alex shook his head. 'What the hell are we missing?'

'I don't think we're missing anything. What we should be asking is what does the murderer want us to see? What is he or she trying to say?'

At that moment Berlin came storming in.

'Alex, have you been in touch with a Noah Johansson over the past few days? A funeral director?'

Fredrika saw Alex go pale, then his cheeks flushed red. At the same time she went weak at the knees and her heart contracted. Noah Johansson was supposed to take care of all the practical details when Spencer was gone.

'Why?'

'I'm asking the questions – answer me!' Berlin snapped.

'Please, you need to tell us – has something happened to him?' Fredrika asked.

Both Berlin and Alex stared at her, taken aback by her reaction.

'He's dead. He was murdered less than an hour ago,' Berlin informed them.

The apartment stank of excrement and the early stages of decomposition. When the initial shock had passed, all Vendela could think about was that she never wanted to be found in the same humiliating way.

'Oh, Henry,' his ex-wife whispered, dropping to her knees beside his body.

Vera had unlocked the door and let out a stench so powerful that it made them retch. Henry was less than a metre inside; they couldn't miss him. They both covered their mouths and noses with their hands as they entered the apartment. In fact they ran in, because hope springs eternal, and even though it was obvious that Henry was no longer alive, neither of them was prepared to accept that. Not until they were close enough to see the empty eyes, the grey pallor.

Vendela backed away; death had made Henry unrecognisable.

'I'll call the police,' she whispered. As if something might break if she spoke in her normal voice.

She went out onto the landing. She could hear Vera sobbing and talking to Henry behind her. 'I told you to look after your heart, Henry. I told you.'

Vendela also started crying. The operator who took her call listened patiently and promised to send a patrol car and an ambulance, just to be on the safe side.

'Try to make sure that no one else enters the apartment,' she said. 'The police will need to preserve the scene of the crime.'

'The scene of the crime?'

Vendela hadn't considered the idea that Henry might have been the victim of a crime. He was in his own apartment, behind a locked door.

'When someone dies at home, the police always have to exclude the possibility of a crime,' the operator reassured her. Of course. It was standard practice. Vendela sat down on the stairs to wait.

No one attempted to go into the apartment, no one came to find out why the stench had suddenly exploded. Vendela was ashamed to admit that she just wanted someone to come and take Henry away, get rid of the smell so that everything could get back to normal.

Slowly she turned her head and looked at Henry, lying on his back with his feet towards the door. His shoes had thick soles, and a dried leaf was stuck to one of them.

Death had taken him when he'd just arrived home. Or maybe he was on his way out.

He must have been so surprised, Vendela thought.

The mobile phone had been in the dead man's hand. The first police officers on the scene had assumed that was how he'd died – with the phone in his hand and terror in his eyes. A woman passing by on the street had heard someone shouting for help – only once, but it was enough. She had kept walking, hailed a taxi and called the police from the back seat as the vehicle sped away.

Thanks to the phone, Alex Recht's name had come up immediately. The investigating officer had established that Alex was one of the last people Noah Johansson had contacted. Alex informed Berlin briefly – very briefly – about his dealings with the deceased. At a later stage, when he knew what was going on, he would tell her a hell of a lot more. Above all he would tell her about Ross.

'Stay away,' Berlin ordered. 'It's nothing to do with you.'

Fifteen minutes later he was on his way to the scene. He left HQ without speaking to Fredrika or anyone else. She rang his mobile, but he rejected the call. He knew she was wondering what had happened, and that she wanted to tell him what she'd found out from Linda Sullivan, but that would have to wait.

Because there's something else I have to do right now.

His chest hurt when he parked outside Noah's funeral business. The brain could tidy things away, but the heart remembered.

His mind cleared as soon as he saw the police tape and officers moving in and out. Alex had no right to be there, but no one else knew that. He walked purposefully to the door, showed his ID and went inside.

Nothing had changed. He recognised the wallpaper, the pale oak parquet flooring, the armchairs in one corner. There was no sign of a struggle.

'In here,' said a uniformed colleague who appeared from nowhere. She pointed to a doorway on the right.

Alex followed her into the office. He couldn't help recoiling when he saw Noah lying on the floor, his head surrounded by a pool of blood.

'We think it was the head injury sustained in the fall that killed him, but of course we'll have to wait for the post-mortem report,' the young officer told him.

Only then did Alex notice the blood on the edge of the desk.

Shit.

He looked around: chaos. Papers everywhere, a total mess. Two cabinets were open, the shelves empty. This wasn't like the other crime scenes Alex had visited over the past few days. This time the murderer had been searching for something, determined to find it at all costs.

'Could the killer have been interrupted?' he asked. 'The victim might have been out, and caught the perpetrator searching his office when he got back.'

'It's a possibility.'

Alex didn't know what else to do. He had no idea what he

was looking for, nor, if he was honest, why he'd felt the need to come racing over here.

He mumbled something about having to get back to HQ, and hoped his colleague wouldn't suddenly come to life and start asking what he was doing there. However, she nodded and smiled, even thanked him. Alex headed for the door, desperate to get out of that claustrophobic office. Someone needed to find out what had happened to Noah, as a matter of urgency. And someone needed to take a fresh look at his brother's move to Australia.

Alex paused in the doorway.

A sheet of white paper was sticking out behind one of the bookshelves.

His pulse rate increased, for some inexplicable reason.

The whole room was full of papers and documents – why bother about a single page that had drifted away?

He didn't understand the instinctive decisions people made, but without hesitation he bent down and picked it up. In fact there were several sheets, folded in half. His hand shook slightly as he opened them up.

He began to read as he set off again. His pulse rate dropped. This was clearly a letter someone had written, a final message to a loved one.

My darling,
   Some months have now passed since we were given the worst possible news . . .

His cheeks flushed with embarrassment. What the hell was he doing? Couldn't he leave people in peace with their most private affairs?

He was about to go back and hand the letter to the female officer – 'Look what I found'. But then he turned to the last page, read the end of the letter.

I am actually trying to take responsibility, in spite of all the years that have passed. As an author once said: I am putting everything right.
  I'm afraid I can't do any more.

I love you more than anything.

Alex could hear his heartbeat pounding in his ears.
  As an author once said.
  I am putting everything right.
  I'm afraid I can't do any more.
  But I can, Alex thought. *I can.*
  Then he read the letter from beginning to end.

This wasn't something he could keep to himself – he realised that immediately. He placed it in an evidence bag and took it back to HQ. Not in accordance with the rules, not in accordance with routine, and definitely not in accordance with Berlin's express orders. For a moment he considered not informing her of what he'd done, but scrapped that idea at once. He couldn't leave her out of the picture.

'What the hell have you done?' she yelled. 'I told you Johansson's murder was nothing to do with you! Nothing, Alex, *nothing*! And you went straight over to the crime scene.'

Alex shrugged, aware that he was acting like a child.

'I found something, and I want to share it with you.'

He showed her the letter, then he told her about the book

they'd found in Malcolm Benke's living room. When she exploded, he realised he'd made a number of mistakes.

'How could you keep this from me? You are unbelievable!'

Her voice reverberated inside his skull. He couldn't bring himself to respond; there was nothing worth saying. They had been planning to tell her about the book, they just wanted more information first. Particularly as she'd said there was no point in going back to Benke's house. Alex took the opportunity to remind her of this.

Eventually they agreed to disagree, and concluded that the investigations must take priority.

'No more secrets,' Berlin said.

It was a clear warning. Everything out in the open. No stone left unturned.

As soon as he got in the car, he called Peder.

Peder who had changed jobs twice in a year. Who had snapped at Alex on the phone, who had almost sounded threatening. Alex just hoped he hadn't lost his grip again.

If he has, someone else will have to deal with it.

Alex had more urgent matters on his mind than a former colleague's mid-life crisis.

The phone rang and rang.

Peder didn't answer.

Alex left a brief message telling him what had happened and saying he hoped to hear from him soon. But by nightfall Peder still hadn't contacted him.

The meat smelled delicious, and there wasn't a peep from the neighbours.

'Either they're out or they can't be bothered to complain,' Fredrika said.

Spencer poured her a glass of red. Wine again. There was no such thing as too much. Not this summer.

'Or maybe they don't want to quarrel with someone who's seriously ill,' he said.

Fredrika put down her glass, horrified.

'Have you told the *neighbours* you're ill?'

Spencer grinned at her.

'Are you crazy? Of course not. Just kidding – you can deal with all that later.'

Later. When Spencer no longer existed.

'*He had a tumour. He died.*'

'*No! How awful! It must have been very quick – we didn't even notice he wasn't well.*'

'*Extremely quick. He took his own life at a clinic in Switzerland.*'

Fredrika snorted. Gallows humour must be God's gift to man.

'Something amusing you?'

'Not really.'

She picked up her glass and took a sip, pushing aside

any concerns about whether she ought to be drinking every day. There was a difference between living as if every day was your last, and living with the reality that it actually might be.

She couldn't stop thinking about what she'd heard before she left work. Noah Johansson was dead. Murdered. She'd been unable to hide her reaction from Alex, and that wasn't good. She didn't really want to reveal her relationship with the deceased.

'What are you thinking about?' Spencer asked.

She swallowed several times; should she tell him? On the other hand, there was no point in keeping quiet. Every one of Johansson's clients would soon realise that he was no longer around. She had no idea of the practicalities involved in changing funeral directors, but someone must know.

'Noah Johansson is dead.'

Spencer froze in mid movement.

'What?'

'I found out about an hour ago.'

'How? I mean why? I . . .'

Fredrika took a deep breath.

'He was murdered, Spencer.'

'Fuck.'

He got to his feet, then sat down again.

'Why?'

'We've no idea.'

'So what happens now? To people like us?'

'I don't know that either, sweetheart.'

She reached out and stroked his arm. 'Are you okay?'

He shrugged.

'This is so macabre. I mean, I didn't really know the guy,

and he didn't know me, and yet he knew a hell of a lot about me. How I want to die, for example.'

He took a couple of gulps of his wine.

'I suppose I'll have to find someone else,' he said.

And then: 'Let's eat.'

Spencer served new potatoes and Béarnaise sauce with the meat.

'You must have left work early to get all this done,' Fredrika said. Neither of them could bear to talk about the funeral director who'd died; it felt as if he'd abandoned them.

Spencer grimaced.

'I had a pretty useless meeting this morning, and I didn't stay around for long after lunch.'

'Good decision. By the way, I need your help with something,' Fredrika said.

She went and fetched her work bag – a yellow fabric backpack that the children insisted on calling 'Mummy's work bag'. Spencer, however, chose to refer to it as 'Mummy's teenage bag'.

She took out a piece of paper and handed it to Spencer. 'There you go.'

'What's this?'

'A colour photocopy of a book cover.'

'You photocopied a green book cover?'

'If you look down at the bottom, you'll see the title.'

Spencer peered closely at the image. 'Bloody hell.'

Fredrika was astonished. 'You know this book?'

'Yes and no. I haven't read it, but I recognise the title and the author's name.'

'What can you tell me?'

Spencer gave a crooked smile. The second smile in one evening.

If this carries on I might not cry.

'A student I was supervising during the spring term wrote her master's dissertation on how writers' views on self-publishing have changed over the last hundred years. Today it's quite common for authors who can't get established publishing houses interested in their manuscript to go down another route, but that certainly wasn't the case a few decades ago. Which is hardly surprising, of course. The advent of the miracle of technology and the internet has made most things possible. However, when Morgan Sander published this book, it was far more unusual.'

Fredrika waved away a wasp.

'So Morgan Sander published the book himself?'

'Exactly. There could be a thousand reasons why a manuscript is turned down, but it's usually because the text is of poor quality. Sander's case was slightly different. The guy could obviously write, but it's just drivel – it makes no sense. This was the only book he published – towards the end of the 1940s, I think – and when it didn't attract the acclaim he'd hoped for, he stopped writing. He died a few years later.'

Fredrika ran a finger around the top of her glass.

'How do you know all this? Why he was rejected and so on?'

'My student visited various publishing houses and asked about authors they'd turned down. Sander had become something of a story; even younger editors knew about him.'

'What's the book about?'

'I don't know, but I like the title. *I Am Putting Everything Right*. A clear statement, no messing around.'

A cool breeze made Fredrika shiver. The fact that the sun was shining didn't help; the Swedish summer was as capricious as ever.

'How do you find an author like Morgan Sander?' she asked.

Spencer picked up his knife and fork again.

'What do you mean?'

'I mean exactly what I say. Who owns his book? And if you don't have a copy, how do you get hold of it? How many were printed, how accessible is it?'

Spencer chewed and swallowed.

'My student found it in the Royal Library, down in the depths of the basement. It was Sander himself who donated it, desperate not to be forgotten. Fewer than a hundred copies were printed. I should imagine most of them have been thrown away over the years as people have tidied up their bookshelves. There are probably a few in antiquarian or second-hand bookshops.'

Fredrika realised they weren't going to be able to trace the perpetrator that way. He might have stumbled across a copy in his granny's bookcase, or in a shop in the far north of Norrland. They would never know.

'Why the questions?'

'Sander's name came up in a case.'

They ate in silence. Fredrika drank more wine, more water. She couldn't help finding it disturbing. The police were looking for a killer who seemed to be obsessed with a writer that hardly anyone had heard of.

Hardly anyone.

Apart from Spencer.

Present: Interrogators one and two (I1 and I2),
Detective Chief Inspector Alex Recht (Recht)

I1: It sounds as if the dead were piling up. At some speed.

Recht: That's exactly what was happening.

I2: It also sounds as if you weren't exactly on top of things.

Recht: Sorry?

I2: Well, with one person after another dying, you'd expect the police to pull out all the stops. That doesn't seem to have been the case in the summer.

Recht: You're wrong. Completely wrong. But it took time for us to work out whether the deaths were connected, and if so, how.
(silence)

I1: We need to come back to Spencer Lagergren.

Recht: He's not part of this investigation.

I2: No, but he was one of very few people who'd heard of Sander's book.
(silence)

I2: You must answer our questions.

Recht: I'm sorry, I didn't realise you'd asked
a question.

I1: Okay, let me put it like this: did it bother
you that Spencer was familiar with both the
title and the author?

Recht: There was a perfectly logical explanation,
which Fredrika passed on to me.

I1: So you weren't in the least concerned?
(silence)

Recht: Not at the time.

I2: But later?

Recht: Later I became very concerned indeed.

THURSDAY

The silence was endless. Dan was still refusing to speak to Malin. He simply observed her as she searched and searched. The knives remained missing. And Malin's panic continued to grow.

When the early morning sun lit up the bedroom, she was lying there wide awake. What time did the sun rise at this point in the summer? Four o'clock? The only thing she knew for sure was that she had to be on her guard, because otherwise she and the children could die.

She was watching Dan. He was on his side with his back to her. She didn't believe he was asleep, and that frightened her. If he was awake too, what thoughts were going around and around in his head? Not the same as the ones stuck in her head, she hoped.

She was so thirsty, her throat felt constricted, she could hardly breathe. The glass on the bedside table was empty. If she wanted water, she was going to have to get up.

And give away the fact that I'm awake.

Malin felt the weariness come creeping in. How long could she manage to stay awake? How many days, how many nights? Sooner or later she would have to sleep. Maybe it wouldn't make any difference. If Dan came rushing in with a knife, no one would be able to stop him.

But God knows I'd try.

Cautiously she slid her legs from under the covers. The house had got hotter and hotter as the weather improved, and she hated it. They couldn't open the windows. She had gone over and over the same questions: What kind of house was this? How could such a place exist? Why had it been built in the first place?

With unbreakable windows.

And impenetrable doors.

Everything that was needed to make the house a home was there: running water, a bathroom, a fully equipped kitchen. A property like this couldn't exist in a vacuum. It was sophisticated. It was real.

Just like the man who'd brought them here, and delivered food supplies at irregular intervals.

Malin had no recollection of ever having met him before, and Dan had quickly said the same. He didn't know who the man was, didn't know why he was punishing them. And yet that was exactly what the man had said when they'd tried to talk to him.

'You,' he'd said, pointing at Dan. 'You know why you're here and how this must end.'

But Dan had simply shaken his head. He had no idea what the man was talking about, no idea how their stay in the house must end.

Nor had Malin, but the weeks went by and it felt as if they'd been away for an eternity. She hated it.

Hated, hated, hated it.

Once again she looked in Dan's direction, stared at his back.

Maybe he did know how this drama must end. Maybe that was why he'd taken the knives.

Malin forced herself to go through her options. There weren't many, and none of them were pretty. If she seriously believed – and she did – that Dan was capable of harming her and the children and was prepared to do so, then she had only two strategies to fall back on. Either she did her best to carry on monitoring his every move, or she got in first.

She shuddered.

If she chose to get in first, what did that mean? Was she going to have to kill him? Or could she lock him up somewhere while they waited for mercy, waited for help?

Which was never going to come.

The man had definitely pointed at Dan, made it clear that they were all being punished because of him. So what would happen if Dan disappeared, if he died? Would the man still want to harm Malin and the children?

Would we be allowed to go home?

She closed her eyes for a moment.

She loathed the man who had forced them to live through this hell.

She loathed his silence, his anger and his fucking gun.

But most of all she loathed the power he had.

Power over life and death. Her life and death.

It was just after eight, and Alex was already at his desk, exhausted after a sleepless night. He contacted the rest of the team and informed them that there would be a meeting in the Lions' Den at nine. A few minutes later Fredrika appeared. She didn't seem as low as the previous day, but nor was she relaxed. There was tension in every line of her body.

She closed the door behind her.

What the hell has happened to you? Alex thought.

He remembered her reaction when she heard that Noah Johansson had been murdered: shock and something resembling consternation.

As if to confirm that he was right to be concerned, she immediately said:

'Have we heard any more about the funeral director? The murder Berlin told us about yesterday?'

Alex moved a pile of papers that were perfectly fine where they were.

'Why do you ask?'

'I was just ... I thought it might be important because of the way she came rushing in.'

'Important in what way? Did you know him?'

Alex sounded more brusque than he'd intended, which provoked a reaction from Fredrika.

'What's the matter with you?' she said.

He slammed a drawer shut.

'I could ask you the same question. I can see there's a problem. Something's been wrong for months.'

Suddenly he was afraid; he hadn't felt that way since he was a child. Why hadn't he considered the idea that Spencer might have visited a funeral director on behalf of his wife? As he had once done. Lena had wanted everything arranged before she died, so they had met Noah while she was still alive. On at least one occasion Alex had gone to see him alone while Lena was at home.

'Sorry,' he said. 'Sorry. I didn't mean to intrude. You don't have to tell me if you don't want to. I . . .'

'It's fine.'

But it obviously wasn't. Alex thought he could see sorrow in her eyes, maybe fear too.

Tell me. Tell me.

The door flew open to reveal Margareta Berlin.

'Same old same old,' she said. 'You two closeting your-selves away with your secrets.'

Alex couldn't deal with this crap right now. He shot out of his chair and strode towards the door, much to Berlin's surprised. He shouted so loudly that he almost frightened himself more than her.

'Out! Get out of here, you mad witch!'

He slammed the door in her face. Had he ever felt this good? He didn't think so.

'Waste of fucking space,' he muttered to himself as he turned around to see Fredrika staring at him, open-mouthed.

'You're crazy,' she said quietly. Then she burst out laugh-ing. Alex laughed too, because he needed the release – not because he felt particularly cheerful. He was still wondering what was wrong with Fredrika.

'Just let me know if there's anything I can do,' he said.

'Thank you.'

As the team gathered, Alex saw Berlin glide past in the corridor. She didn't even deign to look at him, nor did she comment on the fact that they were using the Lions' Den when she'd said only the previous day that it wasn't to be used. Ross hadn't been invited; they would update him later.

'So where are we?' he began. 'Fredrika, could you tell us what you heard from London yesterday?'

Fredrika passed on the information Linda Sullivan had given her. Beata Benke's husband had also been murdered, and they now knew that he'd taken Beata's wedding ring after her death.

'Do we seriously think he died as a result of a random burglary?' Ivan asked when she'd finished.

Eager Ivan. He seemed a little less eager now, which made Alex feel sad.

'No, we don't. Or at least I don't.'

'Nor me,' Fredrika said, which made Ivan's face light up. 'The murderer knew exactly what he was after. On the other hand, I'm not sure if the person who took the ring had intended to kill Beata's husband, or if it became necessary in the heat of the moment, so to speak.'

Alex was trying to work out a timeline. 'When did he die?'

'In June.'

'In June ...' An unpleasant thought was taking shape in Alex's head; the murderer they were looking for had made his plans months in advance.

'That still doesn't explain why Lovisa Wahlberg also had to die,' Ivan said.

He was absolutely right. Nor did they know whether there was a connection with Noah Johansson's death – if it hadn't been for the letter Alex had found. The letter that had kind of hidden itself behind the bookshelf.

Could the words used in that letter be dismissed as a coincidence?

He didn't think so.

He thought it had been written by the murderer.

But what the hell was it doing in Noah's office?

He cleared his throat, unsure of how to proceed.

'Did you want to say something?' Fredrika was looking at him. 'I was going to talk about the book we found at Malcolm Benke's house.'

Alex waved his hand in a gesture of agreement, and Fredrika went over what she'd found out from her husband, the professor. This was news to Alex.

'So there are very few copies of this book around,' she concluded.

'Could it help us to find our perpetrator?' Alex asked.

'I doubt it, unfortunately.'

'It might still be worth contacting antiquarian bookshops in the Stockholm area,' Ivan suggested. 'See if they've heard of the book, if anyone's asked about it.'

Alex glanced at Fredrika.

'Good idea,' she said. Ivan made a note.

Alex took over. 'The murder weapon – we must have more information by now.'

One of the CSIs sat up a little straighter. If she'd been a cat she'd have purred.

'We certainly have. I also took the liberty of contacting our colleagues in London. I didn't want to say anything until we were sure, but now we are.'

'Sure about what?' Fredrika just wanted her to get straight to the point.

The CSI wasn't happy, but she managed to keep her voice steady:

'Sure that Malcolm Benke was shot with the same kind of gun as the one that killed his daughter. A Colt 45.'

A low hum of conversation broke out in the room.

'The same kind?' Alex said slowly. 'Not the same gun?'

'No.'

Alex processed what he'd just heard. Whoever had killed Malcolm had gone to considerable lengths to make his murder match that of Beata.

'Thanks, that's extremely valuable. Now on to something else. Yesterday a funeral director by the name of Noah Johansson was killed. There are reasons to believe that his death could be connected to the others.'

Silence.

Alex knew he'd shocked his colleagues with his brutal statement.

'Another murder?' someone said.

'Yes. Another murder.'

He went on to tell them about the letter. He left out his own involvement, but reported on the content of the letter and its possible significance for their investigation.

'Can we read it?' Fredrika asked.

Her face had lost all its colour. She seemed completely floored by this new information.

'Of course.'

'I don't understand the link to Noah Johansson.'

'No one does.'

'I mean, seriously.'

'I am being serious.'

'Did the murderer leave a message for you?'

Fredrika's question took Alex by surprise. Everyone was looking at him with curiosity.

'No – at least not that we've found so far. And I don't think we will.'

The last few words just slipped out.

The murder of Noah Johansson was something different.

Alex had no doubt that it had been driven by a different motivation from the murders of Malcolm Benke and Lovisa Wahlberg. However, he was equally convinced that the perpetrator was the same person.

Ivan thought for a moment, then said:

'We still haven't found a link between Benke and Wahlberg?'

Torbjörn Ross.

'No.'

'No mutual interests or acquaintances?'

Torbjörn Ross.

'Not as far as we know.'

How crazy was Ross?

Not that crazy. That was the short answer, the only one that mattered.

And as if he'd sensed that Alex was thinking about him, he knocked on the door. Everyone turned around as Torbjörn Ross entered the Lions' Den. His gaze swept the room and he realised this was a gathering to which he should have been invited.

'We've just interviewed Lovisa Wahlberg's boyfriend,' he

said. 'Could you come with me to check on something, Alex?'

'I'm in the middle of a meeting. I'll be along in—'

'Now,' Ross said. 'Berlin wants you there now.'

Alex gave a dry laugh.

'Tell her I'll be there when I have time.'

Neither Berlin nor Ross could tell Alex what to do; they both needed to understand that.

How could such a short document change so much? That was what Fredrika asked herself when she read the letter Alex had found in Noah's office. A three-page declaration of love that also contained a devastating confession. Someone had run over a woman then left the scene of the accident without calling for help. Without getting out of the car to see what could be done for her.

Fredrika felt her deodorant dissolve, felt the sweat begin to pour from her armpits.

Because in the letter were sentences that made her want to set fire to it, make it disappear. Sentences and phrases that glowed as if they had been written in red-hot lava.

> *When you read this, I will be gone . . . It is incomprehensible – impossible to grasp – that I am sitting here writing, yet I am aware that my time is measured out.*

Yes, she thought. *It is incomprehensible.*

She knew exactly who had written the letter. She had tried and tried to find a reason to be doubtful, but such a reason didn't exist. She couldn't even make it up. She read the letter

seven times before she admitted defeat. There was no doubt.
None whatsoever.

Spencer.

Spencer had written the letter.

Spencer was the man who knew he was going to die, and
had therefore written a farewell letter to someone he called
'my darling'. Unless he had more surprises up his sleeve,
Fredrika assumed he was writing to her. But she wasn't sure.
Of anything. Not any more.

> *Do you remember just after our daughter was born,*
> *when I was still recovering from the car accident?*

Oh yes, she remembered.

> *I was careless just once. Once. But that was enough to*
> *ruin another person's life.*

Her memory failed her at this point. Which occasion was he
talking about?

> *I got in the car and drove to Uppsala to meet my boss*
> *in connection with a dinner that was to be held later*
> *that evening.*

Uppsala. Always Uppsala. The place where Fredrika had
loved being a student, but hadn't wanted to stay. The major
sticking point in her relationship with Spencer. He would
have loved to carry on living there, with no need to commute.
Fredrika had won that battle. But at what cost?

*By this point I'm sure you are deeply shocked,
castigating me for my cowardice, wondering what
the hell I was thinking. I was thinking about myself –
that's the short answer. And you and our daughter,
and later our son.*

His fucking ego. *Yes, Spencer. I am castigating you for
your cowardice.*

And that's the way it stayed until a few months ago.

When you found out you were going to die, Fredrika added.

*Others have done similar things, behaved atrociously
and evaded all responsibility, but I don't want you to
remember me that way. That's why I want to tell you
that I'm different from those people. I am actually
trying to take responsibility, in spite of all the years
that have passed. As an author once said: I am putting
everything right.*

At that point Fredrika's heart stopped, every single time she
read the letter.

I am putting everything right.
I am putting everything right.
I am putting everything right.

Only words, taken from a little-known author, but
that was of minor importance. Because certain things just
couldn't be true. It was very simple. The fact that Spencer
was going to die was one of those things. The idea that
he'd turned into a serial killer, driven by guilt, was another.

Wasn't that what he was saying? He was going after people who he thought should pay with their lives, for one reason or another.

It can't be true.

Not one single word.

Waves of panic coursed through her body.

Sick in the head.

That's what he was, quite literally.

But was he sick enough to have lost his mind?

Could the tumour have transformed him into a psychopath?

'For fuck's sake!' Fredrika shouted, and hurled the letter at the wall. The three sheets of paper drifted to the floor, mocking her with their silence.

She hurried over and picked them up, afraid that someone would have heard her outburst and would come to see what was wrong.

She had to pull herself together, try to think clearly.

How the hell was she supposed to do that?

At best she was married to a man who had run over another human being. At worst this incident had turned him into a serial killer.

Fredrika's hands were shaking. Who else would be able to work out that Spencer had written the letter? She glanced through the text yet again, searching for revealing details. It was obvious that the writer was a man with two children, who'd been involved in a car accident and who worked in Uppsala.

Not good. Not good at all.

Then she calmed herself. She hadn't told anyone at work that Spencer was dying and that Noah Johansson had been his funeral director. However, it was only a matter of time before they went through Noah's client records and found Spencer's name.

Her breathing was laboured.

The letter didn't necessarily prove that Spencer was the murderer they were looking for. Quite the reverse. It was illogical to think that Spencer was trying to atone for running over the woman by killing a series of innocent people – people she was certain he didn't even know.

She put her head in her hands, tried to gather her thoughts, which were galloping off in different directions like wild horses. She didn't know what she ought to feel, what she ought to think. There was an infinitesimal chance that some-one else had written the letter, that the man she was married to hadn't left a woman with life-changing injuries. But she didn't believe it for a second. Spencer was the writer, and she was meant to receive the letter after he was gone.

I am putting everything right.

If only it wasn't for those words, particularly in combination with the reference to compensation:

I've tried to compensate my victim, as far as possible at least. I'm afraid that in doing so I have inevitably left a trail.

'What the hell have you done, Spencer?' she whispered. 'And to whom?'

It was going to take weeks to get rid of the revolting stench. Vendela was given this depressing news by the cleaning company the housing committee had brought in; apparently getting rid of the source of the problem wasn't enough.

Vendela had slept for only a few hours. She couldn't shake off the nightmarish memory of finding Henry Lindgren, of how painful it had been to see his ex-wife's reaction. Why had they split up? There seemed to be a lot of love left in their relationship. Clearly it hadn't been enough.

She wandered restlessly around her apartment. On a day like this she could have done with an office. She had to get out, get away, go for a walk. Anything to stop her thinking about Henry.

At that moment the doorbell rang. Vendela padded into the hallway, hating the fact that she felt unsafe. It didn't matter that the police hadn't been particularly worried; they assumed he'd died of natural causes. His death was the issue as far as Vendela was concerned; she hated death.

Henry's ex-wife was at the door. Vendela was about to give her a hug, as if Vera was a long-lost friend she hadn't seen for ages, but managed to stop herself in time.

'I thought I'd go up to Henry's apartment and water his

plants, but I don't want to go on my own,' Vera said. 'Will you come with me?'

That wasn't at the top of Vendela's wish list, but she didn't like to say no to the older woman. What was the point of watering the plants? It wasn't as if Henry had gone away and would soon be back.

'Of course. Wouldn't it be easier if you took the plants with you? I mean, otherwise they'll just end up ...'

She broke off, unsure of how to continue.

Vera fiddled with the keys in her hand.

'I'm not sure what the rules and regulations are. I don't know if I'm allowed to take anything, or even if I'm allowed in. We're not married any more; on paper I'm only a friend.'

Vendela thought for a moment. Would there be a problem if they went into the apartment without permission? Then again, who was there to ask? Surely you weren't meant to bother the police with that kind of thing?

'Okay, let's go,' she said decisively. 'Of course the plants need watering.'

They walked up the stairs in silence, forever united by having found a man dead in his own home.

'I told him to go to the doctor,' Vera said as she unlocked the door. 'Over and over again I told him, but he wouldn't listen.'

Her hands were shaking, her voice on the point of breaking. Vendela placed a hand on her arm but said nothing.

The door swung open. 'So here we are again,' Vera said.

Even though they'd left the windows open overnight, the smell was appalling.

'Jesus,' Vendela whispered.

'It's horrible,' Vera agreed. 'I'll just nip into the kitchen and grab the watering can.'

And that was exactly what she did. She filled the can and turned to water the plants on the windowsill, but then she froze in mid movement.

'What's wrong?' Vendela said, worried that it had all been too much for Henry's ex-wife. Vera was staring at a note on the fridge.

'Look,' she said, pointing. 'Where's that come from?'

Vendela hadn't been in Henry's kitchen before, so she had no idea what belonged there and what didn't. What was so strange about a note stuck on the fridge door?

Vera's eyes narrowed. 'I was here a week ago. Henry and I had coffee on the balcony. And this note wasn't there.'

Vendela shrugged. 'I guess it was something he thought about later.'

'For heaven's sake, can't you read?' Vera sounded unexpectedly cross. 'Something he thought about later? He didn't even know anyone called Alex.'

Vendela gave up and read the note. 'So what do you want to do?'

'I'm going to call the police, tell them what I've found.'

Vendela thought that was probably a mistake, but then the police had more experience than she did when it came to brushing off old ladies with a bee in their bonnet.

'I'll call them as soon as I get home,' Vera said firmly, turning her attention to the plants.

Vendela read the message again; she couldn't imagine why the police would be interested.

Vera, however, was convinced.

'There's something about that Alex. I want to know who he is.'

Vendela wasn't sure what to say.

'I suppose it can't do any harm,' she said eventually.

'No indeed! Let's see if they'll listen to me.'

Maybe she was supposed to feel sad, but Tina Antonsson felt only terror. She'd waited so long, hoping and believing that someone else would get there first. But the days passed, and the headlines didn't appear.

Missing Family – Has Anyone Seen Them?

Tina hadn't been able to shake off the sense that something was wrong after the last time she and Malin had spoken on the phone. Malin hadn't called back as she'd promised; that just wasn't like her. Tina had both texted and emailed, waited for a response. Nothing.

It just didn't fit.

Tina hadn't known what to do. She'd called the police, then hung up. She wasn't the family's next of kin; someone else must be doing something. The problem was that she and Malin didn't have many mutual friends, so Tina had quickly realised that she was on her own when it came to making a decision. Eventually she'd gone to see Noah, even though she'd only met him a few times. It had been both wonderful and terrible. Wonderful because he shared her concern, terrible for the same reason. There was no going back. Malin and Dan were in danger, and only two people in the whole world had realised that: Tina and Noah.

And now there was only Tina left. She'd heard the news

about Noah's murder the previous evening, and had been left paralysed with fear. The papers didn't give Noah's name, but she knew it was him.

The police.

She had to call the police.

Noah had mentioned someone, said there was an officer who might be able to help them. Alex Recht. It was an unusual name, which was why Tina had remembered it.

Alex Recht would listen when she told him what she thought had happened.

Noah was trying to find his brother. Now he's dead. And I'm wondering how long I'll survive.

She sat down on her sofa and called the main switchboard. The apartment door was double-locked, and all the windows were closed. She'd taken some annual leave; she had no intention of returning to work until life got back to normal.

If it ever did.

A young woman took her call.

'I'd like to speak to Alex Recht,' Tina began, unsure of how to pronounce the surname.

'And you are?'

'Tina Antonsson. Tell him it's about the murder of Noah Johansson, and it's urgent.'

After a lengthy wait she was informed that Alex Recht was unavailable.

'I can put you through to another officer. He—'

Tina interrupted. 'I'd rather speak to Alex Recht.'

'And we'd really like to know what you can bring to the investigation,' the woman said. 'Will you have a word with his colleague?'

Tina gave in. After a few seconds she heard a man's voice.

He didn't introduce himself, he simply said 'Hello' and waited for her to respond. Then he went on:

'You're calling about Noah Johansson.'

'I know why he died,' Tina said. 'He was murdered by whoever's abducted his brother's family.'

There was a long pause.

'Noah's brother is absolutely fine. He and his family are having a wonderful time in Australia,' the officer said.

'But . . .'

'You said you had information about the murder?'

'This *is* information about the murder! I went to see Noah the other day because I'm so worried about Malin and Dan. Noah felt the same, and now he's dead.'

Another, even longer pause. Tina had had enough.

'Do what the fuck you want,' she snapped. 'I'm not giving up until I find them.'

She ended the call, her heart pounding. She jumped to her feet, banging her knee on the coffee table.

She couldn't stay in the apartment, she had to get out.

And she knew exactly where she was going.

'Berlin told me to show you this,' Torbjörn Ross said. 'Hurry up, there's something I have to do.'

There was a whining note in his voice; he didn't sound anywhere near as confident as when he'd first tried to drag Alex out of the meeting by issuing an order. Or maybe he'd prefer to keep what he'd found to himself.

Alex stared at the green book Ross had handed him. *I Am Putting Everything Right* by Morgan Sander.

'We found a copy at Malcolm Benke's house,' he said.

'I know that,' Ross snapped. 'Do you think it's a signature?'

His tone was wary, and made Alex wonder what secrets he was hiding.

'We've no idea.' Alex hesitated, unsure of what he dared ask his colleague. Or what he really wanted to know.

Are you the murderer we're looking for, Ross? You seem to be the only one who knew everyone who's involved.

Alex coughed; the dry air was making his eyes itch too.

'There is one thing I've been thinking about,' he went on. 'You said you were convinced Malcolm Benke had been murdered by his son.'

'Did I?'

Alex looked up.

'Yes, you did. And I've been wondering how you could be so certain.'

Ross shook his head.

'You must have misunderstood. I had no opinion.'

Alex waited for Ross to backtrack, but instead he took out his mobile and focused all his attention on the screen.

Alex put down the book. 'See you later.'

He didn't want to be alone with Ross. He decided to go and find a sensible person to talk to – Fredrika.

'You're always so fucking sure of yourself.'

'I'm sorry?'

Ross glanced up from his phone.

'You and your burned hands – I don't understand how you can be so fucking difficult. And I don't understand how you can bear to be reminded of such an epic failure every single day.'

He pointed to Alex's scarred hands. Alex was deeply shocked; he couldn't believe a colleague had just said something so grotesque.

This is sick, he thought, turning away.

Such an epic failure. Every single day.

As if Ross could have done any better.

'Hang on,' Ross said, waving his phone around. 'I just heard from our colleagues in Haiti.'

'Haiti?'

Alex had no desire to hang around.

'They called yesterday, but I asked them to double-check a couple of things.'

'What the hell are you talking about?'

'Lovisa Wahlberg's boyfriend – the guy who got her involved in drugs. I thought it was strange that she'd been given a tattoo just like his before she died, and I wondered if it might have something to do with him. It was a long shot, but I wanted to be able to exclude him. Whichever way you look at it, our perpetrator must have known about the boyfriend's tattoo.'

Our perpetrator. Who could be you, Ross.

'I've been thinking the same,' Alex said slowly. 'We can't see a connection between the victims, but the killer knows a hell of a lot about them.'

Ross ignored his comment.

'So I contacted the narcotics team in Port-au-Prince, asked if they could put me in touch with Lovisa's ex in jail. And that's when I found out he'd died several years ago.'

'Hardly surprising,' Alex said. 'Serving time in a place like that can't be easy.'

Ross gave him a supercilious look.

'I'm well aware of that. Hardly surprising, you say. But you're wrong. The guy didn't die in jail. He absconded after being threatened for a long time. He owed money to several dealers, and asked for protection via his lawyer. He got nowhere, of course.'

Alex waited, suspecting that there would be more twists and turns before Ross got to the point. He wasn't wrong.

'He didn't get very far before they caught up with him. The police don't know exactly what happened, but the day after he did a runner his body was found, badly beaten.'

'Okay, so he definitely wasn't involved in Lovisa's murder,' Alex said.

'The debts weren't just his,' Ross went on. 'They were Lovisa's too.'

Alex suppressed a sigh.

'You think a drugs gang from the West Indies came over here to murder her?'

'No, but I think they inspired our perpetrator when he was deciding how his victims should die. Although I'm not sure how that works.'

Ross held up his phone so that Alex could see the screen.

'Look at this, but make it quick. I'm in a hurry, I've got things to do.'

Alex blinked, moved closer. Then he recoiled.

'They found him on a private tennis court belonging to some guy who insisted the murder was nothing to do with him,' Ross informed him.

The image Alex had just seen was burned on his retina.

The photograph on Ross's phone showed a person who had been buried just below the surface of the tennis court, fingers and toes protruding. In the background was a lawnmower spattered with rust-coloured stains.

Why did the most important decisions always have to be taken when people were shocked and stressed? Fredrika had to decide what to do about what she thought she knew: that Spencer had written the letter Alex had found. That there was a faint chance Spencer could be the perpetrator they were looking for. It wasn't a hard decision – she wasn't going to say a word, not until she knew more, not until she had confirmation. The risk was too great, the consequences for Spencer would be too disastrous.

He was going to die soon anyway.

And the children would be home at the weekend.

The very thought of them made her feel weak. If Spencer was the killer, if she could entertain the idea even for a second, then shouldn't she make sure that she and the children were safe?

But it's not him. I know it's not him.

In spite of the fact that he's putting everything right.

A sharp rap on the door made her jump.

'Come in!'

Alex appeared. 'I thought you'd gone.'

'Gone where?'

'That's what I was wondering – I went back to the Lions' Den because I thought you were in there. With the letter.'

Suddenly he looked very tired.

'Sit down,' Fredrika said.

'I've no idea what I'm talking about,' he said, sinking down on one of the chairs on the other side of the desk and letting out a long sigh.

'What did Ross want?' Fredrika was keen to avoid the subject of the letter.

Alex produced a copy of a photo. At first Fredrika couldn't make out what it was.

'Do you see?'

'No.' But that was a lie; by now she had realised exactly what she was looking at.

'Lovisa Wahlberg's boyfriend,' Alex clarified. 'He escaped from prison owing drug bosses big money, and they murdered him.'

Fredrika pushed away the picture.

'Jesus,' she whispered.

'There's more. Ross told me they found the book by Morgan Sander in Lovisa's apartment. According to her boyfriend, someone had left it on the parcel shelf of her bike.'

Fredrika felt a rush of adrenaline. Her first thought: *Revenge.*

This was someone out for revenge, a killer who made sure his victims died in the same way as individuals they had let down in some way. Who left books and messages.

Two dead. Three if Noah was included.

How many more would there be?

'What the hell is this?' she said.

'It's beyond me. It's obvious how our perpetrator is choosing his methods, but I don't understand why this is happening right now.'

'He's punishing them,' Fredrika said.

'But why only them? If we look at Beata Benke's circle, for example, you could say that several people deserve to be punished, if you're thinking along those lines.'

Fredrika couldn't make any sense of it either.

'The messages to you,' she said.

'I don't understand those either. I haven't a fucking clue about what this mess has to do with me.'

Alex was clearly disturbed by the link between such brutal murders and himself.

If you knew who'd written the letter you found in Noah Johansson's office, you'd realise that I'm scared too.

'There's something I haven't told you,' Alex went on.

Fredrika stiffened, on her guard.

'Okay?'

Alex couldn't meet her gaze. He obviously didn't know how to start.

'It's about Noah. The funeral director.'

Fredrika waited, clutching the armrests of her chair. She wondered if Alex had forgotten he'd talked to her about Noah after Lena's death. He'd praised him to the skies, described him as an everyday hero disguised as a funeral director. Those words had stayed with Fredrika, which was why she and Spencer had chosen Noah.

'He called me. About his brother. He thought his brother, sister-in-law and their kids had disappeared, been abducted.'

Fredrika relaxed a fraction. 'Why did he contact you?'

'I'm the only police officer he knows. He took care of all the practical stuff when Lena died.'

'I remember your mentioning him.'

Fredrika was on the verge of tears, overwhelmed by the situation.

Alex sighed.

'You think it'll get easier over the years. And it does, in a way. But when he called ... All those memories came flooding back.'

'I can understand that.'

Alex remained silent, taking a moment to compose himself.

'The brother. I've checked with our colleagues, looked into Noah's original report. I don't have a good feeling about how it was handled.'

Fredrika sensed there was more to come. She was right.

'Do you know who helped to make the decision that there was no point in proceeding with an investigation?'

'No idea.'

'Torbjörn Ross.'

Fredrika stared at him.

'That's exactly how I reacted,' Alex said.

'Ross. Again.'

'Again,' Alex echoed.

Fredrika's blood pressure rose. Torbjörn Ross. And Spencer? *Impossible.*

'What do you think?' she asked.

'What do you think?'

She smiled, but her cheeks felt tight and the smile died away. If the letter was going to be mentioned, Alex would have to do it.

'You know more than me,' she said. 'Noah's brother's dis-appearance – what's the connection with the other murders?'

Alex spread his hands wide.

'I don't know. We can't even be sure he's actually missing.'

'Surely that can't be difficult to establish? Where do you hide an entire family?'

'You tell me.' In a few short sentences Alex filled her in on what he'd learned so far. As he spoke, Fredrika's unease grew. A father and a mother. A son and a daughter. Gone. Vanished. And no one was looking for them.

'We need to try and get a fresh investigation going,' she said when Alex had finished.

'We can certainly try, but remember – the police have been in contact with the brother.'

Fredrika shook her head.

'No. I'm on Noah's side. He knows, I mean knew, his own brother. I would have reacted in exactly the same way, particularly if the police were seriously relying on one conversation with the brother, which he cut short because he had to attend a business meeting. In the middle of the night. A psychologist. And do they actually know what his voice sounds like?'

She had to rein it in, curb the enthusiasm she was showing for a case that didn't necessarily have any connection with the others.

But it would lead them away from Spencer.

'You asked what I thought,' Alex said. 'But you weren't talking about Noah's missing brother, were you? You were talking about Ross.'

Fredrika fiddled with the necklace she was wearing – a present from Spencer and the children.

'Yes, I was. Why was he so convinced that Malcolm Benke had been murdered by his son?'

'I tried asking him, but he didn't have a sensible explanation. He insisted he'd never said it in the first place.'

'I suppose he might be feeling under pressure,' Fredrika said, thinking aloud.

'Under pressure?'

'He must realise he keeps coming up in one case after another. That could put him on the defensive, even if he's not involved.'

'But that's exactly what we want to know,' Alex said. 'Whether he's involved or not.'

Fredrika felt the hairs on her arms stand up.

'And we called him crazy,' she said quietly.

'Sometimes it's hard to know how right we are,' Alex replied, and this time they both smiled.

Alex got to his feet.

'And I have to stress that we don't know if we're right,' he added.

Fredrika bit her lip to stop herself from speaking. She thought back to the beginning of this conversation, when it had almost seemed as if Alex was about to confess something to her. He'd told her about Noah's missing brother, but was that the whole story?

As if he'd read her mind, Alex said:

'One more thing: I've spoken to Peder Rydh. He called me.'

'Okay ...' She was surprised to hear Peder's name.

'I ... This sounds stupid, but I'd just been talking to Noah, and I needed to run Noah's story by someone.'

'So you told Peder?'

'Yes. And he passed on some information that Noah had forgotten to mention.'

'Noah had been threatened?'

'Possibly, but according to Peder he'd overreacted, exaggerated. If the threat existed in the first place.'

'I don't . . .'

'According to Peder, Noah was kind of volatile, "talked a load of crap", as he put it. I think maybe we should bear that in mind when we're assessing his allegation that his brother is missing.'

'Well, it can't all have been in his imagination,' Fredrika said. 'He's dead.'

'I know, it's a complete mess. Anyway, Noah didn't say a word to me about any personal intimidation. However, he did think his brother might have been targeted by a former client. A father suffering from mental-health issues had sought his help, but ended up killing his entire family, then taking his own life.'

'So who's left to seek revenge?'

Alex looked up. 'I've no idea.'

'Do the Johansson brothers have any other living relatives?' Fredrika asked. 'Why was it only Noah who contacted the police about Dan's disappearance?'

'The parents are dead, but Noah did mention a close friend of his sister-in-law who's also concerned. I made a note of her name: Tina Antonsson.'

'Sounds like someone we need to speak to.'

'Mmm. If we think that's our job . . . ?'

Fredrika could see chaos looming as she and Alex started asking questions, treading on goodness knows how many toes along the way. Although the biggest issue was whether they had time. It seemed unlikely.

'How was he?' she said. 'Peder – was he okay?'

Alex hesitated before answering.

'I don't know. There was something . . . not quite right about him.'

Fredrika rolled her eyes. 'Another marital crisis?'

Alex laughed. 'Maybe. He certainly seems to have had problems holding down a job. I don't know why he can't just grow up and get a grip.'

There was a knock on the door, and Ivan's blond head appeared.

'Have you got your phones switched off?' he said. 'God knows how many people are trying to reach you.'

Both Alex and Fredrika glanced at their mobiles. Both were on silent, both had missed calls.

'Israel,' Fredrika said.

'Renata Rashid,' Alex said. 'She's texted as well.' He read the message with his head down, face closed.

'What does she say?'

Alex swallowed, unable to take his eyes off the screen.

'Alex?'

Fear swept through Fredrika's body like a forest fire.

No more surprises, please.

'I need to call her right away,' he said, heading for the door. Fredrika stood up, desperate to find out what had happened.

'What's it about?' she asked.

Alex looked down at his hands, stared at the hardened scar tissue.

'I don't know.'

Just before he left the room he turned back.

'What do you think we should do about Peder?'

Fredrika shrugged. 'I'm sure he'll call again soon.'

Alex sighed. 'I hope so. Because we need him.'

Peder Rydh's mobile rang just as he joined the E4, travelling north. He checked the display, saw Alex's name and rejected the call. He didn't want to think about the message Alex had left on his voicemail the previous evening.

Five seconds, and the phone rang again.

'Fuck.'

Too many things were going on at the same time.

The kids' school had just called to tell him that Eddie had a temperature. He had no choice but to turn around and pick him up. A few years ago, when Ylva was in the grip of depression, Peder had said he felt like a single parent to their twin boys. He now realised he hadn't had a clue what he was talking about.

He might as well answer; the fucking phone wouldn't stop ringing.

'Peder.'

'Have you got time to talk?'

The voice belonged to Jussi, a fifteen-stone super-strategist. Founder and boss of the security firm Peder had worked for after leaving the Solomon Community, before he took up his current post. A period of his life he preferred not to think about. Nor did he want to think about how Alex had reacted to Peder's chequered employment record. As far as Alex was concerned, there was right and wrong, and very little in between.

Peder viewed life rather differently.

'Not really,' he said to Jussi. 'Keep it short.'

'Of course. Things still the same?'

Peder kept his eyes fixed on the road ahead. 'Yes.'

'I'm sorry to hear that.'

'It is what it is.'

Jussi coughed, as he usually did when he wasn't sure what to say. Peder wasn't interested in his 'sorry to hear that'. It struck a jarring note. Jussi hadn't understood back then, and he didn't understand now. That was why he'd judged Peder so harshly.

'Listen, I'm concerned about a former client,' Jussi said.

It was a comparatively insensitive transition from one subject to another, but Peder didn't comment. Jussi got in touch at regular intervals, always because of work, so this came as no surprise.

'What client?'

'A guy you dealt with. Johansson – one of your last jobs. Do you remember him? He had a brother who—'

'I remember.' Peder didn't like the way the conversation was going.

'He seemed satisfied, or at least ... He went for the less advanced alarm system and the personal-data protection, then said he didn't need our services any more.'

Peder accelerated, flew past several other cars.

'I remember,' he said again.

'The thing is, I usually follow up on former clients just to check that they're happy, and I can't get hold of Johansson.'

Peder passed more vehicles. He remained in the overtaking

lane, noticed that the speedometer had climbed above 140 kilometres an hour.

'Give him a few days,' he said.

'Haven't you read the papers? The funeral director who was murdered? They haven't released his name yet, but I'm afraid it might be . . .'

'I get it,' Peder snapped.

Jussi remained silent for a few seconds, then said: 'What do you think we should do?'

Peder switched lanes; he was a hair's breadth from causing an accident.

'We wait.'

'For what?'

'We can't do anything until they release the name.'

Jussi considered what Peder had said.

'Okay, but then we need to contact the police, tell them what we know.'

'We don't really know anything.'

'Come on, Peder! You were a cop, you know what we have to do.'

'We have to be discreet. That's what we promise our clients, and that's what we have to stick to.'

Jussi was worryingly quiet.

'Hello?' Peder said. He didn't have time to wait, didn't have time to be patient.

'Fair enough. When the name comes out I'll ring the police. We could be sitting on important information without realising it.'

Peder ended the call, then put his foot down.

At first the lock protested when she tried to turn the key; it obviously wanted to keep her out. Tina was holding the key so tightly that her knuckles whitened. She was going to get into this house if it was the last thing she did.

She'd waited a long time, thought she couldn't do what she was doing now. If you gave a friend a spare key to your house, it went without saying that you didn't expect that person to abuse your trust.

'I want you to have this,' Malin had said. 'If we lock ourselves out, or … well, you know. Sometimes we go away, and if anything happens, I'd like someone to be able to get into the house.'

Noah had also had a key, but no one else. And now Noah was gone.

That was when Tina had made her decision – when she heard he'd been murdered. She had to visit the house, take a look around, see if she noticed anything the police or Noah had missed. If the police had even been there, which seemed unlikely.

According to the man she'd spoken to, Noah's death didn't affect their view of Dan and Malin's 'disappearance'. That didn't make any sense to Tina, and she found it deeply worrying.

Will I be the next one to die?

The question kept on going around and around in her head; it was making her paranoid. *Please, please let the door open!* She couldn't stand here much longer in full view, fiddling with the lock.

At last! She let out a little whimper of relief as she stepped inside and closed the door behind her. She locked it and tried the handle, making sure it wouldn't open. Only to be overwhelmed by a fresh wave of panic.

Nobody knew where she was.

Nobody would be coming here over the next few days, maybe even weeks or months.

What if something happened to her in the house? What if she was attacked and had to get out fast?

It was no good, she couldn't bring herself to unlock the door. She would just have to hurry. She had no intention of being there for a minute longer than necessary.

Her palms were slippery with sweat as she left the hallway and went into the kitchen. There were no dishes on the draining board or the table. Had Noah tidied up, or had it been like this all along? Tina checked the dishwasher: some glasses, two cups, four bowls, cutlery. She shuddered. It seemed to her as if the family had got up in the morning, had breakfast, closed the door behind them and never returned.

The same feeling dogged her footsteps in every single room: in the children's bedrooms, the TV room in the basement, Malin and Dan's bedroom, the dining room and the living room. Even the laundry room was tidy, but who moved to Australia for a year and left clothes hanging in the drying cabinet and dirty crockery in the dishwasher?

Noah had warned her, tried to explain why it felt so wrong when he checked out the house.

'Everything was slightly off kilter, and yet it wasn't,' he'd said.

Only now did Tina understand what he'd meant.

She went back to the children's rooms, struggling with the sense that she'd made a mistake, that she shouldn't be here. There was a chance – a remote chance – that the family really were in Australia. How would they feel about her sneaking around their home?

She pushed her qualms aside. She knew exactly why she'd come, and why it had taken so long. That would have to suffice as an explanation. She opened the wardrobes in Hedvig and Max's rooms. They were full of clothes, just as the shelves were full of toys and books and goodness knows what else. She couldn't tell if anything was missing, if anything had been removed. There were two books on Hedvig's bedside table. She picked up the top one, noticed that Hedvig had folded down the corner of a particular page. Tina wasn't comfortable touching the girl's possessions; she knew that Hedvig was very grown-up for a twelve-year-old.

She weighed the book in her hand. Afterwards she couldn't explain why she opened it at the turned-down page; it was just an impulse, something she had to do. The first thing she saw was a note, small, pale grey letters written in pencil.

Hedvig's handwriting.

Tina read the short sentence as she heard a car pull up outside.

He was wearing Wellingtons.

She peered out of the window and saw a brown Saab. The driver's door opened and a man got out. He stared straight at the house, straight at Tina. She quickly moved to one side, dropped the book on the floor.

She didn't dare check to see where he'd gone. She had to get out of the house at all costs. She clutched her mobile in her pocket. Her top was sticking to her back, she was hot and rigid with tension.

She decided not to leave the same way as she'd come in. She didn't want to meet the man in the Saab.

Who was he? And what was he doing here?

As Tina fumbled with the back-door lock, she heard someone insert a key into the front door. There was no time to speculate, she had to get out, maybe make a note of his registration number.

Find out who else has a key.

She inhaled the fresh air, then let out a huge sigh of relief. The door clicked shut behind her and she hurried down the steps, then edged along the wall of the house. Her heart was pounding. When she reached the corner she would peep around, see if the man had disappeared.

Her forehead was beaded with sweat as she leaned forward. *Please let him not be there, please let him—*

She couldn't suppress a scream when she saw him standing less than half a metre away.

What the . . . ?

He gave a chilly smile.

'Sorry. I didn't mean to scare you.'

Tina backed away.

'No problem,' she said, but her voice was far from steady.

He moved inexorably towards her.

'Do you live here?' he said.

She shook her head, still backing away.

'So what were you doing in the house?'

Tina didn't know what to say. She was in the middle of a residential area, and there wasn't a soul in sight. How could she possibly feel so unsafe in broad daylight?

The man's eyes narrowed. For some reason it was clear to both of them that he had the upper hand, that he had the right to ask questions and she must answer. She felt a sudden spurt of anger.

'Are you a police officer?' she asked.

Her tone was rather shrill, but at least she'd managed to say what she wanted to say.

How can you have a greater right to be here than me? Or even the same right as me?

At first he didn't respond, then he said:

'Yes, I am. And I think you and I need to have a chat.'

Only then did she recognise his voice. He was the officer she'd spoken to on the phone, the one who'd dismissed her. And now he was standing here on Dan and Malin's drive, asking her what she was doing there.

Her shoulders dropped.

'Something's badly wrong,' she said. 'I know Dan and Malin aren't in Australia.'

He stared at her in silence. 'I think it's best if you accompany me to the station, then I can take a proper statement from you.'

Tina swallowed. 'Okay.'

He turned and walked towards his car. Tina followed; her car was parked just in front of his.

'I'll drive myself,' she said.

He shook his head. 'No, you won't. Get in the back seat.'

Tina had never had any dealings with the police, didn't

know what was common practice. But just as she knew something wasn't right about Dan and Malin's trip to Australia, she knew something wasn't right about this situation.

She didn't dare walk along the pavement past the Saab. Instead she stepped into the road, intending to approach her car that way, but the police officer blocked her path.

'Didn't you hear what I said? You're coming with me. Otherwise I'll bring in my colleagues, have you arrested.'

Tina's entire body was shaking.

'Fine,' she said. 'You do that.'

Her response took him by surprise; he'd obviously been expecting her to cooperate.

She took her chance and tried to run past him. She didn't have a plan, she just wanted to get into her car and lock the doors. However, he was too quick for her. He grabbed her arm and opened the door of the Saab with his other hand.

'Get in,' he hissed.

His breath smelled of tobacco.

'What are you doing?'

The voice came from a man on a bicycle who'd stopped a few metres away. The grip on Tina's arm loosened.

'Nothing,' the police officer said. 'It's just a misunderstanding.'

A misunderstanding?

Tina gave the cyclist a long look, silently begging him to stay where he was until she was safe.

'I'll take my own car,' she heard herself mumble. At the same time she happened to glance at the back seat of the Saab.

A bobbled blanket, a newspaper. But what really caught her attention and made her heart skip a beat was the pair of green Wellingtons, standing on the floor behind the front seat.

Ten minutes. It needn't take any longer than that. After an endless night with no rest and a morning filled with arguments with the kids, Malin was ready to jump out of the window. If it had been possible to open a window, of course. So she decided to take a shower. Ten minutes. Surely she could leave the kids alone for that amount of time? They'd stopped fighting and were sitting in front of the TV watching a film. There was no point in even thinking about lessons; none of them could cope with that, including Malin. Not when she was putting all her energy into keeping them alive. Herself and the children. And Dan.

He hadn't said a word since he got out of bed two hours after the rest of the family. Malin made no attempt to persuade him to talk. She didn't want to ask him about the knives again, partly because there was no point, but also because she didn't dare.

Because I don't want to hear the dark thoughts inside his head.

She popped her head around the living-room door.

'I'm going for a shower.'

No response.

'Give me a shout if you need anything.'

'Yeah, yeah,' Hedvig said.

Dan was upstairs. That was good; if she left the bathroom door open, she'd be able to hear what he was doing.

Five minutes. She could easily shower in five minutes.

Or maybe she should just have a stand-up wash at the basin?

She hesitated in the doorway. She could see Dan, sitting in an armchair in the bedroom and staring out of the window. He looked contented, almost as if a smile was playing around the corners of his mouth.

Terrifying.

And that was what finally made her reach a decision. She couldn't carry on like this, unable to gather her thoughts. She couldn't stay awake 24/7, day after day. She had already noticed how her heightened state of anxiety had taken its toll. Her hair was greasy and she didn't smell good. She wasn't eating properly either; she hadn't bothered with breakfast.

This can't go on.

She tore off her clothes, dropped them on the bathroom floor. If Dan saw her, he didn't react. The needle-sharp streams of water hit her face, brought her back to life.

Three minutes.

She didn't need ten, she didn't even need five.

After only one minute she turned off the shower and quickly stepped out, desperate to reassure herself that Dan was still sitting in the window. He was.

Back into the shower. She soaped her body with gel, rubbed a blob of shampoo through her short hair, rinsed away the suds. Not exactly a luxurious experience. Without even picking up a towel she checked on Dan again. He hadn't moved.

Her heart was pounding.

This can't go on.

There was water all over the floor, and Malin shivered as she dried herself. A swipe of deodorant under each arm. She pulled on her knickers, trousers, vest top. Hung up the towel, left the bathroom.

And discovered that Dan was no longer sitting in the armchair.

'Another death,' Alex said when he managed to get hold of Renata Rashid, the medical examiner.

'I'm afraid so.'

'Are we sure this has something to do with me? Because if not, I . . .'

'The deceased is a man aged about seventy. I'm not at all sure his death has anything to do with you, but I mentioned something I found during the post-mortem to a colleague, and he said I should call you.'

Alex leaned back in his chair, on full alert. He was in his office with the door firmly closed. A new routine that had been established over the past few days: he and Fredrika worked behind closed doors, together or separately.

Creeping around. Just like Berlin said. I hate it.

'I've got a thousand other things on my plate,' Alex said. 'But if I can help you, fire away.'

Renata was an important person in Alex's professional life. He tried to remember that, give her the time she needed.

'Thank you. So as I said, we're looking at an elderly male. Divorced, lived alone in central Stockholm. The neighbours became aware of an unpleasant smell, and eventually tracked it down to his apartment. I'd say he'd been dead for four to six days by the time he was found.'

Alex grimaced, wondering where the conversation was going.

'It wasn't difficult to work out the cause of death,' Renata went on. 'Not once I knew what I was looking for. There were contusions on his throat suggesting a violent attack, but I didn't think that had killed him. He'd had heart problems for some time, and I was afraid that the blow to his throat had led to a heart attack.'

She paused for breath. Alex was surprised; Renata was usually much more concise.

'But it wasn't his heart either,' he said.

'No. When I turned him over I discovered a puncture wound in the nape of his neck.'

Alex opened up his computer. 'Okay,' he said, mainly to indicate that he was listening.

'Someone had given him an injection,' Renata clarified.

'Strange place to choose,' Alex said as he skimmed the newspaper headlines. The journalists weren't holding back, but he couldn't blame them; an unusual amount of blood had flowed in Stockholm over the past few days.

And I have no idea how to stop it.

'*Very* strange,' Renata said. 'So strange that I immediately regarded it as a deviation. Almost ritualistic.'

Ritualistic?

'Was there any kind of message on the victim?' Alex asked.

'Message?'

'A piece of paper – a book, maybe?'

The brief pause told him that Renata was taken aback.

'No. No message, no book.'

Alex thought for a moment. If there had been a message, the officers on the scene would have noticed it. Or would they? Berlin had imposed a complete lockdown on the inquiry; anyone not directly involved in the investigation wouldn't be aware of the killer's MO.

I need to check that. Alex made a note.

'Anyway,' Renata continued, sounding more than a little irritated by the interruption, 'the injection into the back of the neck doesn't remind you of anything?'

'No.'

'Not even if I tell you that the man who died had significantly elevated insulin levels?'

A faint bell began to ring in the back of Alex's mind, and for the second time within a comparatively short period, he looked down at his scarred hands. The hands he had burned while trying to save a child. A child who would otherwise have met the same fate as two other children. They had been murdered with an overdose of insulin. In one of the cases, where the victim was a baby, the fatal injection had been given via the fontanel. The other child had been too old for that, so the overdose had been injected . . .

. . . into the back of the neck.

Alex's mouth went as dry as dust. He wished he had something to drink.

Then he pulled himself together. From a purely practical point of view, an insulin overdose was an excellent way of murdering someone. The method used in this latest death could be pure coincidence, a red herring.

'A few years ago – well, almost ten – we were looking for a perpetrator who murdered his victims exactly the same way,' he said. 'But all his victims were children. Small children.'

'That's what my colleague told me; he was the medical

examiner back then. And of course this doesn't necessarily mean there's a link.'

No. God forbid.

'I appreciate the call,' Alex said. 'I'll have to ask someone else to check it out – I don't have the time.'

'I just report whatever I find. It's up to you to take it from there.'

'Thank you.'

'There's a lot going on,' Renata said.

'Way too much.'

The last thing they needed was another murder. Even though Alex knew he couldn't take it on, he still had to ask:

'What was the victim's name?'

'Henry Lindgren.'

He ran a hand over his chin, felt the stubble beneath his fingertips. Diana didn't like it when he didn't shave properly.

'Means nothing to me.'

'Good.'

They ended the call.

Alex sat there with the phone in his hand, reflecting on what he'd just been told. *Henry Lindgren.* In fact Alex had partly lied to Renata; the surname meant nothing, but the first name wasn't unfamiliar. The problem was that he couldn't remember in which context he'd heard it.

He had to let it go, prioritise.

The murder of Malcolm Benke.

The murder of Lovisa Wahlberg.

The murder of Noah Johansson.

His conversation with Fredrika had been interrupted before he'd had a chance to find out what she thought about the letter he'd found in Noah's office. He was glad he hadn't mentioned what Peder had said about Spencer, but what did she think about the letter? If it weren't for the letter they wouldn't have linked Noah's death to the other two. And yet it could still be a false trail, because the only things in the letter that had caught Alex's attention were the words 'I am putting everything right' and the reference to an author. What was coincidence and what was worth following up? Alex didn't know.

The man who had written the letter (Alex was sure it was a man) had revealed certain things about himself.

He was dying.

He had children.

He'd been involved in an accident.

He worked in Uppsala.

And he knew of Morgan Sander.

Alex smiled. If you disregarded the first point, the writer could be Spencer Lagergren.

He immediately grew serious once more; he didn't have time for nonsense. They had to consider the relevance of the letter, work out the possible identity of the person behind it. Alex had read it three times, and it still made his blood run cold. It was a kind of confession; the guy had run over a young woman then driven away from the scene of the crime, leaving her to her fate. There was no way of knowing when the incident had taken place. The daughter he referred to could be five years old, or thirty.

The only thing they knew for sure was what he had chosen to put down in writing.

He had done wrong.

And now he was putting everything right.

Is it him? Is this the killer we're looking for? A dying man who once ruined a young woman's life, and is now punishing others?

Torbjörn Ross.

But he wasn't dying, was he?

These days it wasn't easy for the uninitiated to know something like that. He recalled how astonishingly healthy Lena had seemed on the day they were informed that she had less than a year to live.

He decided to call Tina Antonsson, the woman Noah had mentioned. It was an unusual name; she shouldn't be too hard to find.

He was right; Tina lived in Spånga and had both a mobile number and a landline. He tried the mobile first, and she answered almost right away.

'Yes?'

'Am I speaking to Tina Antonsson?'

He could hear her breathing. 'Who's asking?'

The counter-question surprised him.

'My name is Alex Recht. I knew Noah Johansson.'

She let out a sob. 'I'm so glad you called,' she said in a subdued voice.

Alex assumed she was upset because of Noah's death, and began by offering his condolences. His words didn't have the calming effect he'd hoped for.

'Sorry, sorry,' she said. 'But I've been so frightened.'

'Frightened?'

Alex knew that simply repeating the word was stupid, but it just slipped out.

'I think I'm safe. I don't want to say where I am. Not yet. Noah said I could trust you, but I . . . I don't know what to do.'

Alex summoned up his most reassuring voice.

'Let's start at the beginning. You're hiding somewhere?'

There was a long silence, then: 'Yes.'

'I apologise if this seems insensitive, but why?'

Silence.

'I realise you must have been scared when you heard that Noah had been murdered,' Alex said gently. 'He told me you were worried about Dan and his family too, that you think something's happened to them.'

'I *know* something's happened to them. So don't tell me I'm imagining things and need to stop worrying.'

'Absolutely not. I'm far from convinced that Noah's brother is in Australia.'

There was a scraping sound on the other end of the line.

'Let's try again. You know more than I do. So tell me – why are you hiding?'

'Can anyone else hear us?' Tina asked.

What kind of a question is that?

'No. This phone isn't monitored.'

'I don't mean that. I mean are you alone, or can anyone else hear what you're saying?'

'I'm alone in my office with the door closed.'

Alex was running out of patience; he was beginning to regret contacting Tina Antonsson. What possible reason could she have for being so scared?

'Can we meet? So I can see your ID?'

Alex closed his eyes and rubbed his forehead.

What the fuck is going on here?

I don't have time. I really don't.

'I'm a bit pressed for time. Tell me where you want to meet, but it has to be within half an hour's drive of police HQ.'

Tina thought for a moment.

'I'll see you at the OKQ8 petrol station in Johanneshov in thirty minutes.'

'Fine. Is that where you are now? By the Globe?'

'I don't want to say where I am.'

Then she hung up.

'I'm not sure I ought to be calling you, but I'm doing it anyway,' Mikael Lundell said.

Fredrika mumbled about how it wasn't always easy to know what was right or wrong.

'I've been mulling something over since we last spoke,' Mikael went on.

Fredrika was as taut as a violin string; she couldn't handle anyone else's uncertainty on top of her own.

'Go on.'

Mikael didn't answer immediately; her lack of patience had clearly had an effect.

'It's not so much about events in London,' he said slowly. 'It's more about the police, how you work, the organisation.'

Fredrika could have burst out laughing, but she didn't. The organisation? Was he serious?

'I realise this sounds stupid.'

'No, no,' Fredrika assured him. 'We've just undergone a major restructuring, but I'm guessing that's not what you're referring to. Could you be a little more specific?'

'Absolutely. You told me that the police in Sweden weren't aware of what had happened to Beata in London.'

Fredrika shuffled uncomfortably.

'I can't honestly tell you what the procedure is when a

Swedish citizen is murdered overseas, but if no report is filed in Sweden, then ...'

'That's not what I meant,' Mikael said. 'It was more the fact that you had so many questions, when you could have got the answers from one of your colleagues.'

Fredrika was busy moving papers around her desk; she stopped in mid movement.

'Sorry, I don't understand.'

'Malcolm Benke was in regular contact with a detective in Stockholm who gave him good advice on how to handle his daughter's situation. A detective who was a friend of a friend, I think.'

When Fredrika didn't speak, Mikael added: 'At least that's what Malcolm said.'

'Do you remember the name of this detective? Did Malcolm mention a name?'

'He did. It was Torbjörn Ross.'

Alex was nowhere to be found when Fredrika started looking for him. Ivan had seen him heading for the lifts a few minutes ago, so Fredrika tried his mobile.

'Where are you?'

'On my way out. There's something I have to do.'

She thought she might actually explode. *No more secrets, please.* No more than those she was convinced he already had.

There's another reason why you didn't tell me about Noah Johansson's missing brother until today. What was it?

'Alex, tell me where you're going.'

She heard the sound of an engine starting.

'I'm meeting someone who's too scared to talk to me on the phone.'

'Who?'

The engine roared; Alex was on his way out of the underground car park.

'Tina Antonsson,' he said after a few seconds.

'*Now*?'

'Yes.'

Fredrika wanted to protest, point out that they had a thousand other things to do. They had to talk about Ross. That must take priority.

Because if Ross is the killer, then I can let go of my suspicions about Spencer.

She went into the Lions' Den and closed the door behind her. It was colder than ever.

'I know why Ross thought it was Bernhard Benke who'd murdered Malcolm,' she said. 'He knew Malcolm, knew exactly what was going on with Beata in London.'

'Jesus! Where did you get this from?'

'Mikael Lundell.'

Fredrika drew her jacket more tightly around her body, trying to get warm.

'Alex, we need to push this upstairs.'

'You mean we need to make a formal report on our suspicions about Ross?'

'Yes.'

'And how do we do that? Can you provide a simple summary of those suspicions, and the reasons behind them? We have to be realistic. It's a terrible thing we're trying to put into words.'

So terrible that neither of them had actually said what they were thinking, Fredrika realised.

'I still think he's involved,' she said.

'Me too.'

'His name crops up in every single case, and he has links to several of the victims.'

'Exactly.'

'But there's no forensic evidence.'

'And we haven't the faintest idea of a motive,' Alex pointed out. 'If Ross murdered all these people, what's driving him?'

'The MO tells us something. Malcolm was killed in the same way as his daughter, Lovisa in the same way as her boyfriend. As far as I'm concerned, the motive is crystal clear: revenge.'

'Okay, but why would Torbjörn Ross take it upon himself to exact that revenge? And what's the connection with *me*?'

Fredrika thought about the letter Alex had found in Noah's office, about the confession and the assertion that steps had been taken to atone for past sins. Tears pricked at her eyes.

Please don't let it be Spencer, in spite of everything.

'Maybe there are two of them,' she said. The thought came from nowhere.

'Two perpetrators?' Alex's voice was filled with doubt.

'There must be a reason why Ross's name keeps popping up all over the place,' Fredrika insisted. 'If there are two perpetrators it makes more sense.'

However, she was far from satisfied with that hypothesis – for a number of reasons.

'Alex, how many more?' she said quietly.

The question that threatened to destroy her from the inside.

'I'm sorry?'

'Victims. How many more are going to die?'

'I can't answer that,' Alex said. 'But we have to stop this lunatic as soon as possible. Anything else is out of the question.'

Anything else was out of the question.

So true, so difficult.

'I have to go,' Alex said.

Fredrika stared out of the window. Dark clouds were gathering in the sky, ready to party. Maybe the summer was planning to do what it so often did in Sweden: turn on its heel in the doorway and disappear.

'I don't like you meeting Tina Antonsson on your own.'

'It's not ideal, but on this occasion it can't be helped.'

'I'm here if there's anything I can do.'

'Thanks.'

Fredrika was about to hang up when Alex said:

'By the way, does the name Henry Lindgren mean anything to you?'

She thought for a moment. The name Henry rang a bell, but she couldn't pin down the context.

'Do you want me to run a search? I think I've heard the name, but I can't remember where.'

'Same here. Check it out, see what you can find. I'm sure our colleagues have already done that, but I'm afraid they might miss any links to our investigation.'

Fredrika swallowed. 'What do you mean, links to our investigation?'

'A man called Henry Lindgren has been found murdered. He was killed by an overdose of insulin, injected into the back of his neck.'

Fredrika almost dropped the phone.

'Oh my God,' she whispered.

'So you remember that case too.'

'I'll never forget it. But . . .'

'I really do have to go.' And Alex was gone.

As Fredrika left the Lions' Den she met Torbjörn Ross, ambling along the corridor.

'Did Alex tell you what we found in Lovisa's apartment?' he asked.

Fredrika nodded.

Ross was wearing trainers and carrying a pair of Wellingtons. He looked at her for a long time.

'The net is tightening,' he said. 'We'll soon have the bastard.'

It didn't take Tina long to drive from her grandmother's summer cottage in Högmora to the petrol station where she'd arranged to meet Alex Recht. The cottage had felt like a safe place to hide, but was that still the case? It had been locked up and deserted as usual when she arrived. Grandma was no longer around, and Tina's parents didn't like spending time there. They'd hung on to it for Tina's sake.

'Maybe you'll have a family of your own one day,' her mother had said. 'It would be nice for you to have somewhere to escape to in the summer.'

There was so much wrong with that assumption that Tina couldn't even be bothered to respond.

She had been thirty-five when Grandma died; she wasn't exactly a teenager any more. The summer cottage was fun whether Tina had a family or not. Although fun wasn't the right word. It was a place where Tina found strength and joy.

And safety too, on this occasion.

Unless she was wrong, and someone else was able to work out where she'd gone.

This isn't how I intended to spend my holiday, she thought.

She'd been planning to take some of her annual leave later in the year and go over to Australia to visit Malin. That obviously wasn't going to happen.

She felt weak in both body and spirit as she drove. She was wracked with doubt, could hardly breathe.

Should she have stayed away from Noah, realised it might be dangerous to look for Malin and Dan? The answer didn't really matter, because Tina's life had become so much poorer since Malin's disappearance. Nobody could fill the gap she'd left behind, nobody could replace her. It was also a matter of right and wrong; you didn't abandon friends you loved. You didn't stop searching for them if you believed they'd been abducted, taken against their will.

Please don't let them be dead.

Because then I will die too.

She parked at the petrol station. A man was filling up his car, but there was no sign of anyone else. She'd found a picture of Alex online so that she'd recognise him. She positioned herself a short distance away from her car, constantly looking around to make sure she hadn't been followed, checking that the man with the Wellingtons hadn't come after her.

A car pulled off the road and parked not far from the pumps. A tall, grey-haired man got out. He glanced in her direction and raised his eyebrows inquiringly.

Tina nodded.

She couldn't stop thinking about the man with the Wellingtons.

How would she know if she could trust Alex Recht? Noah might have been wrong; maybe Alex was the person behind all the bad stuff.

If he's the one who betrayed Noah, then I've had it.

'Tina?'

She nodded again. She was so tired. Alex took out his ID and gave her as much time as she needed to examine it. He jerked his head in the direction of the man filling up his car.

'Someone you know?'

'No,' Tina said, handing back his ID.

They waited until the man had paid and driven off.

'Why here?' Alex asked.

'It seemed like a good place.' That was the best she could come up with.

'You look tired. Shall we go and sit in my car, have a chat?'

She took a step backwards. 'No.'

'Okay, we won't do anything you don't want to do, or anything that doesn't feel right.'

Tina could see he was wondering why she was afraid to get in his car. She could also see endless patience in his eyes, oceans of calmness and wisdom.

'I went to Malin and Dan's house today.'

'Noah's brother and sister-in-law?'

'Yes. I have a spare key, but I hadn't used it before. Well, I had, but only when Malin asked me to.'

'To water the plants and take care of the post when they were away?' Alex said with a smile.

'Exactly. But this time I went in anyway, because Noah said the police wouldn't listen to him, and I thought I might find a clue, something that would help me work out what had happened to Malin and Dan.'

She fell silent; it had started raining.

Alex glanced towards his car.

'How about this for an idea? You sit in the front seat on the driver's side with the door open or closed, whichever you prefer. I'll sit in the back on the other side. Okay?'

Tina wished she was a little girl again so that she wouldn't have to make decisions, wouldn't have to worry about what was right or wrong.

'Okay,' she whispered.

She waited while he got into the back seat, then she climbed in behind the wheel, leaving the door ajar.

'So,' Alex said gently. 'Tell me what you think has happened to Malin and Dan and their children.'

Tina rubbed her hands together. They were always a little too cold.

What did she think?

It was hard to sum up in a few simple sentences.

'Something's wrong,' she began. 'Very wrong.'

'You don't believe they're in Australia?'

'No. But . . . I can't even guess at where they might be.'

'Hmm. If we play with the idea that they actually are in Australia,' Alex said slowly. 'That for reasons neither you nor I can understand, they feel they have to behave in this way. What might be behind such behaviour?'

She thought hard.

'Nothing. Nothing at all.'

'They couldn't possibly be . . . running away?'

'Running away?'

'As I said, I'm just playing with the idea,' Alex repeated. 'I realise the move to Australia doesn't add up, but I need to work out what the problem is.'

Tina leaned back, keeping her eyes fixed on Alex. He met her gaze in silence.

'Dan's job can make him . . . vulnerable. He's a psychologist, and some of his cases haven't ended well.'

'Are you thinking of anything in particular?'

His tone was too casual, as if he knew the answer.

Noah, Tina thought. *Of course, Noah's already told him.*

'Dan had a client with serious mental-health issues about a year ago,' she said. 'As you perhaps know.'

'That doesn't matter. Tell me about this client.'

'I'd call him crazy, but Dan always says you can't use that word when people have mental-health problems. He was referred by the company he worked for; he was suffering from burnout and needed help. It didn't take Dan long to establish that this guy had far more serious problems, to the extent that he actually tried to have him sectioned; in his professional opinion, the client was dangerous. Unfortunately no one listened before it was too late. One morning the school contacted the police when neither of the children turned up, and they couldn't get hold of the parents. He'd shot his family, then himself.'

Alex adjusted his position in the back seat.

'Horrific. Did he ever threaten Dan?'

Tina shuddered.

'Definitely. Dan cancelled their last session, because the guy wouldn't leave him alone.'

'What did he do?'

'He once turned up at the house in the middle of the night, yelling and banging on the door. And he sent threatening emails and text messages, said he'd harm Dan if Dan didn't make him better.'

'Did Dan report this to the police?'

Tina sighed. 'Malin wanted him to, but Dan's boss chose to handle it differently. The practice works with a security company that provides support when necessary.'

Alex's interest was immediately aroused.

'A security company? Which one?'

'I think it's called Solid Security.'

'British?'

'Swedish, as far as I know.'

'Of course. Everything has to be in English these days.'

For the first time during their conversation, Alex seemed old to Tina. *Everything has to be in English.* Why not?

'You must have been close to the family,' he went on. 'You seem to know a great deal.'

His words made Tina feel sad.

'So did you find anything in the house?'

She didn't answer immediately; her brain had somehow slowed down.

'You said you used your spare key. Did you find anything?'

A police officer. With Wellingtons.

'I didn't think so at first, but then when I went into Hedvig's room, there was a book on her bedside table with the corner of one of the pages turned down. When I opened it, I saw she'd made a note.'

Quickly, so quickly that she stumbled over her words, Tina told Alex what Hedvig had written, and what had happened next. She couldn't stop herself, it all came pouring out. Except for one detail: the fact that the man who'd tried to get her into his car had said he was a police officer. That she'd recognised his voice.

But maybe I was wrong.

'I saw the Wellingtons when I was passing the open car door. I was terrified; if that cyclist hadn't come along I don't think I'd have got away.'

Only then, when she paused for breath, did she register how quiet Alex had gone. He was sitting there motionless, his expression grim and forbidding.

'Where did he say he was taking you?' he asked.

Tina hesitated.

I don't know who I can trust.

'To the police station,' she whispered.

'What?'

'He said I had to go with him to the station to make a statement, but I didn't believe him. Well, I believed he was a police officer, but . . .'

Alex waited patiently for her to continue. His jaws were working, as if he were chewing something.

'I just didn't trust him. I thought he was dangerous, that he was going to hurt me.'

'What was his name?'

'I don't know.'

The rain was hammering on the windscreen and the wind had got up. Tina still wasn't prepared to close the door, and cold air swept into the car.

'But he had a pair of Wellington boots behind the front seat, and that bothered you because you'd just read the note in Hedvig's book about a man wearing Wellingtons.'

Tina shrank down in her seat, feeling stupid.

'I mean, I don't really know what the note meant,' she said. 'Maybe I've got it all wrong, I'm just so stressed out.'

Alex didn't answer. He'd taken out his mobile and was searching for something.

'Is this the man who tried to get you into his car?'

Tina looked at the screen and felt her pulse rate increase.

'Yes. That's him. That's him.'

Alex opened the back door and got out. Tina got out too and joined him in the rain.

'Is he really a police officer?'

Alex was making a call.

'Yes,' he said grimly. 'But not for much longer.'

Where the hell had he *gone*? Malin went round and round the house, over and over again, becoming increasingly agitated with every step she took.

'Dan?'

Her voice was shrill, brought the children to their feet.

'What's wrong, Mummy?'

Max clung to her while Hedvig looked on in silence.

'I'm looking for Daddy,' Malin said, failing in her attempt to produce a smile. 'Have you seen him?'

'No,' Max replied.

'But we heard him coming down the stairs,' Hedvig added.

Malin stared at her.

'You heard him coming down the stairs, but you don't know where he went?'

Neither of the children spoke at first.

'It's happened before,' Hedvig told her. 'One minute he's here, then he isn't.'

Malin's palms began to sweat. She didn't understand what her daughter was saying.

There's nowhere to go.

'Let's all look for him,' she suggested. 'Maybe he's hiding, playing a game!'

Max's face lit up, but there was nothing but fear in Hedvig's eyes.

'Mummy . . .' she said.

'It's okay, sweetheart.' She stroked the girl's arm reassuringly. 'It's okay.'

It didn't work. Hedvig was too old to be fooled by her mother's convenient lies.

Malin shook her hair; it was wet and messy. She'd only given it a quick rub with the towel.

Because I was being as quick as I could, and still it wasn't enough.

She took Max by the hand.

'Right, let's find Daddy.'

It was a stupid thing to say, as if there were a thousand places he could be. That wasn't the case. The kitchen, the TV room, the hallway, the little cloakroom by the front door – that was the whole of the ground floor.

'Dan? Stop messing around, you're scaring the children!'

No answer.

Hedvig opened the cloakroom door for the second time.

'We've already looked in there,' Max whined.

'I want to look again!' The girl's voice was strained; she was struggling to hold back the tears.

'Right, so this is what we're going to do,' Malin said firmly, trying to rescue the situation.

Too late. Max threw himself on the floor.

'I don't like it here, I want to go home!'

He began to sob helplessly, and Malin crouched down beside him, put her arms around him.

'We have to stay a bit longer, poppet.'

'A bit longer?' Hedvig said. 'What does that mean? How much longer, Mummy? How much longer?'

Something caught Malin's attention, the tiniest movement

at the very edge of her peripheral vision. *The closet doors. Had they moved?*

Impossible.

So impossible that it hadn't even occurred to her to look inside, because although the closet was about a metre long, it wasn't very deep. They'd hung their jackets in there when they first arrived, and hadn't opened the doors since.

Because we're not allowed to go outside.

She stared at the closet, waiting for another movement. Nothing.

'Mummy?'

Mummy, Mummy, Mummy.

'Hedvig, take your brother upstairs please,' she said quietly.

If he was in the closet (*he is in the closet*), it didn't matter how much she lowered her voice; he would hear her anyway.

'Why . . .'

'Just do as I say, right now. Go into your room, close the door and push one of the beds up against it. Then sit on the bed and don't come out until I call you. Do you understand?'

Do you understand?

Daddy's in the closet and he's gone mad.

He's dangerous.

She looked Hedvig straight in the eye, wanting to shake her and yell that it was time to stop being a kid, she had to grow up and take care of her brother.

Perhaps Hedvig grasped the seriousness of the situation, because she did exactly as she'd been told. She grabbed Max and hauled him to his feet.

'Come on.'

He let out a howl of protest.

'I don't want to BE here any MORE!'

Malin straightened up, lost her balance, staggered backwards.

The closet doors slid open.

Dan emerged, clutching a big knife.

'Me neither,' he said. 'Me neither.'

Nothing was more sensitive than investigating a colleague, but sometimes it just had to be done. Alex, Fredrika and Berlin were in the Lions' Den. Alex had chosen the location and Berlin had reluctantly agreed. Fredrika had been fully briefed.

'You'll understand why we have to be out of everyone else's way when I explain what's happened,' Alex had said to Berlin when he opened the door.

She certainly understood now.

She was breathing heavily, staring at Alex as she listened.

She's disappointed, he thought. *More than we are, because she likes Ross.*

'I can't believe this is true,' she said when he'd finished.

Alex and Fredrika said nothing.

'Where's the woman who identified Torbjörn?' Berlin demanded.

'Tina. She's in a safe place,' Alex informed her.

'What does that mean?'

'She's left Stockholm for the time being.'

'She's staying with a friend she hasn't seen for over a year,' Fredrika added. Alex had called her first, wanting her spontaneous reaction to what Tina had told him.

'Let's bring him in,' she'd said, but Alex had disagreed. He preferred to put Ross under surveillance, tap his phone, see if he might lead them to Noah's brother. If there was a chance that the family was alive, Alex had to find them.

'He's killing people to punish them,' Alex said. 'Malcolm Benke because he didn't save his daughter. Lovisa Wahlberg because she let her boyfriend pay the price for their joint drug dealings. I'm assuming he's taken Dan Johansson because he failed with one of his clients. Noah had to be silenced because he was kicking up too much of a fuss. Fuck knows how long the list will end up. It's possible that Renata Rashid has another victim on her hands, but we don't know for sure.'

'But we still haven't worked out why,' Fredrika said. '*Why* is Ross the person who's punishing them? And why now? Beata Benke's been dead for ten years – why take revenge now instead of ten years ago?'

Berlin's face betrayed no emotion.

'His daughter,' she said almost inaudibly.

'His daughter?'

'She died back in the autumn.'

Alex and Fredrika exchanged a glance.

'Do we know how she died?'

'He said it was the result of an illness.'

Fredrika frowned. 'I didn't even know Ross had a daughter.'

Nor did Alex, and he certainly hadn't heard about her death.

'So how old was she?'

'I've no idea,' Berlin said.

Fredrika went over to the computer in a corner of the meeting room.

'I'll check the register,' she said as it hummed into life.

Berlin didn't speak or move. She was in shock, and it suited her even less than her usual truculence.

'We need to put him under surveillance right away,' Alex said.

'I'll sort it,' Berlin said, then left the room with her head down.

Two minutes later they had the answer to their question. Ross had two sons, but no daughter. He'd never had a daughter.

The surveillance team had eyes on Ross less than an hour after Berlin issued the order. It was essential not to arouse his suspicions, so he remained in charge of the investigation into the murder of Lovisa Wahlberg. It was almost four o'clock; people would soon be going home, but not Alex or Fredrika. They remained closeted in the Lions' Den; they had a lot to do.

Fredrika gave Spencer a quick call, while Alex made do with a text to Diana:

Going to be late. Will be in touch. Xx

He couldn't stop thinking about the messages he'd received.

I am doing what you cannot do.

I am putting everything right.

He didn't understand what they were referring to, what Ross was getting at. He was absolutely convinced that Ross had written them, but why, for fuck's sake? It was Ross – not

Alex – who'd had knowledge of the cases that had led to the murders the police were now investigating. It was Ross and no one else who could have done something for Beata Benke in London, done something to ensure that Lovisa Wahlberg was prosecuted.

So how can all this be my fault?

Maybe he was misinterpreting the messages? Maybe they were nothing to do with those specific cases, but rather a more wide-ranging condemnation of Alex's competence as a police officer? That made more sense; he and Ross had clashed on more than one occasion.

'What are you thinking about?' Fredrika said when she'd finished her call.

'The messages.'

'I've been wondering about them too. They don't seem to fit with what we think has happened.'

'I want to know more about this daughter who's supposed to have died,' Alex said.

'But she doesn't exist. She never has.' Fredrika was tense and stressed, almost distracted, which irritated Alex.

'Maybe she exists for Ross,' he said. 'Or existed.'

Fredrika shook her head. 'No doubt he's suffered some kind of trauma. We need to find out what it was. I'm not buying this business with the daughter.'

The computer in the corner clicked and hummed, as if to protest that nobody was taking any notice of it.

'Turn the damned thing off, it's getting on my nerves,' Alex snapped.

'I'm just going to look up one more thing,' Fredrika said. Her fingers flew over the keys with her customary efficiency. She waited.

The colour drained from her face. 'Shit,' she whispered.

'Now what?'

'Henry Lindgren. You asked me to check him out.'

Alex held his breath.

Fredrika turned to face him.

'I know who he is. And so do you.'

Once upon a time Henry Lindgren had been the train attendant on an X2000 express between Gothenburg and Stockholm. A young woman, Sara Sebastiansson, had got off the train when it stopped for a while in Flemingsberg. Fredrika couldn't recall whether she'd wanted to have a cigarette or make a phone call, but anyway she'd left her little girl, Lilian, in her seat because she was fast asleep. The train moved off, leaving Sara behind on the platform, distracted by a woman pretending to need help with her dog. Henry Lindgren took it upon himself to keep an eye on Lilian until they arrived in Stockholm, and yet the unthinkable happened. When the train reached its destination, the child was gone. She was found a few days later, murdered by a lethal injection of insulin into the back of her neck.

Just like Henry Lindgren.

Fredrika was more shaken than she was prepared to admit.

Insanity. This is insanity in its purest form.

So far three people had been murdered in the same way as individuals to whom they had once had a connection and an obligation.

Malcolm Benke and his daughter.

Lovisa Wahlberg and her ex-boyfriend.

Henry Lindgren and the child he was clearly perceived to have failed on the train.

But he didn't fail her, Fredrika thought. *It wasn't his fault that Lilian disappeared.*

She allowed herself to be absorbed by the ongoing investigation. This was about preventing more murders. It was about Torbjörn Ross. But above all it was about exonerating Spencer before anyone even considered him as a suspect. Those were Fredrika's priorities.

There was no escaping the fact that another thread ran through all the cases, a thread that the murderer himself had highlighted. *Alex.* Henry Lindgren's ex-wife had found a note on the fridge in his apartment; she'd dropped it off at the station a couple of hours ago. It had reached Berlin immediately after the meeting with Fredrika and Alex, and from that moment things had happened very fast – so fast that Fredrika couldn't remember all the details.

She did, however, remember the note.

Do you understand now, Alex? I am putting everything right.

She broke down the brief message, trying desperately to grasp what the perpetrator wanted them to see.

Do you understand now?

He was looking for an answer to that question.

Do you understand now?

Now?

Now?

It had to be a reference to what the writer assumed had just happened: Alex had heard about Henry Lindgren's death.

Do you understand now – now that you know Henry Lindgren is dead?

Yes, she wanted to yell. Yes, we understand.

The whole thing made her skin crawl. The word 'now' was misleading; it was clear that Lindgren had been the first victim to die, not the last.

And yet the killer had apparently been convinced that he would be found later, after the others. And of course there could be many more. They still had no idea what had happened to Noah Johansson's brother and his family – except that Ross was somehow involved there too.

Do you understand now?

The frustration in that question was unmistakable.

One dead, two dead, three dead. Surely you must understand now, Alex?

Fredrika pushed away the message, smoothed down her hair. She never ran her hands through her hair; that would mess up her plait.

I'm so uncontrollably fucking controlled.

She wished Alex was there, but he was with Berlin, following the surveillance on Ross. Fredrika had been tasked with finding out why Ross had claimed to have a daughter. Had there ever been a child, and if so could her death have unleashed the killing spree to which they now had front-row seats?

She'd devoted a significant proportion of her life to music. She had an unusually good ear, and could reproduce virtually any piece on her violin. She had made good use of this skill in her professional life too. She could hear when someone was lying or withholding part of the truth; something jarred. Exactly the same feeling came over her when she started looking into Ross's dead daughter.

This isn't right.

She found phone numbers for both his current wife and his ex, as well as the two sons he'd had with his second wife.

This isn't right.

She tried to shake off the conviction that she was heading in the wrong direction, mainly because she couldn't work out where it had come from. Ross was the only person who tied up the whole package, the only unifying link between the victims. She felt sick when she thought about what Alex had told her Ross had said about the scars on Alex's hands.

A low blow, to say the least.

It wasn't our fault that Lilian Sebastiansson died. And it certainly wasn't Henry Lindgren's either.

At the same time she felt a bizarre gratitude for Ross's comment, because otherwise they wouldn't have been able to link him to Lindgren's murder. They still needed forensic evidence, of course, and so far they'd found nothing. Nothing. She'd never known a situation like it: a perpetrator who left the scene so clean, yet so striking. She kept on coming back to the same thought. The forensic evidence was negligible. No prosecutor would take Ross to court on the flimsy grounds they had so far.

She looked at her watch; she really wanted to go home.

She had dug and dug, but there was no trace of Ross's alleged daughter. The next move was to contact his family, but that would have to wait. They mustn't reveal that there was any kind of ongoing investigation into Ross, not under any circumstances.

So how could they move forward?

There had to be someone they could call, someone who would talk.

Fredrika went back to the notes Alex had made after his meeting with Tina Antonsson. She'd mentioned a security firm, Solid Security, said that Noah's brother Dan had asked them to deal with threats from a difficult client. Alex had wondered if it was the same firm Noah had used, the one Peder had talked about. With a sense of relief she decided to contact the security firm rather than one of Ross's relatives in the hunt for a non-existent daughter. Well, for the time being at least. They had taken action against Ross because of what Tina had told them, and her only connection was with Noah's brother and sister-in-law.

Which meant Tina was both their weakest and their strongest card.

Fredrika wasn't happy with that.

It didn't take her long to check out Solid Security: a Swedish-owned company that had started up in Stockholm almost fifteen years earlier. They operated nationwide, and as far as she could see, their customers were very satisfied. As she read she felt the darkness descend once more, because the more she found out, the more convinced she became that she'd heard about this firm before.

Spencer had mentioned it.

Spencer.

Again.

We ought to get a burglar alarm. Everyone else in inner-city Stockholm has one.

She could see him in her mind's eye, tall and straight-backed, absolutely certain that the best he could do for his family was to install an alarm system. He had waved a brochure at her, said that Solid Security had an excellent reputation.

It was only a brochure, what the hell is wrong with me?

Pure coincidence. Anything else was unimaginable, so once again Fredrika ignored the sense that something was wrong with the Torbjörn Ross line of inquiry, ignored the knot of fear in her stomach. She called Solid Security's customer-service department and asked to speak to the boss.

'What's it about and where are you calling from?' asked the woman who answered.

'I'm calling from the police, and I think two of your clients have come to serious harm.'

The outcome was entirely predictable. The boss wasn't prepared to say anything over the phone, and requested a meeting instead. Fredrika decided to head over to the office in the Freeport; she could go straight home from there.

Home to Spencer.

Who regardless of anything to do with the murders was not the person she'd thought he was.

How could you run over a young woman, then simply drive away?

She popped in to see Alex on her way out.

'Anything new?' she asked.

'You first.'

His voice was rough, his face set.

Fredrika summarised what she'd done and explained where she was going. On her own, for once – there wasn't time to bring in a colleague.

'Then I'll go home, if that's okay?'

'Fine. We'll carry on looking for Ross's daughter tomorrow.'

'So you believe she existed?' Fredrika couldn't hide the doubt in her voice.

'I'm sure of it.'

Fredrika backed out of Alex's office; she really didn't want to talk about this now.

'See you tomorrow.'

She hurried down to the car park and sped away towards the Freeport.

Solid Security had a visitors' parking area. She slammed the car door and almost ran into the building. A man of her own age came to meet her and introduced himself as Jussi. They shook hands, and he led her into a windowless room. White walls, grey fitted carpet. Someone with a serious lack of interest in interior design must have been given the job of choosing colours and materials.

'This is about two of our clients, if I've understood correctly?' Jussi began.

Fredrika liked the fact that he wasn't wasting time on small talk.

'Noah Johansson and Dan Johansson.' She handed him a piece of paper on which she had written down their ID numbers and company names.

Jussi frowned. 'I remember Dan only too well, unfortunately. A total disaster. Not for us, but for the man who'd been threatening him. But I don't understand why you mentioned his brother.'

'We have information suggesting that Noah might also have been threatened.'

'Who told you that? He's never been our client – only Dan.'

Shit. Fredrika and Alex hadn't known for sure which firm Peder had been working for when he was dealing with Noah. Alex would have to call him back, pin down the facts – and remind Peder that he needed to contact the police and tell them everything he knew about the funeral director who'd met an untimely end, because he'd clearly failed to do so.

Why?

Jussi leaned forward.

'The press haven't released a name, but I'm assuming Noah Johansson is the funeral director who was murdered yesterday?'

'Correct.'

'I'm glad you called. Obviously we're happy to help in any way we can.'

Fredrika wasn't sure how much help was to be gained from a security firm who hadn't worked with Noah, but she didn't want to offend Jussi.

'How did you view the threats against Dan Johansson?' she asked.

'Everything happened within a very short time, but when he came to us we immediately assessed the situation as dangerous. He needed protection right away, and that was what he got. Not from the police, of course, but from us.'

'Hard to provide protection when he never even reported the problem to the police,' Fredrika countered, giving Jussi a long look. He lowered his gaze, embarrassed.

'Was anyone else involved in these threats apart from the man who killed himself?' she went on.

'Not as far as we know.'

Fredrika wondered how to dig deeper without revealing confidential information.

'When were you last in touch with Dan?' She wasn't prepared to admit that they thought Dan might be missing.

'Just before New Year. I tried to call him when I heard about his brother, but I haven't managed to get hold of him.' He paused briefly. I hope nothing's happened to him too? That was what worried me when I realised Noah had been murdered.'

Fredrika hesitated.

'We have reason to believe that Dan and his family may have been abducted.'

Jussi frowned. 'But the person who was harassing him is dead.'

'Exactly, so if he has been abducted – and we don't know for sure if that's the case – then it's down to someone else. Can you tell me the name of the guy who killed himself?'

'Of course – Fredrik Mannerberg.'

Fredrika made a note, and Jussi supplied her with all the details he had.

'I'm glad you called,' he said again. 'I was going to contact the police yesterday, but I spoke to a former employee who was responsible for Dan's case, and he thought we should wait until Noah's name had been confirmed.'

'That was probably good advice. Who was this former employee, by the way? It might be interesting to hear what he has to say.'

'No problem. He used to be a police officer.'

Fredrika frowned.

'A police officer?'

'Peder Rydh – maybe you two know each other?'

Fredrika made a huge effort to control every muscle of her face, not to show her surprise.

'Rydh? Yes, we were part of the same team at one point, but that was quite a few years ago.'

Jussi reacted with interest.

'What was he like back then?'

'What was he like? Competent, hardworking – possibly a little hot-headed, but definitely one of the good guys.'

Jussi didn't respond right away; he seemed to be thinking about what to say.

'I couldn't keep him on,' he said eventually.

Fredrika straightened up. Alex had hinted that he didn't feel as if Peder had told him the whole story.

'Too many problems,' Jussi went on. 'He started with us in late summer, finished in April. At first I believed him when he said he'd left the Solomon Community because he wanted to try something different, but that wasn't the whole truth. He was so restless, so uneasy – that was what drove him. And then when his family . . . he . . . I assume you know what happened?'

Fredrika shook her head slowly. 'I don't – please tell me.'

It was Jussi's turn to shake his head now.

'It's not my place to talk about Peder's private life – you need to ask him.'

Fredrika felt a spurt of irritation. Peder's family, Peder's private life. Had he still not grown out of his very unpleasant habit of bringing his personal problems into work? Was he still allowing his marriage and parenthood to influence the way he behaved in a professional environment?

'He can be pretty immature,' she said. 'We noticed that.'

Jussi expression grew wary.

'I'm not sure what we had to deal with here could be attributed to a lack of maturity.'

Fredrika decided it was time to bring the meeting to an end.

'Just to be clear: as far as you're concerned, Peder never worked with Noah Johansson, but only with his brother Dan?'

'Exactly – but there are plenty of security firms in Stockholm. Peder could have come across Noah through a different company.'

Fredrika thought that was unlikely. Peder had worked for Solid Security, and that was where he must have been employed when he claimed that he'd had Noah – not Dan – Johansson as his client. Had he mixed up the names? Hardly.

Peder was lying.

At that moment her mobile rang: Alex.

'The surveillance team has lost Ross. We don't know where he is.'

What a day – the worst Peder could remember. He'd achieved none of the things he'd intended to get done. Work was fine about him taking time off, so that was cool. But all the rest . . .

Fuck.

His son was coughing so violently Peder thought he was in danger of bringing up his lungs. He couldn't go on like this; someone else would have to take over.

'You can go to Grandma's tomorrow,' he said, stroking the boy's back.

'Are you going to work?'

'Yes – lots to do.'

Grandma had done more than her fair share of childminding lately. *Lots to do.* It sounded so hollow, so pathetic, but it was for the boy's own good. One day when he was older he'd understand why Peder had to put in such long hours, but that could wait.

Peder's mobile rang.

'Are you okay watching TV for a few minutes while I take this?'

His son nodded.

'Drink plenty of water. Any problem, I'm in the bedroom.'

The sound of coughing followed him as he walked away.

'Peder.'

'Shalom – it's Ed.'

Peder sat down on the bed, as taut as a bowstring. Another call from a former boss. He still had a good relationship with the Solomon Community – very good, in fact. However, that didn't stop him feeling stressed whenever they contacted him.

What do you want?

'Can you talk?' Ed said.

'My son's off sick, but yes.'

'Is that him I can hear in the background? Poor kid – sounds bad.'

'Yes, it's not easy.'

The clock ticked, the seconds passed.

Get on with it, for fuck's sake.

'I'm calling about The Sanctuary.'

Peder became very still.

'Oh?'

'You recommended the current leaseholder. It's gone very well, he's always paid on time and we've had no complaints. However, he's now decided to give notice; apparently he won't need the house from the middle of September onwards.'

Peder got to his feet.

'What?'

'Yes, we were surprised too. Anyway, obviously we need to start thinking of someone new. Could you give it some thought, let me know if you come up with anyone?'

Peder was so tense that the veins in his neck were standing out.

'Absolutely.'

A new tenant for The Sanctuary. The house that God had not only forgotten, but deliberately turned his back on.

'By the way, have you any idea what he's been up to out there?' he asked, making a huge effort to keep his tone casual.

'We've made three discreet visits – without going inside, of course. We haven't noticed any deviation from our agreement. A family is living there, just as he said. Two children and their parents.'

Peder swallowed hard.

'Great. It's good to be able to help people in need.'

'It certainly is. They'd be dead by now if they hadn't found refuge in The Sanctuary, poor souls. It's wonderful that there are people around like our leaseholder, people who really want to help others.'

Peder noticed that Ed hadn't mentioned the leaseholder's name. Always the same caution, the same paranoia. It suited Peder very well. He didn't want to think about the man who'd rented the house, or why he'd given notice from the middle of September.

'If there's nothing else, I need to get back to my son.'

'I'll be in touch,' Ed said.

As soon as the call ended, Peder's mobile rang again. Alex, for the third time today. Peder didn't answer.

I already know what you want.

He wasn't happy. He opened up his laptop, skimmed the headlines. The front pages were packed with articles about the murders that had shaken Stockholm, but he couldn't find any indication that a suspect had been arrested.

He wondered how long that would remain the case.

'It's okay if you want to go home,' Alex said.

It was just after seven. Berlin looked tired, but clearly had no plans to leave. A point in her favour – a good captain is always the last to leave a sinking ship.

Alex was frustrated and exhausted.

'I don't understand why we can't find him.'

'Because he's a police officer,' Berlin commented dryly. 'He knows how to stay under the radar.'

'But is he even aware that we're following him?'

'I think that's irrelevant. He knows how easy it is to get caught; he's been so careful right from the start.'

She'd stopped adding the obligatory 'if he's actually the person we're looking for' and 'we mustn't forget that he's only a suspect at this stage'. She was no longer in any doubt.

Ivan appeared. Even he was running out of energy; the fact that things weren't progressing as quickly as he'd hoped was taking its toll.

'Not a single print,' he said. 'Not one strand of hair, not the tiniest trace of saliva. Absolutely nothing in Henry Lindgren's apartment.'

Alex couldn't keep still, couldn't stop pacing.

'It's unbelievable,' he said. 'Completely, totally unbelievable.'

Berlin sat down.

'Not if Torbjörn is our perpetrator,' she said. 'He knows exactly what to do, if you see what I mean.'

Alex nodded.

'We need to speak to the prosecutor,' Berlin went on. 'What – exactly – do we have on Torbjörn Ross right now?'

Alex felt like punching the wall.

'Nothing,' he said. 'Not one fucking thing.'

'He knew all the victims,' Ivan offered.

'Not enough,' Berlin said. She touched her glasses as if she was about to push them up on top of her head, but changed her mind.

'What about the daughter?'

'She doesn't exist,' Ivan informed her.

'Fredrika's going to do some more work on that angle tomorrow,' Alex said. 'We daren't contact Ross's current wife, but we might risk calling his ex.'

Berlin stared at a notice board on the wall, her expression distant.

'Ross went to Malcolm Benke's house on his own initiative on the morning Benke was found,' she said slowly.

'Sorry?'

'I arrived at the same time and sent him back to HQ. I told him you and Fredrika were leading the investigation, not him.'

'So why was he there?'

'I've no idea. He wasn't happy when he found out I'd given the case to someone else.'

'I suppose that's not so strange,' Alex said. 'Given that he knew Benke.'

'And that's a reason to let him lead?'

'Of course not. I'm just trying to understand how the guy thinks.'

Was he thinking? He must be, otherwise he'd never have got this far.

Four dead.

Four missing.

Possibly eight victims in total.

With more to come?

'How the fuck is this supposed to end?'

'Do we really want to know that?' Berlin said.

Ivan was leafing through a pile of documents on the table; he took out the copy of the letter Alex had found in Noah Johansson's office.

'So what do we think about this?'

Alex folded his arms and leaned back against the wall. The gravity of the situation felt like dark, swirling waters closing around him.

'What do you think, Ivan?'

'I think the murderer wrote it.'

The same thought had occurred to Alex, but somehow he wasn't satisfied with that conclusion.

'That means you also think the same person wrote the notes addressed to me.'

'Yes,' Ivan said.

'Why was the letter in Noah's office?'

'I'd say it's a codicil to a will, written by someone who's going to die. And I believe Noah's murder is linked to the fact that he had that letter on file.'

'You mean he had it all along?'

'Yes – he kept a number of wills in a secure filing cabinet, and I think the letter was in there too. The cabinet had been broken open when he was found.'

Alex took two deep breaths.

'According to your logic, the murderer is one of Noah's clients.'

'Exactly.'

'Ross isn't dying,' Berlin pointed out.

'As far as we know,' Alex said.

'But we do know that Ross wasn't a client,' Ivan added.

Silence.

'I checked,' he said. 'There was no Torbjörn Ross on his client database.'

Alex bit his lip, his irritation growing. Ivan wasn't stupid, and he was quick.

'How far back does the database go?'

Ivan looked him in the eye. 'Ten years.'

Which meant Ivan must have seen Alex and Lena's names. His face flushed slightly with embarrassment.

Berlin was getting impatient; she seemed unaware of the sudden tension in the room.

'What are you trying to say, Ivan?'

'I had the letter checked for prints. Noah's were there, and one other person's. I want to know who that other person is, because it isn't Ross.'

'What's your plan?' Alex asked.

'I need access to the wills, then we can check the prints on those against the letter to find a match. Because by definition a will is not anonymous.'

Silence once more. Alex didn't know what to say.

'How are these wills stored?' he asked eventually. 'You mentioned a secure filing cabinet.'

'Each will is in an envelope, and they're kept in suspension files in the cabinet. Some of the envelopes are sealed, some aren't.'

'And you want to open all the envelopes and ask forensics to lift prints from the original documents?'

'Yes.'

'We need to be very clear about what we intend to do with that information,' Alex said. 'We already know that we probably won't be able to link the letter to Ross.'

'I'm thinking that if we get a match on the prints, then we might be able to rule out the letter as a lead,' Ivan said. 'Depending on the identity of the writer.'

Berlin shook her head. 'Good idea, but I can't see the prosecutor agreeing.'

'From a purely legal point of view . . .' Ivan began.

'It's worth asking,' Alex insisted.

'I spoke to our helpdesk,' Berlin said. 'They're already inundated with worried callers who'd been dealing with Noah Johansson. They're fielding queries about everything from postponed funerals to unpaid invoices.'

'Didn't he have any employees?' Alex wondered.

'One assistant,' Ivan replied. 'She's on holiday, but she'll be back this evening.'

Berlin went to fetch some coffee. She stopped in the doorway and turned back.

'Contact the prosecutor. I want those wills opened; we have to find out who wrote that letter.'

B ack in the day, Spencer Lagergren had been a real roman-
tic. He still was, but he was running out of energy, and
more often than he was prepared to admit the pain in his
head was so agonising that he saw stars.

Fredrika was late home from work again. For once he
hadn't cooked a meal. She arrived at seven o'clock. The door
opened, her handbag landed on the floor. The clatter of a
coat hanger falling. He went out in the hallway as she picked
up the hanger and took off her jacket. She must have heard
him, but she didn't look up. Instead she bent down and took
off her shoes.

Something had happened.

Does she know?

That was the question he'd wrestled with for months.
Fredrika's intuition was excellent, and she'd never been stupid.
And yet she'd missed the fact that he'd spent days brooding
over his cancer diagnosis before he told her. Not that she didn't
have the right to know, but because he wanted to make all the
necessary decisions on his own. They shared everything to do
with the life they lived, but death was his and his alone.

'I can come with you to Switzerland, though?' she'd asked.

'Of course. I can't do this without you.'

His throat constricted as he waited for her to straighten

up. It seemed to take forever. She was fiddling with her shoes, her bag, her mobile. Then, at last, she stood up and met his gaze.

Any shred of doubt disappeared.

She knew.

He forced himself to smile.

'Everything all right? I haven't heard from you all day.'

She had two choices. Either she could tell him what had happened, why she hadn't been in touch. Or she could pretend that nothing had changed. In which case she ought to give him a quick kiss and head for the kitchen, saying something along the lines of: 'I'm starving, what's for dinner?'

She stood there motionless, didn't speak.

Then she gave him a quick kiss on the cheek and headed for the kitchen.

'I'm starving, what's for dinner?'

Her voice was too high and her gaze swept the room like a laser beam, as if she was searching for the quickest escape route.

But there is no escape route, not for either of us, my darling.

'How about spaghetti vongole?' she said. 'Or were you thinking of something else?'

He took a step forward. She took a step back, then realised what she'd done and moved forward again. But only half a step.

'Have we got any clams?' Spencer asked.

'I don't think so – I'll just pop down to the shop. No problem.'

No problem. Just as long as she could get out of the apartment.

Spencer felt the dark shadow of sorrow settle over him. He sat down. 'Is there something we need to talk about?'

Fredrika's mouth was a thin line, her eyes a silent scream. *For God's sake, how did it come to this?*

'No. No, nothing at all.'

She walked out of the kitchen, put on her shoes, looped her bag over her shoulder and left the apartment.

Spencer remained behind with the overwhelming feeling that his wife was afraid of him, one thought filling his mind:

If she already knew, then wouldn't it be better to bring things to a close much sooner than he'd planned?

'Ulla's showing a film this evening,' Diana said. 'The one she made about the indigenous population of Canada. It starts at nine thirty, in half an hour. We can make it if we hurry.'

Alex took a sip of his wine. Another thing to be experienced. Another thing he had to say he didn't want to do.

'You don't have to come if you don't feel like it.'

Hurrah.

'Thanks – good to know,' he said.

Diana tilted her head on one side. 'So what are you going to do while I'm out? Lie on a beach and read a book?'

He blushed and she burst out laughing. 'Seriously – you don't mind if I go, do you?'

That smile – it was still amazing.

'Not at all.'

There was no reason for Diana to ditch the aspects of her life that didn't interest Alex.

'Top-up?' he said, reaching for the wine bottle.

'No thanks.' She paused, then asked: 'Did you find out why you got that letter?' She was unable to hide her anxiety.

'No. Well, maybe. I think we're getting closer to some kind of explanation.'

'That's a relief.'

'I can't tell you much more at the moment. In fact I can't tell you anything.'

'I understand.'

'Okay.'

It was a sad little exchange, but it was difficult to bring any humour to that particular topic.

Alex got up and started to clear the table. He thought about Berlin's decision to ask for permission to open all the wills, about Fredrika's search for Ross's daughter. He thought about the fact that they had no idea where Ross had gone, or where Noah's brother and his family could possibly be. Then his phone rang and the brief lull was over.

'Torbjörn Ross is still missing,' Ivan informed him.

This wasn't what Alex had been expecting; they should have located Ross by now.

'That's not good news,' he said.

We want to know what he's up to during the hours of darkness.

'I presume you still don't want us to put out a call for him?'

'No – it's still too soon.'

Too soon?

When more people might die?

Alex ended the call with the feeling that he was standing in the middle of a storm that had no intention of abating. It was a deeply unpleasant experience.

Torbjörn Ross was driving fast. *Keep going, keep going, don't look back.* He blinked several times; he was more tired than he was prepared to admit, more stressed than he'd thought. Every so often he glanced in the rear-view mirror to confirm what he already knew: he'd managed to lose the surveillance vehicle.

He was free to do whatever he wanted.

As always.

How the hell had they worked out what he was up to? He'd killed the police investigation, made it clear that no crime had been committed. That didn't apply to Alex Recht, of course. Why did he always have to go his own way, follow his instincts? And then there was Noah, who'd emailed to tell him he'd contacted Recht. The solution to that particular problem worried Ross. He had his suspicions about who'd killed Noah, but didn't dare investigate the matter any further. Noah's death had certainly made things more difficult for him. He was going to have to work faster, bring his project to an end sooner than planned. He'd already given notice on the house, which had been a mistake. He should have waited until it was all over.

So that no one would start asking questions.

On the other hand, giving notice meant he had a clear

deadline, which was a motivating factor. His mobile lay on the passenger seat, switched off and with the battery removed. No fucker was going to find him through modern technology. Unfortunately it meant his wife wouldn't be able to reach him, which was a worry. She had a tendency to get herself into a state; if he was quiet for too long she'd call the police. Which would be very unfortunate for a number of reasons.

He'd left the motorway just under fifteen minutes ago. The road cut through dense forest; nobody would expect that anyone could live out here.

They can't – they can only die here.

He would be there soon; anxiety and irritation had made him drive much too fast.

But I have to know.

He hadn't thought it would happen so quickly. He'd run a thorough background check on the couple, knew that the man had suffered a period of severe depression a few years earlier. There was no doubt that he would break first, which was the whole point of the exercise. He had to realise that there was no way out of the hell in which he found himself, realise that he must die in order to gain redemption. And that he must take his family with him into eternity so that they could stay together.

The family. The children. Ross didn't like thinking about them. Their deaths were a necessary evil; it wouldn't have worked if he'd left them out of the equation. The punishment would have been disproportionate.

He peered through the windscreen, searching for the narrow track. If he met another car, one of them would have to reverse. Not that that was going to happen; who was he going to meet on a track no one even knew existed?

Two kilometres. That was the length of the umbilical cord between what he referred to as Nothing and the main road. Two kilometres of forest, wrapped around a well-kept secret. A place that could be transformed into paradise or hell, depending on how it was used.

'I'm hoping to provide a refuge for someone,' he'd said when he first spoke to the owners of the property.

They hadn't asked too many questions, not after he'd explained that he wanted to keep his daughter and her family safe – a lie so entirely justified that it didn't weigh him down any more than the air he breathed. And of course he'd provided an excellent reference from a trusted individual who could back up his story, quell any concerns. Ross didn't want to think about what that reference might cost him.

I still have time.

He could see the house now. White wooden panelling, small windows. There was a light on.

He parked on the drive, got out of the car and closed the door. There was no need for discretion. He was alone in the forest, he was sure of it.

His pulse rate increased as he approached the house. It always did. The feeling of having total control over other people never failed to intoxicate him, as did the knowledge that he was making the bastard pay his debt in such a perfect way.

'You're going to suffer,' he'd said when he took the man and his family to the house. 'You're going to suffer just as much as me.'

The man had protested, claimed he didn't know who Torbjörn was and why he was doing this.

'We don't even know each other, for fuck's sake!' he'd bellowed.

Torbjörn had ignored him. He could shout as much as he wanted; Torbjörn knew what was right and wrong. It wasn't his problem if the guy didn't. Not any longer.

He paused at one of the windows and looked in. They were set quite high up, and he had to stand on tiptoe. The living room was empty. The television was on, but he couldn't see either of the kids. Where the hell were they?

He took the keys out of his pocket and continued to the front door. First the entry code, then the top lock, then the bottom one. He drew his gun; he always had it in his hand when he went inside. They'd tried to ambush him once, and once only – right at the beginning before they'd realised that most of the house was monitored by CCTV cameras.

'I'm watching you all the time!' he'd yelled.

That wasn't true, however. There were no cameras in the bathroom or the main bedroom. Or the hallway, which was extremely unfortunate. Torbjörn had managed to work out what they were up to only because the two adults had positioned themselves on either side of the kitchen door. In order to reach the rest of the house from the hallway it was necessary to go through the kitchen, so it hadn't been a bad plan. If they'd stood in the hallway instead, he wouldn't have seen them. That was why his gun had to be at the ready, his mind sharp and clear.

The reason why he'd rushed over was because there had been no sign of the family for several hours. He didn't have time to analyse hours of film, nor to follow their movements in real time. All he knew was that however much he searched and switched between different cameras, he couldn't find them. His only option was to come out here to check what was going on.

He flung open the door.

'Hello?'

He took one step and almost fell over. For a moment the world turned upside down. *What the fuck?* Torbjörn staggered, regained his balance.

He blinked, trying to understand what he was looking at.

Red.

Blood.

Everywhere.

The man. With his eyes open, his throat slit.

Torbjörn inhaled sharply, felt the air get stuck halfway down his windpipe.

The woman and the children were sitting with their backs against the wall two metres in front of him. The woman was clutching a bloodstained knife, her hand shaking.

'We want to go home now,' she said.

INTERVIEW WITH ALEX RECHT
06-09-2016

Present: Interrogators one and two (I1 and I2),
Detective Chief Inspector Alex Recht (Recht)

I1: When did surveillance find Ross
that evening?

Recht: Late, very late.

I2: But you didn't pick him up?

Recht: We had good reason to believe we had more
to gain by leaving him at liberty but
under surveillance.

I2: But he already knew he was being followed.
He'd managed to shake them off once; what
made you think you'd have better luck
this time?

Recht: At that stage we didn't realise he'd
deliberately lost the tail, or that he
knew we had eyes on him. We thought we'd
just been careless. These things happen,
I'm afraid.

I1: We're aware that these things happen,
but this was particularly unfortunate,
wouldn't you say?
(silence)

I1:   We already know how the situation developed,
          but we'd like to hear your summary. Night
          fell, and you had eyes on Ross. Then what?
          (silence)

Recht: Then everything deteriorated. Everything
          and nothing. And the killing . . .
          wasn't over.

I1:   How was Bergman at this point?

Recht: Fredrika was just the same as she always
          was in a professional capacity – focused
          and brilliant.

I2:   You had no idea of what was in store
          for her?
          (silence)

Recht: No, and to be honest I'm not sure she had
          any idea either.

FRIDAY

It was gone midnight, and Fredrika was still awake. Spencer was lying motionless by her side; she could tell from his breathing that he wasn't asleep either.

He's watching me.

She kicked off the covers and got out of bed.

Spencer raised his head from the pillow but didn't say a word.

Fredrika went into the kitchen, drank some water straight from the tap. She was hot and sweaty. The weather forecast had promised thundery showers during the night. A slight pressure that had started behind her frontal bone had grown into a pounding headache.

She filled a glass with water and went into the living room. Sat down on the sofa, tucked her legs beneath her. She felt insecure. Spencer had noticed the change in her mood, but hadn't commented. That bothered her, but she was also angry.

He ran over a woman.

He left her on the road, he didn't even know whether she was dead or alive.

And now he's put everything right.

She felt like going back into the bedroom and putting the pillow over his face, pressing it down. Certain things shouldn't be kept secret within a marriage – like past crimes. Particularly if they were as serious as the one Fredrika believed Spencer had committed.

Believed.

That was a difficult word to have to use in this context. She had gone over the situation in her own mind more times than she could count.

She'd read a letter in which the writer confessed to a crime.

She believed the letter had been written by Spencer.

Which could mean that he was the murderer she and Alex were looking for.

But that probably wasn't the case. It seemed more likely that the perpetrator was Torbjörn Ross.

So why couldn't she let go of these horrific suspicions? The answer was easy: she still had no evidence that the writer had nothing to do with the murders.

I need to talk to Spencer, she thought. *I have to confront him.*

Her sorrow was as overwhelming as her anger. How could he have simply let the years go by? How could he have omitted to tell her what he'd done?

Because I wouldn't have forgiven him.

Fredrika opened up her laptop, which she'd brought home from work. She wasn't going to get any sleep tonight, not if she was sharing a bed with Spencer, so she might as well do something useful. With a bit of luck she might doze off on the sofa, then she could blame work if Spencer wanted to know why she hadn't come back to bed.

Because I don't feel safe next to you.

She opened up her notes from the meeting with Solid Security. Alex had passed on the misleading information given by Peder Rydh, and it chafed like an ill-fitting shoe. Why had he said that Noah Johansson had sought help from Solid Security, when in fact it was Dan? Why had he suggested that Noah was unreliable? And why the hell had he been fired?

She refused to waste any more energy on Peder. She decided to focus on Noah and his missing brother. That was the hardest piece of the puzzle to understand. According to the initial assessment made by the police, Dan and his family were living in Australia, but according to Noah, they'd been kidnapped. Fredrika didn't know what the investigating officer's thought process had been, but she saw no reason to doubt Noah's genuine concern.

So where did you hide an entire family?

And why not assume they were dead?

That was a challenging but important question: why start from the premise that the family were alive?

Maybe because a police officer had allegedly spoken to Dan on one occasion. However, he didn't know Dan, didn't know what he sounded like. It could have been anybody on the other end of the line.

Fredrika changed her position on the sofa. If Dan and his family had been abducted but not killed, where were they?

Ross wasn't the kind to turn his cellar into a dungeon, besides which it would take a very long time to carry out such a project, making major alterations and soundproofing the room or rooms. According to Berlin, Ross had said that his daughter had died back in the autumn. And Dan had disappeared in May.

Forget it.

So: did it have to be so complicated? Had the person who'd

taken the family really invested oceans of time in a complex building project, or did the ideal location already exist?

She shook her head, tried to get her thoughts into some kind of order.

What kind of place would it have to be? Or was the place irrelevant? Ross could have hired guards on the quiet; maybe he didn't need a nuclear bunker.

She heard Spencer leave the bedroom and go into the bathroom.

The uncertainty about what he'd done – or not done – was driving her crazy.

After a little while he stuck his head around the living-room door:

'Are you coming back to bed?'

She didn't look up. 'I have to work for a while longer.'

The clock on the wall ticked.

And yet time seemed to stand still as the man Fredrika had loved for so many years turned and walked away.

A thunderstorm raged for most of the night. One flash of lightning after another lit up the bedroom where Malin and the children had sought refuge. Malin, Hedvig and Max. There were only the three of them left now. Dan was gone, he was never coming back. The man had taken him with him when he left.

'The rest of you are staying here!' he'd yelled.

He had been badly shaken, shocked. As if Dan's death hadn't been part of his plans at all.

'No!' Malin had screamed. 'No, you can't leave us!'

The children had been so traumatised they'd stopped crying, and Malin had been unable to hold it together. She'd broken down in front of them, lost her balance on the slippery blood and ended up lying on the floor while the man dragged Dan away. Hedvig and Max had remained sitting with their backs to the wall as if they were paralysed, until Malin found the strength to get up and take control of the situation. She had to clean up the blood, calm the children. It was many hours before they fell asleep.

Now it was seven o'clock in the morning, and Malin had hardly slept. Again.

Maybe you can get used to it. Maybe you can give up sleeping.

Neither Hedvig nor Max moved when she got out of bed. She found this terrifying, and leaned over them to make sure they were breathing. They were. They were alive. So was Malin. Nothing else mattered.

Nothing else mattered.

That was how she must think from now on. As long as they stayed alive, everything else could be fixed. There were psychologists and drugs for every eventuality.

She went to the bathroom, sat down on the cold plastic toilet seat. She couldn't get rid of the pictures in her head, Dan rushing out of the closet, Dan dying, the moment when she killed him.

It was him or me and the kids.

Madness had burned like a forest fire in his eyes. It had all happened so fast that she hadn't had time to think, not when she hurled herself at him, grabbed the knife, pointed it at him.

'Go on then!' he'd shouted. 'Do it! Otherwise we're all going to die!'

There had been no opportunity to consider the best course of action, no opportunity for reflection. He'd lurched at Malin and she'd used the knife, felt it slice into his throat – so easily, meeting almost no resistance – and watched him collapse. When he sank to the floor she felt a huge sense of relief, which sickened her. Dan was dead. And Malin was *relieved.* Because she and the children had survived, because they were no longer under threat from him. The feeling disappeared almost immediately, because Dan's death didn't actually make the situation better. On the contrary – things were worse. Now she was the only adult in the house, and their debt to the man who was holding them had not been paid.

She flushed the toilet, washed her hands and returned to the bedroom.

Only then did it occur to her that the man hadn't brought any food. She ran through what was in the fridge: very little. In a few days it would be empty.

What happens then?

Surely he wasn't intending to let them starve to death?

Malin got back into bed and drew her knees up to her chin.

He can't let us starve.

He can't let us starve.

Morning briefing was held in the Lions' Den. For once it was pleasantly warm; the air conditioning had been repaired and order had been restored.

Or not.

Only those colleagues who were aware of the investigation into Torbjörn Ross had been invited. Alex signalled to Fredrika to close the blinds at the windows facing the corridor. He didn't want anyone passing by to glance in and think that he or she ought to be there.

He was chairing the meeting even though Berlin was present. She wanted to keep abreast of developments; there was a fighting spirit in her that Alex hadn't seen before. Berlin was on the attack, and it suited her.

'Where exactly is Ross right now?' Alex's question was directed at the head of surveillance.

The team had had eyes on Ross since he returned home at midnight.

'In the toilets on the third floor.'

The odd giggle could be heard around the room.

'Wonderful,' Alex said dryly. 'Absolutely wonderful.'

'Wonderful or not, that's where he is.'

'How long has he been in there?' Ivan asked.

The head of surveillance picked up his mobile and read the latest entry into the log.

'He went in six minutes ago and he's just come out.'

Fredrika smiled along with the others, but exhaustion was etched on her face. Alex couldn't help being disappointed when she passed on what she'd found out from Solid Security – both at the fact that Peder had been fired, and that he'd lied. The guy was a mess; this had gone on for years, and Alex just had to accept it. He'd thought the post with the Solomon Community would give Peder security and clear parameters, but he'd still managed to fuck up. Alex didn't know whether it was that or something else that had caused problems, but obviously family issues had cost him a job.

'Is Ross on his way here?' he asked.

'Yes, he should be here in a few minutes. He's in the lift.'

'Not on his own?' Fredrika said.

'A member of our team is with him all the time. We've brought in surveillance officers from Uppsala, so we're pretty sure he won't recognise them.'

Alex thought his colleague was wrong, but he didn't say so. He had thought long and hard about the fact that surveillance had lost Ross, and come to the conclusion that it wasn't an unfortunate mishap. Quite the reverse. Ross knew he was being followed, and there was no way he was going to lead them to a place of interest while they had eyes on him.

'I presume we've put a tracker on his car?'

'We have; the problem is that he uses other vehicles. When we lost him yesterday he was driving his wife's car.'

'His mobile?'

'Switched off.'

Alex let out a bark of laughter.

'So when he disappeared he was in his wife's car with his phone switched off? And you think he doesn't know he's under surveillance? Do me a favour.'

The room fell silent, then Ivan's phone pinged.

He got to his feet. 'Sorry, back in a minute.'

'Can't it wait?' Alex snapped. That was his way of saying that it *should* wait, but Ivan headed for the door.

'Won't be long.'

Berlin scowled as he disappeared. 'He'd better hurry up or he'll miss what I have to say about the latest decision by the prosecutor.'

'Which is?' Alex prompted her.

'Which is that he's given us the green light to open the wills.' She looked very pleased with herself. Fredrika stared at her.

'What wills?'

'This is something we discussed last night after you'd gone home,' Alex informed her. 'There are fingerprints on the letter I found in Noah Johansson's office, but they don't match anything in our database. Ivan thinks the letter was written by one of Noah's clients, who has also deposited a will with Noah.'

'So we need access to the wills to see if we can match the fingerprints,' Berlin added.

Fredrika was still staring at Berlin as if she'd just said something utterly incomprehensible. She took a sip of water, then put down her glass with a bang.

'We have at least four murder victims. Malcolm Benke, Lovisa Wahlberg, Henry Lindgren and Noah Johansson. Dan Johansson and his family might also be dead, we don't know. But we do know that we have little or no forensic evidence. We don't have a single fingerprint from any of the crime scenes, or a trace of DNA, or a single witness. And yet we think the perpetrator is so fucking clumsy that he's left his prints on a letter that's essentially a confession? Really?'

Her outburst took Alex by surprise.

'We know all that, but surely we have to look into the letter before we can eliminate it?'

Fredrika swallowed.

'Of course. I just mean we shouldn't waste time on the letter as a way of linking Noah's death to the others. We already have a connection through his brother.'

Alex didn't take his eyes off her.

'It can hardly do any harm to check out the wills.'

'Maybe not.'

There was no time for guessing games, no time for mutiny. Alex didn't know what was upsetting Fredrika, but if she wasn't prepared to talk, then she would be overruled.

'Let's move on,' he said.

Ivan reappeared.

'So the prosecutor's agreed that we can open the wills,' Alex told him.

But Ivan wasn't listening. His cheeks were pink with pleasure.

He looks like a child.

'Good news?' Berlin asked.

'I'm going to meet a man who owns an antiquarian book-shop. I rang around several second-hand and antiquarian shops, asked if they were familiar with Sander's book, and if they'd sold any copies recently. This guy sold five copies a few weeks ago.'

Alex could have cheered.

'How come he had five copies?' Fredrika asked dubiously.

'He's the author's grandson.'

Alex slammed his fist down on the table in sheer euphoria. Something was happening at last!

'Well done, Ivan. Show him a picture of Ross – if we can secure a positive ID, we've got him.'

In his peripheral vision he could see that the colour had drained from Fredrika's face for the second time in minutes.

'Do you realise what this means?' she said.

Berlin sighed. 'That we're even closer to our perpetrator.'

Our perpetrator, Alex thought. *Not Ross.* Berlin still had her doubts.

Still.

'Not just that,' Fredrika said. 'Five books. Five. We've found only two.'

Everyone froze.

'There must be one in Henry Lindgren's apartment.' Alex's voice was suddenly hoarse.

'There was a delivery note,' Ivan recalled. 'The postman had tried to deliver a thick package, but it wouldn't go through the letterbox, so he took it back to the sorting office.'

'That's the book. Henry was supposed to receive it before he died, but he didn't pick it up in time.'

In time for his own death, in time for his murderer to get into his apartment.

'Should we put out a warning?' Berlin wondered.

'Are you crazy?' It wasn't exactly polite, but Alex didn't care. 'We have nothing to suggest that these books are being given out with a particular degree of forward planning, plus there would be total chaos if we issued such a warning.'

'On the other hand, there could be chaos if we don't,'

Berlin countered. 'We'll be in a very difficult position if there are more deaths.'

'There won't be,' the head of surveillance stated firmly. 'That's why we're keeping a close eye on Ross.'

'Yes, that's gone really well so far,' Fredrika said quietly.

Her colleague gave her a dirty look, full of excuses no one wanted to hear.

'Henry Lindgren,' she went on. The note on his fridge. I can't stop thinking about the sentence "Do you understand now, Alex?" It sounds like a plea. The perpetrator wants us to see something that's clearly passing us by.'

Alex spread his hands wide.

'I'm so sick of these guessing games!'

He'd also wondered about that sentence; it had haunted him during the night. *Do you understand now, Alex?*

No, he had to confess. He didn't understand. And he couldn't help feeling that the day he did understand he would be deeply, deeply unhappy.

It was decided that Fredrika would accompany Ivan to the bookshop in the Söder district. She didn't say a word during the entire journey. She drove, while Ivan sat in silence in the passenger seat, staring out of the window. He was clearly uncomfortable, but Fredrika did nothing to alleviate the situation. She'd spent the night on the sofa; she was worn out, but totally focused on the tasks ahead.

First of all she wanted to be absolutely sure that it was Ross rather than someone else who'd bought Morgan Sander's books. Then she wanted to get to the bottom of the story of Ross's dead daughter.

She'd put all other thoughts aside for the time being. She couldn't keep brooding over what Spencer had done, couldn't think about the letter found in Noah's office. And she definitely couldn't face worrying about what would happen when they took fingerprints from all the wills and compared them with those on the letter. Why did Ivan have to be so keen?

A young girl had once accused Spencer of forcing her to have sex with him in exchange for good grades. He had been arrested, held in custody, and eventually released, completely exonerated. Fredrika wondered how it would end this time, and how she would cope if he went to prison.

She parked outside the bookshop.

'You're not allowed to park here,' Ivan pointed out.

'Right.' She got out of the car, yanked open the shop door and was overwhelmed by the smell of dust and old books. She usually loved books, she'd spent thousands of hours in libraries when she was growing up. So many good habits, lost over the years.

'Are you Jan?' she heard Ivan say. He was talking to an elderly gentleman with his glasses perched on the end of his nose.

'I am.'

Fredrika wondered if Ivan had realised the same as she had.

The man was blind. Why he was wearing glasses she had no idea; he couldn't see a thing.

Fuck.

Ivan hesitated.

'My name is Ivan Nilsson, and this is my colleague Fredrika Bergman. I'm the one who called you about Morgan Sander.'

Jan nodded eagerly and held out his hand. Fredrika shook it first, then Ivan.

'That was the strangest thing! I mean, we don't even have those books on display; they were in a box up in the loft. They'd been there ever since Father died.'

'You're Morgan Sander's son, not his grandson?' Fredrika said.

Jan raised his eyebrows. 'I'm much too old to be Morgan's grandson.'

'I must have misunderstood when we spoke.' Ivan glanced at Fredrika, wanting to bring the conversation to a close as quickly as possible. This was a waste of time.

'When did you first meet the man who wanted to buy the books?' Fredrika asked.

'He came in one day towards the end of June, after Midsummer. I remember him well; he had a very pleasant voice. He called first, asked about the books. When I told him I'd be happy to sell him five, he was absolutely delighted.'

'So how many copies did you have to begin with? Before you sold those five?'

Fredrika instinctively liked the old man. There was nothing devious about him; he was honest and straightforward.

'Ten, but we wanted to keep the other five.'

Fredrika looked around. The shop was quiet; there was no sign of anyone else.

'You said "we". Who else works here?'

Jan laughed. 'My son and I run the business. I had poor eyesight for many, many years, but when I went blind two years ago I couldn't manage on my own. He'll be back soon – he's just popped out.'

'Did your son meet the man who bought the books?'

'I'm afraid not.'

'Did he say why he wanted them?' Ivan asked.

'Not exactly. He said he needed them for his wife. I assumed she was some kind of collector. It's not my place to poke around in other people's private affairs.'

Fredrika smiled. 'Of course not.' She thought about what Jan had just said: the man needed the books for his wife.

For his wife?

Ivan wasn't prepared to give up. 'Was there anyone else in the shop at the same time? Anyone who might be able to give a description of the customer?'

'No, but I do remember his aftershave. It's the same one my son-in-law uses – Boss.'

Boss?

It wasn't a fragrance Fredrika associated with either Spencer or Ross. She shifted awkwardly from foot to foot, unable to shake off the feeling that they were heading in the wrong direction.

Then Ivan had an idea.

'If I play you a voice, do you think you might be able to tell us if it belongs to the man who was here?'

'Absolutely.'

Ivan took out his phone and searched for a TV inter-view Ross had given a year or so ago in connection with another investigation.

'Okay, here we go.'

Ross's voice was loud and clear.

'*As I've already said, I'm afraid the police are unable to confirm that ...*'

Jan pursed his lips and shook his head.

'No, he definitely wasn't the one who bought the books. Not a shadow of a doubt.'

Fredrika shook her head. *Shit.*

'Are you certain?'

'One hundred per cent.'

Ivan and Fredrika thanked Jan and left. It wasn't Ross who'd bought the books. It was a different man.

Sometimes things happened unbelievably fast. Therese, a member of the Solomon Community, expressed an interest in The Sanctuary, wanted to use it as a writer's retreat during the winter months. Ed, the head of security who was responsible for the house, said that was fine as long as no one who was in need of protection contacted them in the meantime. He was always pleased when problems solved themselves. Therese was the daughter of one of Ed's colleagues; that was how she had become part of the small circle who knew about The Sanctuary and its prerequisites.

He arranged a meeting with her to underline the importance of not inviting any visitors to the property.

'We regard The Sanctuary as our ultimate secure bastion,' he said with deadly seriousness. 'It's a place where those in dire need of a safe haven can go. If such a situation arises you will have to move out immediately. On rare occasions we allow people outside the family to use it.'

The family was his name for the Jewish people. The man currently leasing The Sanctuary was not a member of the family, but he was trusted because Peder Rydh had recommended him so highly. He was a middle-aged detective inspector with many years' experience in keeping quiet about things that must not be said out loud. Ed had immediately seen the advantages of signing a contract with this particular individual.

'I understand,' Therese said. 'As I said, I'm planning to write a horror novel, and I think the isolated spot will be just perfect.'

She smiled. Ed smiled back.

'You'll need to sign a confidentiality agreement.'

'I realise that. Would it be possible to see the place? Mum didn't have any pictures to show me.'

That didn't surprise Ed; there weren't any.

'No problem. I could drive you over there now, but we won't be able to go inside.'

'Because?'

'Because the house is occupied; we have a family living there. It's part of the contract that only the tenant or tenants will enter the house, unless of course we find out that something untoward is going on. Then the agreement no longer applies.'

Therese glanced at her watch.

'Okay, I've got time now – let's go.'

The stillness in the glade where The Sanctuary was located was always overwhelming. No cars, no people, only the forest and the land and the animals that belonged there. As Ed and Therese got out of the car they caught a glimpse of two roe deer.

'Fantastic!' Therese exclaimed.

She inhaled deeply, almost as if she were tasting the fresh air.

'Will you be all right on your own when it's dark?' Ed wondered.

'I think so.'

The sky was overcast, but there was no wind. On the whole it was quite a pleasant day.

'Couldn't we ring the bell, ask if they'd mind letting us in?'

Ed looked at the closed front door. 'No.'

The house was in darkness; there appeared to be no lights on, which worried Ed. If the family had already moved out, he should have been informed. Maybe it would be a good idea to ring the bell after all? Check things out? Then he thought about the tenants and their history. The man who'd rented The Sanctuary had told Ed how much his daughter had suffered, how abusive her husband had been. It was of the utmost importance that she and her children were allowed to rest, to feel safe.

Apparently they would be able to return to normality in the autumn.

'You know how difficult it is to secure a conviction for that kind of behaviour,' the man had said. 'Women aren't safe even if they get away in time. Because there's no such thing as "in time" for them.'

Ed knew exactly what the man was talking about, and was happy to help. However, he couldn't help wondering what kind of life the tenants were living. He came over regularly just to make sure that everything was okay, but the family never seemed to go outside. Not the leaseholder's daughter, nor her children or her new partner. They were always indoors. Ed couldn't understand it.

'There's a lake a few hundred metres away,' he told Therese. 'I can show you the way through the forest if you feel like a walk.'

She nodded, and Ed set off through the tall trees. Therese

Ed reacted instinctively; he ran straight into the water.

It was a man.

A man.

Where the hell had he come from?

Ed turned the body over, dragged it towards the shore. He recognised the man, knew he'd seen him before. Only from a distance, and only through the windows of The Sanctuary, but it was definitely him.

The man with the gaping wound in his throat was one of the people who had sought refuge in The Sanctuary.

followed; after a couple of minutes she laughed and co
mented that it wouldn't be easy to find the way back.

'There's no proper track!'

'You have to keep an eye on the direction,' Ed explained.
'It's to the west of the house.'

That clearly didn't help; it just made Therese laugh
even more.

'You're not bringing me out here to kill me, are you?
Remember, I write horror novels.'

Ed glanced at her and to his relief saw that her eyes were
sparkling. She definitely wasn't scared of him.

'Not far now.'

'Can you fish in the lake?'

'You certainly can.'

They passed a grove of overgrown fir trees, then the lake
opened up before them. The surface of the water was dark
and looked strangely hard without the wind to cause ripples.
As if you might knock yourself out if you tried to dive in.

'It's a good place to swim too – there's a little beach,' Ed
said, pointing.

'Okay.' Therese didn't look as if she had the least interest
in swimming.

'Time to head back.'

Therese didn't move; she stood there motionless, gazing
out across the water.

'There's something floating out there.'

At first Ed couldn't see anything, then he spotted a jacke
A jacket floating on the surface.

'That's odd.'

Therese moved closer to the water's edge.

'Oh my God, it's a body!'

When the first car arrived, Malin was sure that the man in the Wellingtons had come back. Panic made her want to scream. It was over now, she realised that. The man had made his decision. He wasn't going to let her or the children go. Not now Dan was dead; there would be too much explaining to do.

She ran to the bedroom window, trying to see whether he was armed with anything other than the pistol. To her surprise she saw a different man, someone she didn't recognise. And a young woman. She looked strong and healthy, and she beamed when she got out of the car and looked at the house.

As if she wanted to live there.

Malin didn't know what to do. Who were they? Could she trust them?

Will they be able to hear me if I bang on the window?

Her thought processes were too slow. The man was pointing, explaining something to the woman, then they set off through the forest, disappeared. Malin remained where she was, arms dangling by her sides. Should she take a risk? Hope the couple didn't have anything to do with the man who'd kept them here? If so she would be a fool if she didn't seize the opportunity to try and communicate with them.

She turned away. The children were dozing on the bed;

they'd refused to eat or drink. Malin was planning to give them a couple of hours, then she'd have to force-feed them.

'I'm going downstairs for a little while. Back soon.'

They didn't react as she left the room. Her legs only just carried her down the stairs; she had grown so weak.

She went into the living room, positioned herself by the window overlooking the drive where the car was parked. They wouldn't leave it there, they had to come back.

The house was totally silent. She thought about switching on the TV, just to bring a little life into the place, but she couldn't be bothered. She had lost so much energy, lost so much of the person she used to be.

And I thought that everything could be fixed.

There was a horrible stench coming from the hallway. She had mopped it several times, but the smell of blood had seeped into the floor, and she couldn't get rid of it. She felt nauseous, wanted to go into another room, further away.

But I can't.

She waited and waited. Minutes passed, or was it hours? She'd lost all sense of time, but suddenly they were back. The man was soaking wet.

As if he'd been swimming.

With his clothes on.

Malin raised her hands, placed her palms against the cold pane of glass. The one she'd tried to smash with a plant pot.

'Hello!' she shouted.

But the man and woman didn't see her. They got in the car and drove off at speed.

Leaving Malin behind.

I have become invisible. No one can see me any more.

*

Time passed. Time that Malin was unable to count in minutes or hours. She stayed where she was at the window, palms resting on the glass. There wasn't a sound from upstairs. The children were sleeping. Or had they died while she was standing at the window? She began to cry, tore herself away and ran up to the bedroom.

Hedvig was lying on her back, staring at the ceiling. Max was on his side with his mouth open, eyes closed. They were both alive. Neither of them reacted when she walked in.

'Hedvig, wouldn't you like something to eat?' Malin wasn't even sure when she herself had last eaten.

No response.

Malin perched on the edge of the bed and stroked her daughter's hair.

'How about a drink then? Don't you want a drink?'

Hedvig's eyes filled with tears, which slowly trickled down the sides of her face.

Malin swallowed hard, fighting back her own tears. She focused her mind on the man and woman who'd arrived in the car. They'd seen something in the forest, something that had made them take off in a hurry. Maybe that meant they'd come back, or raise the alarm and send someone else?

I have to be ready. Anything could happen now.

As if it hadn't already.

She got to her feet, legs shaking, and went back down to the living room. The TV remote was on the coffee table. She picked it up, weighed it in her hand. It wasn't heavy, but it would have to do.

When they come back, they're going to hear me.

She tapped on the window pane with the remote. The sound she made was negligible; it certainly wouldn't be heard outside. She banged harder, felt her fingers cramp. It didn't matter, she just kept on banging. Even though no one was there, even though no one could hear except her.

And the children.

I'll frighten them.

But Malin couldn't stop. She carried on hammering. Pale red marks began to spread across the glass. She knew she was making her hands bleed. It didn't matter.

I don't need them any more.

'Mummy?'

Malin hadn't realised that Hedvig had come down to see what was going on.

'What are you doing, Mummy?'

Malin hammered and hammered and hammered.

Hedvig tried to grab her arms.

'Stop it, Mummy! Stop it!'

Malin could hear that her daughter was crying, but she was in a trance, she thought she would lose her mind if she left her place at the window.

'Let go of me! Let go!'

Hedvig slumped to the floor. She was sobbing so loudly that Malin couldn't concentrate. She closed her eyes, felt her energy begin to drain away. Her movements slowed, her hands throbbed with pain.

I'm giving up. We're never going to get out of here.

That was when the cars came. First one, then another. Malin tried to wipe away the blood; had she actually gone mad? Was she seeing things that weren't there?

'Hedvig,' she whispered. 'Get up, Hedvig. Can you see what I see? Police cars. There are police cars outside!'

Then she began hammering on the window once more.

The bad news came thick and fast. First of all Fredrika called: the man who'd bought the five books by Morgan Sander was not Torbjörn Ross. Then Berlin informed Alex that the head of security with the Solomon Community had called the police with regard to a suspected murder in a house that belonged to the Community, but was currently being rented by a Detective Inspector Torbjörn Ross.

Alex stood there as if he'd been struck by lightning.

'Another death.'

'Another death,' Berlin confirmed.

'Does Ross know that the Solomon Community has contacted us?'

'No, and I made it very clear that that can't happen. Not until we've taken a look at the house.'

'Do we know who the victim is?'

Berlin nodded and placed a print-out of a photograph in front of Alex. He didn't recognise the man at first; he'd been in the water for almost twenty-four hours, and the face was bloated.

'I don't . . .'

'Dan Johansson.'

Alex blinked.

'Shit,' he whispered.

Berlin picked up the photograph.

'What about the rest of the family?' Alex asked.

Berlin looked shaken.

'Still alive. The head of security called the emergency services and reported what had happened. The first patrol car got out there pretty quickly, but . . . apparently it's impossible to gain access to the house.'

'What do you mean?'

'Exactly what I say. The place has top-level protection against any form of intrusion. It's impossible to force the doors or windows without resorting to a degree of violence that would risk injuring those inside. The officers on site have seen a woman and two children through the windows. They described the woman as hysterical, not surprisingly. We have two cars with members of our team on the way – we'll see what they find.'

Alex felt drained of energy by what he'd just heard.

'I don't understand what kind of house Ross has rented.'

'It's the Solomon Community's safe house. Ross told them he wanted it for his daughter and her family.'

Alex had no idea what to say, what to think.

'But Ross told you his daughter was dead. And Fredrika hasn't been able to find any trace of a daughter, dead or alive.'

'Absolutely, but this is the second time he's brought up this alleged daughter.'

'So why is he pretending that Dan Johansson's wife is . . .'

'I don't know,' Berlin interrupted him.

'Sorry, I'm just thinking out loud. What do we do now?'

'Wait to hear from our colleagues when they arrive at the house.'

'And Ross?'

'He's in his office. If he tries to leave the building, the surveillance team will arrest him.'

There was a knock on the door and one of the admin assistants came in.

'Excuse me, but we've just received a large box of envelopes from Noah Johansson's funeral business.'

'The wills. Send it down to forensics,' Berlin said.

Alex wasn't happy. 'I don't like this. Not one little bit. How the hell did the Solomon Community get tangled up in this mess?'

'It's extremely unfortunate. Could Ross have worked for them at some point?'

'Why would he have done that?'

'He must know people there – otherwise how would he have been allowed to rent their safe house?'

Alex frowned, thought about Peder Rydh who was no longer answering his phone. Who was so unreliable that he'd been sacked from his previous post.

And yet he said:

'Peder worked for the Community for a number of years; he might be able to help us.'

'Good idea.' Berlin sounded distracted.

'We need to question the head of security too, of course. Find out exactly what kind of house it is and why they decided to rent it to Ross.'

'I did a bit of digging, but I don't really understand . . . The house doesn't exist.'

'Doesn't exist?' Alex repeated.

'Not as far as I was able to ascertain.'

A house that didn't exist. A dead man who was Dan Johansson.

'I'll call Peder. Then we need to have a chat with the Solomon Community.'

Peder Rydh was in the car when his phone rang. He glanced at the display: Alex. Again. He rejected the call. It rang again immediately, but this time it wasn't Alex.

'Yes?'

'Shalom,' Ed said. 'Have you got time to meet up?'

The words indicated that it was a question, but the tone of voice made it clear that it was an order.

We are going to meet up.

Now.

'What's happened?'

'I'd prefer not to discuss the matter over the phone.'

Peder was heading north, and was just about to leave the motorway.

'In that case it'll have to wait. I'm busy at the moment.'

Ed wasn't used to Peder being difficult.

'Have you spoken to your former colleagues in the last hour or so?'

Peder stiffened. Alex had called far too many times; had he contacted Ed directly? Peder carried on trying to duck and dive.

'No.'

'Well, maybe you should.'

Peder felt a spurt of irritation.

'Just tell me what's going on, for fuck's sake! I don't have time to play games!'

'You remember recommending your colleague as a tenant for The Sanctuary? The one who wanted to provide a refuge for his daughter?'

Peder was clutching the steering wheel so tightly that his fingers hurt.

'Yes.'

This might be worse than he'd thought.

'I made a mistake,' Ed said. 'And so did you. The man who was living in the house has been found dead. By me.'

Peder had no idea what to say. 'I don't understand. Who's dead?'

'I just told you – the man who was living in the house with his family.'

'You killed him?'

Ed exploded.

'Of course I didn't fucking kill him! I went out to the house to show it to the daughter of a colleague who was interested in renting it as a writing retreat. And we found a dead body in the lake. Do you realise what kind of problems this creates for us?'

Shit.

Why was nothing ever straightforward?

Peder ended the call, switched off his phone and left the motorway at the next exit. Then he headed south, back to the city.

'I'm sorry to bother you, but my name is Fredrika Bergman and I'm from the police. I wonder if we could have a little chat?'

Fredrika hadn't wanted to lose any time, and had gone straight from the bookshop to Torbjörn Ross's ex-wife. Standing outside the door of Mimmi Ross's apartment, she couldn't remember why she'd made the decision. What did lost time matter? They were running around in circles, chasing shadows, taking the wrong turn.

It must be Ross, so who the hell was the man who wanted five copies of Morgan Sander's book for his wife?

Mimmi was a very composed person. She looked at Fredrika for quite a while before letting her into her two-room apartment in Årsta. Fredrika took off her shoes and followed Mimmi into the living room. A small sofa, two small armchairs, a small coffee table. A doll's house for a grown woman.

She sat down in one of the armchairs, felt her body protest at having to keep still. Not constantly moving made her nervous, she needed to be on her way to somewhere else, a place where everything was just the way it used to be, where the letter she believed Spencer had written didn't exist.

Why don't I confront him? she thought for the thousandth

time. And for the thousandth time she answered her own question: *Because I don't think I want to hear what he has to say.*

She explained briefly why she'd come to see Mimmi. In the end she had to lie; the truth was too brutal.

We've got your ex-husband under surveillance, because we think he's murdered several people. What was it like being married to him?

'So Torbjörn's under investigation,' Mimmi said slowly.

'Yes. Unfortunately I can't give you any further details, but ... I'm not quite sure how to put this, but there are a couple of points we think you might be able to help us with.'

Mimmi raised her eyebrows. She had just turned sixty-five, but Fredrika thought she looked older. She had retired about four years earlier, and Fredrika couldn't for the life of her imagine how she passed her time in this tiny apartment.

'How long were you and Torbjörn married?'

'Two years.'

'Is that all?'

'Yes – we both realised it was a mistake. Then he met Sonja, and they're still married of course.'

'How old were you when you got married?'

'I'd just turned twenty-seven.'

'You didn't have children?'

Fredrika already knew the answer, but had decided to ask anyway.

Because somewhere there was a young woman whom Ross referred to as his daughter.

'No. No, we didn't.'

Fredrika allowed herself a moment to think, to search for the right words.

'How many children does Torbjörn have?'

For a moment Mimmi seemed uncomfortable. She turned her face away, fixed her gaze on the wall.

'Two.'

'Two,' Fredrika repeated. 'You're thinking of his sons with Sonja?'

Mimmi looked back at her.

'Why are you asking me about things you already know?'

She was clearly irritated, and Fredrika felt embarrassed by her own lack of clarity, asking awkward questions of someone who lived a lonely life.

'Because I believe there's a different answer. At least according to Torbjörn himself,' she said.

Mimmi was clearly astonished.

'What? Has Torbjörn said that he and I ... that we had a child?'

Fredrika smoothed down her trousers.

'We don't know who Torbjörn had a child with. Maybe you, maybe someone else, but according to him there is, or was, a daughter. And I'm wondering if you know anything about her?'

Mimmi leaned back on the sofa. Fredrika suddenly became aware of the clock ticking on the wall, and all at once the room seemed even smaller.

'Maria,' Mimmi whispered.

'Sorry?'

'Maria. That was her name.'

Fredrika felt her pulse rate increase.

'Did she live abroad?'

Why isn't she registered as a Swedish citizen?

'No, no, she lived here in Stockholm, but her mother didn't

like Torbjörn. They were together for only a short time, just before he and I met. She didn't tell him she was pregnant; she preferred to bring the child up on her own. Or rather with her new boyfriend. I'm not sure if he – the new guy – realised what the situation was; maybe he couldn't count, or he didn't know how long a pregnancy lasts. Or maybe he didn't mind.'

'You mean his name went on the birth certificate?'

'That's exactly what I mean.'

'But Ross knew he was the father?'

'We'd been married for about twelve months when he saw her in town, pushing a buggy. The girl was about two years old. At first Torbjörn didn't react, but his grasp of maths and biology was excellent. He checked the child's date of birth, and the only possible conclusion was that his ex had been pregnant when they split up. He went to see her, demanded to know if the girl was his. She told him the truth, but that was the only time.'

'I don't understand – the only time?'

'Torbjörn went to see her again with the aim of sorting out the legal side of things; he wanted the right to call himself the child's father. At that point his ex changed her story completely, denied everything. Torbjörn threatened her with a court case and God knows what, but this was almost forty years ago; it wasn't so easy to investigate such matters back then, and in the end he had to give up. She threatened him with an injunction if he didn't stay away, and that was that. But he never forgot Maria.'

Fredrika tried to take it all in. So Torbjörn had found out that there was a child who was his, a child who lived in the same city, yet he had no right to see her.

'Was that why you divorced?' she asked Mimmi.

'Yes. He changed completely; there was no reasoning with him. I'm shocked to hear that he's talked about his daughter. As far as I'm aware, he never mentioned her.'

Fredrika lowered her gaze, then looked up again.

'It only happened once. He told our boss that his daughter had died.'

Mimmi nodded. 'So I heard. I meet up with Torbjörn occasionally; the last time was back in the autumn, just after Maria died. He was terribly upset.'

Fredrika stared at a book on the coffee table – an old Sidney Sheldon novel.

'How did she die?'

'You should know that if you're a police officer. She was murdered.'

Fredrika straightened up.

'Murdered? By whom?'

Mimmi took a deep breath.

'It's such a terrible story. Her own husband killed her – and their children too.'

The wheels were beginning to turn in Fredrika's brain.

'He murdered the whole family?'

'Yes, then he took his own life. Apparently he had psychological problems; he'd tried to get help, but it didn't work out. Torbjörn swore that he'd find whoever was responsible for letting Maria's husband down, and hold him to account.'

Fredrika didn't say a word; she was busy processing what she'd just heard.

'I don't know if he managed it,' Mimmi added.

Dan Johansson. Noah's brother, who had misdiagnosed a patient, and who had been missing since May.

The circle was closed.

'I think he did,' she said. She got to her feet and thanked Mimmi for her time.

'What shall I say if I see Torbjörn?' Mimmi asked as Fredrika opened the front door. 'Can I tell him you've been here?'

'No.'

Fredrika ran to her car. Her phone rang just as she was about to start the engine.

'We need to get over to the Solomon Community,' Alex said.

Things were happening fast – so fast that lunchtime simply disappeared, so fast that none of them had time to think. Alex continued his conversation with Fredrika on the phone as he sped towards the Solomon Community, and she told him what she'd learned from Mimmi. As he pulled up he received another call, informing him that the police had finally gained access to The Sanctuary. The woman had given her name as Malin Johansson; she had a number of fractures to both hands, but otherwise she and her two children were unharmed. Physically, at least. Their mental health was another matter. Their stay in the house hadn't been voluntary; none of them had set foot outside for almost two months.

Unbelievable. Sick, Alex thought.

He didn't like having to come back here. The Solomon Community had mourned two dead children and a preschool teacher; was more grief about to come their way?

Fredrika met him at the main door, and listened in horror to the latest news.

'I don't understand how Ross chooses his victims,' she said. 'I mean seriously, it doesn't make sense. It would have been understandable if he'd gone for those he held responsible for his daughter's death – at least as far as the selection process goes. But Malcolm Benke, Lovisa Wahlberg, Henry Lindgren?'

'I guess the job is the common factor. Ross has worked on various cases where he's felt that certain people have got away scot-free, and now he's putting everything right. To use a rather overworked phrase.'

'Very overworked. Which leads us to Morgan Sander and his book – what's he got to do with all this? Why that particular book?'

'Torbjörn Ross doesn't strike me as someone who has a particularly strong interest in literature,' Alex said. 'Could it be his wife who provided him with the inspiration, purely by chance?'

'Maybe. I expect we'll find out sooner or later.'

They'd asked Ivan to check out the information provided by Mimmi Ross. It didn't take him many minutes to confirm the basics. The woman who'd been murdered by her husband, Dan Johansson's former client, had indeed been called Maria. Her parents lived out in Danderyd, and Ivan was on his way over there with a colleague to interview them.

'What if the mother insists that Ross wasn't Maria's birth father?' Fredrika said. 'She might even claim that she doesn't know anyone by the name of Torbjörn Ross.'

'Then we carry out a DNA test if necessary.'

A security guard emerged and checked their ID carefully before letting them in. It was just like before: the security system was testimony to the fact that the Community was part of a persecuted people.

They were shown into the head of security's office, and Ed asked them to sit down.

'Tell us about the house.' Alex got straight to the point.

Ed moved the desk mat in front of him a fraction.

'Can I rely on your discretion? The Sanctuary is important to us. It would be unfortunate if its existence and location became widely known.'

Alex couldn't have cared less.

'Build a new house. Preferably one that actually has an address and appears on a map.'

Ed folded his arms.

'Start talking,' Alex snapped. 'Torbjörn Ross – how did you come into contact with him?'

'He got in touch with us, asked about the house, wondered if it would be possible to rent it.'

'How did he know about the house in the first place?' Fredrika said. 'You can't exactly see it from the street.'

'He was fishing on the lake; I think he came ashore for a pee, then decided to go for a walk.'

'And stumbled across The Sanctuary.'

'Yes, and not only that – our former head of security happened to be there, and they knew each other. Apparently they used to work together.'

Alex's eyebrows shot up. 'When was this?'

'Last summer.'

'And what was the name of your head of security?'

Ed's eyes narrowed. 'You already know that.'

'Peder Rydh,' Fredrika said.

'Exactly.'

'As I understand it, The Sanctuary has always been a well-kept secret. What did Peder tell Torbjörn Ross?'

'Not much, but Ross worked it out for himself.'

'Then what?'

Ed sighed impatiently.

'Ross contacted Peder again. Six months had passed since

they'd bumped into each other at the house, and Peder was no longer working for us. However, he and I had kept in touch, and he knew The Sanctuary was empty. Ross was wondering if he could rent it; he had a daughter who was abroad at the time, but when she came back to Sweden she would need protection, a place to hide. Peder passed his request on to the Community, and we decided to say yes.'

Alex and Fredrika exchanged glances as they tried to sort out the timeline without saying too much. Fredrika took the lead.

'When exactly did Ross ask to rent the house?'

'In February. He came to see it in April, but didn't move his daughter in until the end of May.'

'Did he pass on his daughter's personal documentation?' Ed was clearly irritated.

'Yes, but it was of no interest to me. Ross told me a very personal and tragic tale, which Peder confirmed. The girl's mother hadn't allowed Ross to be registered as her father, so someone else's name was on the birth certificate. She was living under threat, so her details were protected anyway. The name didn't get us very far; I mean, Malin Johansson is pretty common in Sweden.'

'Isn't it just,' Alex said.

He could have added that Ross's daughter wasn't called Malin Johansson, that his daughter was dead, and that Malin had completely different parents.

This doesn't make sense.

How could Peder have confirmed that Ross was related to the woman he alleged he was trying to protect? They didn't even know each other. Alex took out his mobile, hoping there would be a missed call from Peder. Nothing.

'It seems as if the Community puts a great deal of trust in Peder Rydh,' Fredrika remarked.

'We do indeed, and I can't see any problem with that. He was an outstanding head of security, and we miss him.'

I can't see any problem with that.

Strange. And Peder's continued absence and lack of contact were even stranger.

He's got himself into some kind of trouble again. Same old same old. And now he's ashamed of himself, trying to hide away.

'The man I pulled out of the lake,' Ed continued. 'I assume he was living in The Sanctuary too?'

'Yes, his name was Dan Johansson. He was married to Malin.'

'Ross's daughter.'

'Ross doesn't have a daughter,' Fredrika said.

Ed frowned and his face lost some of its colour.

'You never met the family?' Alex asked.

'No.'

'We'll need to speak to you again.'

'Hang on a minute – so who were the people Ross lent the house to if they weren't his daughter's family?'

'He didn't lend the house to anyone. The family were not there of their own volition. They were being held captive by Ross for reasons I can't go into right now.'

Ed's face froze, his expression betraying a mixture of shock and anger.

'Just tell me if Rydh's mixed up in this too,' he said.

'We have no reason to suspect his involvement at this stage,' Fredrika reassured him.

However, Alex could see what she was thinking. Peder

was the kind of person who made mistakes, then refused to take responsibility. The fact that he wasn't a suspect needn't necessarily mean that he wasn't partly to blame for what had happened.

Alex's mobile rang: Berlin. She didn't bother with any small talk.

'I've had to have Ross arrested. He's admitted kidnapping the Johansson family.'

Time stood still. Alex took several deep breaths. Once upon a time he had hung out with Ross, gone fishing with him. Now he was in custody, having confessed to a terrible crime.

'Jesus.'

Fredrika caught his eye. Alex got up and left Ed's office, mouthing 'back in a minute'. Out in the corridor he continued the conversation with Berlin.

'What about the rest? Has he owned up to the whole lot?'

Berlin didn't answer right away.

'You should have seen him, Alex.'

'What do you mean?'

'He was completely floored when I listed all the crimes he was suspected of. He denies everything except the kidnapping.'

Alex tried to understand. He failed and shook his head.

'Surely he's not denying the murder of Dan Johansson?'

'He claims it was Dan's wife who killed him. He also swears that Noah's death was nothing to do with him.'

Alex took a deep breath. 'We need to talk to Peder Rydh. He—'

'Peder's here now,' Berlin informed him.

Yet another surprise.

Quite a big surprise.

'He's giving a statement; he's very upset at the way Torbjörn abused his trust.'

Alex felt a pang of sorrow. Peder had gone to Berlin rather than to him.

'He's embarrassed,' Berlin added quietly. 'Peder, I mean.'

'And so he should be.'

Then, with some hesitation, Alex asked the question he didn't really want to know the answer to:

'Are we going to be able to nail Ross for the lot?'

'Doubtful. Very doubtful, unless we can come up with more forensic evidence.'

'I'll come and see you as soon as I get back to HQ,' Alex said. 'I'm still at the Solomon Community, and—'

'One more thing. We've got a match between the prints on the letter and one of the wills from Noah's office.'

'Okay.'

'Not okay. It's the last will and testament of Fredrika's husband, Spencer Lagergren.'

The courier arrived just as Spencer was on his way out. He accepted the beautifully wrapped bouquet of flowers with surprise, and thanked the girl who'd delivered them.

'I think they need to go in water right away,' she said.

'Okay.'

He went into the kitchen and found a vase. Tore off the paper and saw a card.

Thanks for all your help! I'd never have completed my dissertation without you. Have a wonderful summer!
  Eva-Lotta

Spencer smiled. Eva-Lotta was going to do very well. She'd done a magnificent job of researching the history of self-publishing in Sweden.

I'd never have completed my dissertation without you.

Spencer thought that was an exaggeration. Eva-Lotta would have worked well with any supervisor. She had the drive, the fire in her belly. Her attitude reminded him of Fredrika when she was a student. A student who'd fallen head over heels in love with Spencer. He always blushed when he remembered how he'd pushed her away at first.

I never imagined that she'd be mine. Marry me, give birth to my children.

His eyes filled with tears as he arranged the flowers. There would be no more students to follow in Eva-Lotta's footsteps. No more lectures, no more dissertations. Everything he did was for the last time. His days were measured out, coming to an end. And in the middle of it all, his funeral director had been murdered. Talk about irony and black humour – it was like something out of a _Monty Python_ sketch. The funeral director who died and left the dying in a pickle.

Spencer had been off to see a new funeral director when the courier turned up with the flowers. He'd chosen someone who was part of a larger chain, a company that didn't stand or fall because of one individual. After all, who knew what else might happen? Death behaved like a drunk in a crowded bar, cannoning straight into whoever got in the way without even apologising. Spencer had had enough surprises. Other people talked about getting their lives organised; he just wanted to organise his death.

He left the apartment and headed towards Sankt Eriksplan. At least he was in control of the most important thing: settling his debt. Not that the debt had been paid in full, but he had reduced it significantly. That would have to do, both for him and for the young woman concerned.

He felt a kind of peace when he reached his destination and took out his phone. One quick call, then he'd be ready to meet another of death's entrepreneurs.

Noah Johansson's assistant answered almost immediately; she'd just returned from her holiday.

'Spencer Lagergren. I left you a message about my will.'

'Oh yes – you're not the only one, I can assure you!'

'Of course. I realise how busy you must be; I'd just like to know when it would be convenient for me to call in and pick up my envelope – or rather envelopes.'

There was a rustling sound on the other end of the line; the woman was doing something else at the same time. Or was she playing for time? Spencer had no idea where that thought came from, but he didn't like it.

'Hello?' he said.

'The thing is, I don't quite know how to tell you this, but the police have been here and taken away a load of stuff.'

'That's understandable, but I'm sure they haven't taken the wills.'

'I'm afraid that's exactly what they've done.'

Spencer couldn't speak for a moment. 'But they're confidential,' he managed eventually. His objection sounded pathetic.

'I know, and I'm very sorry, but they promised to return them very soon.'

Spencer ended the call.

The police had taken all the wills. To read them, to examine them? He had no idea. What was clear, however, was that whoever opened his two envelopes would find out way too much.

Exhaustion overwhelmed him.

Fredrika, he thought. *How the hell am I going to get out of this?*

This situation required resolve, strength, willpower. Those attributes had largely ebbed away. He was too tired, too ill. Maybe even too old.

He stood there on the pavement for a long time before making a decision.

The children. He would go and pick up the children.

'He took my daughter away from me. I lost her for the second time. He destroyed her life, it's his fault that her husband shot her. I don't know what else you need to hear.'

Torbjörn Ross had become a very small person – so small that Fredrika was afraid he would simply vanish if she blinked.

One second he was there, and then he wasn't. Very strange.

She and Berlin were questioning Ross. Alex had removed himself from the equation as soon as they got back to HQ, answering evasively when she asked where he was going, what was so urgent.

'Alex can't be part of this interview,' Berlin had said firmly. 'Obviously – because of the messages he's received.'

Fredrika agreed, but that didn't explain what was happening now. She couldn't shake off the feeling that Berlin was pleased to have her there – not because she valued what Fredrika could bring to the table, but because she wanted her exactly where she was, away from the rest of the department.

'Did she know she was your daughter?' Berlin asked Ross.

His expression grew blank.

'No. Her mother didn't want me to tell her, and that was the end of that. I couldn't go against her wishes.'

'But you were always close by,' Fredrika said.

'Always.' Ross's voice was thick with emotion. 'I often sent money when she was growing up. Her mother is useless when it comes to finances. She can't do anything right. Money disappears in no time – it just runs through her fingers.'

'So what did you do? Once you'd rented The Sanctuary, how did you get the Johansson family out there with you?'

Ross narrowed his eyes.

'Difficult for you to work out if you've never been armed. Do you know how people react when you draw a gun on them? They're terrified. I took the Johanssons the day before they were due to leave for Australia. If they hadn't been planning that trip, I'd have taken them earlier in the year, but it was worth waiting, so much easier knowing that no one was going to miss them. They did exactly as I said. The two adults were very helpful; they didn't hesitate to tell their children how to behave. "Come along, let's do what the man says." I tied them up with cable ties and put them in the back of a van with no side windows. I'd borrowed it from a friend. They couldn't see where we were. I drove around for something like five hours before I let them out at the house.'

'And the rest?' Berlin said. 'Apparently you've dealt with their emails and a phone call.'

'We live our lives through our phones. It was perfectly simple to answer questions from the few people who got in touch. As for the phone call, I was lucky. I was in The Sanctuary at the time, and I forced Dan to speak. Once again, Australia was a very welcome bonus.'

Fredrika hesitated, but she had to ask.

'What did you intend to happen in that house?'

Ross responded without hesitation, but his voice was far from steady.

'The same thing that happened to my daughter. To Maria and her family.'

Fredrika felt sick.

Berlin's mouth was no more than a thin line as she listened. She was angry, which wasn't good. Her anger was a sign that she was taking this personally, and that kind of conflict was inappropriate. Fredrika, meanwhile, was beside herself with anxiety. Alex had behaved so oddly since Berlin called him while they were at the Solomon Community, and Berlin herself was definitely hiding something. Ross was clearly the perpetrator they'd been looking for – Ross and no one else.

Not the man who'd bought five copies of Morgan Sander's book *I Am Putting Everything Right* in the antiquarian bookshop in the Söder district.

And not Spencer.

Two men who could each be linked to the fateful words that had haunted the police throughout this case. But where was the link between Ross and those words?

Berlin had identified the same logistical gap, and tried to fill it.

'Why Morgan Sander's book?'

Ross was taken aback by the change of subject.

'I don't know what you're talking about.'

'The book we found a copy of in Malcolm Benke's and Lovisa Wahlberg's homes.'

'You're out of your minds, both of you. Absolutely fucking crazy.'

You can talk, Fredrika thought wearily.

Berlin sighed.

'It's not that we don't sympathise with what you've been

through – the daughter you knew about, but weren't allowed to contact. I get it, believe me. But . . .'

She shuffled the papers in front of her.

'. . . I can't even pretend that makes it okay to murder people one after the other.'

Ross didn't answer at first. His white shirt made him look even more ashen; he was almost swallowed up by the pale walls.

'I didn't do any of that. You can't lay any of those deaths at my door.'

'Apart from Dan Johansson's, you mean?' Fredrika said.

'It wasn't me who killed Dan Johansson. It was his wife.'

Berlin slammed her fist down on the desk.

'Enough!' she yelled.

'It's true! He was already dead when I arrived. There was blood everywhere – I nearly slipped and fell.'

Slowly Fredrika realised that he was telling the truth. He hadn't murdered Dan.

Jesus, what kind of life had they been forced to live in that house?

'Do you understand what you've done? Do you understand what you've put that family through?'

'Nothing they didn't deserve.'

Berlin had no intention of listening to that kind of nonsense.

'Noah Johansson,' she said. 'Did he also deserve to die?'

'No.'

'So why did you kill him?'

'I told you, I didn't!'

They were getting nowhere.

'What was your plan?' Fredrika asked. 'It still doesn't make any sense to me.'

Ross lowered his gaze.

'It worked out more or less the way I wanted – although I was hoping for more.'

More?

'You wanted them to start killing one another?' Berlin said.

'I wanted Dan to take his own life, but not until he'd killed his family. I wanted him to realise that was the only way he could be free.'

Fredrika's brain was threatening to overheat.

'Was this really the first thing you came up with when you started planning your revenge? Find a bunker and lock them up?'

Ross shook his head, tears glinting in his eyes.

'My first idea was to shoot the bastard, but then I thought about the house. I knew it existed, how it could be used. I wasn't sure I'd be allowed to rent it, but then it all worked out and . . .'

Fredrika leaned back. They were looking for a man who claimed he was putting everything right. Ross insisted he wasn't that man. He was admitting to only one crime: kidnapping the Johansson family. The crime that was different from all the others. A crime scene with no message to Alex, no copy of Sander's book.

Surely there couldn't be another perpetrator?

Doubt was lurking in the shadows of everything they didn't know, everything they couldn't prove.

There was a knock on the door and a younger colleague came in.

'Can I have a quick word with the two of you?'

He nodded to Fredrika and Berlin; Ross was no longer a part of the team.

They went out into the corridor. Berlin slammed the door behind her, leaving Ross alone.

'We're carrying out a search of Ross's house at the moment.'

'I know,' Berlin said. 'I was the one who asked the prose-cutor for a warrant.'

The young man ignored her.

'I've just had an initial report from the scene. They've made a number of discoveries, including two copies of Morgan Sander's book hidden at the back of a wardrobe.'

Fredrika let out a long breath. At last, solid ground beneath her feet.

At last.

She could see there was more to come; the corner of their colleague's mouth was twitching with eagerness.

'And they found a revolver.'

'A Colt 45,' Berlin said quietly.

'Exactly.' He was beyond excited. 'It's being fast-tracked to the National Forensics Centre, of course, but I think we can be pretty sure it's our murder weapon.'

Berlin was clearly shaken. Fredrika's head was spinning, and the solid ground was shifting slightly. Aftershocks, noth-ing to worry about.

'Where was the gun found?'

'In the garage.'

'Where in the garage?'

'Behind a pile of winter tyres.'

'And did they find Ross's prints on it?' Berlin asked.

'They only found it fifteen minutes ago, so no, not yet.'

'I don't think we should expect too much in terms of prints,' Fredrika cautioned. 'We've found no trace of Ross at any of the crime scenes. He's been very careful.'

'Maybe.' Their colleague nodded and walked away.

'So that's that,' Berlin said.

'Looks like it.'

But Fredrika was picturing Torbjörn Ross in her mind's eye, an ageing man with heavy Wellington boots and the lack of sharpness in his eyes that came with the passing years. He would never have managed to build the kind of house he'd been lucky enough to rent from the Solomon Community. Never.

'What are you thinking?' Berlin wanted to know.

That this is more than Ross is capable of.

'That I'm not convinced.'

Was that really her own voice she was hearing? Ross was the perpetrator. It *had* to be Ross.

'Why not?'

'I don't think Ross is the kind of person who can flit about between various crime scenes like a ghost. I'm sorry, but the fact that he's left no traces anywhere . . . it just doesn't fit.'

Berlin shook her head.

'It's always the same with you. Always the same lack of respect.'

Fredrika glanced up in surprise. 'I'm sorry?'

'You don't understand police officers, especially not the older ones like Torbjörn and Alex.'

'Hang on a minute, I—'

'Torbjörn is one of the most competent colleagues I've ever worked with. If there's anyone who could commit a series of murders like this without being found out, it's him.'

Fredrika was lost for words. Of all the things Berlin could have chosen to say, this was the most astonishing, the most ridiculous and the most childish. In the end she had to point out the obvious.

'If he could do all that without being found out, how come he's sitting in an interview room right now? And how come he's owned up to one crime without offering any resistance, but not the rest – even though he knows the game is up and he's not going to be able to get away with it?'

'He knows we don't have any evidence of his involvement in the other cases. But of course he's unaware of what's been found at his house today.'

'He's a detective, for fuck's sake!' Fredrika snapped, feeling her cheeks flush. 'He knows how we work, he knows we'll be carrying out a search. And if he couldn't come up with anywhere better to stash the books and the revolver than in the wardrobe and the garage, then he must realise we're going to find them.'

Berlin stared at her as if she'd lost her mind.

'Are you saying someone planted the books and the murder weapon?'

Fredrika didn't bother pointing out that they didn't actually know whether the gun was the murder weapon, even though it seemed likely.

'Yes. Yes, I think we have to consider that possibility.'

Berlin was having none of it.

'Go back to the department. I'll finish the interview on my own.'

'Fine by me.'

Fredrika turned and walked away. Away from Berlin, away from Ross.

Back to the department, where she was sure Alex was following a lead he had no intention of sharing.

'They've got him,' Ivan said.

Alex looked up. 'Who?'

'Ross. They've found two copies of Morgan Sander's book in his wardrobe, plus what looks like the murder weapon.'

Alex dropped the papers he was holding, stared at them as if they'd just burst into flames.

'Thank God.'

The fingerprints had shown that Spencer Lagergren was the most likely person to have written the letter Alex had found in Noah's office. Spencer, who Peder claimed had attacked Noah on a previous occasion. Noah, who had been threatened and had turned to a security firm. Noah, who was economical with the truth. All this was according to what Peder had said to Alex, but when he'd gone to see Berlin that same afternoon, Peder hadn't mentioned Spencer, or the fact that Noah had needed help with security issues. Peder had lied to Alex.

And now both the Johansson brothers were dead.

Alex wanted to believe they'd been murdered by the same person.

And that that person was Torbjörn Ross.

'So what do we do with this?' Ivan gestured towards Spencer's letter.

'We know Spencer Lagergren wasn't involved with Dan Johansson and his family, and we haven't found the slightest connection between him and any of the other victims,' Alex said.

He didn't want to think about the rest of it, the indication in the letter that Spencer was going to die in the near future.

'He does say he's putting everything right,' Ivan pointed out. 'Quoting an author he doesn't name.'

'True, but Spencer is a professor of literature. He told Fredrika he'd supervised a student during the spring who had looked at Morgan Sander's work, among other things.

'We need to double-check that,' Ivan said.

'Fine, but try to be discreet. Then we'll drop it.'

They sat in silence for a moment. Alex thought back to the last time Spencer had been dragged into a police inquiry; a young female student had accused him of sexual harassment. He had been arrested on that occasion; they must have taken his fingerprints, fingerprints that had been wiped from the system because he'd been completely exonerated. If Ivan hadn't gone through the wills, they wouldn't have been able to identify Spencer. Alex almost wished that had been the case.

'Don't we have to do something about his admission in the letter?'

'What do you mean?'

'He says he ran over a woman then drove away from the scene.'

Alex lowered his chin. 'We have no idea how long ago that was.'

'Yes we do – it says their daughter had just been born.'

Ivan wasn't stupid, and that wasn't always a good thing.

'Let me give it some thought,' Alex said. 'I mean, he doesn't name the woman. Any kind of legal action would be problematic if the letter is all we have.'

'They might still have the same car – in which case we could bring it in, let forensics take a look at it.'

Alex stared in silence at his colleague. Ivan's shoulders slumped.

'Although obviously this all happened years ago,' he said.

'Indeed.'

'I saw his name in Johansson's client database the first time I went through it.'

'And you saw mine.'

Ivan flushed. Alex took a deep breath, unsure whether to share what was on his mind.

'We need to tread carefully with this. Not leap to conclusions based on what we think we know. Okay?'

'Okay.'

'Not only because Fredrika's involved,' Alex went on. 'Absolutely not because Fredrika's involved, in fact, but because we must never, ever jump to conclusions based on too little material. The consequences for the individual can be devastating.'

With those words Alex closed down the discussion about the letter. If he had his way, it would never be spoken about again.

'Where are the rest of the wills?' he asked.

'With forensics. People have already started calling, wanting them back.'

'Return them right away. We don't need them any longer.'

Ivan picked up the phone immediately and passed on Alex's instructions. Alex listened in silence. Noah

Johansson must have been killed because he kept on pushing to find out what had happened to his brother. Anything else was unimaginable. That could also explain the chaos in his office. Nothing was missing, nothing had been stolen. Someone had messed the place up to make it look like a robbery gone wrong. Or as if the killer had been searching for something. But what was there to search for at a funeral parlour? Surely there was nothing of value, nothing worth stealing?

No, Alex thought. *What the killer wanted was Noah's silence. And then he went after Tina Antonsson, but she got away, thank God.*

Ross and his fucking Wellingtons. How could he be so stupid?

'Do we tell Fredrika?' Ivan said.

'No. That's up to Spencer.'

The more Alex thought about the letter, the more concerned he became. The change in Fredrika over recent weeks, the anxiety he had seen in her eyes. Spencer had written that he knew when he was going to die, that his time was measured out. Alex was struggling to understand. Was Spencer ill? If so, why hadn't Fredrika said anything?

Because she always keeps things to herself.

Ivan picked up the letter. 'She must have realised.'

'Fredrika?'

'Yes. She must have realised who wrote the letter. Even if she wasn't aware of the car accident, she must have known.'

The thought hadn't occurred to Alex. Fredrika had read her husband's last confession here at work. Learned that he'd done something terrible, something he was now putting right.

Alex's mouth went dry.

Fuck.

She must have had the same reaction as Ivan and Alex.

She must have thought she was reading a murderer's letter.

But unlike her colleagues, she knew who'd written it.

She must have been so worried, so frightened.

Alex knew he had to speak to her, reassure her before they went home for the weekend. The man she lived with had certainly committed a crime when he ran over a woman and left her lying in the road, but he was no serial killer. If she hadn't worked that out for herself, then Alex would make it clear to her.

The perfect opportunity soon presented itself. Alex had just sat down at his desk when there was a knock on the door and Fredrika came in.

'We need to talk,' she said.

'Take a seat.'

She closed the door and sat down opposite him. Alex was intending to get straight to the point, but Fredrika beat him to it.

'I think we're wrong. I don't think Ross is lying. He didn't kill Malcolm Benke, Lovisa Wahlberg or the other victims.'

Alex was more than a little surprised.

'Didn't you hear that they've found two copies of Morgan Sander's book in his wardrobe, and a gun in—'

'Someone could have planted them – it means nothing.'

Alex leaned forward; it was time to free his younger colleague from her demons.

'Fredrika, I know,' he said quietly.

She stared blankly at him.

'I know,' he repeated. 'I know it was Spencer who wrote the letter we found in Noah's office, but believe me, he's not our killer.'

Fredrika blinked.

'Do you seriously think I'm sitting here hinting that Spencer is our man?'

Alex shuffled uncomfortably.

'Sorry – I didn't put that very well. But in that case who . . . What are you suggesting? I don't understand.'

Fredrika's cheeks flushed; she was clearly upset by Alex's words.

'I don't know who the perpetrator is. It just seems so unlikely that Ross of all people would be capable of carrying out such complex murders without leaving a trace of himself behind. I said the same thing to Berlin, and she told me I had no respect for more experienced police officers, but please believe me – that's *not* what I meant.'

'Of course not. It's a long time since we had that kind of discussion.'

Alex wanted to get back to Spencer, explain why he'd said what he had. But he was caught up in Fredrika's assertion that Ross was an unlikely candidate. Was he too old, too unsophisticated, or had they underestimated him? Ross with his stooped posture, his Wellingtons. Who knew what he was capable of, what was concealed behind the façade.

'We can't ignore the fact that he managed to abduct an entire family and keep them off the radar for two months. That's quite an achievement.'

Fredrika shook her head.

'He didn't build that house, Alex. His revenge was served up on a plate; all he had to do was kidnap the family. And he didn't have to be particularly careful, because he didn't expect anyone to start looking for them. They were supposed to be in Australia.'

Good point.

'So what have we missed?' Alex said. 'What do you want to take a closer look at?' This gave him another chance to talk about Spencer.

'The man who bought the books,' Fredrika replied.

'The man whose voice wasn't Ross's.'

Alex touched the scars on his hands for the thousandth time. Henry Lindgren's death was the most terrifying of them all. A crystal-clear link to the past, to one of Alex's failures as a police officer.

'I'm not sure, Fredrika. We can be absolutely certain of two things: the man in question knows me, and he's familiar with the background of his victims on a level of detail I find absolutely horrific. Who else fits those criteria, apart from Ross? Who else have we managed to link to all the victims, apart from Ross?'

Fredrika thought for a moment.

'No one,' she admitted eventually. 'On the other hand, we haven't looked very hard. We can't rely on the principle that "it can't be anyone else". That's not evidence, and it won't stand up in court.'

'I'm well aware of that, thank you.'

Alex hadn't meant to snap, but Fredrika withdrew into herself, closed down.

'My apologies,' she said.

Silence.

Fredrika, I know.

They had to talk about the letter, about Spencer.

'What was Ross like when he was younger? Was he good at his job?'

The question sent Alex spinning back through the decades, made him think about all those years that had disappeared, all the capabilities that had dwindled.

'He was one of the very best,' he said hoarsely.

'One of the very best?'

He nodded. 'It's his judgement that's changed, become skewed. In terms of pure skill he's still got it.'

'In that case maybe you're right. Maybe he really is our perpetrator.'

'I think we have to accept that,' Alex said. 'And we just forget about the man who bought the books, unless of course he was buying them on behalf of Ross. We'll probably never know.'

Fredrika managed a wan smile.

Alex took a deep breath.

'I know, Fredrika. I know that you know Spencer wrote the letter we found in Noah's office, I know you're worried that he might be involved. Listen to me: Spencer might have done foolish things in the past, but he has nothing to do with any of this. Okay?'

Tears sprang to Fredrika's eyes.

'Okay.'

It's always the same. We always excuse those we love the most, yet at the same time that unconditional love opens us up to a doubt we would not allow ourselves in a different context. Because we can't possibly be wrong, not when it comes to our nearest and dearest. Where they're concerned, we have to be absolutely certain. We cannot let evil creep into our closest circle.

Alex leaned back.

'How is he?'

'Fine.'

Alex wondered if she'd understood the question. 'So he's not ill?'

'He's dying. He has a brain tumour.'

Time stood still.

Of all the things she could have said.

Of all the things he'd expected to hear.

He wasn't ready for this, wasn't ready for the realisation that Fredrika was going to have to watch the man she loved deeply die.

You have no idea of the hell that's waiting for you. But I do, I've been there.

'I'm so very sorry.'

'Me too. Me too. And you have to believe me, Alex, if I'd had the strength ... you would have been the first person I confided in.'

He couldn't say a word, he merely nodded. He didn't want her to feel for one second that she owed him an explanation for her silence.

'You've got a lot to tell me,' she said in a broken voice.

'Whenever you're ready,' Alex assured her. 'Any time, day or night. I'm always here for you.'

As soon as Peder Rydh missed Ylva, he would go and visit her. Sometimes he took the boys with him, sometimes he didn't. Today he was alone.

'I did the right thing,' he said in a matter-of-fact tone of voice. 'I went to see Berlin, had a chat with her. Told her what I needed to tell her. But I missed out the stuff about Spencer – too messy. He's going to die soon anyway.'

It had stopped raining, which was a good thing. It meant he didn't need that fucking umbrella. It was ages since he'd seen Ylva indoors.

'I know what you're thinking. I should have done it earlier, I'm not taking responsibility. But you're wrong. This time I've taken all the responsibility anyone could wish, and more besides. Deep down, you realise that.'

A bird flew past, so low that Peder automatically ducked.

'Bastard fucking bird,' he muttered.

He'd always been afraid of birds; they were so unpredictable. His brother Jimmy had felt the same way. The fact that Jimmy could also feel scared had frightened Peder when he was a child, because Jimmy was the kind of person who hardly ever found things unpleasant. He didn't have nightmares like Peder, he didn't insist on sleeping between his mum and dad. Then the accident happened, and everything changed. If Peder closed his eyes he could still see his brother's body being thrown from the swing, landing on the hard ground and hitting his head on a stone. He could still remember the pool of blood that got bigger and bigger, how warm Jimmy's head had been when he held it between in his hands. Jimmy would never be the same again, but Peder didn't realise that until he grew older and the gap between him and his brother – who remained a child for as long as he lived – became too wide to bridge.

He carried on talking to Ylva. 'You know when I shot the man who killed Jimmy? I don't remember the details, it's all kind of blacked out, but I do remember the feeling, I was certain I was doing the right thing. I still think so today.'

The ground was soft and damp beneath his feet. He moved gently across the green grass, felt each blade bend with his weight.

'It came over me again – I told you. That feeling. The same as when I shot Jimmy's murderer, but more . . . real. It lingered for longer this time, it went deeper. I . . . I'm ashamed to say that I couldn't get my act together at first. I failed in everything. I know I've said this before, I know you know I got the sack. But things are different now. I'm in control, I'm good with the boys. And Jussi, my boss at Solid Security, he didn't get it. He started hassling me, telling me I wasn't normal, saying I was unreliable after what happened to you. He came straight out and said I was damaged, that taking me on had been an error of judgement. Fucking arsehole, there was nothing wrong with me back then. There's nothing wrong with me now either. But we talked about how I felt last summer, when I wanted to change jobs. I couldn't stop brooding over Jimmy's death, what I'd done, in spite of the fact that you reminded me of how many years had passed. I tried, I really did. But it was no good, not even when I got a new job. I couldn't free myself, Ylva. I was stuck fast. For a long time.'

Peder was breathing heavily.

'One day when the boys are older I'll explain it all to them. I can't do it right now, I'm sure you understand that. I ... Shit, Ylva, I was supposed to put everything right, but I didn't get as far as I'd intended. Not even close. I'll come up with a new plan, I promise. After all, this was meant to be a lifetime project, not something that took one week in the summer.'

Peder heard voices approaching. They were no longer alone.

'I have to go now. I'll come back with the boys in a few days. They miss you so much, they talk about you all the time. But ... we're fine, really we are. It's important that you know that.'

He leaned forward and brushed away a leaf that had drifted down onto Ylva's gravestone.

'By the way, did I tell you about Ross? I did, didn't I? What a fucking idiot – you won't believe what he's done! But he feels the same way I do – he's convinced he did the right thing.'

He stepped back; time to go.

'You're the best thing that ever happened to me,' he whispered.

The apartment was bursting with life when Fredrika arrived home. The children whirled around like restless summer butterflies, giggling and shouting. The smell of garlic was coming from the kitchen. Fredrika put down her bag and grabbed Saga as she raced towards her.

'Daddy came and fetched us!' Saga informed her, clearly delighted.

'That's wonderful!'

Fredrika picked up the little girl and held her close. Soon she would be too big for that kind of thing, wouldn't want Mummy cuddling her like a soft toy. The days could be endless, but for some reason the years just flew by.

She went into the kitchen. Spencer had his back to her. He was chopping onions and didn't turn around, even though he must have heard her.

'Hi.'

'Hi,' said Spencer.

Spencer who was going to die, Spencer whom she'd loved for so long, who wasn't the murderer they were looking for. But he was still a man who had once run over a young woman and left her lying in the road without calling for help.

Saga insisted on being put down, then ran off to find her brother. They headed for Saga's bedroom like a mini-tornado.

'Did you miss them?'

'Terribly.' At last he turned around. Fredrika struggled to hide her shock at his appearance: he looked exhausted, hollow-eyed. Almost gaunt.

'I called Noah Johansson's assistant today. I wanted my will so that I could pass it on to the new funeral director, but I couldn't have it. Apparently the police had taken all the wills to examine them.'

Fredrika didn't move, didn't say a word.

'I know that you know,' Spencer said. 'I know you've read the letter.'

Fredrika still didn't speak. She'd kept a little spark of hope alive, she realised. Hope that he hadn't written the letter, hope that he had nothing to do with any of it, hope that he hadn't run over that woman.

Shit.

'How could you do that?' she whispered. 'Run over someone and just leave her lying there?'

'What was the alternative? Go on, tell me! I'd finally managed to get out of my miserable marriage, finally embarked on a life with you. I even had a child. Do you understand how miraculous that was for me? And then I'd had that terrible accident; I thought I was going to die right there in the car. I didn't, but it was a long road back. It was hell.'

Fredrika remembered. That had been the most difficult period of all, but the fact that it had made Spencer indifferent to the lives and wellbeing of others had passed her by.

'You wrote that you've put everything right now,' she said. 'What did you mean by that?' She hardly dared breathe.

'I've made a bequest to Miranda, and I wanted you to know why.'

'Miranda?'

'That's her name.'

Fredrika stood on a piece of Lego. It hurt and she kicked it away. The apartment had once been so clean and tidy that you could walk around barefoot; these days she was grateful if she managed to get from one room to the next without falling over something.

'Couldn't you have made it clearer? Explained that that was what you meant?'

'What did you think I meant?'

That you'd murdered several people.

'I don't know.'

'What did your colleagues say? They must have recognised my name.'

'I've only spoken to Alex. He's very sorry you're ill.'

The water boiled over on the hob and Spencer turned down the heat. Fredrika could see that he was trying to hurry, and yet everything happened so slowly. His right arm was stiff; had it been that way before, or was this something new?

'Need any help?'

'No thanks.'

And suddenly she remembered what he'd said when he told her about the tumour: he didn't want to see the day when he couldn't manage on his own, when he needed help.

'I don't do impotence and humiliation,' he said. She'd nodded and said 'of course', told him she'd have felt the same, even though she hadn't been at all convinced. Until now. Looking at Spencer and the boiling water, she knew for the first time exactly how she felt. She was like Spencer. She too hated the idea of impotence and humiliation so much that she would choose death in Switzerland over the alternative.

'Say something, please.'

'About what?'

'About what I did, what I didn't do.'

Fredrika scratched a mosquito bite, contemplated the pile of toys on the floor and listened to the children's excited chatter from the bedroom. She was the one who would be left. The one who would have the privilege of continuing to live this everyday life.

'What's done is done,' she whispered.

Spencer froze in mid movement. His face was filled with such sorrow that she wanted to caress his cheek. Once, twice, ten times. Over and over again before the flight to Switzerland at the beginning of September.

'Are you sure?'

'We have so little time left,' Fredrika said. 'I choose not to quarrel, just as you have chosen how you're going to die.'

A single tear ran down Spencer's cheek. Fredrika went over and wrapped her arms around him. Held him close, so close. For once it was her turn to bring him solace.

Margareta Berlin was well known for two things: she was tough on those who were tough, and she was tough on those who were vulnerable. She wasn't proud of the latter, but it was undeniably true. Sometimes she had gone in way too hard, which was indefensible. That aspect of her character had cost her a great deal. She wasn't stupid – she knew she wasn't popular with her colleagues. For a long time she'd told herself it was because she'd risen through the ranks too quickly, that she hadn't served her time as a foot soldier. However, as the years went by she had to accept that there must be other reasons why people didn't like her, why she was never included in social gatherings.

'You don't listen, you don't want to hear what others have to say. Which means you end up alone and lonely.'

It was Torbjörn Ross who'd come straight out with it, told her that the fault didn't lie with others, but largely with herself.

She had hated him – and respected him in equal measure, because he'd had the strength and courage to voice what everyone else was thinking but didn't dare say. For that reason he had secured himself a special place in Berlin's heart forever. Not that she ever gave him the slightest hint, but it had influenced her decision-making on key issues. She had become his protector, without the slightest hesitation.

Until now.

She couldn't understand what had gone wrong, how he could have gone off the rails like this. The thought that Ross had kidnapped an entire family was beyond ridiculous. She still didn't quite believe it. Ross had revealed few details, and the interview with Malin Johansson had had to be postponed. She was shocked and traumatised, as were the children. All three were in hospital, with the press lurking outside like predators, desperate for a glimpse of The Missing Family, as the headlines were calling them. Which didn't really make sense – they weren't missing now, they'd been found. In spite of the fact that only Noah and Tina had been looking for them.

Berlin was still in her office. She didn't want to go home, but she didn't want to carry on working either.

It wasn't meant to be like this.

Alex Recht and Fredrika Bergman had done a good job, she had to give them that. However, Fredrika had overstepped the mark earlier with her fantasies and her total lack of respect for experienced police officers.

Ross wasn't smart enough, that was what she'd implied.

Sorrow burned in Berlin's breast. Torbjörn Ross was most definitely smart enough to murder without leaving a trace of himself behind. Everyone who'd known him for a long time would agree – and that didn't include Fredrika.

The shrill sound of her mobile interrupted Berlin's train of thought.

'Sorry if I'm disturbing you at home on a Friday evening,' the prosecutor said.

'No problem – I'm still at work.'

Berlin immediately regretted her words. She hated sounding lonely and bitter.

'I'm going out for a late dinner,' she added.

'No chance of going home as far as I'm concerned,' the prosecutor replied. 'I've got far too much to do.'

'Absolutely, same here.' Berlin didn't want her to think she didn't care about the job.

'I'd like a word about Torbjörn Ross.'

'I thought that might be it.'

'This can't go wrong. The stakes are too high, the interest from the outside world is too great. So let me ask you this: are you absolutely certain we can't come up with any more evidence?'

'Apart from the books and the murder weapon?'

'We can't tie Ross to any of the crime scenes except the Solomon Community's safe house. And we both know that's a problem. There *has* to be something else,' the prosecutor insisted.

Berlin glanced at her watch, then at the darkening sky. Then at her watch again.

'Give me another two hours.'

'Two hours? You've got days, maybe weeks. We have enough to charge him, but I want this to go all the way. I want him convicted of the whole lot.'

'I'll be in touch,' Berlin said, ending the call.

Torbjörn Ross was asleep when Berlin walked into his cell. He sat up looking dazed. Berlin realised he hadn't slept for a long time.

I saw him every single day, and I didn't even notice.

He made a move to get up.

'No, we're staying here.' Berlin closed the cell door and leaned against the wall. A boring green wall. 'I have a problem.'

Ross looked at her, his expression faintly amused.

'We haven't found a single trace of you at any of the crime scenes. Nor in the place where Lovisa Wahlberg was found.'

'That's because I was never there.'

'So who hates you enough to plant a murder weapon in your garage? And books in your wardrobe?'

Ross lowered his gaze. 'It's not my place to answer that question. It's your job to find the guilty party, not mine.'

'I've already found the guilty party. He's sitting right in front of me.'

Ross didn't answer. He started picking at a cuticle that looked infected. Berlin suppressed a shudder.

'You've always been a better police officer than me,' she went on. 'Help me out here, Torbjörn. Point me in the right direction.'

The cuticle began to bleed. Ross pressed a finger onto the sore to stop the blood.

'You wouldn't have asked that question if you really believed I was the perpetrator,' he said quietly.

'In one case there's not a shred of doubt.'

'You're right, I abducted Dan Johansson and his family. But all the rest . . . no. It wasn't me.'

Berlin thumped the wall with her clenched fist.

'So who was it? Don't you realise how this looks? I gave you Lovisa Wahlberg's case, and if you didn't kill her, then you must have taken the job seriously. So what did you find? You've had days – how far did you get? Or were you too busy with your kidnapping project?'

Ross sighed. The paper sheet beneath him rustled.

'What did you find?' Berlin repeated. And was completely floored when Ross replied:

'A police officer.'

Berlin stiffened.

'A police officer?'

'Think about it. No signs of a break-in at Malcolm Benke's house, or Lovisa Wahlberg's apartment, or Henry Lindgren's. What does that tell you?'

'Oh, come on! It tells me that all the victims recognised their killer – you. I certainly don't believe for a second that it was a police officer they'd never seen before, and that they let him in just because of his police ID card. It's too simple, too naïve.'

'Too simple? For fuck's sake, Maggan, it's always simple. Take a look at the most famous cases in Swedish history and you'll find the most banal explanations as to how certain things happened.'

Berlin shook her head. This was a bad idea, she should never have come.

'If your only theory is that it was some unknown colleague who murdered those poor souls, then there's no reason for me to stay here.' She turned away, ready to leave.

'I didn't say it was some unknown colleague.'

Berlin paused.

'Who?'

'Check it out for yourself,' Ross said. 'There's one name that comes up in every single investigation.'

'I don't have time to go through every case,' she snapped. 'Tell me who you're talking about.'

Ross took his time.

'When Beata Benke died, the Met police contacted Stockholm. Since I had a personal relationship with her father, I asked a younger colleague to answer their questions. The same colleague was by my side when Lovisa Wahlberg was accused of drugs offences later that year. And the same colleague worked with Alex when Henry Lindgren was involved in the investigation into Lilian Sebastiansson's disappearance.'

Berlin's heart skipped a beat.

'*Who?* You have to give me a name!'

Ross's expression was tortured.

'He's called me several times during the spring and summer. Asked for favours in return for his help when I needed a reference to secure the lease on The Sanctuary. His desire for information about our progress has been insatiable.'

Berlin could hardly breathe. She was finding it difficult to hear what Ross was saying, kept missing vital details.

'An officer who wasn't part of the team has been asking you for information, and you just passed it on? You didn't report him? Are you out of your mind?'

'I thought he wanted to come back. I thought he wanted to be ... part of it all. He's so bitter.'

'Who?' Berlin shouted. 'Who the hell are we talking about?'

Ross got to his feet and moved closer.

'Who worked for the security firm that provided Dan Johansson with protection? Who helped me to lease The Sanctuary?'

'Oh my God,' Berlin whispered.

She opened the door and ran to call Alex.

When Alex arrived home he found Diana reading in the living room. She seemed to be absorbed in her book.

'Everything okay?' he said.

Diana put down the book.

'Not really. It's a bit depressing, sitting here reading in the armchair. It would be much better on a beach.'

'I'm going to keep hearing that, aren't I?'

'Difficult not to keep repeating such a fantastic sentence,' Diana said with a smile.

Alex sat down in one of the armchairs Diana had picked up at an auction. Most of the furniture was hers. He hadn't brought much when he'd moved in; he'd passed on a few things to the children and got rid of the rest.

Diana pushed her hair back from her face.

Alex thought about Fredrika and what she'd told him about Spencer. Death had no compunction.

'Has something happened?' Diana asked him.

'Yes and no.'

He didn't want to tell her, not until he'd got used to the idea. What would the consequences be? Fredrika didn't see the police as her natural environment, and she would be left alone with two children. Would she stay on as part of Alex's team, or would she look for a new job, since her life was going to change beyond recognition?

If she goes, I'll have some lonely years ahead of me until I retire.

His body tensed as soon as it heard any talk of retirement. He intended to dig his heels in, refuse to leave. There was a dire shortage of police officers; surely they couldn't get rid of someone with his experience who wanted to stay on in the new organisation?

Diana shifted in her chair.

'I went to the graveyard today. To visit Rebecka.'

Alex reached out and placed his hand on hers.

'How was she?'

'She was absolutely fine,' Diana said, her eyes filling with tears. Her daughter Rebecka was the reason why she and Alex had met. She would always have a special place in his heart, even though he'd never met her.

'I saw one of your former colleagues there,' she went on.

'Oh yes?'

He was surprised; Diana didn't know many of Alex's colleagues.

'Peder.'

'Peder Rydh? What was he doing there?'

'I wondered the same thing. I don't think he saw me, he was completely focused on what he was doing.'

'And what was he doing?'

'It looked as if he was standing talking to someone. Nothing strange about that – I talk to Rebecka. But – and this sounds really stupid – when he'd gone I went over to the grave. I don't know why, I suppose I was just curious.'

Alex sat up a little straighter without realising it.

'Was it his brother? They were very close, and he died in extremely traumatic circumstances.'

'No, there was a woman's name on the headstone. Ylva.'

Alex recoiled as if she'd slapped him.

'But that's his wife.'

'You didn't know she was dead?'

'I had no idea.'

What the hell?

Alex had spoken to Peder – how come he hadn't mentioned something so important?

Then he remembered what Fredrika had been told at Solid Security, and his blood turned to ice. Peder had been fired because he wasn't doing his job properly. Because of something that had happened in his family.

That was the last thing he needed.

'You look very shocked,' Diana said.

'I am. I . . . I don't know what to say. Did you notice when she died?'

'Back in the autumn. November, I think.'

'Back in the autumn . . . There wasn't anything about how she died?'

'On the gravestone? Of course not.'

Alex felt stupid, but for reasons he couldn't put into words he felt it was important to find out.

At that moment his mobile rang: Berlin.

'I have to take this.'

'I'll make us something to eat,' Diana said, heading into the kitchen.

'Alex, can you come back in? Right now?' Berlin sounded stressed.

'What's this about?'

'We've got a new lead.'

'Someone we can link to the crime scenes?'

'No, but it's someone we can link to all the victims.'

'We've already got a candidate who fits that category. We found the murder weapon in his garage, if you recall.'

'We don't yet have confirmation that the gun in Ross's garage is the murder weapon, but in any case this is something we have to follow up.'

There was something about Berlin's voice that bothered him. It was as taut as one of Fredrika's violin strings.

She's scared. He felt a sudden pressure in his chest.

'Who are we talking about?'

'Peder Rydh.'

Perhaps the answer should have floored him, but it didn't. Not because he'd expected it, but because he'd just been sitting here thinking about Peder, had sensed that something was wrong. No, not just wrong – disastrously wrong.

I had him within reach all along.

He called me.

And I didn't understand.

'You have to come in.'

Alex got to his feet.

I'll never forgive myself for this.

'I'll be there in half an hour.'

They called Fredrika too. She tore herself away from her home, her family, to work a few more hours.

Alex didn't think they should have brought her in. Now he knew the situation at home, now he understood the significance of the letter, he wanted to leave her in peace.

They met in the Lions' Den. Alex felt numb. He knew what Berlin was going to say before she uttered a single word.

Ross wasn't their man.

It was Peder. Broken Peder. Lost Peder.

'First of all,' Berlin began, 'we've received important information earlier than expected. There's no doubt that the Colt we found in Ross's garage is the murder weapon.'

Alex nodded. Good to know, but it added a further complication.

'Ivan has collected the package addressed to Henry Lindgren,' Berlin went on. 'The one that was too large to fit through his letterbox.'

'Morgan Sander's book?' Fredrika said.

'Exactly.'

One piece of the puzzle after another, but the picture still wasn't complete. Not until Berlin took a deep breath and continued:

'Peder Rydh. I'm sorry to tell you that his wife died in the autumn. She was in her car when a drunk driver crossed over onto her side of the carriageway. He left the scene; she didn't stand a chance.'

Alex heard Fredrika inhale sharply. It was obvious that this information had come as a huge shock; she'd clearly had no idea what the meeting was about until now. Or to put it more accurately – *who* the meeting was about.

Do you understand now, Alex?

Yes, I understand.

'Did they find the driver?' he asked.

'A witness took down the number of his car. He was charged and convicted of causing the death of another person, but took his own life days before he was due to present himself at the prison to serve his sentence.'

'How did he die?'

'A combination of tablets and alcohol. The official cause of death was registered as suicide; it was assumed that his guilty conscience got the better of him.'

'But you no longer believe that.'

Berlin shook her head. 'No. I think he was forced into it. By Peder.'

Fredrika took a deep breath.

'Hang on, how did we get here? I don't understand – have we completely given up on the idea that Ross is our perpetrator?'

'I sent Ivan to see the man who sold five copies of Morgan Sander's book,' Berlin explained. 'Ivan played him a recording of Peder's voice, a snippet of an interview.'

'And what did he say?'

'He wasn't sure. It might have been Peder who bought the books, but he couldn't be certain.'

Fredrika looked distraught.

'He lost his footing when his brother died.' Her voice was thick with tears.

'He lost it long before that,' Berlin said.

Alex wanted to protest, but couldn't bring himself to do it. Peder had been like a son or a younger brother to him. Someone he cared about, someone he liked having around. The current situation hurt far more than he could have imagined.

He heard his own voice: 'I should have done more.'

Fredrika placed a hand on his arm. 'So should the rest of us.'

'I couldn't have imagined ...'

'Nor could anyone else.'

Fredrika removed her hand. 'I wonder if he's done.'

'With the murders? Of course not. He's busy tidying up; I think there will be plenty of names left on his list,' Berlin said.

Alex was turning into a pressure cooker. This was worse than anything he'd experienced in the past. 'So what do we do now? We have no evidence linking him to any of the crimes.'

'We start a new round of interviews, we knock on doors.' Berlin was resolute. 'He must have made a mistake somewhere along the line. I've already got him under surveillance, because as I said, I don't believe he's finished.'

'So we wait for the next murder and take him then?' Alex said.

Berlin's face lost its colour.

'You do realise we might have to wait for quite some time?' Fredrika pointed out. 'Peder isn't stupid; he knows we've arrested Ross, which means he stands a chance of getting away with it if he keeps his head down, doesn't rock the boat.'

'My feeling is that his desire for revenge has become an itch he just has to scratch,' Berlin replied. 'He knows he can get away with it, but he has so much more to do. So much more to put right.'

Alex couldn't stop thinking about the messages they'd found. The messages that were addressed to him.

'Shit,' he whispered.

Berlin gave him a surprisingly sympathetic look. 'I believe this will be over before the week is out. It's Friday today. We'll have him by Sunday.'

'I think you're wrong,' Fredrika said.

It was just before midnight when Peder Rydh went to bed. The boys must have sensed his unease, because they woke up more than once during the evening. Peder went into their room, stroked their backs gently and whispered:

'It's all right, I'm here. Everything's fine.'

Everything's fine.

And that was the way it would stay.

He had to stop now, he realised that. In the middle of all his hard work. Otherwise he would get caught. His mother had looked increasingly anxious each time she turned up to babysit. She didn't ask any questions, but Peder knew she was wondering how he could possibly have so much to do in the middle of summer, why he'd had so much on his plate for so long. Deep down he was eternally grateful to her. Who else could he have called when he went over to England to pick up Beata's wedding ring?

No part of Peder felt good; the fear and anxiety seemed to be howling inside his head.

But I did the right thing.

The only right thing.

Commitment, efficiency, availability. The three key principles of police work. Peder liked to think he'd been a good soldier. His commitment recently had been indisputable. His efficiency impeccable. And he had certainly been available.

No one he'd killed had been innocent. He'd seen so many people get away with it over the years – parents who had failed in their responsibility to their children, those who had stood by passively, well aware of the crimes of others, those who had committed crimes themselves, those who in one way or another had made it possible for someone else to do the most terrible things. He put them all in the same category as hit-and-run drivers, and there were so many of them. Hundreds.

When Ylva died, it was as if the last part of Peder that had been whole was shattered. He'd fought so hard during the years that had passed since he shot the man who'd murdered his brother, tried to find a path to reconciliation with what had happened, but such a path did not exist. Jimmy was gone. And Peder was a murderer. His action had been justified, but he had still extinguished a life. Outwardly he pretended that he was at peace with what he'd done, but a war was raging inside him, a war that escalated with each passing year. He couldn't shake off the fear that he had joined the ranks of evil, and in the end that was why he declined Alex's offer to speak up for him, try to get him back into the police. Peder didn't belong there.

And then that bastard came along, smashing into Ylva's car then driving away. He had also extinguished a life (Peder refused to think about Ylva inside the burning vehicle), but for no good reason and without the slightest inclination to take responsibility for what he'd done. A cowardly little shit who couldn't face the consequences of his actions. And Peder sank. He hadn't been on solid ground since he left the Solomon Community, and after Ylva's death things got steadily worse. His behaviour rang alarm bells with his employers, who begged him to seek help. Eventually they had to let him go. Which was fine. Peder hadn't enjoyed working there anyway. Might as well start over somewhere else, but first he had to pull himself together.

He didn't realise until much later, but ironically it was Ylva's death that released him, in a way. That was when he understood what separated him from others who killed, and he was satisfied with that difference. Peder had killed to make the world a better place. Somewhere deep down he knew why the law must be written as it was, why the state didn't kill its own citizens. However, the law was one thing, the duty of the individual another. Something that Bernhard Benke had grasped, for example, but not his worthless father.

But now he knows. Now I've helped him to put right everything he did wrong.

A long series of decisions had simply made themselves. This was about duty, nothing more, nothing less. Ylva's murderer was never going to be allowed to get away with it, no fucking chance. Peder made sure he got in first, took him before the court got the chance to fuck everything up with a pathetic eighteen-month sentence. As far as Peder was concerned, it was essential that the punishment, the revenge, was proportional. And it was. Afterwards he acknowledged that he had now become a double murderer. He had felt a little uncomfortable, but there had also been a sense of pride, particularly when he got away with it so easily. That was when the next thought was born: what else could Peder do to achieve justice for those who had been wronged?

If only he'd known there were others who thought the same way. On a smaller scale, admittedly, but the basic principle was the same. It was in the early summer when he'd first realised there was something wrong about Torbjörn Ross and The Sanctuary. He was busy with his own preparations when he began to wonder what Ross wanted with that horrible place. It was pure instinct, he couldn't explain it. Ross wouldn't leave him alone, and Peder had found it hard to resist his pleas. He needed The Sanctuary and its unique properties, that was how he'd put it when he contacted Peder, begging for his help to persuade the Solomon Community to let him lease the place. His voice breaking, he had told Peder about the daughter he'd never been allowed to call his, the daughter who was now living with the threat of death hanging over her. Like Peder, Ross had sought alternative methods when he was looking for a solution to his daughter's problem.

'I'm the only one who can fix this,' he'd said. 'You understand what I mean, don't you? She's abroad at the moment, but when she comes home later in the spring, I have to be ready.'

Peder had nodded, and had vouched for Ross's background and credibility with the Solomon Community.

But then came that nagging feeling that he really hadn't understood anything at all. Peder had visited the house several times after Ross had taken over the tenancy. He had his own plans to take care of, a timetable he must stick to. He didn't want Ross dragging him into any of his crap – he had to keep the summer free. The first time he didn't believe his eyes. He had peeped in through a window and seen a whole family, just as Ross had said. But this wasn't just any family.

Peder immediately recognised Dan Johansson, and his first reaction had been to take action. Ross had gone crazy and kidnapped an entire family.

Fucking lunatic.

But then he'd given himself time to try and throw some light on why Ross had done such a thing, and Peder had changed his mind. He didn't really have a problem with Ross's actions, even though he would have preferred it if the children hadn't been involved. He also knew that one day he would probably need someone to blame. Ross was the ideal candidate, and had therefore dictated Peder's choices to a certain extent, albeit unconsciously. Peder restricted himself to people who had a link to Ross. Little by little he began to protect Ross, make sure no one realised what was going on. It was fairly straightforward; the only person who seemed to think that something had happened to the family was Dan's brother Noah. No one else contacted the police, anyway. Peder got into the habit of driving past Noah's funeral business, keeping an eye on things.

The second time he went by, he saw Spencer Lagergren standing there. Peder had been very surprised; why would Spencer be visiting a funeral director? He had to know, so the following night he broke into Noah's office, causing no damage, leaving no trace behind. His most important discovery was Spencer's last will and testament, along with an accompanying letter that made Peder furious. Spencer of all people had seriously injured a woman by driving while under the influence. Without incurring any punishment – it had been years since the accident. The time scale didn't matter as far as Peder was concerned; under no circumstances was he going to let Spencer get away with what he'd done.

Until he read the letter again, and grasped that Spencer was dying. Peder had many sources, many methods of accessing people's private business. Through his various jobs he'd built up a solid network of informants in hospitals and other institutions; he also used Ross. It transpired that Spencer had a brain tumour and was refusing treatment. He had even arranged the date of his death, so Peder decided that fate clearly took care of certain things without the need for human intervention, for which we should all be thankful. However, Peder kept Spencer in mind just in case Ross didn't work out as his scapegoat, in case he had to abandon his mission earlier than planned, before Spencer died. The last few days had been tricky. Ross had failed to monitor Noah properly, hadn't realised what steps he'd taken to find his brother, along with his newfound friend Tina. Peder had had to fix that too, check Noah's emails, keep tabs on his contact with the police. And finally he'd had to stop him when he threatened to go too far. There was a risk that Alex would believe him, and that couldn't be allowed to happen. Peder had tried to destroy Noah's credibility, convince Alex that he was a complex, volatile individual who couldn't be trusted.

It had never been Peder's intention to kill Noah. He'd only wanted to scare him into silence. He'd explained that unless Noah stopped playing detective, Dan and his family would die, but Noah's reaction had been totally unexpected. He had been furious, attacked Peder, yelled that Peder had to tell him where Dan was, why he'd taken him. That had enraged Peder – he wasn't the one who'd abducted Dan!

'You're not blaming me for your fucking brother's

misfortune!' he'd shouted, giving Noah a hard shove. Noah had fallen backwards, hitting his head on the sharp corner of the desk.

Shit.

After that there had only been one way forward: to continue according to his plan. He made as much mess as possible in Noah's office, making it look as if there'd been a break-in. Finally he took out Spencer's terrible confession, which had proved a great source of inspiration the first time he read it.

Because that was where he'd found the words that suited him so perfectly. *I am putting everything right.* That was exactly what Peder was trying to do. He had been so pleased when he realised those words were also the title of a book. *As an author once said: I am putting everything right.* The book wasn't easy to find, but after a few days Peder had managed to pick up several copies. Spencer's letter had given him the perfect link; Peder's concept had its unique signature. And now he was going to have to break off, in spite of months of preparation, after just a few days.

But what days they had been.

At some point in the future he would resume his task, he knew that. However, there would be no signature, no books left behind. Maybe he would also review his modus operandi, consider killing his chosen victims in a different way from the one in which those they'd let down had died. He didn't regret his messages to Alex; quite the reverse, they were important. Alex in particular must understand that there was an intelligent person behind everything that happened. Peder felt no sympathy for those who'd died; they didn't deserve any better. Alex would agree, if only he sat down and thought about it. He might even forgive Peder for having lied to him, necessary white lies to keep the police away from him and Ross, but also from Noah.

You understand that, don't you, Alex?

Eventually Peder fell asleep. The fluttering butterflies of fear and anxiety had settled.

He hadn't done anything wrong.

And as long as he behaved himself, he wouldn't get caught.

AUTUMN 2016

The sun shone on the day Spencer Lagergren died. In fact it shone uninterruptedly, wherever Fredrika Bergman happened to be. First of all in Switzerland, then in Stockholm.

Alex rang her when she was sitting on the kitchen floor, crying. Five days after she came home from Switzerland with Spencer in a coffin.

'I just wanted to see how you were,' he said.

'Terrible.'

'And the children?'

'They're with my parents today.'

'But they'll be at the funeral tomorrow?'

'That's the plan.'

'Sounds like a good idea.'

Alex ended the call, got in the car and drove over to see her. And that was how it came about that on a September afternoon, not one but two people were sitting on the kitchen floor crying. Fredrika would always be grateful to Alex for that.

'I miss him so much I think I'm going to die,' she said. 'But I don't. I go on living, and I just don't see the point.'

Alex wiped the tears from his cheeks.

'I felt exactly the same after I lost Lena. I couldn't leave the kids, though. And when a little time had passed I realised that I wanted to stay around after all. Dying is so ... definitive.'

'Horribly definitive,' Fredrika agreed.

She had cried so much that her head was aching and her eyes were swollen. That's how it is when someone you've loved for more than half your life dies. Grief poured out of her body, disguised as tears. How she could possibly go on without him was beyond her comprehension. And yet, in an astonishing way, it simply happened. *Extraordinary*. However much she wept, however much pain she felt, however impossible it was to imagine a future without Spencer. Time passed, days which the previous evening had been the future became the present. Fredrika found this fascinating. To think that a person could die of a heart attack, but not of a broken heart.

'Are you really going to move to London?' Alex asked.

'I think it'll be good for both me and the children to experience something different. A friend of mine has moved there with her family, and my brother's working there during the autumn. The children can attend the Swedish school, and ... I'm sure it will all work out.'

'And what will you do with yourself?'

'I haven't given it much thought. Play, I suppose.'

Fredrika and her violin.

'I'd like to hear you some time,' Alex said.

'I'm sure that can be arranged.'

He stroked her arm.

'How much leave do you have?'

'Berlin gave me six months, but she said I could have more if I need it. Anything at all as long as I don't resign – that's what it sounded like.'

Alex couldn't help smiling.

'So Berlin's not all bad,' he said.

'Just mostly.'

They sat in silence for a while. That was one of Alex's many positive qualities, in Fredrika's opinion. He understood the art of silence.

'Anyway, how are you?' she said, tired of thinking about something that couldn't be changed. 'How was Österlen?'

'Really good – sick,' he said.

Fredrika burst out laughing, even though she sometimes felt as if she would never laugh again, as if it was the wrong thing to do.

'Sick? I've never heard you say that before.'

'My kids say it all the time.'

Alex placed a hand on her arm.

'It'll be all right,' he said quietly. 'Eventually. You won't be lonely forever.'

Fredrika stiffened.

'Do you seriously think that's something I'm worrying about right now?'

Alex shrugged. 'I did.'

'In that case we're very different.'

For a long time Fredrika had been convinced that people could just as easily live alone or as part of a couple, and therefore she had never compromised when it came to love and relationships. Love was a bonus, not an essential, and it definitely wasn't something you could order up with a click of the fingers. The years with Spencer had changed her. She had begun to love being part of a couple. Not just any couple, but the two of them. The idea of replacing Spencer was as ridiculous as the thought of replacing her mother if she died.

It was impossible, it couldn't be done. Love wasn't something to be pursued, as far as Fredrika was concerned; it simply created itself, and sometimes people were lucky enough to experience that process. She couldn't imagine it happening more than once in a lifetime.

'Tell me about tomorrow,' Alex said.

'The service is in the afternoon, then dinner. Lots of people will be at the church, but not everyone will stay around.'

'So the apartment will be full of overnight guests?'

'No. Some of Spencer's friends from overseas are coming, but they're staying in a hotel.'

Alex looked at Fredrika.

'I'd love to visit you in London.'

'I'd like that too. I'll even play for you.'

They sat in silence again, then Alex just had to say what had been on his mind.

'Peder.'

'I think about him sometimes,' Fredrika said.

'We'll never nail him.'

'But at least Ross's trial is due to start soon.'

'The prosecutor is going for a custodial sentence of twelve years. I can't see Ross being able to handle that,' Alex said.

'But the Johansson family – they're okay?'

'Not the father, obviously.'

'No, but ...'

'The others are okay, but no more than that.'

Fredrika hesitated, but she had to ask.

'What do we do if we bump into Peder? What do we say?'

Alex shook his head. 'I've no idea.'

*

The funeral took place the next day. The sun shone once more, and Fredrika dressed the children in bright clothes. The church was full, and she wondered who all these people were. Alex and Berlin were in the pew behind her, and when the cantor began to play the introduction to the first hymn and Fredrika burst into tears, she felt Alex's hand on her shoulder.

'It will get better,' he whispered in her ear. 'Trust me, it will get better.'

Maybe that was true, maybe not.

Two weeks later Fredrika was on a plane heading for London, with a child on either side of her.

Saga had the window seat, and pointed at the big, fluffy clouds beneath them.

'Is that where Daddy is now?' she asked.

Who knows.

'Yes,' Fredrika replied. 'Daddy's there now instead of with us.'

'Let's wave to him!' Saga said.

So they did.

Two months later, Alex flew to London. No one could understand why the hell he was going there in November, but he missed Fredrika as a friend and colleague, and wanted to see how she was getting on. That was reason enough for the trip. He took his daughter with him; she didn't know Fredrika, but he wanted company, and they didn't see each other often enough. Diana understood, and stayed at home.

Alex adjusted his jacket, thought about the note in his inside pocket. The note he was going to show to Fredrika, a final message from Peder.

I'm stopping now.

It had arrived in the middle of August, and Alex had taken it straight to Berlin.

'What does he mean?'

Alex thought it was perfectly clear; Peder meant exactly what he said. There would be no more murders.

'Do you think Fredrika's okay?' his daughter asked. 'I've thought about her a lot, about how fragile life is. I realised that when Mum died, but you kind of forget, don't you?'

'You do. And it's probably just as well.'

His daughter took out her book and settled down to read while Alex looked out of the window. Eden Lundell had called him just as they were about to board. She asked if there might be an opening for her in Alex's department, if he knew of any interesting senior posts. He did, because rumour had it that Berlin was on her way out.

'Could you seriously cope with me as your boss?' Eden had said, laughing.

'Yes. You couldn't possibly be worse than Berlin.'

Which was a little harsh. Berlin had improved, upped her game, but she was still a long way from the kind of boss Alex wanted to work for.

His daughter gave him a nudge.

'You didn't answer my question. Do you think Fredrika's okay? And what do we do if she's in a total mess when we arrive? What if she can't cope?'

Alex stretched, fixed his gaze on one of the clouds.

'Fredrika Bergman will always be able to cope,' he said.

AFTERWORD
AND ACKNOWLEDGEMENTS

I think you've just read what will be the last Fredrika Bergman novel. I say 'think', because of course one can never be sure. Both Fredrika and Alex are alive and in good health, so who knows – maybe one day they will be reunited in the hunt for some dreadful criminal. But the way things look right now, there are no plans for such a reunion.

In the late summer of 2007 I began writing *Unwanted* [*Askungar*], the first book about Fredrika. Little did I imagine that what had been my hobby since I was seven years old – writing – would change my life and become my full-time occupation. Nor did I have any idea how many stories I had within me. It wasn't until I gave up work that I (and everyone else, I presume) got the full picture of what my writing looked like. Wild and unruly. Passionate and driven. These qualities have made me productive, and perhaps rather unpredictable. My writing is different from that of many other authors. I have loved to write ever since my first year in school, and it is impossible for me to spend all my time in Fredrika Bergman's world, never to be anywhere else. That's why I wrote the books about Martin Benner. That's why I wrote a horror novel. And that's why I started to write children's books.

When will the next Fredrika Bergman book be out? That question has haunted me since the spring of 2013, when *The Chosen* [*Davidsstjärnor*] was published in Sweden. And now I understand why; so many of you have accompanied Fredrika on her journey. So many of you want more of her. But it's like this: books must be longed for by the author who writes them just as much as by the readers who are waiting for them. And I didn't start longing for Fredrika until shortly before Christmas 2015. A new wave of longing seems incredibly distant at the moment, and Fredrika seems to be getting on fine without me. She and the children have a good life in London. And Alex will soon retire, whether he wants to or not. Maybe he'll find that beach and lie there with a good book.

Anyway. Whatever happens to Fredrika, I will carry on writing, of course. You don't just dump good habits that have been around for so many years. I'm not finished with Martin Benner; I want to know more about him. Nor am I finished with horror, and certainly not with my children's books. There are so many stories to tell, so many characters to bring to life. I've only just begun.

* * *

There are many people to thank, as is always the case. First of all, warm thanks to my friends. Too many to mention each one by name, but thank you for being part of my life and for making me strong and happy. Special thanks to Sofia

Ekholm, who continues to believe that I can do anything, and do it well.

Warm thanks also to my family, who continue to show their loyalty and joy when it comes to my work. Special thanks to my parents, who tirelessly travel to book fairs and other literary events to hear me talk about my writing and my books. It means so much to me to see you sitting there in the audience.

Thank you to all those who help me to produce my books and ensure that they reach as many readers as possible:

To Salomonsson Agency, who continue to promote my books across the world. It's always a celebration when the translations of my novels land on my doormat! Special thanks to Karin Lindgren and Julia Angelin.

Thanks to Mirja Turestedt, who records my audio books and fills each story with voices.

Finally, thanks also to my wonderful publisher Piratförlaget. I'm so happy that you were the ones who decided to believe in me and Fredrika! It's a great gift to have you in my life as a writer. Special thanks to my editor Anna Hirvi Sigurdsson, without whose meticulous attention to detail this book would have been much less readable. Special thanks also to my publisher Sofia Brattselius Thunfors, whose listening skills, enthusiasm and knowledge are invaluable resources.

Thank you.

HAVE YOU READ THEM ALL?

Discover the entire series ...

Unwanted

When a little girl is abducted from a crowded train, Alex Recht thinks it looks like a classic custody row. But young Investigative Analyst Fredrika Bergman is convinced the case is more complex. Then the child is found dead with the word UNWANTED scribbled on her forehead. Will Alex and Fredrika manage to put aside their differences and work together to find the killer, before it's too late?

Silenced

A teenage girl is assaulted and raped. Fifteen years later, a man is killed in a hit and run. At the same time, a priest and his wife are found dead in an apparent suicide. Fredrika Bergman and Alex Recht are assigned to the seemingly unconnected cases. But the trail leads them to a different crime, one whose consequences will reach further and deeper than anyone ever expected.

The Disappeared

The body of a young woman is found dismembered and buried in a forest glade in an innocuous Swedish suburb. Alex Recht and his team soon find that someone has been returning to the same spot to bury his or her victims year after year, decade after decade ...

Hostage

Shortly after a crowded New York-bound flight takes off from Stockholm, a bomb threat is found on board. Anonymous hijackers demand that the Swedish government revoke its decision to deport a Moroccan man. If their demands are not met, the plane will explode when it attempts to land. As the hours pass, the US and Swedish governments are running out of options, and the plane is running out of fuel ...

The Chosen

On a cold winter's day, a teacher is shot dead in front of parents and children at the Solomon Community, a Jewish pre-school in Stockholm. Just a few hours later two Jewish boys go missing. A figure known as the Paper Boy keeps popping up in the investigation, but who is he? And could he possibly have resurfaced in Stockholm, claiming new victims?

Or discover Kristina Ohlsson's other books ...

Buried Lies

Five brutal murders in two countries. A woman confesses to the killings, then leaps off a bridge to her death. Her brother insists she was innocent, and wants the case reopened. But how do you vindicate a deceased, self-proclaimed killer?

The Lies We Tell

Stockholm criminal lawyer Martin Benner is chipping away at the false confession linking the deceased Sara Texas to a string of killings. Mio, Sara's four-year-old son, is missing. Meanwhile, someone is trying to frame Martin for murders he didn't commit. When it becomes clear that the identity of the killer and that of Mio's kidnapper are one and the same, Martin realises that he cannot save both Mio and himself. He has to choose ...